FREEDOM'S QUEST

The New World-Florida.
The Castillos

by Bruce Ryba

Copyright © 2022 by Bruce Ryba

All rights reserved.

ISBN: 978-0-578-36738-5

Table of Contents

Prologue 1: *Flood* v
Prologue 2 ix
Prologue 3 xiii
Book One: Part 1: Castillo 1
Book One: Part 2: Luis Francisco Castillo 8
Book one: Part 3: De Soto 22
Book one: Part 4: Assignment... 32
Book one: Part 4: Cowboy 42
Book one: Part 5: Tanatacura 58
Book one: Part 6: Freedom 64
Book one: Part 7: Plague... 67
Book one: Part 8: City of Mounds 74
Book one: Part 9: "Pensacola"... 87
Book one: Part 10: Tainted Mountains of Florida................. 92
Book one: Part 11: Tanatacura Elk Beasts 103
Book one: Part 12: Bitter words 108
Book one: Part 13: Stew 111
Book one: Part 14: Wife... 114
Book one: Part 15: Fur... 116
Book one: Part 16: Colt.. 118
Book one: Part 17: Tampa.. 124
Book one: Part 18: Calusa.. 135
Book one: Part 19: Ais 141
Book one: Part 20: Manny 148
Book one: Part 21 Panther 156
Book one: Part 22: Mother's milk.. 160
Book one: Part 23: Oath... 178
Book one: Part 24: Flint Trader 183
Book one: Part 25: Shoots Ducks 194

Book one: Part 26: Hurricane 199
Book one: Part 27: Wreck of Gods Banner, Cape Canaveral 205
Book one: Part 28: Conquistador..222
Book one: Part 29: Matanzas inlet...234
Book one: Part 30: Demands 241
Book one: Part 31: Spoils of war 245
Book one: Part 32: Christian...249
Book one: Part 33: Savochequeya 255
Book one Part 34: Ulumay..281

Prologue 1: *Flood*

Sandridge west of Merritt Island, East Coast of Florida. Seven thousand years before the present.

Skins-Llama stood upon the sandy ridge overlooking the bowl-shaped prairie and the willow-lined stream that twisted snake-like through the close-cropped grasslands.
The panicked animals below him could, at any moment, turn uphill towards him as had the recent wolf pack.

At length he squatted, holding his two spear-darts and shell-topped dart thrower ready to hurl flint-tipped death.

Never had the sandy Bison Ford seen such use, he marveled.

Bison Ford was the favorite ambush spot of his, his father's, and all the grandfathers before him. Skins-Llama was overcome with sadness. The resignation and awareness that never again would the clan's favorite ambush crossing be used.

Mine will be the last kill at Bison Ford, thought Skins-Llama.

Below him on the short grass prairie, herds of horses and llamas splashed across the stream as if running from a smoky grass fire.

Both the spotted and the stripped types of horses raced back and forth, back across the ford. No decision could be made upon which side of the stream possessed the greatest safety. The horses were aware of the dangers of wolves' teeth and jaguars' claws.

This new threat?
Chaos reigned. Nothing like this had ever happened before. Or perhaps it had?

Turkeys ran along the stream, then flew over the water when spooked by running bison.
A jaguar slipped across the ford without a splash, completely ignored by the horses. Following the jaguar, a great lumbering bear that was ignored by both cat and horse.
A white-tailed eagle reluctantly left its kill and flew overhead, uttering a shrieking call of protest.

Skins-Llama watched as a panicked llama avoided the crowded ford and attempted to swim the stream, only to be immediately pulled into a death roll by a grandfather alligator.

Deer and more wolves crowded through the ford and a small deer was pulled into the water with a great splash.

The Grandfather's feast today, thought Skins-Llama.

The animals fled as if from a lightning fire; however, there was no smoke on the horizon, yet flocks of ibis and cranes took flight at the approaching danger.

Next, the secretive animals of the forest and prairie appeared; foxes, rabbits, and bobcats. They ignored the ford, sprinting north towards an unknown sanctuary.

A young panther appeared from the willows to grab a rabbit and sprint north following the trail of fox and bobcat, the squealing rabbit still held in the whiskered mouth.

"By all the Grandfathers!" swore Skins-Llama.

His eyes opened wide in surprise as a family of mammoths appeared from the willows and crossed the stream.

The Giant alpha bull wielding huge ivory tusks.

Mammoths had not been seen since the childhood of his talented grandfather, known by the clans as 'Ivory-carver'.

Mammoth skulls and curved tusks were found throughout the land; however, these were the first of the giant beasts that Skins-Lama had seen alive.

Suddenly the grass around the feet of the shaggy mammoths wavered and the family of mammoths cried out an ear-splitting cacophony.

"I have heard that call before," uttered Skins-Llama.

Never having learned in all his wide hunts, what type of animal had made that call.

Below him on the prairie, the bull mammoth stomped his foot, and water splashed around the shaggy legs! The bull again echoed his call of protest.

Skins-Llama marveled at the volume of the sound. Only the thunder of dark storms rivaled the sound.

But the water!
The prairie grasslands disappeared as a tide of water swelled out of the stream to spread over the cropped vegetation.
The invasive water spread as would an animal bleed red when struck by his dart; the stream bleeding as if the very earth made water.

Did a god weep?

Flocks of quail took flight from their hideaways and in the short time-span of a few breaths, the water had grown so wide he could not cast his spear across to the far side of the flood!

Through the spreading flood tide, the mammoths strolled unfazed, while a multitude of small animals lost footing to be carried north by the ever-spreading slow waters: opossums, raccoons, turtles, and peccaries.

A sloth even taller than the mammoths sloshed its way onto dry land with its own contingent of small animal refugees clinging to the stiff fur of its back.
Alligators drifted lazily from the willows, unfazed at the growth in their environment. Otters played in their new domain.
On the far side of the flood, as on his side, llamas, deer, and horses snorted uneasily and the grazers fled the rising water, running towards the forest edge, away from the grasslands.

"Saltwater," marveled Skins-Llama

The flood tide was saltwater, he knew. For the east prairie had flooded less than a moon-rise ago, eventually topping off, creating a vast inland sea. The new sea eventually spilled over into the prairie below him.
The result was that the land on the far side of the flood-tide was now an island.

Skins-Llama watched as the new sea grew wider and the alligators pulled the small animals underwater; the willow trees were islands of safety, jutting from the flood and decorated with crawling, climbing things.

What if the water keeps rising and covers the ridge he stood upon?

"Will the water swallow the world?" asked Skins-Llama.

If such were the Creator's wishes,-so be it. For the world had flooded in another age, easily demonstrated because of the wealth of ocean shells and sharks teeth found inland of the ridge…*So be it.*

That is why his people buried the deceased in the inland ponds. Water *would* cover the world again, the ocean *would* rise and the ancestors *would* be reborn.

That, however, was the trade of the shamans.

My trade is the hunt, thought Skins-Llama.

Assuming the water would stop below the ridge upon which he stood; how were he and the hunters to cross to the new island to hunt llama and horse?

Below him, the mammoths called again as they splashed away from the rising water. Skins-Llama notched his dart to dart thrower and walked downhill, his belly growling.

Grandfathers before his time, now resting in the burial pond, had passed the knowledge about how to hunt the dangerous mammoths.

The calf.

The small calf mammoth guarded by the herd was more meat than his people could use in a week. However, as always, he would share his kill with wolf and eagle.

His clan would once again feast on mammoth.

"My name is Skins-Mammoth," he whispered, beaming with pride.

Outside of his sight, the prairie continued to flood, a great salt lagoon in the making.

Prologue 2

Kennedy Space Center, Florida, September 12, 1992

Brian.

"Which launchpad is it?" whined Brian George.

No one answered him.

He was hot and bored. NASA was actually a pretty boring place.

His Grandfather seemed to be enjoying himself. Some old man was droning on about really dull stuff.

"I worked on the Apollo program, over there, in the VAB," said the old man. The speaker was an ancient white man with a huge pink bulbous nose; pink the color of one of those Florida spoonbill wading birds. The pink nose and face were traced with miniature hieroglyphic blue-black bird tracks stamped across the old face like a map.

Uhh so ugly, thought Brian.

Pops, however, seemed to be actually interested in what the red-faced geezer was saying. Pops even studied the gigantic VAB building and asked pink face questions about Apollo!

Brian however couldn't give a darn about some old Greek or Roman god. He sighed, looking towards the other members of his family.

Eddie had the Walkman headset over his ears, staring at the expansive river to their front but tapping his feet to the music.

Mom and Dad were angry again and were doing their darnedest not to talk to each other.

Big sis, well Mary Ann was gawking at the boys in the crowd, gathered to watch the space shuttle blast off.

"Which launchpad is it?" repeated Brian

There were lots of launch pads to be seen, although the crowd kept staring at two faraway launch pads across the blue-green water.

"Which launch pad?" he asked again. No one would answer him.

Nothing was happening since the loudspeaker had blared the countdown was on hold. There were clouds at the Trans-Atlantic landing site.
But that had been over an hour ago. *An eternity.*

"Can I go down the water?" asked Brian of his parents.

"No!" his mother said too quickly, "There are alligators in that water."

Yes! Alligators!

Eddie had heard "Alligators" over the music and glanced at Brian, a mischievous grin on his face. Both Eddie and Brian picked up pieces of crust from the Domino's pizza box and began to meander their way towards the water.

However, his grandfather, sparse white hair contrasting with his walnut dark skin, spoke quiet instructions.

"Boys, back here."

Crushed, Brian sat down and stared longingly at the water, but saw no alligators. At least that would have been exciting-feeding pizza crust to a man-eater! *Yes!*

But there were other children by the water, chasing grasshoppers and long-legged white birds. How dangerous could it be?

Mom is in a bad mood, he thought. She and dad had fought on the drive to Kennedy Space Center. Heck, mom has been in a bad mood for a year!

The George family sat in their folding chairs, mostly quiet, enjoying the sun, and like the thousands of other spectators stared at the distant launchpad. Perhaps a thousand cars or more were packed tightly onto a causeway in the middle of a wide river, or perhaps it was a lake or the ocean.

A large gray fin appeared in the river catching their attention.

"Shark! Yes!" exclaimed Brian, excited at last.

"Don't think so Brian," said his father, Cornelius George. "That *shark* just exhaled." Pops chuckled.

"It's a dolphin or porpoise; tastes like chicken," said Pops. Brian's sister Mary Ann punched her grandfather.

"Pops! That was terrible," said Mary Ann.

The loudspeaker attached to a tall pole crackled to life.

"TAL sites are clear of clouds and a go for a trans-Atlantic landing. Entering the two-minute hold." The crowd applauded, relieved more than animated that the space shuttle launch countdown was proceeding.

"Sit down boys," said Cornelius.

But the crowd rose as one, and so did the George family, anticipation mounting. "Ninety seconds," crackled the speaker.

Like a hive of angry bees, the noise of nervous hubbub gradually blended into a ragged chant.

"Ten! Nine! Eight!" Then the chant grew louder, more ardent. "Seven! Six! Five!" Brian stared hard over the water and the small launch pad.

"Which one, which one!" he squeaked with desperation.

"We have main engine ignition!" came from the speaker. Brian stared across the lagoon.

"And we have lift-off!"

Brian's disappointment was palpable, as eternally long seconds passed and nothing was happening.

"There!" yelled his sister, pointing at a small cloud of white smoke across the river.

"Lift off of the Space Shuttle, Endeavor!" the speaker called out.

The crowd around Brian cheered as if they were at an Astros ball game.

A small object appeared to lift from the horizon, chased by orange fire so bright, that Brian had to shield his eyes. He was awed that astronauts rode the top of a rocket.

Rode that bomb.

The flame and little dot atop the fire seemed to roll over, picking up speed, leaving a huge column of smoke tracing the space shuttle's ascent, passing through wispy clouds.

The sound began to push him.

First, only a rumble, then noise, like thunder, grew louder than the crowd's excited yells. An explosive reverberation of pulses that drowned out even the speaker-as if ten-thousand shotgun blasts had fired one after another, engulfing him, each blast a pressure felt on his arms and chest.

Felt inside his body!

"Holy Crap!" Brian yelled.

And he found himself cheering along with his parents, Pops, his brother, sister, and the crowd.
The smoke column grew larger, twisting, and curling, like a giant white sky python. The space shuttle lifted ever higher, followed by its giant snake cloud seeming to curve away.
The crowd hushed, waiting for something.

"My son works on the solid rocket boosters," said a nearby man, his voice cracking with raw emotion.

"The boosters will separate from the orbiter at two minutes," said another with worry.

Another man with binoculars mumbled about the Challenger. The speaker kept up a steady stream of NASA rocket talk.

"Endeavor on its historic mission to the International Space Station."

"Holy Crap!" said Brian, repeating himself only to see his mother give him a disapproving glance.

"Holy Crap is right. Haven't felt percussion like that in… well since Korea," exclaimed an enthusiastic Pops.

"Godspeed Endeavor," said someone behind them.

"Come on, separate, *drop* those solids," said another person off to their side.

"There!" yelled an excited spectator.
The crowd roared its approval as two dots of fire dropped away from the distant shuttle and three smoke trails billowed and curled long after the shuttle with its orange rocket had disappeared into space. Sounds of laughter and mirth came from a thousand spectators and more rocket talk blared from the speaker poles.

Cornelius George beamed with a bright smile of pleasure, knowing that his children had witnessed, had participated in this historic event. The first female African American astronaut on the space shuttle. Hell, they might not realize how historic for years to come.

Prologue 3

Mosquito Lagoon, Florida Space Coast, 1992

"William Bartram, while residing in Florida in 1776-77, explored Mosquito Lagoon by canoe, seeing 11 bears in one day and many deer." -- Historic Marker at Eddy Creek, Canaveral National Seashore.

Eddie
The fishing guide's motor roared to life and the Flats boat pushed out onto the mirror-glass-smooth water of Mosquito Lagoon.

The sun had not yet risen but Eddie George did not regret the early morning trip. Of course, his father had driven the entire way to the east coast. He had fallen asleep almost the moment his Grandfather, Father, and little brother had climbed into the family SUV for the drive to the lagoon.

His mother and older sister had opted to sleep in and lounge around the hotel pool; it was just the "men" who were going on the fishing adventure.
The fishing trip would be the top of an already fantastic week: three fun but exhausting days at Disney, then viewing the awesome launch of the Space Shuttle, and today fishing for 'Redfish'.

Eddie held tightly onto his hat, his eyes squinted from the wind as the guide's powerful Flats boat raced across the smooth lagoon. To the east, the gray sky was just showing orange.

His fervent wish was to see a wild Florida alligator.
They crossed the wide lagoon in only ten or twenty minutes. The guide turned the engine off and standing on a raised platform, he used a long pole to push the boat silently towards a series of stumpy islands, on the eastern side of the Lagoon.

The water was no longer glassy-smooth, instead, the lagoon almost boiled with fish.
    "Those are Mullet," explained their guide, Captain Charley. Pointing at the jumping and swirling fish.

"They are good to eat and easy to net, however, this morning we will be fishing for the king of the lagoon, the Redfish," said Captain Charley.

Captain Charley reached his chosen spot and silently placed the push pole in its holder. He baited three rods and presented them to Eddie, his brother Brian and his Grandfather. His father had opted to stay out of the way of flailing fishing rods and flying hooks. There would be plenty of time during the day to catch fish.
But in truth, his father was bursting with pride for his family.
Cornelius George, a communications engineer at Lackland Air Force Base in Texas, had saved for over four years to do this vacation right. And the lagoon fishing trip was just the icing on the cake.
His priority for the vacation had been taking his children to watch the Space Shuttle launch, with the first female African American Astronaut on board.
Ironically, he suspected his children had not even noticed that one of the Shuttle astronauts was of African descent.
The country was looking up, literally.

Of course, America had not considered *his* skin color when the Army had shipped him off to fight in Panama.

The sun jumped out of the east to shine brightly over a wide lagoon, sprinkled with low islands. Eddie saw his alligator, in fact, by his brother's and his reckoning, they counted *nine* blackish colored 'gators and they caught fish, lots of fish!

His father laughed with gusto at each fish pulled to the boat and repeated appreciation of the fishing guide several times during the morning.

"Captain Charley, you're worth every dollar of your charter fee," said Cornelius George.

With full daylight, the boat Captain pushed his boat quietly through the clear shallow grass flats to where huge Redfish dined on crabs and finger-sized mullet. The "Red's" pinkish fins and spotted tails pushed above the surface as they schooled and hunted the grassy lagoon floor.

Once hooked, the fish made the drag setting on the fishing reels squeal in protest.

When the Reds, worn out and exhausted, were eventually reeled to the boat, they proved to be bronze in color, instead of red as their name implied. One of the Redfish brought in by Pops was over three feet in length!

Captain Charley took a picture of each fish and carefully nursed the exhausted creatures until they were strong enough to swim away.
For the boys, the Reds proved to be too much to handle, so Captain Charley found sandbars where they caught plenty of smaller fish; spotted sea trout, yellow-finned Jack Crevalle, and enjoyed Silver Lady fish that jumped acrobatically when the hook was set.
Once a giant catfish appeared from the green depths to seize a speckled trout as it was reeled to the boat.
As the morning progressed, ospreys and pelicans dropped from the sky into the shallow lagoon. Bottle-nosed Porpoises and Manatees surfaced near the boat to loudly exhale. Demonstrating to everyone that they were not fish but mammals.

Large mullet jumped out of the water and schools of smaller mullet would ripple the water in unison whenever a low flying Cormorant or gull spooked them. Brown Stingrays and blue-clawed crabs could be seen almost everywhere in the shallow clear water.

For lunch, Captain Charley guided his boat into the south end of Mosquito Lagoon where he pulled up on a small sandy island and opened a cooler with ham and cheese sandwiches and unlimited sodas.

The Atlantic Ocean could be heard, off to the east, unseen waves breaking on the nearby beach. Charley pointed south.

"Those are the Space Shuttle Launch Pads 39A & 39B, on Kennedy Space Center," explained Captain Charley.

"We saw the space shuttle launch!" said Brian George.

Eddie looked north and the lagoon extended to an endless hazy blur on the horizon.

After the lunch break, Charley cruised the west side of the lagoon, searching for a final Redfish or a large fish, oddly named "Black Drum," before heading back to the parking lot.
Eddie finally had to speak up about his full bladder; the two sodas he had finished at lunch were ready to burst out. He had to pee.
Despite the joking from his father, Eddie was too embarrassed to urinate off the back of the boat and pleaded to be put on the shoreline where he could unzip out of sight.

Captain Charley did not mind, whatsoever, and piloted the boat up an old channel, right to the tree-covered shoreline.
Brown ducks and pink Spoonbills feeding in the shallows took flight at the boat's approach; while defiant Great Blue Heron stood its ground until finally leaving with a flourish of giant wings and a dinosaur squawk of frustration.

Cornelius George took in the sights of wildlife, the palm trees, breathing deeply the aroma of decaying turtle grass and mangroves.

"This sort of reminds me of where our unit was dropped off in Panama," he said to his father. "Pops" George looked across the wide expanse of water dotted with birds.
"Don't remind me of anything in Korea," said Pops.

Father and son laughed at some joke that was only humorous between the two of them. Captain Charley helped Eddie to the sandy shore.

"Keep an eye out for Rattlesnakes," warned Captain Charley.

Eddie wasn't sure if the boat captain was joking as he walked into the shaded canopy beyond the water's edge.
The lagoon breeze did not penetrate the forest and almost immediately, mosquitoes began hovering around him. Nevertheless, he could not help but notice how the land rose sharply inside the tree line and it seemed there was a hill made entirely of diverse seashells.

Eddie emptied his bladder against a cedar tree and quickly climbed the mound of shells. On top of the hill sat the concrete remains of a house. Vines and creepers had reclaimed most of the home. However, before Eddie could inspect the ruins further, the mosquitoes made him retreat towards the water. Climbing carefully down the shell hill;

Eddie noticed a pale blue marble lying between the shells and he skidded to pick it up.

Oh cool.

He pocketed the marble as a keepsake for an amazing day and a wonderful vacation.
Back out on the shoreline of Mosquito Lagoon, Eddie excitedly told his father of his discovery of the ruins and the hill of seashells.

Eddie climbed in the boat and Captain Charley, standing in the shallows, turned the boat around so the bow was pointed towards open water. Jumping into the boat he picked up the long push pole steering the boat into the old channel. Stingrays darted like jets from around the boat.
Captain Charley talked while he pushed the boat.

"The house, well there are actually a lot of old houses hidden in that tree line. I'm thinking around 1964, the government came in and took these folk's land to create the Space Center. Some of the houses were moved to the mainland but most just rotted away."

Charley placed the push pole in the holder on the side of the boat and started the boat motor. He talked while slowly idling to deeper water.

"The shell mound? Well, there are *lots of them* around here also. Found an arrowhead on one of them! Those mounds were here long before the houses and I've heard there were Indian villages at each mound.
A couple of really *big* oyster shell mounds on the north end of the lagoon, "Seminole Rest" in Oak Hill, and "Turtle Mound" at Canaveral National Seashore. Some of the old netters tell stories about a killer hurricane that tore a new inlet between the lagoon and the ocean and drowned all the Indians in these parts. Just stories you know. It was so long ago I don't think anyone really knows what happened to those mound folks," said Captain Charley.

"Everyone hold on," warned Captain Charley. The guide pushed on the throttle.

The flats boat jumped onto the plane and roared north, eventually passing the wide Haulover Canal that connected Mosquito Lagoon to the Indian River.

At the boat ramp, the Captain helped his customers from the boat; their legs wobbly from being on the water all day. Cornelius George paid Captain Charley's charter fee and an extremely generous tip. Everyone thanked him and said goodbye.

On the drive back to the hotel; Eddie twirled his blue marble and wondered who had dropped the glass sphere on the mound of shells.

Book One: Part 1: Castillo

Siege of Granada, Spain, 1491 A.D.

There was weeping in Granada, the crimson sun to the west, Praise called out to Mary, or pain called to Muhommad.
The Koran carried out the gates, the sword hilt of the Cross, the final test. And here the Christian verse and there the Moorish curse.
Ravens in their nests scoured the walls, their final jest.
-Old Spanish Ballad

He was suddenly aware that the cannons had ceased their bombardment. The Spanish assault began, with calls to Saint Sebastian failing again.
The Christians retreated from the desperate fight in the fresh wall breach; stumbling over the casement rubble, the wounded limping or crawling away.
Others unable to move, called upon Christ, or Mary. Others cried out for their own mother. One man in torn armor simply screeched "Kill me!" over and over.

His men, greatly diminished in numbers, were too weary and hungry to cheer or give chase after the Christians. However, they had also learned to respect the sting of the Spanish counterattacks.
Few survived for very long once leaving the safety of the battered fortress walls.

From the wreckage wreathed in a cloud of stinging black powder smoke and choking dust, as if arising from the dead, there appeared heads with wide eyes under helmet visors. Unwounded footmen precipitously appeared from shell craters or fallen walls and scampered after the retreating warriors.

"Weaklings!" growled the man.

Weaklings who had cowered in safety while their brethren had attacked the gap created by the cannonade.

Unreasonable anger gripped him as he watched the cowards scurry to their own earthworks and trenches.

The enemy that would face him, Halberd in hand, piss water running down their legs, he could respect. However, no man on either side of the conflict who had by luck and skill survived the confusing clash of spear and shield could abide cowardice.

If he had had a bow or gun he would have shot down every one of the cowards.

Chasing after them, of course, was out of the question.
For simply stumbling over the tumbled red wall was torture on his old thigh wound. *'Healed but never healed.'*
Each uneven painful step forced a sharp inhalation.

Suddenly a low moaning, growing to a crescendo, hid the wails of the injured.

A mournful cry poured from along the shattered walls, morphing into deep wailing of grief and then into high-pitched keening that spread from the parapets and through the beleaguered city.

A corresponding cheer and shouts of "Santiago!" emanated from the Spanish earthworks.

For upon the tallest red battlement of Granada, the summit of Torre de la Vela, the flag of King Muhammad had been lowered, and in its place they lifted the banner of St. James.
Lastly, the flags of Castile and Aragon were lifted above the war-torn city.

So it was over.

He hissed, his old wound throbbing as he sat down on a stone and wiped his sword on the legging of a fallen soldier.

What would happen now?

One thing for certain, he had decided no matter how, or what he would have to do. His time as a slave was *over*.

Nearby, a handsome youth, a Spanish man-at-arms sprawled on the rocks. The Spaniard half sat, half lay in the uneven rubble, silent and staring, intent on holding together his intestines and a gaping wound. A losing battle. Loops of gut slipped between slick palms and fingers.

Thigh aching, he stood up slowly and walked on unsteady feet to stand above the wounded Spaniard and questioned him in one of the Spanish dialects.

"What is your name, son?"

The Spaniard replied in a voice surprisingly steady for one with such a grievous wound. "Castillo, name is Castillo," said the wounded Spaniard.

Neither man spoke for a length of time, one grimacing at the pain in his thigh and one facing the terrible prospect of a slow painful death.

Cheers of victory still echoed from the Spanish earthworks.
Finally, the standing man spoke.

"I'm sorry, Castillo. I am offering mercy. Go with God."

He placed his sword upon the wounded man's jugular and leaned hard on the blade.

"Go with God," he repeated for himself and the dying soldier. *The coup de grâce given after the battle often the only memory of the actual sword blows. The act to be repeated in sweat-filled dreams.*

In the distance, a horn sounded calling them from the walls.
To his ears, it was the sweet sound of freedom.

"Captain Diego Lopez Del Castillo," he said aloud to a priest.

Captain Diego Lopez Del Castillo, *his new name*, the Spanish words rolled off of his tongue easily enough.
It *was* the speech of the enemy and yet it was now his language.

All who had chosen to stay in Spain had to select a new Christian name and so he had taken the name of the last man he had killed as a slave.

A chill crept upon him as he fingered his new crucifix. Staring dourly at the distant white-capped ocean and flecked with tiny sails; the fading fleet of the armies of the Moors sailed from Iberia in defeat.

Forever?

Could anyone know the future when the gods of opportunity rolled their bowl of carved bones? Certainly, the bickering nobles of the Emirate of Granada and King Muhammad the XII had not foreseen the absolute victory of the Christian armies with their powerful Frankish cannons.

Most certainly, they had not foreseen the wholesale desertion and conversion of their warrior slaves.

The Trickster God at play again, he mused.

Around him, to his front and rear, kneeling on the cold dusty plain were a thousand soldier slaves. Now *Free men*, all pledging allegiance to the victorious kingdoms of Aragon and Castile, to the Catholic Monarchs, King Ferdinand and Queen Isabella, and finally the oath of fealty to the Christian Church.

Like him, the warrior-slaves had chosen uncertain freedom with the victors, over uncertain slavery with the defeated.
Nearly all the thousand were from the Ivory and Ostrich lands south of the great desert.
Dark Moors, the Spaniards call us.

Enslaved, taken as youths from their homes on the east and west coasts or from deep within the great continent and transported down muddy rivers or tethered as human trains behind camels and marched across the dry wastelands to be sold to the Moors or Berbers for warrior stock.

Brutally trained in the fierce arts of war. Sent to guard the northern reaches of the Emirate of Granada, and when necessary, do battle with the diverse Christian kingdoms of the Iberian Peninsula.

The very same kingdoms whose Hidalgos and nobles now proffered gold and silver for *their* services as trained mercenaries.
Free mercenaries. We made a good showing holding the cannon breaches to the Granada walls.

"So help me, God," repeated the thousand new Christians.

Completing their conversion as one, stood to their armored feet with a roar as free men. Castillo stood with assistance from others, hissing at the pressure upon his old thigh wound, once girdled by a Hidalgo horseman of Leon.

I gutted that bastard. Nevertheless every day the ghost of the slain Hidalgo returned in the form of a leg that burned with pain.

A thousand sets of Moorish armor and blades scintillated across the dusty January plain. Deafening cheers caused ravens and carrion eagles to take flight, momentary leaving behind their grisly meals.

A visceral throbbing pressed on Castillo's chest. *Freedom!* A concept still not to be readily accepted or grasped.

Stone-faced priests wearing dusty robes, suspicious of the Dark Moors, walked among the new Christians, seeking out any whose conversions might be false.

Not in this thousand, thought Castillo, who proudly displayed his costly silver and blue crucifix. Those slaves who had stayed true to Islam, the religion of their former owners, had boarded the ships with the other devout refugees of the kingdom of Granada.

My own brother, Ahmet, had chosen Islam and slavery over Christianity and freedom. He was on one of those distant ships.

What would happen to those men, to his brother and the other faithful soldier-slaves? Surely the exiled king turned beggar would no longer be able to feed and house all those devoted slaves.

Castillo suspected the best warriors would be sold to the Egyptians to bolster their never-ending war against the savage Turks.

The remaining slaves?
Rumors had spread that some would be sold for galley slaves alongside captured Christians or simply marched deep into the Sahara and turned loose to the mercies of the sand, heat, and scorpions. *Their freedom.*

Castillo glanced for a final time at the fading sails disappearing over the clouded horizon.

God is with you Ahmet and turned to face his questioning men.
Free men.

As commander of a hundred men, now to be named *Captain* in the Christian manner of military rank, he studied his men.

Gaunt ebony faces looked to him for guidance. Some were strangers; few of the original one hundred remained, many wore bloodied wrappings and were painfully thinned by the long siege upon the fortress.

During the brutal ten-year war for the kingdom of Granada, the maimed and dead had been quickly replaced with a dizzying assortment of faces and names, speaking strange words of unknown villages.

Ten years of guarding the northern frontier against the advancing Christians had been costly in men and material. In the final three years of conflict, the Moors had forgone the expense of training and sent in newly enslaved herders and rice farmers, youngsters, and old men directly to the war.

Barely one in twelve of the untrained survived their first moon against the hardened Spaniards. Well, there *would* be no more replacements from Africa, but there would now be wives, sons and daughters, and their sons and daughters.

The Moors had not permitted their slave-soldiers to marry. Instead, demanding of them absolute loyalty to the caliphate. Replacements from the south of the great desert had been relatively inexpensive.

Musa Ag Ihemma, a young man of Tuareg ancestry, a slave by way of the great desert and the quickest left-handed knife fighter he knew, still alive, was fretting at their future.

"What will happen now, sir?" asked Musa.

The question implied the unspoken death sentence that Islam placed upon all apostates.
The Imams, frothy spittle flying from thick beards, had placed the penalty of death on *them*.
He rested a callused hand on the young man's chain-mailed shoulder, reassuring him.

"Musa," he quickly corrected himself. The lad had chosen the most Christian of all names. "De Jesus."

"De Jesus, my fine left-handed killer, *we have* selected the correct path. Already the gentry of Castile, Leon, and Aragon proffer gold for our service. *A lot of gold.* These Spanish kingdoms, like the Arabs and Berbers, are forever at war with someone," said Castillo.

Castillo paused, contemplating the fate of the thousand free men.
Logistics.
Simply to feed so many mouths, we have to be split up. Some will be thrown at the Portuguese border. Others to the northern mountains and the boundary with the Franks and Basques.
Some he knew, would have to stay in Granada to watch over the Moors and Jews who had chosen conversion over exile.

Finally, merchants from across the Mediterranean but especially the Genovese were always in need of guards, sailors, and interpreters.
The Turks were ever a scourge in the east, disrupting both Christian and Moslem trade.

"We will go as free men, to whatever wars, cross whatever oceans or mountains that King Ferdinand and Queen Isabella deem a threat to Christendom," explained Castillo.

However, there would be wives, sons and daughters, and their sons and daughters. Castillo smiled broadly, then burst into deep laughter at their prospects.

Book One: Part 2: Luis Francisco Castillo

De Soto Expedition: Unexplored lands west of the Florida Apalachee Mountains, 1542 A.D.

Like *wildfire* or the black plague, the excitement spread quickly throughout Spain and Portugal, and then to the outlying corners of Europe, that one, Hernando De Soto, a conqueror of golden Peru, was personally funding the grandest army since the crusades to subjugate for God, the great empire of Florida.
Florida, a pagan territory, understood to be superior in treasure and grandeur to any of the conquered realms of the new world.
Drawn to his standard came the sons of noble birth on fierce steeds, bastards, and commoners, but most important, came the mercenaries and professional soldiers whose iron-shod feet had trampled both city and plain across the known kingdoms.
All came to offer up their service for gold and Christendom.

"Of the slaves....
Soto brought from the forests of Florida over five hundred unhappy Florida men and women, secured with chains, driven by keepers, and made to transport the effects of the expedition. When any of them became sick, died, or escaped, it was his policy to supply their places at the first town upon which he marched. He always, however, distributed among the principal Indians, presents, which were gratifying to them, and left as many of the town's pairs of swine to stock the country." - Journal of Elvas

The fight at the fortress of Mabila in the country of the Alabamas:

"The Indians fought with so great of spirit that they, many times, drove our people back out of the town. The struggle lasted so long that many Christians, weary and very thirsty, went to drink at a pond nearby, tinged with the blood of the killed, and returned to the combat."

"Breaking in upon the Indians and beating them down, they fled out of the place, the cavalry and infantry driving them back through the gates, where losing the hope of escape, they fought valiantly; and

the Christians getting among them with cutlasses, they found themselves met on all sides by their strokes, when many, dashing headlong into the flaming houses, were smothered, and, heaped one upon another, burned to death...."

"They who perished inside the walls, there were in all two thousand five hundred, a few more or less. Upwards of five thousand bodies lay outside on the plain. Of the Christians, there fell two hundred... Of the living, one hundred and fifty Christians had received seven hundred wounds..."
  - Journal of Elvas

With a final gasp of frustration, Luis Castillo, grandson of a Moorish Captain, pushed away from his slave woman and lay on his back.

My manhood does not work, thought Castillo.
It is as if I am already in my fumbling gray hair years. The Indios have a berry for this problem he knew.
No, it is this expedition to conquer Florida. *It affects me.*

He almost laughed at the thought. Nightmares of the worst sort, sleepless nights, and now his manhood? However, he did not linger long in the rare moment of silence and self-pity and began fumbling for the cords to lace up his leather breeks.

I had best be ready because, without a doubt, the guards would be coming soon to escort me to the Governor-General.

The Indian woman near him, a tribute gift said to be from the Ar-Kansas nation, *west* of the great river, began to weep softly.

I cannot worry about her now, thought Castillo.

Foremost in his mind; there was no alternative but to deceive the Governor-General. Weave a falsehood of deceit to the man that he had readily followed to the ends of the new world.
At length, he looked over at the Indian. Her silhouette and buckskins were just barely visible in the shadows.

"*Mary*. I will call you Mary," he panted out her name.

I have owned her for four days now?

In the dim light of the nameless hut, in some godforsaken nameless Florida village, he christened his new woman "Mary."
He briefly attempted to recall the faces of the previous Marys he had owned since the landing in Florida.

"Six, or was it seven?" he muttered.
The last Mary, his favorite, a gift from the Okmulgee people, had died at Mabila, a sharp stone hatchet buried in her pretty black hair. Murdered along with numerous other slaves and captives.

At length, he gave up the futile game of recalling faces because of the one face that kept coming back to him: Mary of the Pensacola or Oconee nation, no, Ani-Yunwiya Cherokee?
He blew out a deep breath.
It didn't matter, her clan did not matter.

It had been the Mary who had taken her own life by leaping into the flood tide of a great muddy river.
And she hadn't been the only slave to take advantage of the river's offer of freedom from the Spanish. The foaming brown current had quickly pulled her and others beneath the swirling waters; however Mary's face, *her eyes*, her final defiant glance at him. She had the look of, well, *victory*, as if she had just won a great battle.

That triumphant gaze had troubled him for many days and dream haunted nights, dredging from deep within him confusing thoughts of good and evil.

It didn't matter.

With a sigh, he considered trying again to use his woman. I am young. *No*, I will require the Indios palmetto berries to correct… *the problem.*

And there was the need to choose an additional name.

Shifting to easier thoughts and furrowing his brow in contemplation, he considered male names for his new squire. The new Mary had come with a brother.

I chose to keep the brother as a servant rather than turn him over to the expedition slave pens and undoubted mutilation.

The Army was in a foul mood after the calamity of Mabila. The army was desperate to replace the baggage slaves killed in the hurricane of flint-tipped arrows.

The charitable gesture to save Mary's brother may have been lost on her, but it was for the better.
If, when she found her brother chained, mutilated, branded, or worse, as were the majority of the expedition's slaves; well, I *might lose* another slave woman to the next river crossing.

So, what would he name the brother? Guess it does not matter.

Mary, for her part, did not respond to her new name. She simply rearranged her buck skins and huddled
in a corner away from him.
He had noted even in his frustration, that her firm legs and brown belly had the marks of having born a child.

"Mary, what happened to your child?" he asked in the shadows.
No response.
Of course, she could not understand a word he said.
Not one single word. Only a few of the other Marys had lived long enough to learn more than a few sentences of Spanish.

A longing swept over him.

How long had it been since he had had a real conversation with a woman? Flirted, enjoyed the bright tinkle of their laughter at one of his clever jokes?
In fact, he thought darkly, not since the army's departure from Cuba had he heard the nourishing laughter of women.
Wailing, yes, screams, yes, and tears always tears.

Castillo shuddered and smacked his temple at the unmanly thoughts and stepped outside squinting at the strong afternoon sunlight.

His horse and Mary's brother were both tethered nearby.
It was readily apparent that Mary's brother, like all-new Indian servants, was still terrified of the strange animal. The braided tether holding Mary's brother was stretched taut, the Indian staying as far as possible away from the horse.

As well he should be.

The magnificent Andalusian warhorse was both thrilling and powerful but possessed of a savage bite and hooves that had killed many men. His stallion, hugely expensive and exquisitely trained for war, yet, perhaps it could be justly said, the stallion was not tame. The horse simply *allowed* him to climb upon his back.

He approached the horse and the stallion's ears went flat against its head, nostrils flaring in defiance.

The action caused Castillo to laugh at the insolence. He jerked the hackamore twice with two quick tugs then scratched behind the ears and patted the powerful neck.

"Adelantado, so just who is the ruler here?" said Castillo to his warhorse.

Turning his attention to the Indian, he unsheathed his dirk and gently cut the leather rope.

"So Juan," for that is what he decided to name his new servant. "How am I to train you to be a squire when we can't understand each other and you are devil be scared of horseflesh?"

Juan did not reply.

The woman, or rather the *new* Mary, possibly concerned about her brother, walked out of the hut and stood obediently next to Juan. The brother, while rubbing his numbed wrists, had retreated even further from the intimidating horse.

Not a word of Spanish between them, Castillo thought glumly.

Knowing there would be no answer, he still asked the brother and sister. "Just where in the hell is Ar-Kansas?"

He sighed; once again he had the demanding task of explaining how to pull rations and *at all costs*, avoid the slave kettles where the baggage slaves were fed.

Still, he had good intentions for both Mary and Juan: the army would need interpreters once they crossed the mother river into… well into the Ar-Kansas area of Florida on the West Side of the great river, still roughly two hundred leagues distant.

Interpreters had value in a brutal campaign where the natives of Florida had no value, except as baggage carriers to be disposed of when they could no longer carry their back-breaking loads.

A slight echo of disturbance, a few catcalls of greeting reverberated through the nameless Indian settlement.
That would be the Governor's guards, Castillo thought.

The little Indian settlement was situated on a small rise near good water. A clear spring bordered by a large green meadow and a small river that had overflowed its banks where the brown water flowed through the adjoining forest.
Castillo and the other scouts, out of necessity for forage, always pastured their horses well away from the main Spanish encampment.

Just as expected, the guards, but *only two* of the Governors' personal bodyguards, threaded their way in his direction, through the small encampment of Spaniards and Indian slaves.

The victory at Mabila had been costly, so very costly; the expedition losing a third of the *remaining* fighting men, and the murder of most of the freeborn herdsmen of Hispaniola and Castile.
All of the army's cattle and many of the swine, all the Mastiffs, and nearly all of the slaves, both Indian and African had perished.

Anyone or thing caught without armor had been hit with a withering storm of arrows. The damage to the horses was still too terrible to even contemplate.

He and his men had been spared the initial attack and arrow storm as they had been returning from a patrol sweep around the fortress and surrounding villages, their instructions to search out any signs of treachery. The men rightly grumbled about missing the celebration taking place both inside and outside of the walled city.

The feast, a celebration of the union of the Christian expedition and the Choctaws and Alabama nations of Mabila. The celebration promised singing, voracious feasting, and willing maidens.

The patrol had witnessed the soldiery and the wealthy Hidalgos; the surviving free herdsman and African slaves all celebrating with a boisterous crowd. The commanding officers departed with Governor De Soto to feast with the Cacique Tuscaloosa.

A frenetic ball game between at least two hundred men rolled back and forth across a glade off to the side. Cheers and guffaws were hooted at the scrambling players.

Only the patrol scouts and sullen sentinels walking before the town walls or guarding the nervous herds and the chained Indian baggage slaves did not partake in the celebration.

For everyone else of the Florida expedition, food was aplenty; endless plates of roasted venison and Spanish hog. Whole bass and catfish were spitted over red coals, giant frogs burned crispy, bowls of stewed dog-exceedingly prized by the Indians; steaming maize and gourds, dishes of tomatoes, peas and beans, baskets of peaches, plums, paw-paws, orange pumpkins, and green melons. Shelled walnuts, hazelnuts, and pecans mixed with dried berries and muscadines were passed around the roaring fires and ball game spectators.

From the tall gates, the Cacique's beautiful wives emerged, dancing and spinning, clapping enormous clamshells in a sinuous rhythm. Following them, a group of maidens decked with wreaths of wildflowers, naked from the waist up wearing bracelets of freshwater pearls, beaded necklaces of carved turtle shell, claws of panther, and bear or the talons of birds.

Spanish Priests scowled, but a lusty cheer rose from the soldiers and freemen alike. For the dancing maidens like their mistresses, were of pleasing aspect, their foreheads high, eyes lustrous, ebony hair lathered with bear grease; their beaming countenances full of willing promises.

"Surely they are sorceresses?" A soldier whispered gleefully to Rybowski.

But then searched nervously to see if any of the sour-faced priests had overheard his exclamation.

Castillo kicked his stallion and led his men away from the cheering crowd and jostling leering soldiers. On the circuit out and most of the way back towards Mabila, Cowboy wined incessantly.

"It's just not fair; we get the shit duty all the time," said Cowboy.

Ortega, for once, agreed with Cowboy. They had indeed been singled out for patrol duty while the entire army was feasting.

Castillo was still in a melancholy mood and not in the mood for feasts or maidens after his restless night of ill dreams. *Again*, the nightmare of their first year in the Florida Mountains.

Castillo shivered and sighed.

"Well Cowboy, if you had been born a wealthy Hidalgo, you would not have a saddle sore ass. Wealth has its privileges; even the Governor knows how far he can push his rich cavaliers. Rybowski is a bastard and Ortega is an Indian. So *we* ride. There will be food and women enough when we return from patrol," said Castillo. Ortega snorted in derision but did not comment. There were Frenchmen in the Grand Expedition.

Frenchmen were the source of the weeping pox that turned one's cock into so much spoiled meat and he *never* touched any woman who may have lain with the Europeans.

Rybowski held his tongue. He wasn't just angry, he was enraged. Other scouts could have helped and lessened their burden. However, with each village, his irritation melted, consolidated into a growing lump of disquiet.

"Things were not right," he had explained later. "In the villages, we passed through, where were the children? Their mothers?"

The scouts had observed only the unfriendly faces of old men, dwarfs, even once a blind albino had cursed unintelligible words at them causing all four scouts to make the sign of the cross.

However, the grumbling by the scouts had immediately ceased at the sudden uproar. A distant, but a rising cacophony of bellowing, panicked cattle echoing incomprehensibly through the pine and oak-studded hills.

The scouts had looked at each other first in wonder and then increasing concern as they, at last, recognized screams of the dying cattle.
Unknown to them, the harsh bellowing overshadowed the simultaneous screams of the butchering of men.

Kicking their horses into a light cantor, it would do no good to reach the origin of the noise on blown horses; they at last crested a small knoll where they had gawked open-mouthed at the impossible scene below them.

Thousands, perhaps *ten thousand* Indian warriors had surprised and then swamped the Spanish camp. Here and there, small knots of Conquistadors had formed squares, shields up, the rat-ta-tat sound of stone-tipped arrows breaking upon shields, and helm rolled over the four scouts on the knoll.

Only steel and sheer stubbornness kept the squares from being overrun.

A fire had broken out inside the fortress of Mabila; huts blazed, dark smoke billowed into a sky where storm clouds threatened the horizon.
The army's supplies had been staged *inside* the walls.

Charging down the knoll, they reached the melee on the outskirts of the fortress, just as the Captains; including Governor de Soto and his personal guard hacked their way free of the confining walls and into a horde of raging Indians.

That day Castillo and his scouts had gained the Governor's favor by riding directly into the fiercest and costliest battle of the campaign. The Scout's horses kicking and biting forged a bloody pathway over twisted and broken bodies, enabling the hard-pressed Captains to reach the uncertain safety of one of the hastily formed battle squares.

Nevertheless, in only one treacherous battle, albeit a bloody long, but victorious fight; the Florida expedition with two years of dazzling victories, had been in essence, crippled.

Well, Mabila was in the past, the consequences of today's events had to be paid, thought Castillo.

Familiar faces.

Castillo recognized the guards coming to fetch him, *Ortiz and McCulloch*, recalling their names. They, like himself, were also veterans of the conquest of Peru.

All three bore the Seahorse Tattoo of Conquistadors. However, he had never been friends with these two infantrymen. Never had sat down and shared wine or mead.

He nodded his head in acknowledgment of their approach.

To the ordinary Spaniard, the Mahogany-skinned Ortiz and the azure-eyed, morose Scotsman, McCulloch, were almost giants.

It was sometimes unsettling that many of the Indian warriors, especially of the Timucua tribes actually towered above these two intimidating Conquistadors. However, no Indian was as deadly as the Governor's picked guards.

Castillo stood nearly as tall, and his skin was the same Mahogany shade as Ortiz, yet his lean form could not match the bulk of either of these two imposing infantrymen.

They were killers who had proven their salt by cutting De Soto clear of the trap at Mabila.

The Scotsman wore his heavy blade upon his back, a heavy unwieldy weapon of his homeland. A quiet man, McCulloch would never be called bright; but in a fight the man could cut a corridor through any army in the world, leaving a trail of human destruction in his wake.

Ortiz, now *he* was the clever one. Beady dark eyes set deep in a thick shaved head with no neck; his preferred weapon was a poleax. In skilled hands, the poleax was the deadliest weapon any man could face.

But Ortiz also had the adroitness to read people, to see the truth of them, no matter the patina of polished courtly manners; consequently, he had both friends and enemies at headquarters.

Ortiz, his tongue seldom held in check, could be as prickly as his pole-arm.

Ortiz glanced admiringly at the warhorse, his infantryman's sense keeping him far enough away from any straying hooves or gnashing teeth.

The Scot, however, had another opinion of horses in general. They were good to eat and they usually carried assholes.
The Spanish version of knights--*Hidalgos*, the majority of them flat out useless. Oh, there were some good fighters sprinkled among them, but mostly they acted more like Englishmen than Spaniards. Spoiled popinjay assholes who complained incessantly if they had to walk anywhere.

This Castillo they had been ordered to retrieve was one of those wealthy popinjays, although grudgingly, he was no coward and a superior horseman who rode that beast.

Neither guard took any heed to the Indian servants.

"Well, Castillo," said Ortiz, who leaned heavily upon his scarred pole-ax.

"Not sure what you did to piss off the second in command, but the little weasel-faced bastard has the Governors' ear and we've been sent to bring you in," said Ortiz.

Ortiz paused for an instant, for the first time noticing Mary, quickly inspecting her from head to toes and not bothering to look at Castillo, as he mumbled his opinion.

"Personally I think the second wants your horse," said Ortiz.

"Wants your horse," no words could have had a greater blow, like a booted kick to his groin. What was worse, the words had the ring of truth to them.

Armando Martinez De Algarabejo, the diminutive but admittedly talented second in command of the Florida expedition.
There *had been* coarse jokes about the supply nag that Martinez had been forced to ride. His horses, a tough gelding, and Berber mare had both perished along with many of the expedition's other horses in a hail storm of arrows at Mabila.

"Fuck," said Castillo and then sighing, "I'll leave my stallion and servants with the Pole. And we will see the Governor."

From his pouch he removed a rag, unwrapped his silver and blue crucifix, draping it around his neck. The crucifix pleased Governor De Soto and his priests, and so it was openly worn during his visits to Headquarters.
Other than his official visits, the cross was too heavy and bulky for horseback riding or scouting in general.

His father, a hard man, had given him the cross on his last day in Mexico.
It was the only thing besides bruises that he could recall ever receiving from his father.

The crucifix,-gaudy and old-fashioned, had originally belonged to his Grandfather, however, Castillo had promised himself many times that once back in Havana or Mexico City; he was trading the heavy ornament for warm spiced rum or if lucky, *two whores.*

They located the Pole, Ortega, and Cowboy outside of the ruined village.

Castillo's scouts were camped upon a meadow of fresh grass, their well-used horses grazing above the flooded stream. Equipment and clothing spread across the pastureland to dry in the afternoon sun.

Two days of torrential rain storms had brought misery to everyone and death to many of the wounded. Cowboy, the youngest of the four scouts, combed prickly burrs from his Mustang mare, while her colt pranced about, snorting in alarm at the approach of the Governor's escort.
Ortega crouched over smoky coals tending to the roasting ribs of a savory Elk, his bare arms and chest covered in the tattoos of his faith. His right arm covered in an elaborate crucifix and his left, a cruder tattoo of a seahorse.
Across his hairless chest were stenciled various Latin phrases from the Bible. Words of power and magic.
He shook his head in a wry smile at Rybowski's comical attempts to teach his new Indian servant short sentences of Spanish.

"Lord, mighty killer of Turks," repeated Rybowski, to his uncomprehending servant, as if trying to teach one of the Mayan yellow and crimson talking birds.

The servant, a tribute slave, said to be from Missouri, another clan west of the great river, spoke hesitantly.

"Tki-ler au Turcs," said the Missouri Indian.

"Yes, Yes! That's me, Count Rybowski!" yelped the animated Pole.

The Missouri servant almost smiled. However, the strangers-of many-hues, with their giant dog-beasts, were still too odd.
He, along with Castillo's two Ar-Kansas servants, had been woefully mistreated captives of the Chickasaws until finally presented as gifts to the Spanish scouts who ranged far afield of the main expedition. The scouts had, in kind, presented a handful of colored ribbons that were greatly admired by the Chickasaws.

At the approach of Castillo and the guards, Rybowski ceased the juvenile game with the Missouri Indian.
He recalled the two guards from the battle at Mabila, their armor, beards, and weapons sheeted in blood, gasping, stopping only long enough to slake their thirst from a stream that flowed pink, before returning to the melee and killing.

Rybowski gestured towards the Governor's guards.

"They are here about this morning?" asked the Pole. Castillo nodded.

"I'm guessing so… I need one of you to look after Adelantado and the servants," said Castillo.

He withheld the fact that he might have to give up his stallion.
Instead, he guided the big horse to Cowboy who was well aware of the stallion's tendency to bite, cautiously set hobbles around Adelantado's legs, and turned the stallion loose to graze with the other horses.
Castillo pulled up a clump of thick grass, shook off the dirt, and fed the sweet grass to Adelantado. Perhaps for the last time.
Ortega and Rybowski exchanged rumors with the Governors' guards, thereby allowing Castillo a few minutes with his horse.
The Cavaliers and their horses…they were weird like that.

"Luis," said Cowboy in a hushed voice, "Just want you to know that I agree with what you did this morning at that village."

Castillo nodded at the young man. However, he was not sure if he approved of his own actions; *in fact, the morning events had left him confused and drained.*
Absurd as it seemed, some days his mind felt like a fine coat of chain mail that had stopped too many arrows and link by link was slowly unraveling.

"I'm done with this expedition, believed it would be an adventure, but I just want to go home. Marry Anna, raise some children, perhaps a few cattle and horses. Don't want no gold; just want to go home to my Anna," said Cowboy in a hushed whisper.

Cowboy and a few of the Priests were part of the very few who had not taken Indian women as slaves, choosing instead to stay true to his promise given to his betrothed.

Castillo winced at the words, spoken just out of earshot of Ortiz who was laughing heartily at one of Ortega's jokes.

He studied the young man before him, handsome face leather tanned, not yet twenty years of age, but his eyes had the faraway look of any veteran of the Peruvian Mountains.

Desertion, for that, is what Cowboy spoke of. Deserters were treated harshly, flogging or execution and besides, in the vast land of Florida, *there was nowhere to desert too.*
Castillo placed a strong hand on Cowboy's shoulder.

"If, *no*, when you get out this Florida, I want you and Anna to come to my family's estate in Mexico. Tell my brother Ernesto, that I said, he should give you lifetime employment. We always need good men on the ranch," said Luis Castillo.

Cowboy acknowledged the proffered offer; realizing it had been given in the context that Luis may not be present.
However, he understood. Watching with concern as Castillo walked away with the two giant infantrymen in the direction of the main camp and an uncertain meeting with Governor De Soto.

Book one: Part 3: De Soto

Castillo inwardly shuddered at the approach to the main encampment.

Because of his responsibilities as a mounted scout and Lancer, Castillo was duty-bound to eat and sleep in the small outer camps required to forage the horses, thereby avoiding the horrors of the main Spanish encampment.
Even after his promotion, he sometimes sent the Pole to headquarters to report for him.

Now, however, under armed escort, he could not avoid the camp and mistreatment of the slaves. The expedition required four to five hundred Indians, slaves, manacled, ill-fed, worked nearly to death, and then quickly replaced. The countryside was even now being shaken and dredged to replace the slaves killed in the recent battle.

For reasons impossible to understand, he had begun to be physically ill at the treatment of the slaves. The problems had begun even before the army's exit from the frozen mountains and growing *forbidden* suspicion that there may not be any gold in this savage land, named Florida.

The mountains, that is when he had begun the restless nights of difficult sleeping; plagued by evil dreams of a bloody field of tubers and crimson-eyed creatures. Dreams that often ended with him waking up with a start or shriek.
Then the distressed nights were followed by days when a heavy foulness smothered his normally bright disposition.
By ranging far afield on his stallion, he had been able to control the growing disquiet, his burgeoning revulsion of the actions of his own countrymen. But then, the loss of Captain Vasquez by a single stone-tipped arrow.

The recent death of his friend and captain had forced his unwanted promotion to leader of the scouts and the *requirement* that he report in person to headquarters.

Each subsequent visit had left him with a sour burning knot in his gut and an ache that gnawed at his very soul.

Without his horse... He shuddered at the possibility that he would be assigned to the ranks of the foot soldiers or slave guards.
Of course, the Army had not changed, it had been much the same in their subjugation of Peru; of which he had actively participated.

But I have changed. I tire of the uselessness of it all. Of the butchery of the expedition.

After passing by a lone sentry; the familiar ordinary odors of any encampment washed over him: slit
trench latrines, vomit, horse manure, offal from gutted game, and an undertone of cloying sour-sweet rot of gangrene that would make one retch if dwelt upon. The rot only slightly masked by the cleansing odor of wood smoke and the mouth-watering aroma of roasting elk or dog; *there would be no pork or beef for the foreseeable future.*

However, it was difficult to adjust to the new reality of the camp being shockingly reduced in size after their *victory* at Mabila.

Still, the onslaught of diverse languages assailed him and his escort. The spectacular gold-laden victories of Mexico and Peru had drawn fighting men, adventurers, and bastard sons from all corners of Europe, eagerly gathering at busy ports, crossing the gray Atlantic as if on a new holy crusade. Albeit a crusade to conquer unexplored Florida and not Holy Jerusalem or the dusty lands of the Saracens.

At the periphery of the main encampment, someone, one of the soldiers, perhaps a prince or failed priest, someone who was possessed of too much education and a twisted sense of humor, had scrawled upon the peeled bark of hickory: *"Lasciate ogne Speranza, voi ch'intrate"*.

Castillo, whose father had forced upon him the importance of reading in addition to the martial skills, recognized the well-known phrase from Dante's Divine Comedy, repeated the words.

"Abandon all hope, ye who enter here."

He almost laughed, except his sense of humor was muted.
For his dilemma, the ownership of his warhorse might very well depend upon the falsehoods he would have to weave.

Fortunately, his father had also beaten into his stubborn son the vital skill of lying.

Thank you, Papa, but you're still the heartless bastard son of a swine who sold mother when at length you had tired of her.

Like a Hell in Dante's inferno, he was led from the outskirts of the camp and ushered through a camp of dispirited soldiers, most with festering wounds. Sullen men who paid little, if any heed, to the escort.

Guided through concentric circles of misery: despair, torture, murder, past groups, or lines of closely guarded Indian slaves, the most beautiful women of Mabila, rousted out of the forests, weeping at their new status of concubines.
While the male slaves, dependent upon their status, ranged, from sullen and quiet to anxious or terrified or wailing in mutilation.
Castillo grasped at his seldom-used crucifix, seeking some type of alleviation. However, there was none.

Blacksmiths hammered chains onto a growing line of Florida Indians that curved out of sight. A pack of dogs growled over ownership of a growing mound of human noses.

"Lasciate ogne Speranza, voi ch'intrate" muttered Castillo and received odd looks from his two guards. Finally, he was escorted to a large native dwelling, guarded by De Soto's Halberdiers, to meet the man who was responsible for the multiplicities of human suffering.

The Halberdiers, having been given word to expect Castillo and his escort, waved the three men inside without challenge and into the presence of the Governor.

Governor De Soto, in burnished armor, falcon-eyed, dark beard immaculately trimmed, wearing a warm alpaca robe burned crispy black at the edges. His fine Incan robe once belonged to the Emperor of all the Andes, being the only item of his wardrobe that had been salvaged from the ambush in the ruined fortress of Mabila.
The Governor-General sat perched upon a bench covered with the tribute pelt of a bison, his attention focused upon a group of Indians and a priest who translated their words into Spanish.

The Governor did not notice the three newcomers. However, his second, Armando Martinez De Algarabejo, who missed very little, frowning, his amber green eyes only briefly acknowledging their entrance, nodded slightly towards a corner of the spacious building, towards bearded soldiers stiff with attention, their crossbows cocked with stubby quarrels.

The iron-tipped quarrels were pointed at warriors armed with tall war bows, their hair tangled with hawk and owl feathers, and bodies painted in stark combinations of fierce crimson or vermilion, solid black, azure, and saffron.

The warriors stood behind their leader, a Cacique of proud bearing, his impressive mantle of checkered Jaguar skin, high tattooed cheekbones, and polished mica earplugs, looking every bit the part of a regal barbarian king.

The escort had interrupted a meeting between De Soto and a Chickasaw Cacique.

The Chickasaw leader apparently arrived to pay homage or suggest an alliance as the Chickasaw people were sworn enemies of the Alabama and Choctaw clans so recently defeated at Mabila.

However, through some misunderstanding or abuse, the forces of the Spaniards and Chickasaws had skirmishes with losses heavy on both sides.

The conversation between the Governor and the Cacique had to be spoken through the tortuous process of three translators, each who could only speak one or two of various Florida languages.

Castillo watched the translation with interest, for during his work as an advance scout, he had participated in hundreds of similar difficult conversations.

The proud Chickasaw Cacique spoke for a great length of time.

A Choctaw prisoner, who professed to speak Chickasaw, translated his words to a valuable Appalachee slave, who understood both Chickasaw and Timucuan.

The Appalachee slave spoke the Timucua words to one of De Soto's supplicant priests, a tonsured man who claimed to have learned one

of the Timucuan dialects to save the souls of the Indian slaves from the wiles of Satan and the fires of hell.
When the Applalachee finished, the priest turned to the Governor-General.
The priest, his face devoid of nearly all emotion, translated the words of the Chickasaw leader to Governor-General De Soto.

"The Indio Cacique says as follows my lord," explained the priest.

"Mighty De Soto, to whom all of Florida owes obedience, I grovel before your Lordship for my treasonous actions. Ruler of all Florida, just lord, be mindful of my weaknesses and proclivity towards evil, for I know not the true God and his saintly mother. I beg clemency for the recent battle with the Christians, even though I have not earned a pardon. My wish is to serve your Lordship and Holy Church. To offer my bravest warriors for your bidding. To crush your enemies, to serve and obey you in all ways. Lord punish me as you see fit and order me as your own but allow me to serve as your faithful bondsman."

The priest-translator ended with a flourishing bow.

Castillo, who although not up to Ortiz's caliber of judging people, nevertheless was still very good at reading people, especially Indians, whispered his opinion.

"Horseshit," said Castillo.

His father, a celebrated conquistador who had accompanied Cortez in the conquest of Mexico, had always stressed "Know thy enemy." The actual statement had been "Know thy fucking enemy and kill them."

The Chickasaw leader had *absolutely* not made that adulation to the Governor.
Ortiz, for all his reputation for talking too much, knew when to be quiet and lightly punched his charge behind the head.

"Shut up!" hissed Ortiz.

Of course, Ortiz also recognized horseshit when he heard it hit the ground. Yet the translated words had greatly impressed Governor-General De Soto.

"Tell the savage that he is indeed forgiven. Tell him that he is pardoned for past actions, that thenceforth and in the future, we would consider him a friend, brother, and protect him in all his affairs," said General De Soto.

Soto waited for his words to be translated.

"Finally, to cement our new friendship, the Chickasaw must supply women, slaves, corn, and venison. Then our two peoples, the Chickasaw, and Christians will move together to crush the remaining Choctaw and Alabama nations," said Governor De Soto.

The Governor nodded at an assistant who presented the Chickasaw Cacique a small round mirror, who at first seemed greatly impressed with the trinket.

However, even before De Soto's words had been fully translated; the face of the Chickasaw leader turned to stone, black eyes turned deadly and a string of angry words shot from the Cacique's twisted mouth.
The cheap mirror was dropped purposely on the packed earthen floor.

The three translators, agitated, with cautious glances at both the Chickasaw and the Governor, conversed urgently among themselves, and at last, the priest replied; his head bowed.

"I'm sorry, my lord, the Cacique's last words are not understandable." Observing De Soto's scowl, the priest hurried forth an explanation.

"The Applachee slave refuses to translate the Caciques words sire," said the Priest-translator. Placing the failure of communication fully upon the Indian slave.

The Chickasaw Cacique and his painted warriors turned and departed the hut without another word. The crossbowmen followed the Chickasaw out of the building.

The Governor considered the priest for a long moment before speaking. "Kill the Apalachee slave," ordered Governor De Soto.

Armando Martinez De Algarabejo, always close at hand and whose task it was to temper and advise the Governor, leaned in and spoke quietly.

Soto, still glaring at the Priest, nodded and amended his command.

"Kill the slave, *after* you find a suitable replacement or we move out of the lands where we will require questionable skills," said Governor De Soto.

The falcon's eyes bored into the priest's cold fish's eyes to make him aware that he bore the lion's share of responsibility for the failure in language skills.

"And Priest. Arrange for a gelding of a slave, not the translator. An example must be set for those who displease me," said Governor De Soto.

Martinez leaned over and spoke again. The word "Castillo," audible in the large building. The Governor scanned the room, alighting on the escort and their charge.

"Esteban, Liam, bring Luis to me," ordered the Governor.

Only in private did De Soto use personal names. Such was the nature of keeping control over a mercenary rabble.

The three men approached the seated Governor and nodded their heads in respect.

"Thank you for bringing our guest," said Governor De Soto to his guards.

"Now would you be so kind as to monitor the savages that just departed so brusquely? If need be, you have my leave to kill them or chain them with the baggage slaves."

And with a gesture, barely a shrug, he dismissed the escort. Governor De Soto turned his attention to Castillo.

"Luis, you do us a disservice by staying away too long from our presence," said the Governor-General.

"Yes, your lordships," said Castillo with another nod of the head. Acknowledging both the Governor and his second in command, Martinez.

"Luis, I have a new assignment for you and your squad. However, there is a…. an *unpleasantness* we must correct," said De Soto

Governor De Soto stroked his beard in contemplation and then nodded to his clerk, the same priest who had muddled the Chickasaw translation.
The priest who had eyes of a dead fish, quoted from memory the "unpleasantness", apparently now an official charge against Castillo.

"On October 20, 1541, Anno Domini, it is reported that you, wantonly and with full knowledge of standing orders, released slaves that were the sole property of his most just Governor Hernando De Soto."

Castillo briefly wondered who had been the person who had reported him?
Not his men. It had to be one of the foot soldiers assigned to him to raid the town; a wild guess… it was that broken-nosed Saxon bastard Webber.
However, it did not matter, because the charges were true.
He listened quietly as dead fish eyes completed the rendition of the charges against him.

"The accusations are true, your lordship," admitted Castillo.
The admission brought him back to the morning, clear and dewy.

They, the horse and foot soldiers, had expertly surrounded a small town. No, not a town, just some hamlet with perhaps ten families. So complete was the surprise, the trap, that the Indians had not the chance to raise arms to defend themselves. One of those rare occasions when no natives were killed or *at least not when the trap was sprung.*

The Indians were herded together, the huts searched for food. A poor showing of corn, tubers, and dried fish and that not even enough to properly feed the men for more than three days. A few martin and

fox skins of minimal value were found. It was as expected with such a small community.
Still, it was an adequate capture of slaves considering the remoteness of the wilderness through which they trekked.
The extraordinary thing was how ordinary the raid was. The same as a thousand other raids since the landing in Florida.

Yet it had been different.

He had sat upon his stallion watching as the food was collected and the infantry grinning at the approaching bloodfest. Their spears and halberds leveled; an encircling ring shrinking ever tighter around the new slaves.

Castillo's involuntary jerk startled him.

He had a vision? A spell? It was as if a Gypsy had offered him a vision of the future.
But no, it was not really a vision. No, it was only that he was looking at dead slaves and they simply did not understand their death yet.

In his vision of the future, armored men of the expedition stood over dead or dying Indians: Infants and toddlers lay crumpled and broken. Blissfully unaware of the ravenous wolf packs that would be drawn by the blood.
The older children and the elderly, those fortunate enough not to be of any use, had been quickly stabbed with efficient strokes. The soldiers saved their energy for the rapes.

Castillo shuddered at his future prescient vision.
His vision included the future of the remaining slaves, those of minimal work value, taken to the main camp to die slow torturous deaths, starved, whipped, branded, or their nose and ears sliced off to signify their slave status.
That woman *there*, she would topple over dead, whipped and emaciated, hauling firewood while fighting with curs for small pieces of foul vomit. Her husband, that man over *there*, haunted by his children's murder would burn on a stake for insulting a priest.
The hungry flames cheating both starvation and pestilence.

At last, Castillo rubbing his eyes, driving his thumbs deep until the pain made him scream, "Enough! Enough! Enough, I say!" screamed Castillo.
Kicking his stirrups, charging his horse forward, knocking spears and halberds askance, the wooden shafts rattled upon each other, breaking the encirclement, startling both Spaniards and Indians who scurried to get out of the way of the big warhorse.

"Let them go! Enough of this murder!" yelled Luis Castillo.

Spurring his stallion forward again when the captives did not move fast enough,
"Run damn you run!" yelled Luis Castillo.
He herded the prisoners towards a small flooded stream. The Indian women wailing as they snatched up their children and scampered away like rabbits, finally breaking into a full panicked run to escape.

"Run, damn you, run," he said with a final whisper.

A concerned Count Rybowski rode alongside him and grasped the stallion's hackamore. "Luis?"

"I have to get free of this," whispered a sickly Castillo.

Book one: Part 4: Assignment

Governor De Soto brought him back to the present.

"Well what do you have to say about this serious accusation?" asked the Governor.

Castillo still shook at his unexpected behavior at the village; however, with passion presented his prepared excuse for having disobeyed De Soto's standing orders.

"Very exalted and very excellent Lordship, whom the King in his great wisdom presented with the Governorship of all of Florida and the care, the disposition of its people and control of its riches."

Like there was anything in this land but beasts and hostile savages.

"Lord, we gathered your slaves at the unnamed village in preparation to secure and conduct them back to your camp and their disposition of your just ruling."

Castillo paused for effect.

"Forgive me, sire. As I sat upon my horse I began to have suspicions that the Indians of this village had been involved in the atrocities committed at Mabila.

"Sire, my thoughts went to our soldiers who had been captured and how we found them eyeless and castrated. I recalled the battle, stepping over our slain herds and the screams of the horses impaled with a hundred arrows.

"I recalled my anger at the treachery attempted upon your very person. However, you are blessed by our just Lord God who protected your life when so many good men of Portugal and Spain perished.

"Black hatred carried me, swept me over as if in a great tide and my only desire was for the death of your servants. I was consumed and wished nothing but honor-bound vengeance.

"Sire, only the briefest fleeting moment of reason returned and I realized I was about to execute your servants. Kill them *without* your consent. In desperation, I freed your Indians, *before* in my haste I put them to the sword.

"We can catch them or others in the morrow. But *had* I ordered them killed, they could never be brought back to serve you, sire," explained Castillo.

Castillo dropped to one knee in front of De Soto.

"August father and ruler of all the peoples from the coasts and mountains of Florida to the far lands of New Spain, and whose inhabitants rejoice in thy just righteousness, your lordship, our refuge, and strength in this untamed territory of pagans, forgive me."

Governor De Soto was quiet for a few minutes studying Castillo. At length, the Governor turned to his clerk with a dismissive gesture.

"Father Enriques. Note that Luis Castillo, Captain of the Scouts is pardoned of unspecified infractions," said Governor De Soto.

Castillo wondered, *did I see a hint of irritation in dead fish eyes?*

De Soto turned back to Castillo.

"After all Luis, I just pardoned that ill-bred savage. He was a Chickasaw?" Soto asked Armando Martinez.

Martinez nodded.

"Yes, sire," said Martinez.

"A Chickasaw who I will end up killing anyway. How could I do any less by my best scout and lancer?" said Governor De Soto with a flourish.

A hint of a smile, but then the falcon eyes returned.

"However, Luis, let me stress our situation. The success of our expedition depends upon slaves for labor, their *fear* of us. *Our* victory is a three-legged stool, dependent upon slaves, allies, and tribute to supply our needs," said the Governor.

De Soto had a faraway look. As if he was still staring across the endless Inca Empire.

"I understand, sire. Your humble servant will not fail you again," said Castillo.

Governor De Soto nodded his head in satisfaction and turned to Father Enriques.

"Please arrange for a geld punishment for the translators' failure. Assemble *all* the slaves and Christians to witness the punishment. Choose an Indio at random. However, have the geld completed before sundown *today*," ordered Governor Soto.

"Yes, sire," replied the priest-scribe.

Dead fish eyes genuflected and departed the building.

The Governor dismissed all his bodyguards leaving only the three, himself, Martinez, and Castillo for a private meeting.

De Soto walked to the doorway and watched as the guards herded the Indians to the sprawling open ball field.

However, the falcon eyes were actually examining the area for anyone eavesdropping, and at last satisfied that no one was within listening distance, turned to Castillo.

"Luis, I have a task that requires your sworn silence. A task that is vital to the very success of the expedition," said Governor De Soto.

And he gives me something this important after my performance this morning? wondered Castillo. "My word, sire," Castillo replied.

Coming to the attention stance his father had taught.

Governor De Soto paced the hut seeking the proper words, *words were important.*

"You followed me into Peru, those tall mountains fraught with unknown perils; I know you can be trusted. Do you recall when we boldly marched into Cuzco?" asked De Soto.

The falcon eyes had returned as he spoke of their shared past.

"Yes, sire, I recall," said Castillo.

For with his share of Incan gold, he had purchased his beloved War Horse. The Governor abruptly turned and asked a question.

"You have read the chronicles of Cortez and the defeat of the Aztecs?" said Governor De Soto. The abrupt change in subject surprised Castillo and caused him to stammer.

"Why of course, sire," *And had to listen to it every day of my life.*

"My father, as you are aware sire, was with Cortez when they captured Tenochtitlan, and he also made the chronicles of the conquest required reading for all his children," said Castillo.
So we could bask in his glory, but how father had despised mad Cortez.

"Ah, good," said the Governor, "So few people can read except priests or merchants," said Governor De Soto.

Governor De Soto peered at Castillo reassuring himself that the tall scout who stood before him was not from one of those classes.
"Then you may recall what happened to Cortez's ships?" *asked the Governor-General. So it had come to that.*

"Yes, sire, there had been a mutiny. A mutiny by soldiers loyal to the Governor of Cuba and they attempted to steal a ship to return to Cuba. To prevent further mutinies or temptations, Cortez had the ships scuttled. Except for one to be used to communicate with the royal court," said Castillo.

A look of mad inspiration washed over De Soto's face. Castillo had seen that look once before.
When together they beheld a room, *an entire building* of Inca gold that was the ransom for the Inca King. The King who had been murdered once the room had been filled with treasures.

"Renown and affluence require great risks. And even *greater* commitment. Cortez *understood* that, and so he had his ships scuttled. *There was no retreat*, and no turning back," explained Governor De Soto.

"Yes, sire," said Castillo.
A cold sweat ran down his back. He chanced a brief look at Martinez.

Had the Governor gone mad?

"Luis, I have pre-arranged orders with captains of the supply ships.

An agreed-upon code word in the event of a disaster such as Mabila. The ships are to pull back to Cuba. There can be no... *there will be no* retreat of this expedition. No mutiny, no turning back. No desertions. We succeed like Cortez!" said Governor De Soto.

The Governor placed a strong hand upon Castillo's shoulder.

"You were with me at Cuzco. You have been tested and are trustworthy. I need you and your men to find those Brigantines and order them back to Cuba," said Governor De Soto.

The hand squeezed tightly to Castillo. A swordsman's grip.

"Our ships are reported to be at the bay of the Pensacola. The recent rains... if the rivers have subsided; you should be able to make Pensacola in seven days if you give your horses no rest. The rains? I understand the river crossings and fords the army used may be flooded from the storms. However, if the rivers prove to be a barrier to completing your assignment, you will turn inland until you locate new fords," explained Governor De Soto.

Castillo thought of the hill over the flooded river where his men camped.

"Of course," continued the Governor, "I am striking *North* in the morrow. North and west before the corruption of mutiny can set in."

Governor De Soto smiled confidently.

"I'm certain you and your scouts can catch back up to the army in a few days. However, if the ships *are not* at the bay of Pensacola, you will have to travel south to the Bay of Espiritu Santo, to our first Florida landfall. *Luis, you will find the ships for me*" said Governor De Soto.

Stern dark eyes bore into Castillo.

"The code word the captains will be waiting for is 'Cortez,'" said Governor De Soto. Castillo nodded his head in understanding.

"Yes, sire," said Castillo.

No mention was made about returning if they traveled to the Bay of Espiritu Santo.
However, a great weight had been lifted from his shoulders and he turned to Martinez. "Then you do not want my horse, sir?" asked Castillo.
Martinez was startled at the unexpected question but only smiled.

"Lord no! Only an idiot would want your horse, and only a damn fool would get on that beast," replied Martinez.

Castillo smiled at what he took as a compliment.

"But," continued Martinez, "We, the expedition, we need your horse and the horses of your men. Find those brigantines and return them to Cuba," said Martinez.

"And Luis, your orders, your destination, are not to be told to anyone but those whom you trust with your very life," added Governor De Soto.

An implied threat? A gradual dawning, as Castillo realized the castration about to take place was not just a lesson for the Indian slaves, but also a warning for both the potential mutineers or those who failed the Governor-General's assignments.

"Yes, sire, we will find those brigantines or galleons and give the code word to send them back to Cuba," said Castillo.

Castillo's head was spinning with details and the distance.
It had taken the expedition two years just to get to Mabila, albeit much of that time had been spent in the misty mountains of Florida searching for golden kingdoms or fighting off hordes of archers in the maize-rich kingdoms.

Castillo genuflected and departed the Governors' hut to find the entire camp assembled in rough formation.
He quickly picked out Rybowski's snow-white hair, and standing near his horse was Rybowski's

Missouri servant, and the two Ar-Kansas slaves, Mary and Juan.

Governor De Soto and Martinez watched Castillo depart the building and enter the assembled crowd.

The Governor hissed,
"Working with broken tools," and turned to Martinez, "So what do you think, will they make it?" asked Governor De Soto.

Martinez, a deep thinker, and lawyer by profession mulled over the question that had no real answer.

"Cannot quite figure out what happened this morning at that village. A breakdown perhaps. Extended campaigns can do that to the best of men. *There will be more breakdowns of course.* And perhaps a mutiny to put down. As to his excuse? Well, a lie of course. But a grand one worthy of a royal presentation. Leadership quality in that excuse. Well, lawyer quality anyway," said Martinez.
A shadow of a smile.

"And, I might add, far and above the talents of that arse kissing priest you have as a translator. As to Castillo and his scout's chances? Well they have to journey hostile territories and a wild coast to find eight ships," replied Martinez.

Martinez inspected the crowd of soldiers and slaves that had gathered upon orders of Governor de Soto. The wounded, the dispirited, and the mad.

"Odds are about the same as for the scouts you sent out last week to find the ships. I would prepare the next group of scouts to follow Castillo, send them out five days hence. As planned, send more the week after that. *Someone* is bound to survive to locate the ships at Pensacola or Tampa, ah the Bay of Espiritu Santo. But *it is* a damn shame about losing that stallion to some savage for food," replied Martinez.

Governor De Soto winced, nodded his head in agreement and they both walked from the hut into the fading afternoon sunlight and the geld.

Castillo walked around a crude formation of closely guarded chained women, the recently captured lamenting maidens of Mabila. He pushed his way through nervous male slaves, shackled in groups of twos and threes, or personal servants who no longer required chains.

His mind was on the upcoming journey. They would need pack horses, spare… everything, crossbows, food, water bags, and he was stopped dead in his tracks as the slaves were no longer allowing him to pass.
A living wall of bodies that hindered his approach to his scouts.

The Indio slaves were planted to the ground in terror. For the priest with dead fish eyes walked among them to do what evil they knew not.

Following dead fish eyes were four soldiers, technically they were Ibo, African slaves who had been with the expedition since Cuba, purchased by De Soto for their legendary strength.
However, the Ibo now wore burnished armor, helmets, and clumsily carried halberds. The losses at Mabila having forced the army to free the Ibo and train them as soldiers.
As new soldiers, they were assigned the crap work to assist in punishment. Not coincidentally an up-close lesson for any recruit.

Dead fish eyes stopped where Rybowski, Cowboy, and Ortega sat astride their mounts and studied the Indians standing nearest to the scouts.

He's looking for someone in particular, thought Castillo. Hey asshole, it's supposed to be a random pick.
However the priest was planted in front of his slave Juan; staring intently at the Ar-Kansas Indian, then at his sister, then back to the three scouts. The priest glowered with uncertainty.
The priest scanned the crowd of slaves until he, at last, spied Castillo and moved slowly around making false gestures with long thin fingers, to which each slave cringed and gasped.

Governor De Soto's clerk-priest finally stopped near Castillo searching to see if any particular Indian served the scout. At last, the priest pointed to an unchained Indian. A Hidalgo's personal servant who just happened to be standing in front of Castillo. A Spaniard behind him began to protest and quickly stopped.

The four guards grabbed the wailing man and pulled him to the center of the crowd, stripped off his meager clothing, and held him adjacent to the physician who stood near a pan of red smoking coals and an iron used to cauterize wounds.

Dead fish eyes locked eyes with Castillo, baring crooked teeth in a cruel smile and at length turned and followed the guards.

Asshole.

An audible sigh of relief came from the slaves who had avoided punishment for an infraction unknown in origin or severity of punishment. Few of the slaves understood Spanish but many had their noses hacked off for reasons they could not comprehend.

Castillo for reasons unknown could feel both hands shaking and budding nausea in his gut. However, he knew better to turn away from the discipline when the Governor-General had ordered all to attend. He gripped his Grandfather's silver and blue crucifix so hard his fingers hurt.

Governor-General De Soto followed closely by Martinez marched into the plaza and with the authority granted by the King, spoke to the assembled peoples.

"This man, my servant, has displeased me," said De Soto in a loud commanding voice. De Soto turned slowly making eye contact with slave and soldier alike.

"If he were my enemy I would kill him and raze his town. However, he serves me under God's watchful eyes. So, he will only face my just discipline. Geld him an example of my mercy," ordered the Governor.

Dead fish eyes produced a well-gnawed piece of rawhide and a curved geld knife from beneath his stained robe. The slave begged in one of the Muskogee dialects until the folded leather was forced into his mouth.

The Priest expertly grasped the slave's testes applying downward pressure and with one quick motion severed them. The gelded man's body went rigid and passed into merciful unconsciousness.

The physician, or rather the physician's assistant, for the physician, an unconverted Jew, who nonetheless was an excellent healer had perished from a dozen or more arrow piercings at Mabila. The assistant sloppily applied the red iron to the bleeding ruin of the slave's genitals, inadvertently burning both thigh and penis, but cauterizing the fresh wound.

Acrid smoke, carrying the scent of burned flesh wafted through the crowd. One of the African slaves made into a soldier vomited. A few jokes and guffaws were heard from the assembled soldiers.
The Governor-General looked disgustingly at either the sick soldier or the incompetent physician. However, the lesson had been taught.

"Take the slave's nose," commanded the Governor-General.
Governor De Soto and Martinez walked away as the surrounding guards herded the shocked slaves to their pens for the night.

Book one: Part 4: Cowboy

Castillo pushed his way through grim-faced soldiers and fearful slaves, manacles, and armor clinking in the dusk.
Upon reaching the three scouts and the three slaves from west of the mother river; the Pole was silent, holding Castillo's warhorse.
Ortega was crossing himself and Cowboy refused to make eye contact. Instead, he rubbed the neck of his mustang and held tight a leash with the jumpy colt.
No one asked although he knew they wanted to know about the meeting with de Soto. Castillo mounted his stallion and spun him tightly around.

"The Governor graciously accepted my apology and has forgiven me. Let us get back to our camp. We have a new assignment," said Luis Castillo.

Castillo waited until full dark, the stars' brilliant overhead before explaining to his fellow scouts about their new assignment.
The campfire crackled brightly, the scouts soaking up the comforting warmth and sharing the slab of elk ribs. Old stories were spoken quietly.

Rybowski, a bastard son of a Polish Count, repeated his oft-made observation.

"Why do the Spaniards treat these people in the same manner that the Turks treat their Christians? I have fought beside the Royal Spanish Musketeers when they were sent to help stop the Turk at Vienna.
Those Spaniards were *honorable* and brave men who did not butcher simply for the enjoyment of seeing crimson on their blades.

In fact, the mettle of those musketeers was one reason I crossed the ocean. To fight alongside such men," said Rybowski.

Ortega, a man of easy laughter who found humor in most things and God in all things, joked with his foreign friend.

"*Sure*. Their mettle and the lure of Incan Gold," said Ortega.

Rybowski, as usual, denied the accusation that his motives were purely mercenary.

"Of course, I do not have the title of count. However, I received a goodly portion of my family's fortune. Like *you* and Castillo, I have money. I am here *only* for the adventure. Just that I have never quite adjusted to the Eastern type butchery practiced in Florida daily."

Rybowski pointed at the three Indian slaves who silently chewed upon their rib bones.

"These Indians. They are like the Slavs. Both peoples have discovered that wealth actually lies in the family, in God, and one's honor. Not the yellow gold, furs, or amber that gives wealth and power but only fleeting happiness," said Rybowski.

Castillo warmed to the old banter, the shelter of the brotherhood of the scouts. An unguent who had supported him through the difficult campaign.

He recalled the first time he had met Cowboy and Rybowski.

It had been soon after they had landed in Florida, at the shallow Bay of Horses. A spring flood tide allowing the Galleons and Brigantines to be pulled up close to the palm-shrouded shoreline.
By the third day in Florida, the sailors had at last completed the complicated and dangerous task of unloading the expedition's horses and other livestock and began the arduous work unloading supplies and crate upon crate of manacles and chains.

Except for the hardened veterans of Lombardy and Peru; the expedition's Lancers and Cavaliers, numbering over two hundred, were in foul moods with shortened tempers. Many of the pampered Hidalgos had even refused to assist in the unloading of their own horses.

Tempers had flared. Not only had they several times been attacked by the arrows of unseen savages; already a servant to one of the noblemen had been bitten by an enormous viper whose tail rattled like a gourd full of pistol shot.

Then some of the Cavaliers had learned to their great consternation, they would have to walk, *walk* with the infantry until their horses weakened or injured during the crowded journey from Cuba had sufficiently regained their strength to carry armored men.

To add to the insult, the upstart Commander of the Cavaliers, one "*Captain Vasquez*", an experienced veteran of the Peruvian Campaign, had *demanded of them* that all the Cavaliers would have to pull additional duty as Scouts.
Scouting was dangerous and difficult, subject to the whim of the climate while offering up small rewards and *no* glory.

Scouting was a task of peasants.

The Cavaliers of both Spain and Portugal had sold or taken loans on their holdings to finance the expedition expenses and journey across the Atlantic.
They had come for the *Grand Charge*, the sweeping away of barbarian armies and reaping harvests of golden treasures. They had not risked the crossing of the vast ocean to perform the tasks of commoners. And so, the embittered knights had quickly spread the rumor and even faster yet, believed their own rumor that Captain Vasquez was a fatherless bastard.

A peasant bastard.

They were justly incensed that a bastard and a commoner had ordered they perform peasant work that would quickly wear out their horses and gear.

A slight muttering of mutiny and the demand to see Governor-General de Soto would correct the stain to their honor.
In fact, Captain Vasquez *was* a bastard. A shame that had been considerably reduced by his return from the Andes with a fortune in Inca gold.
Vasquez was said by some to be a man of the "New World". A handsome mixture of Castilian, African and Indian.
Some veterans whispered the victory in Peru would not have been possible without Vasquez and his horsemen. That Vasquez had saved the Governor-General's ass from the Inca hordes.

Accordingly, despite vehement protests of the high born; Vasquez had been placed as the leader of the Lancers.
For his merit and not birth status! A stunningly illogical and dangerous concept.

The horse soldiers in any army were always a moody lot; however, the Governor had personally appointed Vasquez to lead the difficult Cavaliers *because of Vasquez's performance in Peru.*

And once ashore in Florida had come the ultimatum from Governor De Soto.

"Obey the requests of Captain Vasquez as if they had come from me. Mutineers and trouble makers will forfeit their mounts."

The loss of one's horse was *always* of paramount concern to any Cavalier, Hidalgo, knight, or scout.

Consequently, the Hidalgos, discontented, insulted, *dangerous even,* were again insulted when another peasant had without proper announcement, audaciously ridden into their company.
The peasant, a mere horse trainer from Hispaniola, dismounted and secured his horse to a palm tree and approached them as if an equal!

"Sirs, I need to talk with Captain Vasquez," said the peasant.
He required '*their*' bastard, Captain Vasquez.
It had become painfully obvious to those of the old families; that all of the New Spain peasants needed schooling in respect of their betters.

Sneers were followed by insults, horsewhips, and slim knives were drawn by the Hidalgos.

The horse trainer, a youthful peasant of little means who had been hired to care for the herds of horses and cattle, backed away in alarm from four immaculately dressed Cavaliers who surrounded him.
He reflexively pulled his own blade, a broad-bladed heavy-tanged fighting knife, and dropped into a crouched fighting position.

Even the Hidalgos had to pause at the sight of the big knife. Peasants were normally not allowed to carry fighting weapons, except when conscripted to fight for their lord or king. Or an invasion of Florida.

The leader of the Hidalgo assailants, Francisco de Tejeda smirked. He dropped his whip and withdrew his thin saber. Pushing aside his good friend, Don Queipo.

"My turn," he said, savoring the easy fight and cementing his leadership of the minor nobles.

However, a foreigner with silver yellow hair interjected himself on behalf of the peasant and without drawing his own large blade, backed the nobles away from the peasant. The foreigner was from the distant eastern lands. A Pole of unknown temper and fighting ability.

Steely eyes filled with haughty anger greeted the foreigner. *Another* problem with the Florida Expedition in the opinion of the Hidalgos, too many damn foreigners.

To the Spanish nobility, fighting alongside the Portuguese was humiliating enough, but De Soto had encouraged adventurers from all corners of Europe: Austrians, Italians and Lombards, Saxons, Minorcan and Corsica islanders, Low Country Dutch and Flemings, Franks, *English, English!* and hordes of unwashed barbarians-Moors and dark Moors, Danes, Scots, Welsh, and Irish. In small numbers from the alien east came fierce men with heavy mustachios and harsh accents: Poles, Finns, and Lithuanians.

"Savages all, Christian in name only," had mumbled De Soto's fuming priests.

Now, this Pole suited in outlandish armor had interrupted their disciplining of a mere peasant. Francisco de Tejeda sheathed his saber with a disdaining glance.

"The Governor-General has forbidden dueling among ourselves. I'll not stain my family's steel on this savage or that peasant" said Tejeda in subdued Spanish.

Don Queipo considered challenging the foreign knight to a duel, but grudgingly followed the lead of Tejeda. The Pole might be dangerous. *A dangerous cur,* he thought.

The "foreigner," Count Rybowski, had watched the youthful peasant ride into the camp of the Cavaliers. The young man dismounted gracefully, *a natural horseman*, and was almost immediately assaulted by the four finely dressed bullies.

Rybowski, *who was not actually a count,* only a bastard son with a strong dislike for bullies. But he possessed an even stronger dislike for those who had been born lucky enough to inherit a title without any connection to talent or effort. Inheritance awarded simply upon their mother's marital status.

He almost hoped the laced nobles would push the issue.

However, he had seen their hesitation when just one young man drew a blade in self-defense. And so he was confident and proved correct, that his armor alone would back the bullies away.
Rybowski addressed the young horseman in courtly Castilian.
"I will take you to see the Captain," said Rybowski.

Sitting beneath a sweeping oak of gigantic proportions, Captain Vasquez, Castillo, Hector, and Ortega planned the upcoming days. The four friends were experienced veterans, *survivors* of the Peruvian campaign. They were acutely aware of the manifold duties that would be demanded of the Cavaliers: scouting, rear and advanced guards, messengers, foragers, trailblazers, testers of river fords, finder of towns, catchers of slaves, and locator of pasture land for the livestock. Then, as needed, assist the herders to move the stock.
These duties would be in addition to the usual tasks of Lancers. Breaking ambushes, harass, flank, terrorize and finally pin the enemy in place so the infantry could crush them.

The sheer size of the De Soto army was a logistics nightmare; the most ambitious and well-funded expedition ever to come ashore in the New Spain territory of Florida.
Setting ashore onto the white sandy shores of Florida were over one thousand foot soldiers, two hundred Cavaliers, over one hundred skilled workers -- gold and ironsmiths, doctors, slave overseers, cattle herders, and horse trainers.
Herds of cattle, horses, and swine had been unloaded.

Consequently, due to the demands of food and clean water, the expedition would at any given time, be divided into five to twenty distinct groups, coming together only for the requirement of large pitched battles.
Hernando De Soto had estimated it would take five hundred Indian slaves to move the expedition forward. As it was, the separate hosts, like ravaging locusts, would strip the land of everything edible and foul freshwaters in their wake. So it would be the Cavaliers and scouts responsibility, to act as the glue that held the disparate armies together.

Vasquez deliberated their situation and his absurd hope that even as Captain of the Cavaliers and scout he would still be able to range far afield with the other three veterans.
However, it had become apparent that the obligations as Captain and the headaches caused by the disgruntled Hidalgos would keep him stranded to a central location where he could deal with difficulties as they arose.
At least until the spoiled noblemen either "hardened or perished."

Hector was going to be pissed, thought Vasquez.
Pissed by his decision to promote him as a replacement second in command. His sworn second, Rojas had, on stepping ashore in Florida, taken a fishbone-tipped arrow to the Jugular.
Rojas would recover if the arrow was not poisoned, however, for the foreseeable future he was confined to the dubious attentions of the Barbers and Physicians.

"Hector, I need you here with me as my second. Ortega and Castillo will have to be paired up with others," said Vasquez guiltily.

All three men were disappointed by the reassignment.
Into their shaded conference came two riders; the Pole on a big charger, followed by a young peasant on a tough-looking Mustang mare.

The Pole, *Rybowski is his name*, thought Vasquez.

The stranger wore the alien armor of Eastern Europe. Armor dented and worn from use, repaired in the correct places, the Pole's weapons, armor, and his confident bearing screamed "professional soldier." In fact, Vasquez had already marked the Pole as a veteran from the oft-talked about wars against the encroaching Turk and so placed him in a separate class from the majority of Cavaliers composed mostly of pampered Hidalgos.

For who knew what challenges lay before them in Florida?
The Expedition and scouts needed professionals *now*, with no time for waiting to see which of the royalty would shape up to honor their family names.

Rybowski reined his horse to a halt.

> "Captain Vasquez, good day to you," said Rybowski. Vasquez nodded, "Rybowski."

Rybowski let his horse graze and gestured to the rider with him.

> "This young man," in fact Rybowski was only a few years older than the youth on the mustang, "wished to see you, and required assistance to get away from your Spanish knights," said Rybowski.

The term "knights" was used as in the old-fashioned northern European meaning of the term, and not necessarily as the modern Spanish, "*Hidalgo*."

> The youth took offense to the foreigner's announcement that he had been requiring aid and protested. "I needed no help to handle those four cowards!" snapped the young horse trainer.

Rybowski smiled at the young man.

> "I do believe you are correct. No offense was intended," said Rybowski.

Even though it was the rare warrior who could face four men, even four cowards at the same time.

> "Actually Captain, my timely intervention offered up to *your* knights a chance to back away from this fellow's pig sticker and retain some sense of honor," said Rybowski.

> Captain Vasquez, curious, gestured at the weapon on the young man's belt, the 'Pig Sticker'.

49

"Let me see your knife," requested Vasquez.

The peasant handed the blade over to the Captain, who inspected the weapon, simple bone handle, wide blade, sweeping to a curved point, and with a broad tang to guard the hand and wrist.

"I'd guess it was made by a village smith; the maker is somewhat an artist," said Vasquez. Balancing the fighting knife, "The tip is too heavy," he said in contemplation.

"*But* if you had to punch through a leather jerkin, that extra weight would help. So then the maker knew a thing or two about fighting," said Vasquez.

He handed the blade back to its owner.

"My uncle sir, Raymond Acosta, he made the blade, he is our town smith," said the youth with evident pride.

"I'm Pablo Acosta of Aguadilla."

"Well, Acosta, you wished to see me?" asked Vasquez

"Yes, sir, horses, I found horses sir, *wild* horses. Three, perhaps four hours ride to the west," explained a nervous Acosta.

It took a couple of seconds for the others to realize Acosta was not talking about the Expedition horses, but *other* horses, *and* this Acosta claimed to have traveled three or four hours west of the camp and returned alive.

"So… Acosta, *you are aware* that we have been attacked four times in three days?" asked Captain Vasquez.

"Oh yes sir," said Acosta, apparently nonplussed by the sudden attacks by the Florida tribesmen.

"I smelled them long before I saw them. They had lathered on some rancid bear grease. Otherwise, they would have gotten closer to me before I saw them, but they weren't expecting me outside of the camp and they slipped by, about nineteen of them, naked, greased, armed with bows and arrows tipped with fish bones," said Acosta.

Acosta, worried at the looks of incredulity, hurried with an explanation.

"I'm sorry sir; I could not get back to the camp with a warning. They cut me off until they came running back. Only fourteen of them came back and one of your Lancers was chasing after them. They were scattering like rabbits. I think that was the third attack," said Acosta.

Castillo gave a short laugh.
"Why were you out there anyway?" asked Castillo.

However, Captain Vasquez cut him off.

"What duty did you hire on as?" asked Captain Vasquez.

Acosta was not sure if he was in trouble. The soldiers had proved to be a prickly lot.

"I hired on as a cowhand sir, but I'm working with the horses now. *Horses* are what I do best. What was I doing out there? I was looking for pasture for the herds. The cattle and horses might die by arrows, sir. But they will die of starvation if we don't find them better grazing," said Acosta.
Vasquez was intrigued.
The young man was correct of course. The Governor had sent teams of scouts in all directions, seeking forage for the herds and food sources for the slaves.
Not all of them had returned.
But *horses*; wild horses could be an asset to the expedition or even a potential source of profit after the current adventure was over.

"Show us these horses. *But*, let us proceed with caution. The Florida natives may have discovered your trail," said Vasquez.

Captain Vasquez looked at Castillo and Ortega.
"You two, scrounge, steal or borrow two lightweight crossbows," ordered Captain Vasquez. The two conquistadors returned shortly with two crossbows and a dozen quarrels each.
Ortega, who cared little for the existence of untrained horses, was far more interested in learning about the easterner, obviously a professional soldier, someone who would have his back in a fight.

"Alright 'Cow-boy' show us your horses," said Ortega. Captain Vasquez and his scouts mounted up.

"Rybowski, if you don't have any current duties, would you come with us? I think we would like to hear something about your experiences," asked Captain Vasquez.

The Pole mounted his charger and they let Acosta guide them west, out of camp.

"Well, the first thing you should know, Captain," explained Rybowski, "So you heard it first *from me*. I was born a bastard. My father is the Count, and he provided for my upbringing, even money, however, my half brother received the title and estates."

To the Spaniards, except perhaps Ortega, being called a bastard was second only to being called a coward or cuckold.

Duels were fought for far fewer words.

Castillo and Acosta were shocked and embarrassed at the admission. Vasquez, also born a bastard, only nodded his head in understanding.

"A difficult admission. Unlike some of the cavaliers, *we* scouts have no issue with who inherited what titles," said Vasquez.

Ortega, even though his family had adopted all things Spanish, could not comprehend the Spaniard's problem with children born out of wedlock.

Any infant born through the difficult process of childbirth should be celebrated.

Furthermore, the fact General De Soto had chosen Vasquez, *a bastard*, to lead his Cavaliers, only pointed out the foolishness of the entire dispute.

Of course, Rybowski had heard the rumors spread by the Hidalgos and decided to use the fact that he was also a bastard to get in closer to the command structure of the scouts and perhaps get away from the pampered nobles.

He had his fill of following spoiled princes *and* amateurs that could get one killed or ransomed.

"So, exactly because I am the Count's son, *but not the heir,* I've been fighting since I could ride. Fighting Turks, lots of Turks, but also those bastard Swedes and Finns, the Serbs, Croats, the German Princes, Cossacks, and Muscovite Rus and Janissaries, that would be the Turk's Janissaries," said Rybowski.

Upon leaving the camp proper, all four men were silent. They were entering into the home territory of a little known opponent.
They threaded their way through a lowland wood of seemingly endless palm trees; the thin trunks crowded tightly together, the broad overlapping leaves shutting out the sunlight, following a well-used animal trail into a grove of immense cloying cedars, where they anticipated flights of arrows at every shadowed turn.
Hidden in the cedars, twisted a small river of the clearest waters that Castillo had ever seen. Small fish and turtles darted through emerald green water plants that rippled like strands of a mermaid's hair.
Acosta, who had temporarily accepted the demeaning name "Cowboy," guided his mare down the snow-white sandy bank and into the cold translucent water, surprisingly deeper than it looked. A family of otters barked in alarm, diving away with a series of splashes.

Cowboy allowed his mare to drink deep but pulled the horse back when she began to paw the water.
    "Let me show you the *whales*, they are not far from here," said Cowboy.
There was excitement in Cowboy's hushed voice.

Crossing the river to the opposite bank and turning upstream. The terrain steadily lifted, leaving the cedars behind, the forest transforming into towering oaks and sycamores.

    "I was watching the whales play, sitting sort of quiet-like when I picked up the scent of bear grease and pulled back into the shadows," said Cowboy.

At the top of a small rise, they could see the large oval pool edged with limestone ledges where twenty or so small black alligators sunned themselves. From beneath one of the ledges, a spring bubbled forth, the force of the water rippling the bluish waters in which swam immense green-brown forms.

A pair of nostrils lifted out of the clear water and exhaled strongly.

"Seals? Walruses?" asked Rybowski, studying the animals with their large tail flukes.

"Sea Cows." Castillo and Ortega both said the name of the giant creatures.

"Good eating, if we can't get venison," explained Vasquez.

"The Arawaks and Caribs call them Manatee. *Lots of work* to get one of those things out of the water. Let's move on to the horses before we get caught out here after sundown," suggested Vasquez.

Cowboy led the captain and scout lancers out of the forest onto a plain of waist-high broom grass, intersected with muddy trails of wolf, deer, and *human track*s, across another clear stream bordered by swaying cypress.

In the distance, impossible to tell how far away, an immense wildfire consumed prairie and forest. A vast and ominous smoke plume billowed up to the heavens, rising to co-mingle with cotton and gray rain clouds. The giant plume eventually consumed all stray clouds within its reach.

The scouts emerged from the second stream and spread out onto another plain; a burned pasture land where tender green plants pushed up from the blackened ashes of broom grass and palmetto.

The fire perhaps a month in the past had cauterized the plain and the new green sprouting from the dark ashes attracted grazers of all shapes and sizes. Herds of deer bounded away, their white tails shrinking until disappearing into the far distance.

Fierce-looking wild cattle, shaggy, and horned snorted at the horsemen. Rybowski reined in his horse uttering an odd phrase in Polish. He struggled to find the word in the Iberian language, at last spitting out the word *Bison*.

"Those are bison! The aristocrats of my country hunt bison in their forest preserves. More dangerous than boar, those things," said Rybowski.

Riding a wide circuit around the alert and snorting bison, they startled a pack of wolves resting in the shade of a dense stand of cypress trees.

The pack darted away and the scouts came into the hearing range of two screaming animals that everyone recognized.

Horses.

The sounds of two stallions doing battle caused their mounts to perk up, snorting and whinnying.

"Adelantado, heel!" snapped Castillo.

His stallion eagerly pressed forward to join in the unseen battle. The party of scouts continued around the cypress and onto another open prairie, stopping within an easy bow shot of a herd of wild horses.

Two dark-coated stallions, sweat-streaked and bleeding savagely kicked and bit at each other. The winner would gain control of the herd of mares. To the cavaliers, connoisseurs of horseflesh, they were surprised to see the excellence of the horses.

"See, as I told you, Barbs and Arabs!" said Cowboy. "I know my horse flesh."

A boisterous Ortega interrupted Castillo's reminisce, forcing him back to the present. To the company of his friends sitting around the fire and the Governor's new assignment.

"Wait, wait!" said Ortega. "Do you know the difference between a Spaniard and a Lawyer?"

Rybowski and Cowboy groaned and guffawed.

"We've heard that joke a thousand times," said Rybowski.

Castillo tossed his rib into the crackling fire.

"We have a new assignment from the Governor," explained Castillo. The scouts were suddenly serious and attentive.

"We are to back-track the trail of the expedition. Follow the coast, locate and deliver a message to the supply galleons," said Castillo.

They contemplated the perils of the assignment. They were used to traveling far ahead of the expedition. Their duties were to meet suspicious and occasionally hostile clans.

But to journey *back* over the army's trail where *all* the nations were riled like a nest of ground hornets… The Florida nations had suffered mightily under the yoke of Spanish demands. They considered the dangers of their new assignment to locate six to eight ships along

a wild uncharted coastline rife with hostile natives, *hostile nations,* and without knowing the galleons' exact locations.

"What we know is the boats are using both Pensacola and the Bay of Horses, the bay we landed the first day, as supply depots. The smaller ships, perhaps frigates or brigantines are patrolling the coast looking for signs of the expedition. We only need to find one of the boats," said Castillo.

Castillo looked upon his men in the flickering firelight. Yes of course they understood the danger and would not shy from the orders.

Did they realize he needed to get away from the butchery of De Soto?

"The ships have standing orders to shadow the army. All we have to do is find them. If needed, we will make our way to the Bay of Horses," said Castillo.

The unlikely prospect of any success caused Ortega to comment.

"Like finding a virgin in a nunnery is what we got ourselves," said Ortega. He received chuckles and guffaws.

"Oh well, it gets more interesting. Not only do we have to locate these ships; we are to give them the code word that will turn them *back* to Cuba. Temporarily marooning the expedition in Florida," explained Castillo.
Three questioning faces stared back in dull comprehension.

"*Mutiny.* The Governor rightly fears a mutiny. With the ships returned to port, he can better control any unpleasantness that may arise. So the ships have to return to Cuba. But first, *we* have to find them," said Castillo.

Rybowski, ever thinking things through to the end, only had one question.

"And what are our orders? What are we supposed to do when the ships depart for Cuba? Go with the boats or try to catch up with the expedition that will be moving away from us the entire time we are heading east in the opposite direction?"

Castillo had wondered about the same question himself.

"I guess that depends on what type of shit we are in when we meet the ships," said Castillo.

Book one: Part 5: Tanatacura

First, the miscarriage of the twins, and then the death of her son.

The tears had dried on her cheeks. Her offering to the rain god no longer flowed and she carefully arrayed shells and tiny arrowheads next to her lifeless son. At length, she kissed him a final time and pushed red earth over his poxed face.

Tanatacura buried her son next to the twin girls that she had miscarried in the season of the new leaves and yellow jackets. Yet, it felt as if a dozen summers had passed. In the woods and fields, other women buried their children in secret places.
Only the children of the royalty or priests were blessed to be entombed in the holy mounds; the pathway between earth and the heavens.

Across the city and periphery clan villages, a keening wail rose to the heavens. Dogs howled to match the wailing of forlorn parents. The disease of boils had taken nearly all the children of the vast Coosatchee Town.
And it had only been one day since the coming of the fever boils.

Only yesterday her son lived and the maize farmers had caught a thief skulking around their fields. Upon summons, the farmers had brought the trussed thief before the king and priests.

A curiosity.
For the maize thief had the same glistening walnut dark skin like that of the elk-dog warrior whose skin now adorned the king's wall of trophies.

Word was sent that the king wished for the dark-skinned thief as his slave. However, when the thief was presented before the king; frightened priests had pointed to the boils across the dark man's neck and chest.
Boils that leaked fetid pustulence and the priests insisted the captive be taken *outside* of the city and sacrificed to the gods.
The king flayed those who displeased him. However, the boils had turned the thief's skin the color of charred pine.

"There is witchery and demons in the weeping boils. Remove him from the city!" hissed his major wife.

His major wife whom he had not bedded in years; at times offered wise counsel. The king consented to the sacrifice. When both the priests and his major wife offered the same warning, he heeded their advice.

Word spread rapidly that the stranger would be sacrificed on the level ball field outside of the sunrise gate. An immense crowd had gathered outside the city, farmers and midwives, artists and tanners, warriors and priests, naked slaves, and rich merchants. Nearly all who lived in Coosatchee Town were present for the sacrifice.
Excitement filled the air; crispy muskrat skewers were passed about for families to pick at. Yellow dogs fought for the bones and screaming babies were given nipples to suckle.
Archers on the tall walls-having the best view, watched with interest as the priests directed sweating slaves to set a post in the ground and secured the dark-skinned thief with leather and sinew.

Tall spear-men formed a rough oval around the sacrificial post and arrow impact area.
Tanatacura and her friend, Whistling Duck, held their children high to witness the occurrence. Bodies crowded close together and one warrior pressed up too close behind her, keeping his hands above him, waving unstrung bow and arrows, yet pushing his groin forcefully against her backside.
It was not unpleasant and she pushed back, matching the movements and feeling the erection of the not-so-shy stranger.

The king, followed by his many wives was carried to the gathering wearing shirt-of-a-thousand-pearls that gleamed iridescent in the midday light. Huge mica earrings cut in the shape of birds, flashed back and forth blinding people as was his right. The king and the sun, one and the same.
A mighty cheer arose from the assembled peoples, for their king was the god incarnate ruler of the fertile Coosatchee lands. His personal blood offerings caused the maize to grow and their enemies to flee.
The king's slaves set the royal litter on six posts, set so the king could witness the sacrifice.

From the ridge west of the city, Natchez merchants drove forth their slaves, captured Mobile and Houma fisherfolk to be sold in the markets. The merchants were relieved to have reached the protection of the city and avoided Chickasaw raiders.
Slave merchants and slaves alike stopped to stare at the immense gathering and sporadic iridescence that flashed from the center of the crowded plain. The Natchez licked their lips in anticipation. Such a gathering would make their sale of slaves quick and profitable.

Centered around the dark man and post, tattooed priests chanted holy songs. Festooned in fur and feathers, the priest's elongated earlobes adorned with the heads of red cranes or the long-nosed god, swayed with the rhythm of their chanting.
Select archers assigned to the sacrifice, danced, stomping the packed earth with steps-of-power praying to the god of archers for an accurate shot.

Priest acolytes carried platters of dried elk-dog meat. Passing out to all who wished to attain the essence of the speed and strength of the riding beasts from the south.

Interspersed in the assembled crowd; swayed and stumbled the maize farmers who had first captured
the dark thief. The farmers had sprouted their own boils after wrestling the dark man to the ground. The
multitude gathered for the sacrifice, pushed and shoved the fevered farmers, pushing upon the leaking pustules and unknowingly spreading the fluid of the boils throughout the vast crowd.
Whistling Duck grabbed two pieces of elk-dog and shared them with Tanatacura and her son. The toddlers greedily sucked upon the half-dried meat.

"May they grow to be fleet warriors," said Whistling Duck.

"May they grow to kill the enemies of the Coosatchee," replied Tanatacura.

Whistling Duck gave an annoyed glance at an older warrior who had pinched her breast. ,

"I miss Strikes-with-flint. I hope the warriors return soon," said Whistling Duck.

Tanatacura wiggled pushing back on the warrior behind her.

Whistling Duck might miss her husband, Strikes-with-flint, but she certainly did not miss her husband, Runs-with-lightning.

In fact, no one had struck her since her husband had left to war upon strangers at Mabila. She wiggled again, a coquettish grin upon her face. Yet she *did* worry for both Whistling Duck and her child. Who would feed them during the approaching winter?

There had been no word of the three hundred and sixty warriors who had left weeks ago to assist their sometimes ally, the king of Mabila. When the runners from Mabila had arrived with a request for archers, the priests of Coosatchee had declared three hundred and sixty warriors - *one for each day of the year*; and journey south, each with three hundred and sixty arrows.

Shawnee war captives were required to carry such a vast quantity of arrows. Yet the Shawnee slaves had gone armed and eager for a fight. Bravery in battle would gain their freedom and even official adoption into the vast Coosatchee Empire.

The King in his pearl shirt nodded to begin the sacrifice.

A cheer rose from among the Coosatchee as the first warrior stepped between two priests, drew his powerful Osage bow, and released an arrow straight into the heavens.

The crowd cooed, holding their breath, straining to follow the flight of the arrow until nearly out of sight, to mark that holy time when the god-who-had-brought-the-bow, gripped the arrow at its peak and, momentarily holding it in invisible hands, then released it with a blessing, to plummet back to earth.

Priests and archers alike shuffled away from the incoming arrow.

The arrow thumped into the earth only a few paces from the dark man, and the crowd cheered in approval.

Gamblers waged slaves, flint, or rare shells on how many arrows it would take to kill the thief. The gamblers wagered on how many arrows would hit the crowd, what fletching would be used on the arrow, or bet upon their own clan to gain the renown of hitting the man tied to the post.

Each new warrior took his turn, stepping up to the priests, firing their arrow straight up and the crowd hooted the name of bird feather fletching and yelled in excitement as the arrows plummeted back to earth.
Goose and eagle, red tail hawk and sea hawk, crane, buzzard, wood duck and mallard, raven, woodpecker, heron, owl, crow, and turkey.

Anticipation and excitement grew with each shot.

Each time the crowd roared, Tanatacura felt the warrior's hand between her legs, searching, touching, the sensitive spot that her husband always ignored.
She could not exactly recall when the warrior standing behind had first caressed her, for the crowd pushed and swayed with each shot. Only that she looked forward to, she needed each arrow that lifted towards the heavens and the subsequent roar of the crowd.

A warrior of the raven clan stepped between the priests; fired his arrow and it came down to sink into the post, mere inches from the prisoner's head, and the crowd roared.

"Crow! Crow!"

She groaned with the crowd.

Another arrow was shot into the sky, wavering, and came down into the packed mass of spectators. Thudding harmlessly into red earth, the people scattering, pushing and shoving, screaming in the exhilaration of the near-miss.

And the warrior behind her groaned with her as his hand found her under her cotton apron…

Another warrior stepped up, released his arrow and a fierce scream erupted from her mouth as an arrow dropped from the heavens to sink deep into the shoulder blades of the dark man.

Tanatacura gripped her son, eyes closed tight as she shuddered and leaned heavily on strangers crowding around her, while the Coosatchee fell into a frenzy chanting "Turkey! Turkey!"

The warrior behind her vanished into the chanting crowd and Whistling Duck gave her a wry look.

A priest acolyte climbed upon the sacrificed thief and pulled the arrow free, tossing it to the frenzied crowd, and the arrow was passed from men to women, warrior to child, each touching the bloodied arrow for a blessing from the god-who-had- brought-the-bow.
Tanatacura and Whistling Duck both touched the arrow and rubbed a small dab of blood across the forehead of their children.

On the post, the dark-skinned stranger now dead was ignored, blood congealing across the contagious boil the arrow had pierced on its path to the dead man's heart.

Book one: Part 6: Freedom

Before sunrise, their horses were saddled, while two pack horses, which had been relinquished from the expeditions dwindling supply of horses, were loaded with spare weapons and supplies of Indian pemmican and jerked venison.

Rybowski, already mounted on his big warm blood, his shock of white silver hair stood out among the Spanish camp.
As did the pair of eagle wings across his shoulders.
His 'Turk killing wings' he called them and were only worn for important events or upcoming battles.

Rybowski dwelt upon the Ogeechee woman and the fire. His woman that he had become fond of. She had been impressed by the magic of his warrior wings. She who, when given the opportunity, had taken up arms and had fought *against* the Spaniards at Mabila and subsequently perished in the air stealing inferno as the Indian fortress burned.

Castillo checked the girth strap on his horse, giving it an extra cinch, and mounted his stallion. He patted the war horse's neck, whose ears had gone flat at the nearness of Rybowskis roan horse.
The other scouts mounted up, Ortega and Cowboy each taking the rope of a packhorse, followed by their three slaves on foot.

On the outskirts of the camp, the infantry sergeant Webber drilled the four African soldiers with Halberd and sword. Webber's practiced eye took in the loaded packhorses and spare weapons, *no short patrol.*

"Them Indian slaves are just gonna slow you down; might as well give them to me," said Webber. The infantryman was greedily apprising Mary's legs.
Castillo chose to ignore the Saxon but nodded to the Africans, men he had befriended when they were slaves.
His mother, also of the Ibo people, had come from the same country - might be cousins and he had felt some small connection to the Africans.

The new soldiers, sweating already from their practices, had carved crude sea horses into the flesh of each other's arms, the sign of the Conquistador.
How they had lived through Mabila...... well they earned their new tattoos, by simply surviving that chaos.

Castillo held up his tattooed arm in recognition of their new carvings. Rybowski, who had killed nearly as many Germans as Turks, stopped to converse with the Saxon.

"You see Sergeant, those three... " said Rybowski, indicating the Indians following the pack horses,
"... are for my lance practice. You have to drive the lance in just so without snapping the shaft or let's say the wood does not break, an unskilled stab could get the lance ripped out of your hand, or even break your wrist. This is a skill that must be practiced on real targets," explained Rybowski.

Rybowski continued talking about saddles and spurs, Turkish Cavalry, and the benefits of a curved saber versus a straight blade.
Webber growled, becoming ever more agitated.

"I have duties!" blurted the Saxon.
Rybowski chuckled, immensely pleased at having irritated the Saxon.

"Have a good day, Sergeant," said Rybowski.
He kicked his horse into a light gallop to catch up with the other scouts.
After traveling ten leagues from the main camp, they halted on a meadow with burned and scarred hickory trees.

"This location will suit," said Castillo.

Castillo and Rybowski loosened their lances from rawhide holders and gestured the three Indians forward to the front of the horses.

Castillo opened an elongated case that held an extra spear and an unstrung Indian bow quiver, with four feathered arrows, a small flint knife, and a leather bag containing pemmican.
He tossed the items on the ground and gestured to Juan to pick them up.

Then Castillo pointed west towards the distant mother river that some of the slaves named Mississippi.

"Go," said Castillo. "Take Mary and go home to whatever godforsaken country you came from."

Juan hesitantly took up the bow and expertly strung the weapon.

The act of stringing the Osage bow impressed the Europeans because except for Rybowski, only some of the Welsh and Scots were powerful enough to string the Indian weapons. The average Spaniard could neither string nor draw the powerful native bows.

Juan began to string an arrow when Castillo's lance pricking his neck, drawing a tiny bead of blood. . Castillo wagged his head in the universal symbol of *No.*

"Go home," said Castillo.

Rybowski tossed his Missouri slave a small stone hatchet, some animal snares, and a bag of food.

"Go," said Rybowski. Gesturing to the westerly direction.

"Run like the devil is after you, cause if the Spanish bastards catch you... Well you have already witnessed hell on this earth," said Rybowski.

The Indians understood not a word of it.

When all four horsemen yelled "Go!" the three Indians turned and made a slow lope into a stand of persimmon trees, spooking a noisy flock of quail. The servants were gone.

I'm gonna miss my topping, thought Castillo, turning his horse towards the east.

Book one: Part 7: Plague

On the second night, a pronounced lament, a keening wail echoed between tall mounds and off crenelated walls.

The King-Who-Is-the-Sun had died.

Yet she cared naught for the loss of her sovereign god. She cared naught if the sun or moon failed to rise. Her tiny son was gone and she tended her friend Whistling Duck, the only person alive in the whole green world that she cared for.

My son. Would be that she was in a terrifying dream and she would awake to her son's mischievous laughter?

No.

She had covered his face with red earth.
Grief-stricken she had ripped handfuls of hair from her head trying to release the pain that threatened to drown her in sorrow.
He had been so healthy and strong!

Only Whistling Duck's needs kept her from taking her own life.
With the clan healers themselves dead or dying, she burned sacred tobacco in a carved soapstone vessel; the curative smoke curled about the rafters of her wattle-and-daub hut, ejecting the menage of sprites and unseen demons that had brought on the killing sickness.

Tanatacura rocked beside Whistling Duck, grasping her friend's discolored hand until finally Whistling Duck went rigid, coughed blood, her last breath a throaty gurgle, and voided her bowels in death.
Whistling Duck, no.

Around her, in a thousand huts, parents still grieving at the loss of their children watched helplessly as their parents were next to quickly succumbed to the pox.
Around her, in two thousand huts, nearly every adult watched in fascinated horror, the painful progression of boils, the steady growth of swellings of joints that they knew foretold their rapid death.

Except for the empty hollow feeling inside of her, she grew no boils, felt no fever or weakness.

She rose and stumbled outside of Whistling Duck's hut, sinking to the packed earth, and watched dully as ill neighbors, relatives, and slaves covered in weeping boils fled the dying mound city.

It was there that the priest, "Falls-Star" and his warriors found her. Falls-Star, a minor priest but the only priest immune to the sickness, had been assigned to collect workers, free or slave, anyone who could still walk. And bring them back to the center of the city to take up flint spade and woven baskets of red dirt to bury their King in his temple mound.

However frustratingly few people could be located, most of the Coosatchee, at least those who could walk or paddle and with no parent or child to hold them in place, had already fled the dying city in panic.

She did not resist the warrior's spear prompt and accompanied an assortment of people, most ill but some like her, who suffered no effects.

Ill or not, they were nevertheless prodded deeper into the city by warriors, some so weak they dragged their flint-tipped spears to the royal mound.

The royal muralist, Rains-on-Fires, protested loudly as the warriors pulled him away from his painting, leaving paints and brushes untouched.

An angry warrior thwacked him across the forehead with a spear shaft and Rains-on-Fires quieted as blood streamed down his face.

Falls-Stars would broker no protest.

The King-who-is-the-Sun, required bodies to carry earth, and the King-who-is-the-Sun required blood to nourish the earth. Blood was required.

> "And I will not fail in my obligation," uttered Falls-Stars.

His warriors hunted the emptying city, gathering up both free Coostachee and slaves, Koasati and Choctaws, with their distinct flattened heads. Anyone who could still walk.

Often dragging wailing free women away from lifeless husbands and distraught fathers from their lifeless children or teenagers from still parents. Dealing out strikes and blows as needed for the King-who-is-the-Sun could not be denied.

At the King's earthen mound, slaves were carving out an earth chamber; while others, the least sickly, carried the body of the god-king, covered in a blanket of pearls and bear claws to his resting place. Tobacco was burned in carved bowls to clear the space of ground and air spirits.

A line of male slaves followed by the King's wives were guided or pushed up to where the king lay, covered in pearls and tiny flint arrowheads. Many of the wives tore their hair, wailing in despair for their lost god-king.

Priests carrying conch shell cups of the sacred black drink, made from the leaves of the holly tree, forced to be entombed with the king to purge themselves.

The King's wives and male slaves drank the bitter broth and almost immediately vomited. A priest, pale with fever, approved of the purification rite and led each victim to kneel in the pit next to their king. Falls-Stars dismayed that the elder priests had died or were too weak to perform the ceremony; nevertheless repeated the litany that would return the King to the home of the gods and bring forth his replacement to step into view upon the highest mound.

"How you have fallen, Morning-Star, Son of the dawn! You who brought forth the maize! You who once laid low the Cherokee and Shawnee!" spoke Falls-Stars.

He nodded his head, and the royal executioner bludgeoned a slave with a heavy ax of hematite. Next, the weeping wives were sent home to their sun king.

"Is this the man who shook the earth and made kingdoms tremble, the man who planted the wilderness, who overthrew his enemies and would not release his captives?" asked Falls-Stars.

He nodded his head again, and another slave was dispatched. The royal executioner, peppered with angry boils, swayed as he broke open the skull.

"Go now, return, ascend above the tops of the clouds. Sit enthroned on the utmost High. Beloved Sun, scent of cedars, winged-hunter-falcon who brings the ducks, fire-in-blood rattlesnake, Father of crawfish, web builder, and wolf. Send us the new Sun to rule over us!" begged Falls-Stars.

Falls-Stars paused; was it not now the time when spider would block the sun in the sky and a new sun on earth would be designated? When no shadow passed over the yellow sun, he continued the prayers he had been taught.
Who will be your successor?

"Pearl bright shining dew in the morning sun! Ruler of the Rivers. Keeper of the honey. Singer of the ground hornets. You who had eyes of the owl. Speed of the swift. Wisdom of the winter geese. You who taught jay and raven to screech. You who taught wood-pecker the secret of grubs-in-trees. The Shrike to hunt, the hummingbird to sup nectar. You who brought forth acorn and oak, you whom the gray squirrels changed to scarlet to honor your very presence" spoke Falls-Stars.

Even as he felt no effects from the pox that was ravaging the city, he was sweating, nervous.

How much blood was required?

Falls-Stars gave the final nod and all the terrified slaves to be interned with the Sun King were killed. Lesser priests, weak with wet carbuncles, arranged the kings twenty-four wives and five male slaves around the king and red ocher powder spread across all.
Priest acolytes, the few remaining, carried a variety of grave goods and set them over the slaves' bodies.

Arrows, an arm span long, tipped with deer horn or razor-agate, two feathers twisted about the shaft. Elegant bows of Osage, axes of polished hematite, and razor-sharp shark tooth war clubs. Bison horn and whelk-shell cups. Gold beads and copper gorgets, pipestone carved into the shapes of frogs and jaguars, huge baskets of tobacco. All to be available when the great sun returned home.

Tanatacura saw that the ground was dug up, as if in a forest bison rut,-the path leading to the temple mounds.

Taking this footpath, they met the honor guard of fifty archers who guarded the remaining slaves, men,

and women of many nations- Alabama, Coosa, Ocmulgee, Oconee, Cherokees, Mobile, Pensacola, and Uchees.

The free Coostachee were ignored until at last directed to work side by side with the slaves to carry heavy baskets of dirt and cover the King-Who-Is-The-Sun, his wives and servants.

Tanatacura carried earth to cover her king.

Falls-Stars was distressed.

For he had said the words, had made the blood offerings, yet the sun still shone as brightly as if no offerings had been made.

More blood, there would have to be more blood.

An Ocmulgee gray hair-exhausted and sick stumbled, fell sprawling across the ochre-coated bodies and Falls-Stars nodded at the waiting executioner.

Still not even a hint of change in the sun.

"All of them, kill all of the slaves. And if need be, the Coostachee. Our sun demands blood!" commanded Falls-Stars in desperation.

The priests, the executioner, and the archers, many who had laid their weapons on the ground, began to kill the ill and dying, those slaves who were easy to dispatch.

Yet for many of the slaves, they had had enough abuse and began to fight back.

"Dog talker," a Cherokee, "Owl," a Choctaw with a flattened head, "Bison Jumper," of the Uchees, and "Serrated-Arrow," of the Shawnee, each immune to the effects of the pox, attacked their tormentors with heavy flint spades.

A wave, the avenging slaves pushed forward, hacking and chopping everyone in their path. Rains-on-Fires grabbed Tanatacura,

"We must flee! The slaves will spare no one!" said Rains-on-Fires. Under his breath, Rains-on-Fires mumbled,

"And I don't trust those priests!"

He pulled her away from the King's burial, towards the city's southern gate.
Only when the archers had retrieved their bows and showered the melee with stinging arrows, did the slave uprising stall and finally, every slave was slain.

Falls-Stars lifted his hands to the heavens.

Is this enough blood?
Still, Spider did not block out the sun and bring forth the new sun-god.

Rains-on-Fires and Tanatacura ran through the gate and she pulled the artist to a stop.
A pack of red muzzled dogs barked at them and two warriors, immune to the sickness, passed them with a warning.

"Ware! Shawnee raiders to the north," warned the warriors.
The warriors armed with powerful Osage bows and full quivers of arrows sprinted north towards the smoke-filled horizon.

"Where do we go?" asked Tanatacura, for her home was in the great city.
Rains-on-Fires spoke without hesitation,

"The Shawnee are to the north. Therefore we go south to the ocean."

And they joined other stragglers fleeing the city, south towards the nations of the Pensacola.

Falls-Stars watched as the last of the bodies were covered in red dirt. Still, the gods were not satisfied. More blood was demanded.
An alarm was called out that echoed through the emptying city.

"Shawnee! "Shawnee!" Shawnee! Persistent enemies like craven wolves around a bull elk were always harrying the northern borders of the city.

He realized the folly of the offering of slaves. The gods demanded the blood of warriors spilled upon the earth.

To the archers and the few remaining Coosatachee, he gave new orders.

"The Gods! The Gods have demanded we go forth and slay the Shawnee. Everyone who can walk will go forth to slay the dogs of the north. Only then, the new Sun-King will return to bless us," ordered Falls-Stars.

Until the return of the Sun-King, he would rule the Coosatachee.

Book one: Part 8: City of Mounds

At the intersection of two great rivers, one flowing muddy brown and one with waters sky cobalt clear, they came upon the first body.

The horses snorting in protest at the sight of the woman slumped across the path.
The woman, newly dead and who had probably seen the red dawn that morning, lay upon the foot-worn trail, her face peaceful as if sleeping.

A peace disturbed by the scarlet pustules that covered her body. Boils still oozing glistening pink viscous fluids.

A flurry of swear words and the four scouts made the sign of the cross.
"Jesus wept," muttered Cowboy. For the pox had entered the land. Seeking a ford, the scouts traveled along to the broad river, which kept its two distinct brown and blue torrents until at last combining into one solid color of opaque green.
More bodies lay on the trail.

One man sprawled face down in the muddy trail as if slurping for a final drink of water.
The deceased, nearly all adults with only a few children, were covered in crimson boils. The bodies had not yet begun the process of decay, conveying they had only recently perished.

Where the river waters blended to green, they guided the horses up a small ridge and for the first time in a year, spied the distant Apalachee Mountains.

Yet, it was the city spread out before them, vast and somehow noble upon a cultivated plain, that took their breath away.
A magnificent sight to behold; over one hundred earthen mounds blanketed in emerald green, some topped with houses, had been forced inside a tall crenelated palisade, the log wall plastered white that reflected the afternoon sunlight at them.

From the center of the mounds flowed a cerulean spring, twisting between the man-made hills and under the white wall, to flow between neat rows of thatch-covered huts that numbered perhaps in the thousands. Fields of emerald and golden-eared corn spread out along the river until fading away into the distant river plain.

"Food enough to feed the Army for a year," muttered Cowboy.

At spaced intervals, towers and arrow loops covered the approaches to portcullis-protected gates. To their soldier eyes trained to such thoughts, they took in the height of the wall, the towers, and were admiring of the defenses.

Castillo had the distinct impression of the Yucatan, of the Mayans, their temples now abandoned and mined for the construction of haciendas and churches.

Ortega however, groomed on the stories of Tenochtitlan, and the legends of his people's greatness was briefly saddened.
Dreams of my fathers, he thought, never having actually seen the white city on the lake in all its glories. And never would, as Tenochtitlan, no longer existed. Renamed Mexico City, a mere shadow and hesitant reflection of the glory of the Mexica, now stood on a lake slowly being drained. God's decisions were not to be questioned.

Rybowski pointed at the trail of bodies leaving the city.

"Comes to mind, a summer lightning strike upon a tall pine tree, the tree being killed outright, but little fingers of lightning spreading along the ground, trailing out in all directions, the green grass turning brown in each of the myriad of fingers, of which one could, if wished, trace the dead grass back to the tree trunk and source of its death," said Rybowski.

So it was with the city below them.

From several gates issued trails of bodies, spreading out in all directions as if not one thing guided them. The gates to the city having the greatest amount of bodies and thinning out the further one traveled away.

The four scouts traced one such twisted trail of death to the very ridge upon which they stood. Beyond the city and fields, a smaller town sat on the other side of the river. There had to be a ford, but they would have to journey through this valley to reach the ford.

"Look, survivors!" exclaimed Cowboy.

But quickly realized his first impression was very wrong.

For below them at the base of their ridge, there was motion vast and sinewy, the trail shimmered with movement.
Dark shapes tugged and pulled along the road of death. And the dawning reality, ranging from horror to simple acknowledgment and expectations, gained from observations of other pestilences in other cities. The motion coming not from survivors but from the actions of feasting buzzards. Many of the birds, too full to take flight. They simply perched and preened upon their unholy feast.

The scouts kicked their mounts into motion. Dark fascination drew them down the ridge to the city, even as collective sagacity screamed at their subconscious to flee and never return.
Ortega was calm as he rode into a poxed land, bolstered by his belief in the Spanish God.
The Lord is my rock, and my fortress, and my deliverer; my God, my strength, in whom I take refuge; my shield, and the horn of my salvation, and my high tower.

His family belonged to the small number of people who were immune to the myriad assortment of Spanish illnesses.
In fact more immune than the Spaniards themselves.

The obvious explanation had been to assume that his family's immunity to the European diseases was a simple result of embracing the god of the cross. Despite his people, his neighbors had equally accepted the god of their conquerors, yet those pious converts continued to suffer from the plagues which decimated entire regions.

Ortega's family had come from an important lineage of Eagle warriors, elite and proud, yet upon the fall of Tenochtitlan, his father had quickly adapted all things Spanish. Relinquishing his Aztec heritage and marrying his daughters off to key Spaniards, who came to rule New Spain.

Important marriages that kept him and his sons from the brutal slave gangs that were used to demolish the myriad of temples construct the new cathedral and rebuild the new Mexico City.

The marriages also protected his family from accusations of witchcraft. A serious allegation, yet proved to be unfounded.

His son, Alfredo Ortega, had also embraced the culture of the victors, both good and bad: the belief in the Holy Church, reading, falconry, the necessity of thrashing servants, and the love of alcoholic spirits. Trained to the use of fine steel and horsemanship, like other conquistadors, he adopted the cotton armor of the Meso-Americans, forgoing the hot and cumbersome steel plate.

Ortega had gone off to the Andes to assist his European comrades in their destruction of yet another empire. The cotton armor being the only external reminder that his family had once spilled blood in opposition to the Spaniards and their seemingly unstoppable expansion, north, and south.

He had returned wealthy with Peruvian silver, another sign of God's approval.

So Ortega rode into the valley of death and mounds with slightly less concern than his comrades for whatever variation of the pox had doomed the inhabitants.

The Lord is my high tower.

Still….

Enormous flocks of crows and ravens took flight while overstuffed buzzards hopped painfully away or made comical attempts at flight. Hardened veterans as they were to all manners of Spanish death, each man avoided looking into the hundreds of empty eye sockets and distended bellies waiting to burst or torn open.

Upon the plain proper, the scouts were inundated with the odor of death, tainted and miasmatic, making the horses nervous and difficult to control. However, the horses were also veterans of Spanish death and tightened reins and sharp quiet commands kept them moving forward.

On a well-trodden road to the western gate, stood a post the size of a small tree, and tied to this tree was a dead man. Brown blood had dried upon the man's darkened skin.
The dead man wore striped trousers, a pattern that had once been popular with the gentry of Seville, but now out of fashion.

"It's Rios," said Ortega, "He had been so proud of those ugly pants."

True enough, they could just make out the dark skin, now turned black and swollen.
Rios, one of the African slaves had fallen ill with fever, unable to travel and the Governor-General had ordered him to be left with friendly Indians.
Perhaps he had sought his freedom, slipping away to this distant city. For they were now far off the route the expedition had taken.

"Should we cut him down and give him a Christian burial?" asked Cowboy.
"Look closer, you cow fucker," snapped an agitated Ortega.
He, along with Castillo, had liked Rios and often during their long journey into the Florida mountains had slipped Rios and the other Africans extra food or hides.

"I'm not touching him," warned Ortega.

Immune to the pox his family might be, there was no need to take useless risks with the little devils that spread the pox.
Rios, like the Indians around him, had the pox red pustules spread randomly across his body.
Like most of the Europeans, the Africans could and did weather the pox with only permanent scars, albeit not attractive scars, but one would live.

The Indians however…

At the approaches of the west gate, the archers' towers standing high above them, they encountered dogs. Hundreds of dogs, the yellowed Indian curs that were a favorite food of Spanish and Indians alike.
Some dogs sauntered away, some ignored them completely, while others barked frantically at the intruders, but all the dogs had fed well

upon bodies of the poxed inhabitants. Their yellow muzzles stained red-brown, small in stature, looking like giant rats.

Ortega quoted scripture.

"I will appoint over them four kinds of destroyers, declares the Lord: the sword to kill, the dogs to tear, and the birds of the air and the beasts of the earth to devour and destroy. Jeremiah 15:3-4."

"You know brothers, I may not eat puppy for a long while," Castillo replied wryly. They passed through the gate entering a city of ghosts and silence.
Scary silent except for flocks of ravens and grackles that cackled noisily from the palisade, and the dogs had not followed them inside, the scent of horses and smell of the Spaniards being too alien and food upon the plain too plenty.
However, the city itself was strangely empty of bodies, suspecting of a great panic that must have gripped the populace in their failed attempt to escape the pox.
They rode between towering mounds, some flat-topped, some pointed, marveling at their height, reminiscent of the pyramids of New Spain, only guessing at the toil of human generations and sweat it had taken to construct such temples to whom….. The devil? For what else could they be?

Interwoven between the grassy mounds were buildings of unknown purpose: shrines, temples, or prisons, their walls coated with stucco and painted with scenes of both beasts and royalty, but most impressive were the delicate copper reliefs, huge in size, polished bright like nobles armor and secured to partitions.
The reliefs; pagan in aspect and varied, the largest most ornate, depicting a winged warrior, hatchet in one hand, and the head of an enemy or slave in another. Smaller reliefs depicted familiar animals and birds, a hawk or eagle, turkeys, woodpeckers and buzzards, rattlesnakes, and spiders on great webs.
These lower temples contained the greatest amount of native metals the Conquistadors had seen, since their arrival in the vast land of Florida, although the copper sheeting in itself possessed little value except as a novelty.

They brought their mounts to a halt at one unfinished painting, small bowls of paint still sat below the image, as if the artist had been interrupted.

Upon the wall, in great detail, a brown bay horse with black main and tail. Upon the horse's back, an empty saddle.
The painting itself was not a surprise, the expedition had been ranging Florida for two years and plenty of Indians had seen horses.

The portrayal could even be of an escaped horse of the Panfilo de Narvaez expedition of Florida, some fourteen years previous.

A breeze began to twist through the silent mounds, gray clouds blotted out the sun and finally, thunder crackled in the distance.
Cowboy, handing the rope of his packhorse to Rybowski, rode his mare up a steep mound, the hooves gouging great chunks of red clay and grass from the hill. The colt followed him up the slope, tail straight out in enjoyment of the game. At the top of the earthen mound, he gauged the size and speed of the approaching storm.
He wanted out of this city of pestilence.

"Damn," said Cowboy.
He talked to his Mustang, as most scouts were wont to talk to their horses.

The oncoming thunderheads were large. Large enough for hail or even a spinner in the tempest. Already, the ridge from which they had first viewed the city had disappeared under a fast-moving rain squall. They would not be able to get out of the city before the rain was on them.

Personally, he would rather face a miserable night in the storm than spend one more minute within the gates. However, that decision would be up to the Captain.
Perhaps he could talk Rybowski into convincing Castillo to leave.

A freshening wind, rich with ozone, tugged at his clothes and he turned his mount around and carefully leaning far back in the saddle, went down the slope.
However, upon reaching the plaza below the mound, a lightning bolt flashed, striking the hill that he had just vacated.

The urgent thunderclap which followed was of such violence that all the horses spooked in panic and only with great difficulty were they brought under control.

"Alright then, let's find shelter to wait this out," said Castillo.

Near the spring they found the lavish home of a Cacique or head priest.
The building, an enormous structure, the wide entrance through which they rode without bothering to dismount, guiding their horses into the darkened interior. Castillo judged the building which included a vast empty council room that could hold upwards of three hundred warriors.
Outside a great roar, as a deluge dropped from the angry clouds making any speech inside the building nearly impossible.

Lightning flashed and crackled again, briefly illuminating the inside of the room and row upon row of red ceramic human faces.

"Death Jars," the painted sculptures were actually trophies; the scouts had seen plenty of death jars in the Florida of the western side of the mountains.
Each jar, portraying the full-sized face of a vanquished foe, the eyes mere slits to represent death. The jars symbolized the capture of their enemy's strength or soul.
The outraged priests had smashed such images when they could, their actions greatly angering the Indians who still lived or were free of the expedition's manacles.
So great was the anger of the natives, that Governor De Soto had to rein in the holy men, forbidding the further destruction of the pagan trophy jars.
Castillo dismounted, and shouted over the pounding rain,
    "Ortega, get a fire started!"
Castillo and Cowboy secured the horses and colt to a huge post, an entire tree that had been planted to support beams of the great room. Ortega removed flint and steel, a box of tinder from his kit, and expertly kindled a small flame. A quick search found flint-tipped arrows, lots of arrows that were slowly added to the budding fire. Other wooden objects were stacked near the fire as fuel: spear-throwers, darts, lances, ax handles, an exquisitely carved panther,

masks, and phallic carvings that brought much-needed strained laughter before eventually being tossed on the growing flames.

With each item added, further sections of the immense room were illuminated.
Out of the darkness appeared additional faces of death, more trophy jars, and the arrangement of exotic statues, both ceramic and wood, tobacco pipes in the shape of animals, horned masks, and upon the walls, skins of animals.

Cowboy pointed with surprise at the hide of a crocodile, a familiar creature in his home island of Hispaniola, but perhaps it was the skin of the other variety of water dragons, so common in Florida.

Castillo gestured at the skin of a great cat, checked in yellow and black.

"I had hoped we had moved beyond the range of those brutes," said Castillo.
At various times, all of them had been woken at night; the scream of the Jaguar, like a cold breeze bringing forth brief uncontrolled shivers. The growl of panthers would also wake them, but it was the roar of the Jaguar that caused the most anxiety for both Spaniards and their native slaves.

Sitting around the blazing fire, Castillo conversed with Rybowski about their route come daylight while Ortega studied the death jars with renewed interest. Cowboy fed the fire, staring into the dancing yellow flames and orange-red coals, thinking about home, but afraid to look away from the fire, knowing he would see a spirit or wraith in this city of ghosts.

From the shadows, Ortega commented on a clay trophy head.

"Hitchiti," holding up a painted jar with the face of a fallen warrior. "See the way the war paint was applied? A Hitchiti warrior," said Ortega.

Setting the death jar down, he picked up another.
"Look at this one, these symbols - Miccosukee, yes, look at the hair and paint. One of these bastards killed Vega with that knotty cudgel," said Ortega.

Ortega gestured at a row of clay trophy heads.

"This could be Cherokee; that might be a Muskogee, a guess; this handsome fellow could be an Alabama. Here, this is a Timucua. Bastards!" spitting out the last word and tossing the jar to shatter on the packed floor.

"Except that one still had his nose," said Ortega. He picked up another jar.
"Look at this ugly mug. Not even a guess as to this clan. Shawnee? Missouri?" said Ortega.

He tossed the head underhand into another three clay faces and heard the satisfying shattering of ceramics.
The priests had insisted these trophy jars were an abomination in the eyes of God.

Cowboy winced at each jar shatter, wondering what spirits were being set free. Ortega gestured around the wide room, at the rows of faces still in the shadows.

"The people of this city. They have as many enemies as us," said Ortega.

Castillo pushed his gear away from the roaring fire and leaned back on his saddle.
Had *a lot of enemies, thought Castillo. Had any survived the pox?*

"So, I have to wonder, where was the screw-up in translations. Seemed that the different tribes always tried to direct us towards their favorite enemy. Yet we missed this city altogether," said Castillo.

Rybowski chimed in, "Might have been best that we missed this place. Looks as if this city could have fielded twice the number of warriors as were at Mabila."

Ortega, his demeanor grim, walked into the firelight carrying a painted trophy head. The eyes were slits of death, like the other trophies, yet this jar had been painted ebony. "Could this have been Rios?" he asked.

In the flickering light a ceramic face distinctly ethnic, unmistakably African, stared back at them. "Put it back," ordered Castillo. Not sure if he should be angry.

The thunderstorm passed as quickly as it had come upon them and during the hours of darkness, the city was silent except for the crackle of their fire and the steady tap, tap, drip of water from unseen buildings.
Outside on the plain of poxed bodies, sounded the deep howl of wolves and the higher-pitched yipping of their little cousins.
However, the nocturnal songs of wolf and coyote were comforting and familiar, hinting that all was normal and eventually allowing for a much-needed sleep.

The crepuscular dawn skulked slowly over the tall walls and into the mounded city giving the scouts time to scrounge for supplies and prepare corn tortillas for breakfast.
Food, there was plenty and the packhorses were re-supplied with cornmeal, jerked meats, and pemmican; for the delay of swollen rivers had time after time forced them north, deep into the unknown interior and eventually to this silent city, each detour depleting their supply of provisions.

With full daylight, they could see the enormity of the room, the trophies, collection of weapons, and hides of beasts, in which Rybowski took great interest.
Having come from old Europe, he was familiar with the beasts of his native forests of Poland, for in the ancient forests there still dwelt bison, brown bear, and red deer. However creatures such as lions and griffins, now only existed on the standards of great houses.
He ran his hand over the patterned jaguar lion fur, marveling at such a beast, one of god's majestic creations.
To the wall, apparently dedicated to pelts and hides of beasts, were pegged, the jaguar, an outsized black bear, the Alligator, a complete elk with broad antlers still attached.
Rybowski paused in front of four unique skins.

Two of the skins were surprisingly large, perhaps the size and girth of bison. However, the beasts were of different colors: speckled roan and brown bay with flowing manes and tails draped straight down. Rybowski turned cold, gingerly stroking the long stiff mane, having curry combed horses all his life. Turning his attention to the other skins upon the wall.

Why hadn't he recognized the skins of men immediately?

The flayed men, like the horses, were also of two separate colors: tan and walnut brown, the brown having a distinct tattoo of a seahorse on the right arm.

"Fuck," was all he could say.

Castillo studied the flayed men and was not greatly concerned or surprised by the skins. The practice of flaying was done by both Indians and Europeans.
The Spaniards were especially vicious when they believed gold was hidden from them.
But, "I know him," quickly correcting himself, "I knew him. See the scar that disfigured the Sea Horse, and the ear, do you see the ear?" said Castillo.

Attached to the dark head, the ear was disfigured.
Turning, he walked quickly to the rows of trophy jars until he found what he was looking for.
"See, look at the ear!" said Castillo.
Holding up the Death Jar with the African dark features, pointing to an ear that had not been fully completed on the jar.

"He lost part of that ear to a Mayan obsidian knife. This is Hector! Hector Santana Oyola, one of our scouts!" said Castillo.

Cowboy and Rybowski, realizing they were not looking at the runaway slave Rios, both spoke at once.

"The Governor sent other scouts before us!"
Castillo and Ortega nodded in agreement.

It was upsetting to all four scouts. They had just lost their prideful status of being personally sent on an imperative mission by the Governor himself.

Instead, they now realized that they were just as expendable as the Indio slaves. Tools to be used and discarded, tossed haphazardly into the wilderness searching for fleeting ships.

And there were nagging questions that had no answers, how many scouts had De Soto sent ahead of them, and had those other scouts *already* found the galleons and returned them to Cuba?

Were they on a fool's errand and abandoned in Florida?

At last, Castillo spoke.

"Let us leave this place of death. We have boats to locate." Gesturing at the immense room around him, he said, "Burn it."

Dogs and buzzards greeted them outside of the city gate.

At the river ford, they turned to see a giant black cloud rising above the empty city of mounds and the tall whitewashed walls aflame.

Book one: Part 9: "Pensacola"

"It is a grand bay," muttered Rybowski, at last reaching the sweeping bay of the Pensacola.

Castillo pondered De Soto's orders; how much it must have pained the proud Governor to order the supply ships away from this Pensacola. Stranding his great army in a hostile land with only the guidance of the story of perhaps a mad, but successful Cortez, to reassure his decision to return the Galleons and Brigantines to Cuba.

Nonetheless, more than one conquistador had chosen difficult but bold decisions. And true, God had favored the bold.

For three days, the party of scouts followed the morning sun, fording numerous rivers and lacking the assistance of a local guide, used only the sun and stars as their cynosure.
Florida was an immense land and when the tired horsemen judged they had traveled far enough towards the sunrise, they randomly selected a large black water river and turned south towards the ocean. The worn river trail took them into desolate pine uplands nearly empty of life, except for noisy crows and screeching jays. Far below the trail, the sinuous dark waters had chiseled bluffs as much as sixty feet in height.

On the desiccated trail to the heights, they again encountered the dead. Bodies covered with the weeping boils of the pox; however other bodies also lay upon the trail, slain, bearing more familiar marks of battle or ambush: arrow wounds and crushing blows from hardwood war clubs.

The manner of dress and accouterments of the dead, those that had not been stripped of clothing, suggested the ambushed had been refugees fleeing the sickness at the city of the mounds.

Soon they encountered survivors.

In the shaded pine barrens, normally empty of people, despondent Indians with parched and cracked lips, sprawled in the soft pine needles, lacking the energy to hike down to the ribbon of water below the bluffs.

Others had slid their way to the river yet lacked the strength to make the steep climb back to the trail. Many of the prone Indians, chiefly the dying, suffered from the boils of the pox.

While those refugees who possessed a shred of vigor, those few who possessed a natural immunity to the sickness, fled down the slopes in panic at the approach of the horsemen.
However, most Indians simply lay or crawled upon on the trail, mewing in abject terror at the apparitions of the horses or begging and gesturing for water, helpless to move more than a few feet, if at all.
Starvation and dehydration, twin devils, slowly bringing an end to their suffering, finishing what the brutal pox had begun.

Directing and kicking skittish horses, the scouts reined their mounts around the quivering obstacles; the scouts themselves having grown immune to the suffering and impotent to help the dying.
Ortega fingered his rosary, offering up prayers for their souls, for these Indians, like his ancestors, lacking the blessing of the Holy Church were bound for the fires of hell or at best bleak purgatory.

The scouts having judged the distances correctly and at length, the black river emptied into the blue-green bay that was the destination of their orders.

Saddle-sore and weary, they traversed a large open meadow, a lighting burn atop a low summit. The picturesque bay of the Pensacola opened below them.

It is a fine bay, thought Castillo, sharply reining in his stallion with effort, the horse had been difficult these past few days, not only because of the odor of the dead or the grasping hands of desperate refugees but because Cowboy's mare had come into season again.

His war horse had his own priorities and frustrated, the stud with ears flat back against its head had become very vocal in protest; biting and kicking at any man or horse that dared come within its reach.

Pensacola, a fine bay and sheltered inlet, indeed in the far distance could be seen the white-capped ocean where waves broke upon a pearl ribbon of beach. Still, as they noted on their journey down the slope, the fine bay was *empty of any ships.*

His eyes swept the bay from one end to the other, admiring the red clay bluffs and multiple high points. This is where I would place fortifications if I were a settler. Three forts would control access to the bay.
The land below him was the location the Governor had at last chosen to establish his colony, however, the expedition had found no gold-laden kingdoms to conquer. And the grand expedition pushed west seeking a Tenochtitlan to conquer.

Even before the disaster at Mabila, the Indian slaves had suffered terribly. The sheer weight of the Army's equipment and supplies, lack of food to adequately feed the slaves, malignant fevers, numerous serpents, and the endless harassment by flights of flint-tipped arrows, had decimated the Indian slaves faster than De Soto's army could capture replacements.

Occasionally, the lack of slaves had halted the army's forward progress. The slaves had been flogged to the bone and mounted cavaliers sent forward to clear ambushes, yet finally, the frustrated Governor-General had issued the orders to bury all the unnecessary equipment.

However, there could be no doubt that the blue-green harbor spreading out before them, would someday be an important town. Obviously, the inlet would be a goodly shelter from the summer hurricanes that swept the lower Caribe islands and Cuba every few years.

The sailors who explored this coast before the invasion had sworn that exactly every seven years the same giant storms savaged this land, called Florida.

Leaving the red bluffs behind them, the scouts traveled the coastal flatlands weaving their way through chessboard patterns of tangled shorelines, abandoned villages, feasting on fields of un-harvested corn and pumpkins.

Cowboy whistled his signal of alert, bringing the others to his discovery of tracks. Horse hoof prints of what could only be another scout or cavalier sent by the Governor.
The single set of tracks indicating a lone horseman had arrived at Pensacola before them. The cowboy looked to Castillo.

"What do you think Captain, had this rider been sent before or after our departure from the camp?" asked Cowboy.

For the very question again indicated the Governor-General had lacked faith in their success. Castillo studied the hoof prints, considering if there was even a rider on the horse.

"I would put forward that the horseman was sent after our leaving," said Castillo. Castillo hauled back on the reins of his stallion, the stud pawing at Cowboys mare.
"We wasted over a week, turning inland seeking fords for those flooded rivers. If this fellow had left a week after us, those same rivers could have been fordable and he would have beat us to the bay," said Castillo.

"I agree, the rider left camp after our departure, but he would have not come alone. Somehow he was separated from his companions," said Ryboski.

"Or skint," said Cowboy.

His reference to the two flayed scouts in the city of the dead.

The sighting of the tracks caused mixed emotions; in some ways, they felt pride for the lone scout, a comrade on an alien shore, determined to carry out the commander's orders, perhaps dying in the process. Perhaps even now the horseman was dead and the tracks, like a ghost, were all that remained of the brave scout.

At length they all agreed, the bay had been empty of European ships when the unknown scout arrived, else the horseman would not still be heading south and east towards the Apalachee lands.

Still, the very nature of their mission was troubling; had the commander sent them and the other scouts on an assignment that could result in one or more of them stranded in a hostile land?

For if other scouts reached the ships before them, there would be no pick-up, no brigantines, or Galleys to offer assistance.

Furthermore, if they succeeded and delivered their message, would they not be stranding the greatest army ever assembled north of New Spain, to perhaps perish at the hands of brutal savages?

They followed the tracks east around the empty bay. No matter who it was they followed or when the horse rider had departed Governor de Soto's camp; what was certain, the spotted pox had beaten him to Pensacola Bay.

Or perhaps the fevers had arrived with the army but remained after their departure to complete its deadly work.

Whenever the epidemic had arrived, the results were much the same as the city of mounds. In some of the coastal settlements, less than one in forty of the population had survived. Some villages had fresh burial mounds to mourn the deceased, yet other villages only showed signs of pillage and raiding.
Hamlets had been torched and bodies strewn about showing the wounds of both combat and pox.

The tribes that had given name to the Pensacola bay had perished or perhaps migrated, fleeing and carrying the sickness with them to new lands, but leaving their homes intact, boats remained beached, nets spread to dry, fields of crops unharvested, and hordes of yapping beige dogs wandered wild, dining upon unholy remains.
At the approach of the sixth coastal settlement, the first five being deserted except for dogs, they were mildly surprised to discover survivors.

Upon sighting the four scouts on their tired horses, the natives set off a series of conch shell warning blasts, and the pitiful and stunned natives scattered like spooked rabbits; well aware of the Spaniard's jealous god and their habit to chain and enslave everyone unlucky enough to be caught by them.

However, more disturbing than the behavior of the panicked survivors or the empty towns and bloated bodies were things the scouts had all observed first hand across Florida, the results of the fevers and poxes on the natives. More ominous was that the bay, such a grand sheltered harbor, was empty of both native canoes and European ships.
For even though at their first sighting, the harbor was empty, they had somehow expected a masted ship, at any moment to steer into the bay, flying the colors of the Crown.

Book one: Part 10: Tainted Mountains of Florida

Reluctantly, they continued their easterly circuit of the bay, fording rivers and navigating sucking marshes, often intersecting the churned trails of the Grand Expedition's varied armies and livestock herds.
Yellowed bones of cattle, hogs, horses, and slaves, scattered by scavengers, marked the conquistadors' passage through Pensacola the previous season.

Seven days out of the city of mounds, they passed through another uninhabited town, this one set at the base of a small bluff that wept rivets of water from a limestone cliff.
Fields planted with tall stalks of tuber artichokes cloaked the village, the plants higher than a man swayed in the afternoon wind.

The unnerving silence of the lifeless village was broken by the abrupt onslaught of unexpected clamor, the sounds of a deadly ambush.
The four scouts and their horses perked up at the familiar sounds yet were unable to pinpoint the exact location of the fight.
Screams and blows echoed off the weeping cliff, and the tall plants muffled and hid the sounds of fighting.

Castillo acknowledged the anticipation of Rybowski, Ortega, and Cowboy, and the four scouts crossed a small river, directing their horses cautiously through the towering plants, straining to locate the fight.

The Governor-General had levied upon them the task to find the ships, orders which only implied not to get involved in local disputes, nevertheless, had not implicitly forbidden them to do so. And the lone Christian scout they had been following might require their assistance.

The art of scouting was necessarily a task that carried vague instructions and implied greater autonomy than most soldiers or Cavaliers. Successful scouting was based upon curiosity and courage. And flight on tired but fast horses was always an acceptable alternative to getting involved with unknown antagonists of unknown size.

Ready to run, fight, or rescue as the situation warranted, curiosity drove them forward through the artichokes. They loosened lances and or set arrows on bows, eager, hopeful but not actually expecting to participate in the fight.

Sitting high on their mounts, over tops of the tall weeds, they spied an Indian warrior, blood-splashed and armed with a spiked war club, giving the coup-de-grace to wounded men and women. The warrior methodically moved from body to body crushing skulls, as if breaking pumpkin gourds. Around and behind him, other Indians finished off the remaining refugees they had ambushed.

A group of five warriors harried a woman who had sheltered upon a large boulder.

The woman, evidently the only survivor was young, short of stature, and broad-shouldered, had scrambled up on the boulder and was ably defending herself with a knotty club, methodically smashing the hands and fingers of each of her attackers as they attempted to climb the stone sanctuary.

However, two warriors howling like wolves, each armed with long bloody lances, ran towards the circling five, roughly jostling the others out of the way to impale the woman on her boulder sanctuary.

Rybowski's great roan snorted at the fresh iron odor of blood and the Indians turned as one, upon hearing the familiar sound of the hated or feared Spanish horse-elk-dog.

Cut noses. A brief inspection of the Indians who had been circling the boulder confirmed they were all escaped or perhaps even released slaves.

The snarling faces were at once familiar and horrifying.

The Indian warriors were missing both noses and ears. The scouts immediately recognized the disfiguring marks of the Indian slaves of Governor de Soto's Grand Expedition. The quickest method to break a man to servitude was castration, however, the gelding of a slave required up to a month of recovery before the slave could be fully worked, and the Army had needed tame usable slaves immediately upon landing on the sandy coast of Florida.

Facial disfigurement, branding, or removal of the nose was the next best method to break a man and required virtually no recovery time.

The Cut noses bore other savage marks of their enslavement, scarred backs, and branded cheeks. Some even still wore the iron shackle that had been welded around their necks. Like a savage pack of wolves, the Cut noses, turned from their prey trapped on the boulder and howling in rage, pain, or excitement, charged towards the Scouts.
The blood-smeared warrior who had been smashing the heads of the wounded pivoted to stare into the artichoke weeds and the Spaniards whose helmeted faces and wide-eyed horses could be seen jutting over the swishing weeds.

The warrior, Leaping Crow, once a proud member of the Egret Clan of the Ocala People, was a survivor. He had survived the battle where his nation's best warriors had been defeated by the invaders. He had survived disfigurement and torture, survived his family's enslavement and eventual death, he had survived starvation and fevers, endured frozen mountains, attacks by hostile tribes, and for nearly three years carried back-breaking loads of equipment as a slave to a race of demons.

Only when his racked body could no longer serve his Spanish overlords, was he was freed with other worthless Indians. Set free upon an unmarked trail, with no food or clothing, and a thousand miles from his homeland.
However three years of hell had not killed him, and despite lack of food or shelter, his body healed. Yet Leaping Crow's very survival had come at a steep price, and that price had been his sanity. The Ocala warrior screamed a nasal war cry and charged the horsemen.

The warhorses, excited by the odor of blood, burst through the weeds and onto a scarlet stained meadow.
As one, the horses leaped cat-like over unseen, unexpected bodies, landing amid a massacre that surprised the Spaniards, as much as the Indians were surprised by the sudden appearance of the Elk- Dog- horses.

The scouts were nearly unhorsed by the sudden and unexpected swerving of the horses attempting to and failing to avoid stepping upon the prone bodies of men, women, and children that littered the meadow. By their manner of dress, some fallen Indians were refugees from the city of mounds, having found no shelter along the great bay. Yet others wore only the simple deerskin cloak and leather leggings of the Pensacola fishing clans.

Ortega, whose Mixtec ancestors had conquered the old civilizations of Mexico and whose father had accepted all things European, was as skilled a horseman and lancer as any from Lisbon to Krakow, kicked his steed into action and easily pinioned the blood-stained warrior charging him with a grisly club. He expertly withdrew his lance as his horse bowled over the cut nose and wheeled towards the next Indian.

"Holy Mary, mother of God, forgive our transgressions, now and at the hour of our death," Ortega repeated his battle chant.

The words spilled from his mouth as he charged the escaped slaves who had obviously forsaken Christ and were, therefore, enemies of God.

For the Pole, the game was afoot, a damsel was in distress and Castillo said nothing as Rybowski released his bowstring, his arrow striking true to sink deep into the mouth of a slave who had crept up the backside of the boulder and had with strong dirty finger,s grasped the ankle of the young woman; yanking her off of her feet to land painfully on the boulder.

The woman whose attention had temporarily been turned to the incredulously alien sight of horsemen screamed at both the gripping hand and the horribly scarred face that lacked a nose. And then screamed again at the white-fletched arrow that suddenly appeared in the man's mouth.

Rybowski reached for another arrow as Cowboy, with a yell, charged his nimble mare into the remaining Indians, saber held high and slashing to either side.

Yet Castillo sat astride his impatient shuffling warhorse, momentarily keeping himself as reserve, scanning the meadows and riverbank for any reinforcements by the ambushers and ready to call retreat. They were after all only four in number and someone had to keep the supply horses and colt steady.
He quickly tallied the dead, construing how the ambush had progressed by following the pattern of bodies, an obsession he acquired since the first winter in Florida.

The counting and interpreting the 'map of battle,' disguised his main obsession, always searching for the 'sign'… searching for the sign, even as he had the day after the great fight at Mabila.

He had not found the sign at Mabila, even though he had counted eight thousand, nine hundred and seventy-three Indian dead, both inside and of the ruined fortress and out upon the trampled plain.

A shadowy blanket of melancholy swept down heavily upon Castillo. In its wake, leaving him with tremors that shook his hands so greatly that the lead ropes to the horses fell from numb fingers.
Sadly, in this little meadow bordered by tall weeds and with perhaps only three dozen bodies, he found what he had searched for and the very thing he always dreaded finding.

For as Cowboy's mare jumped panther-like over a fallen body, a Cut nose scrambled upright brandishing a bloodied flint knife.
Cowboy's saber swiftly struck the Indian's neck, too late noticing the iron slave collar nicking his blade and sparking the sword as it scraped off of the neck collar to slice deeply into the whip scarred chest.
The sticky flint knife and what the man had been grasping in his other hand, tumbled to the ground. Strips of fresh-cut meat fell slowly to land in the grass beside a slain youth.

The slave had been in the process of butchering a child when the scouts burst out of the tuber field.

While his whirling comrades, shooting, and slashing, finished off the Cut noses, Castillo wretched up his last meal. The three scouts briefly turned their attention to the woman on the boulder but then rushed to their Captain who vomited from his saddle, doubled over as if shot by an arrow.

Castillo attempted to catch his breath, unable to take his watering eyes from the butchered child.

It had all gone wrong in the cold mountains of the Apalachee, their first spring in Florida.

He recalled the day it had all gone wrong because variations of that day had haunted his dreams ever since.

The morning had been wet and cold as he guided his horse through the busy camp after attending the Captain's meeting. The weather had been freezing, recalling that he had savored the steaming heat rising from his stallion and digging his stiff fingers into the warmth of the horse's thick mane.

He always looked forward to meeting with the leaders of the expedition, trading jibes, and jokes with the other professional soldiers.

His family name, his stallion, and his reputation in Peru were recognized and admired by the true conquistadors. Some of the grizzled veterans had even served with his father in the Mayan uprisings. That morning, his mind on the recent captain's meeting, consequently he was nearly thrown from his horse.

The odor of wood smoke and cooked meat permeated the mountain camp and the more than four hundred surviving Indian slaves stood in a dozen ragged lines, queuing up at the cook fires or great boiling kettles, hoping for a scrap of food or bowl of weak stew.

The difficult mountainous terrain had hampered both the Indian and army game hunters, and even though elk, bear, and innumerable raccoons had been brought in to be butchered, there was not nearly enough food to feed the Governor-General's grand army composed of soldiers, friendly Indian warriors, and guides, hired European servants, African slaves, baggage slaves, and women captives.

The herds of swine and cattle brought from Cuba at such huge expense had been left under strong guard in the lowlands, while the majority of the De Soto's Army searched the Appalachian wilderness for gold or Inca-like temples. Indian leaders in the corn lands had sworn there were golden temples in the mountains. They

had even shown the Christians the gold baubles they wore, said to be from the mountains.
Consequently, the captive Indians manacled to carry the expedition's equipment suffered greatly; the slaves that could always be replaced, were given the least amount of food whenever there was a shortage of supplies.

Icy rain fell upon the shivering slaves, washing away mud and ashes while a heavy misty fog hid the towering Florida Mountains that shortened daylight by blocking both the sunrise and sunset.
The rain dampened the Army's enthusiasm, their bowstrings, cook fires as well as gunpowder.
However, the freezing rain sapped the strength of the already weakened slaves. Each frigid dawn, the smiths were called to strike manacles off the stiffened bodies that had perished during the night. The slave captives from hundreds of clans and ruined towns, malnourished and ill-dressed for the frigid mountains, desperately cued up in food lines for a slice of venison or bear.

Likely to be the slaves' only substance for the day, small pieces of meat, charcoal black on the outside but nearly raw inside, were doled out by the hired slave trainers. The slave trainers were free men brought from across New Spain, their specialty, the breaking and care of Indian slaves.
Small amounts of smoldering meat were dropped into shivering manacled hands and despite the scorching that blistered hands and tongue; the slaves gobbled the morsels before other grasping hands could steal the precious substance.

The slave tenders, warmed by their cook fires, made sport by purposely missing outstretched hands and laughing uproariously while the desperate slaves scrambled in the mud, swinging iron manacles at faces that lacked noses or ears.

Castillo rode past the slaves' food lines, admiring a great black bear and doe that hung from a large walnut tree, while the slave trainer leaders sheltered behind a windbreak, a great canvas taken from one of the ships and hauled at a terrible cost in human suffering into the tall mountains.

His war horse suddenly reared up on its back legs as a group of slaves, chains clinking, pushed into the horse's path scrambling and shoving for a piece of muddy meat.

The stallion reared, screamed with ears flat, eagerly striking and caving in the head of a slave with sharp hooves.
The Indian collapsed silently to the ground.
Castillo would have been tossed from his saddle were it not for his hands woven into the stallion's mane for warmth. Getting thrown into the mud and excrement was the very type of embarrassment the jealous Hidalgo Cavaliers hungered for.

Francisco de Tejeda had been slain by an arrow but in his place had stepped the irritating son of a Marquès, one Don Queipo Antonio Primo de Rivera, who complained endlessly about the low-born scouts and foreigners.

There was bad blood between the veteran scouts of the Peruvian campaign and the untrustworthy newcomers from Spain and Portugal. The Hidalgos, while not quite cowards, were still spoiled bastards who ceaselessly complained.
Of course, there was smug satisfaction from the professional soldiers, the lancers, and infantry who joked at the whining of the better-bred gentleman cavalrymen. For the pampered lifestyles of the Hidalgos had not prepared them for the harsh Florida expedition.
Odd, Castillo had often dwelt upon the fact that their sires and grandsires and their grandsires had fought the invading Moors, stubbornly holding onto Christianity in desolate mountains, such as these very misty slopes of Florida.

It was obvious the Governor-General had not the foggiest notion of how to repair the conflict between the hardened veterans and the pampered Hidalgos.
Hernando De Soto needed them all to conquer vast Florida.

The war stallion pranced sideways to avoid stepping on the body of the fallen slave and then savagely bit at the two slave trainers who had rushed out of their shelter towards him.

Castillo cursed and reined sharply as two slave trainers, themselves cursing the rain, pulled the body across slick mud to the edge of a small ravine behind their windbreak; to the offal pit that every camp had to have.

"Dumb asses," snarled Castillo at the slave trainers. *Had they not just witnessed one of the slaves killed by his horse?*

But no, the freezing trainers focused only on retrieving the body of the Indian, paid no attention to how or why the slave had been killed. Their responsibility began when the captives were brought into camp and ended once the bodies were disposed of.
And completing the disposal quickly meant they could get out of the icy rain.

The trainers' other responsibility was feeding the slaves. Under the canvas awning, blocked from the bitter wind, slave trainers butchered a hanging doe, tossing meat into a basket that was carried to a huge iron kettle, hanging over glowing coals.
Nearby, one of the trainers sat miserably in the rain and wind, ladling soup from another steaming kettle.
Anger and curiosity turned to horror, as a trainer walked to the Indian just recently struck by his horse, rolled the body on its belly, and expertly removed the back strap and thigh muscles. With a kick, the trainer tumbled the body into the ravine, carried the meat to the fire, and tossed it into the boiling kettle for the slaves!

Castillo, not quite believing what he had just witnessed, kicked his horse and guided the stallion to the edge of the ravine.
On the steep slopes lay the butchered bodies of deer, elk, turkey, bear, dogs, raccoons, opossums, *and people.*

Bile tasted bitter in his throat.
He wanted to kill the slave handlers.
Instead, he turned his mount around to inform Governor de Soto of the magnitude of inhumanity.
Yet before he dismounted, he sat in the cold rain watching the camp; the normality of camp life around him.
Of course, they all knew. The Governor-General would also be aware of what the slaves were being fed.

In fact, as much as he tried not to focus on the subject; Castillo was cognizant that these particular slaves would not live to see the spring and another five hundred would take their place.

Fuck.

He turned his stallion around and cantered for the outer camps, aware that he would never be able to clean the filth that shadowed his soul. This army, his army was going to roast in the pits of hell for their sins.

That freezing morning in the misty mountains,-now two years past?

That had been the embryonic crucible, the dismaying, sleep-depriving enlightenment of how far man could treat fellow men in the name of gold or god.
The experience had been a festering thorn, an unremitting remembrance, malicious and tainted, that had blemished his outlook of the expedition and indeed the luster of the leader who allowed such an obscenity as had been witnessed at the edge of that frigid ravine.

Even in a world where massacres and enslavement were common, that deed, cannibalism, surpassed all notions of depravity.
There had also been the dishonoring humiliation, the involuntary realization that it could never be denied, he was part of the horror of the so-called "Grand Expedition" and consequently, when allowed, he had pushed his scouts far in advance of the slow-moving army, taking advantage to admire the various towns and people, before Governor de Soto's unstoppable army forever sullied them.

Cowboy pushed his way through tall tuber plants, risked being bitten by the horse, and grasped the hackamore of the volatile stallion. Urgency and worry in his voice.

"Captain, are you wounded?" asked Cowboy. Castillo shook his head.
"No," said Castillo.

Raising his eyes from the butchered boy, he saw blood splatter on Cowboy and the other two. He himself, although not stained with battle gore, felt filthy to his soul.

"Look at what those bastards were doing to that boy," snarled Castillo. He unexpectedly vomited again from his saddle.

"Clean your gear and horses," said Castillo.

He wiped his face and pushed his way towards the cleansing river. The colt frolicked about the tall weeds, and cantered to the river's edge, jumped down a small bank, pawing and splashing about, oblivious to the bloody meadow and waving tuber plants.

Book one: Part 11: Tanatacura Elk Beasts

The fight between the half men-half-elk beasts and the mutilated men, ended as suddenly as it started.

Tanatacura scrambled back to the top of the boulder, her tail bone aching after one of the mutilated men had managed to avoid her wild blows, lunged for an ankle, and pulled her hard onto the unforgiving stone.

Before she could free herself, the snarling man-with-no-nose, was struck by one of the beast-men's white fletched arrows and uttering a nasal squeal twisted away out of sight.
She scrambled painfully to her feet gripping the sticky war club in both hands unable to catch her breath and watching the fight raging across a meadow strewn with the bodies of the refugees she had followed from the great city.

Rains-on-Fires lay in the river where he had been stabbed in the back attempting to flee. She was certain she should have felt sorrow for his death, but no emotions surfaced from her well of sorrow. A dry well.

The beast-men, mythological creatures, half men-half elk, had burst out of the tuber field and began killing the mutilated men.
With strange arrows and spears, three of the monsters quickly dispatched the mutilated men, while the remaining monster, perhaps a priest-king, stood over the fallen, and like her, observed his monsters efficiently dispatch the mutilated men.

She would have sworn to the twin Rattlesnake God, that she could have not been further surprised than seeing six-legged beasts.
However, to her astonishment, another animal, smaller resembling more of a doe, than the spear and bow carrying larger creatures, sprinted from the tall weeds and whinnied.
One of the beasts responded with a corresponding whinny - an alien sound, reminiscent only of an elk bark. Mother-monster and child?

Her own child was buried outside a dead city.

She readied her club as one of the monsters galloped past her boulder to trample the last of the mutilated men. The man-with-no-nose, panic in his tortured face, emitted a nasally scream as he attempted to flee across the stream; however, the beast-men were fast as elks.

She felt no pity for the mutilated men; in fact, she was happy to see them die. Several times since fleeing the city, the mutilated strangers, apparently insane, most missing noses and ears, had attacked the refugee group of which she had been forced to join. With each attack, her group had been whittled down in size. Finally, the mutilated men had trailed and ambushed the remaining refugees on the edge of the tuber field and like dogs, trapped her upon the rock.

The fighting over, Tanatcura the only survivor, looked across the meadow where mutilated men and refugees lay sprawled in poses of death; a few still lived, moaning as their lifeblood leaked to a crimson puddle into the grassy field.

The tubers would grow well next season, she thought.

An absurd thought, considering the fevers that had swept the land and now elk beasts with bows. Was she, at last, losing her mind as had so many of the refugees and mutilated men?

Yet the monsters paid her no heed, instead, they congregated around the body of a child, a Pensacola boy who had been killed at the beginning of the ambush. To her amazement, the monsters spoke to each in an alien tongue, harsh and incomprehensible, like that of the Cherokee slaves.

However alien the sounds, nevertheless, they used the words of men and not the growls of a bear or raccoon as she expected.

The Priest-King-Leader became animated gesturing towards the boy and then back to one of the mutilated men, then regurgitating his last meal. At length they slowly turned towards the stream, only once glancing in her direction, but showing little interest in her.

The fight over, Tanatacura wanted to flee, wanted to scream, however a lifetime of stories of bears and wolves had taught her it was best to remain quiet. So it was that she held her place on the stone, sitting down to wait for the beasts-who-talked-like-men to move on.

Yet she was not prepared when the four monsters separated into eight! Four of the monsters walked like men and four resembled the doe-like younger version that pranced about in shallow waters of the river. Before she could again question her sanity the smaller man-like creatures removed their head coverings to show that indeed they were only men. Strange men true, but nevertheless, men not beasts.

Completely ignoring her, the strangers stripped naked and cleaned their unusual weapons, clothing, themselves, and finally cared for their riding beasts. The riding beasts pawed at the water while the naked men washed and combed their manes. Even administering a mud poultice to a small wound on one of the riding beast's forelegs.

Tanatacura was not surprised at their complete lack of modesty, that was how warriors acted on a raid, but she was fascinated at the dissimilarities in the men. Unlike her people, the Coosatachee, who were generally of the same size and coloring, the four strangers were as varied as their riding beasts.

All four were muscled like warriors, but there the similarities ceased, one was handsome, but the others were curiosities. The handsome one with high cheekbones, his features resembling those of a Choctaw or perhaps a Natchez nobleman, was covered in striking tattoos, he wore his dark hair short and was in fact, the only stranger who occasionally shot curious glances her way.

The other, the one she had assumed was the priest-king, was taller, his skin dark, the color of old walnuts. Yet another of the strangers-his hair matched that of ripened corn and similar colored fur covered his face! That one removed his blood-stained clothes and while his hands and face were tan, the rest of his body, incredibly was the ill color of snow!

The final stranger appeared to be the youngest, but his head was balding or shaved like an Osage, yet his chest and back were covered in fine brown fur, like a beast!
A revelation came upon her and she chided herself for stupidity.

The naked warriors bathing in the river must be the invading people, that at the behest of the king of Mabila, her husband had gone south to assist the levies of Choctaws and Alabamas.

My son is dead and my husband disappeared. My city is dead.

The strangers reminded her that she was alone on a rock.
A reminder of the illness had then swept the city killing nearly everyone in three days. The panicked survivors fleeing to the four corners of the Coosatachee kingdom.

But Rains-on-Fires had insisted they journey south, following other refugees through the dry hills and to the assumed shelter with the fishermen of Pensacola clans.
As it turned out, however, they found no sanctuary with the Pensacola, as the weeping boils had also decimated the fishing clans. She and Rains-on-Fires had stumbled east, continuing their flight towards the rising sun and until at last, the final meeting with the men-with-no-noses.

With studied patience, for she had nowhere to flee, she observed the strangers. Apparently only these four had survived the confrontation with the Mabilians and her husband's warriors.
After they had cleansed themselves and their beasts, the four strangers crossed the small river to set up a camp for the night. Clothes were hung to dry on willow branches, the handsome tattooed stranger kindled a fire and collected firewood, the hairy man saw to the riding beasts, placing small hoops of ropes upon the animal's legs and letting them graze on the thick grass of a riverside meadow. The other two- the snow white and the dark man disappeared into the tuber field, soon returning with two more riding beasts apparently loaded with provisions for both man and beast. They spoke very little and followed a seemingly well-rehearsed pattern of camp activity.

In a cloudless sky, the sun passed the western treetops while the four strangers dressed in damp outlandish clothing took turns to stand next to the drying fire. At last, the strangers gathered in their riding beasts, tethered them close to the fire, and quietly shared a meal between themselves

Tanatacura sat on her boulder, watching the sun turn crimson and sink below the horizon.

She had never felt so alone. Her opportunity to slip away had come and gone. However, she was paralyzed with indecision.

Her entire life she had been part of a family or group. Married young to an older warrior who beat her when displeased, she had at least taken comfort in her status in the clan as wife and mother.

Even in the refugee group of gruff and despondent strangers, she was at least *part of something*.

Now….. She sat on her boulder hugging herself, growing colder; feeling forsaken as the first evening stars slowly appeared overhead.

Book one: Part 12: Bitter words

Castillo stood with his back to the drying fire. His guts had been burning since the fight and at last, he hurled the bitter words that had been trapped inside him for so long.

"The fault for this devastation lies entirely with us. We brought the cannibalism, the pestilence, enslavement, and disfigurement of entire fucking nations. We brought murder and death to these people- who were simply living their lives, wishing only to be raising their children," stammered Luis Castillo.

Rybowski and Cowboy, who actually agreed with most of the things Castillo had said, were at a loss as to how to respond.

"I just want to go home and marry Anna," said Cowboy meekly.

Rybowski, who been for some time disgusted at the conduct of the expedition's Spaniards; the people of Iberia who were in most ways the most devout of all Christians tried to talk to his captain.

"Well, we have been right bastards, but I would not blame everything on us. Certainly, we bear no responsibility for the pox and fevers. And, it is quite evident the people inhabiting Florida are at least, as warlike as the stories of Ortega's people. Hell, tally our wounded at Mabila. The Turks could have scarcely done better. I can truthfully state, that we did not bring the corruption of violence to these folk," said Rybowski.

Ortega, who had been circling the fire, stopped pacing to stand across from the fire from his distraught captain.

He would be heard.

"Luis, you could not be more wrong. True, these people have suffered. But what you speak of, is simply how the world is. Each day the Lord tests everyone and everything and every day the road created by the Lord God progresses to something new. It is no different than the cycle of day and night or lightning and rain. Birth and death. The very act of shedding tears and blood renew mankind in God's eyes," said Ortega.

The three scouts stared intently at Ortega, who continued speaking. Cowboy narrowed his eyes in suspicion; what Ortega had just said, was something that an Aztec pagan priest might say, not a converted Christian Mexica. The church might, the church had burned for similar sentiments. *The Aztecs had shed blood for their gods.*
Ortega attempted justification of his declaration.

"I think, because it has only been a few years that my people were conquered by the Spaniards, and my people still suffer greatly from the Spanish maladies, so I have a different perspective. The world created by God is little different from when a baby comes into the world. There are pain, screams, blood, and tears, sometimes even death, but from the suffering and blood, a new child is born to replenish mankind.

This is the story of man.
My people, the Mexicas, like the Hebrews of the book- wandered out of the wilderness bringing fire and arrows to conquer the ancient civilizations. Out of the ashes, they formed the Aztec nation, powerful and wicked. Our enemies were as numerous as the stars.
Then, like the Hebrews, we, ourselves, were conquered, and as foretold by our pagan priests, out of the east came the Spaniards with steel, with horses, gun powder, and the banner of the true God to conquer both the Aztec and our enemies. Was there not blood and tears, death, and rebellion at your coming?
Most certainly. But it cannot be denied that out of the ashes and pain came a better civilization, one graced with the teachings of our Lord Jesus" said Ortega.

Ortega briefly paused to think.

"Or... What of your Spaniards' storied struggle, 'The Reconquista' a seven hundred year war of freedom from the tyranny of the Moors. Seven hundred years of bloody war and you Luis, point out the invasion of Florida that has not yet seen its third year? Forget not also, according to the Lord's Book, from the forge of the Roman conquests and slavery came hence our lord savior; as well as the enchanted words of Latin and even your numerous languages of Spain.

"This Florida, yes you have witnessed blood and suffering, disease, and even cannibalism, but from the fires will be new nations, new hopes. Then one day, new people will come from the wilds, from the north or south, or east following the Spaniards, and the new people will conquer again, spilling blood in the birth of a new nation.

"Luis, all you can do, is all anyone can ever do.....Love, raise children, enjoy the beauty of your horse and grow old in the arms of the nation you have helped to create," said Ortega.

In Castillo's tortured mind he still saw the youth's body lying in the tall grass butchered like a doe and was not persuaded by Ortega's words.

Ortega, you're more goddamn Aztec than you realize. He kept the statement unspoken.
    "Perhaps you are correct," said Castillo.
However Ortega's words "Grow old in the arms of the nation you have helped to create." The very words were thick with falsehood as if the very words were slick with lard. For he doubted he would ever grow old.

Book one: Part 13: Stew

The handsome man, his tattoos now covered by a shift of exotic looks, stood up from his fire holding a bowl of steaming stew. He crossed the stream approaching her rock with caution but stopping at a distance as not to cause alarm and placed the bowl upon a patch of bare earth.

He was indeed handsome, boldly meeting her eyes, appraising her and she felt her throat constrict. For the first time since the burial of her son, she worried about her appearance. *He had just bathed.*

Unconsciously, she pulled back a loose wisp of hair and straightened her travel-stained dress. She must look horrible. Painted with a coating of dust, charcoal, tears, and others' blood. Yet she held her club at the ready.

The stranger spoke several words until at length she thought she understood one heavily accented word in the Coosa tongue: *Wolf.* When she did not respond, he used the sign language of the flint traders, yet she had never needed to learn the hand language.

When she still did not acknowledge him, he pointed at the bodies sprawled around the meadow then pointed to the surrounding forest, cupped his hands, and quietly howled like a wolf.
"Wooooooo-Rooooo."

He pointed to their camp, gesturing an invitation, turned and re-crossed the river collecting branches and sticks during the return to the fire.
The wolf caller sat upon the ground with his back to her.

Tantatacura cautiously slipped off the boulder, scrutinizing the four strangers for tricks.
She snatched up the bowl and scurried back to her safe haven. Hungrily slurping down the stew, it was plain fare-corn mush, thickened with acorn flour, with a few wild onions and chunks of elk, yet it was the first warm meal since her flight from the city.

She licked the bowl considering that the stranger's simple act of kindness was something that she had never once received from her missing husband.

While the strangers remained seated by their fire, she slid off the rock again, hiked up her skirt, and squatted in the bushes. Straightening her clothes she took the bowl to the stream and used it to gulp down water. She washed the bowl and used it to wash layers of dust off her arms, legs, and face. Unsure of what to do next, she climbed back onto the boulder.

The stars turned brilliant, filling the night sky as full dark and cold air settled in around her. She jumped at the song of a wolf family howling in unison.
They were close. Shortly thereafter the growling began as the wolves tugged at the fresh bodies of refugees and the mutilated men.

She sprang up grasping her club, straining into the darkness, when two unseen wolves began fighting over the mutilated man below the boulder.
As the growling morphed into a savage fight, she slid down her rock and sprinted towards the river, checked herself and returned for the bowl, and again dashed towards the water, moving cautiously down the riverbank and stepping carefully over slick rocks, painfully banging an ankle on something hidden below the chilly water and guardedly approached the fire.

Three of the strangers were curled in blankets sleeping, while the tattooed man, spear across his lap, had taken first watch to guard their beasts. She cautiously entered the circle of light. Savoring the primordial protection of fire and relished the envelope of heat that greeted her.

One of the riding beasts snorted at her and the dark man lying on the ground lifted his head but only glanced curiously at her and dropped back to sleep.
Nevertheless, she was tempted to flee into the night. However, the growling and feasting of the wolves and the ink-black darkness beyond the light gave her an excuse to stay with the strangers and their shielding firelight.

The tattooed man spoke quiet words to her in an unknown language.
He slowly stood up and she gripped her now-familiar club.
Had she made a mistake?

He tossed a heavy blanket to her and sat back down on his side of the fire.
The blanket reeked of an unfamiliar sweat, the heavy scent of a foreign animal; nevertheless, she gratefully wrapped the smelly blanket around her shoulders.

Animal furs always smelled so it was easy to ignore the exotic odor permeating the blanket.
As her shivering slowed-she had not realized she had been shaking; but as the tremors ceased profound exhaustion seeped from deep within her and with a will of their own her eyelids crashed down upon her.

Book one: Part 14: Wife

Ortega sat at the fire listening to the pack feed.

There was no danger to the horses as the meadow alone would feed the wolves for a week. He did however worry about Castillo. The captain was coming unraveled as a frayed bowstring. *Sooner* or later it would snap if the tension was not lessened. Sooner, he thought.

As he had predicted, the woman came wandering in out of the dark. "For God said, Let light shine out of darkness," he mumbled quietly. His only surprise was that she had remained as long as she had with the wolves feasting and fighting.

But then his wife would be strong and fearless.
She came limping in from the dark, her dress soaked from the knees down, the club in one hand, and his bowl in her other hand.

"I knew you would be coming in to get away from that pack," said Ortega.

He tossed her the blanket he had reserved just for her. The Pole had wagered she would not come in.
Ha, you owe me Rybowski.

The woman shivered under her horse blanket, her wary eyes boring into him.
Ortega stared back mesmerized, he was certain that he had never seen eyes such as hers-dark eyes, reminiscent of smoldering coals flecked with dancing embers and like the glowing coals of a twilight fire.
One could easily stare into those eyes for hours.

Those smoldering eyes were what bore hunters to hurry home after searching out game in rain or sleet. Or bring a man home to hearth and family after a difficult campaign.

He recalled his inspection of her when he carried the stew across the river. He had scrutinized her closely, confirming that she was free of the pox.

Like his family, the woman on the rock was one of the rare natives of New Spain, possessed of immunity to the diseases of the Spaniards. Her face had been marked though; tears had cut through ravines across her pretty dust-coated cheeks, the rivulets striping her face like a falcon.
He liked that.

There was a minor stirring in his groin.

She had also washed before coming to his fire, proving she was of civilized races and he liked that also. The style of dirty dress confirmed that she was a refugee from the city of mounds. His grandfather and the fathers of his ancestors-killers all had based the mettle of a people by counting their enemies and this women's people apparently had vast numbers of enemies.

The mettle of her people was also confirmed in that she faced him with a cudgel and when he had first spied her she was fighting for her life. She had not lain down and simply given up as so many had. Here was a woman worthy of his own bloodline, that of an Eagle Warrior of the Aztec Empire and Conquistador from New Spain. *He* had found for himself a wife and mother of his yet unborn children. Of course, she would have to be baptized in the true faith.

Book one: Part 15: Fur

She awoke once in the night; a habit ingrained and required to care for her son, her little boy whose ghost now walked among the city with her ancestors.

She lifted her head to see that the tattooed man was curled in a blanket near the low fire and the dark-skinned man had replaced his spear across his lap watching over their riding beasts. However, the wolves on the other side of the stream were silent. Having fed and departed.
The rare feeling of security, unproven among these strangers. Also odd, security had been lacking since the death of her son. Security, the feeling enveloped her and she faded into sleep again.

Tanatacura awoke again to the sound of camp breaking up, the riding beasts snorting, stomping, and whinnying. The dawn too far away to make out other than fuzzy silhouettes until someone added branches to the small fire they had kept burning all night.

In their strange language, the four men exchanged quiet words and she was assaulted by the sound of a riding beast urinating and the stinging odor of a male animal wafted over her.
The four warriors strode to different corners of their camp and also made water, at least one of them groaned as he urinated.
Each minute that passed brought additional daylight and at last, she could make out their faces clearly. For the first time, she was able to observe them up close and see exactly how alien they and their beasts were. All four men were attractive in their own freakish way, the tattooed man being the only
normal-looking person.
Her fear lessened somewhat as she watched, still, except for the one, they were the oddest looking people she had ever seen. Their clothes, weapons, skin color, odor, but what stood out the most was the facial hair.

Three of the four warriors had great amounts of facial hair each having a distinct color and texture. The men of her clan would occasionally grow small amounts of facial hair. But these strange warriors had pelts of fur on their faces; evidently, they were more kin to the fur-faced wolves or dogs than perhaps men.

The man with yellow hair and beard spoke unintelligible but reassuring words and handed her a bowl of corn porridge with acorn flat cakes. He gently pulled the blanket away and placed it upon the back of a riding beast.

Other than the giving of the porridge and the taking of the blanket, the warriors ignored her.
Although she could not understand the sounds of their speech, she could tell there was trouble. The dark-skinned man sat by the fire speaking passionate, yet distressing words.

Apparently greatly affecting two of the warriors who mirrored the dark man's words in tone and volume. While the normal-looking man paced around the smoking fire, apparently growing impatient with their conversation.

Finally, the normal-looking warrior, whom she now suspected to be a Cherokee, sat next to the dark man and spoke calm words. Even though Tanatacura could not understand the words, she was greatly endeared by the intensiveness of his foreign speech and his obvious concern.

Book one: Part 16: Colt

Ortega tried not to be angry.

There was an illness about the captain that was little different from any fever or pox. This morning's disagreement was worse than yesterday and the other two were not being of any assistance.

Cowboy was a useless fuck anyway.

For what did it matter if Castillo's words were accurate in every way?

It would still not change the fact that they had been sacrificed by De Soto, sent into dangerous regions to locate missing ships. Missing ships that common sense decried had already pulled back to Cuba. It was only a matter of time before the four of them reached a hostile town or clan that had not been devastated by the pox.

Mary, Mother of God! It had taken the entire army two hard years to cut their way deep into the heart of Florida.
What could four *scouts* do when they, at last, encountered a force of fleet warriors?

What will happen is we will gallop our worn-out horses for perhaps ten miles *that would kill them*, and then these Florida warriors would run us down.
Hell, these people r*un down elk!* A travel-weary horse carrying a man would be easy by contrast. When that day arrived… well, he knew better than to be taken alive by these godless pagans.

Ortega looked at the new woman. She was watchful, curious, and most likely terrified. Her attention wavered between studying the men and horses.

Ortega reached down and pulled up a clump of green grass, shook out the dirt, and waved at the women to accompany him.

She cautiously stood up and followed him to where the colt grazed. He clucked-clucked to the young horse and the colt cantered over with its ears up. The colt eagerly ate the grass from his hand. Ortega handed a clump of grass to the woman and she tentatively held out the grass to the colt, which ardently devoured the fresh grass.

The woman smiled at the colt and then at him.

The *first time* she had smiled, he realized.
He spoke to her, gesturing an open palm to his chest, and said "Ortega."
Ortega repeated the gesture twice more and last she hesitantly pronounced his name. This time he smiled and received a smile in return.
He left her with the colt, saddled his horse, and shifted equipment into the saddlebags of the supply horses: his leather and mail jerkin, crossbow and quarrels, spare weapons, and food. Transferring weight off his horse so his mare could carry both him and the Indian woman.

All the while he kept glancing at the woman.
She needs a name he thought, a name to be used until she could be baptized with a Christian name. He liked the hawk-like markings that had been on her face yesterday and now washed away. She reminded him of the diminutive little hawk that preyed upon songbirds, the Kestrel. Kestrel, no *Kessie*- Her name for now anyway. Pretty and brave.

He warmed at the memory of Kessies's smiling eyes when the colt nuzzled her palm.

Cowboy saddled his own horse, watching suspiciously as Ortega relocated the gear; the damn Aztec was showing moon-eyes towards the new woman.
He stomped off to Castillo like a little bantam rooster.

"Captain, are you going to let Ortega slow us down with that new slave?" asked Cowboy.

Castillo was adjusting the cinch strap on his stallion and exhaled deeply. Unhappy at the interruption. He looked at Cowboy, *What was eating at him?*

"Yes, she won't slow us down at all," said Castillo.

He knew that was a lie, but he just did not care anymore.

"At least one Indian will be happy when we have departed this blighted land," said Castillo. Cowboy did not know if the Captain was speaking about Ortega or the slave woman.

However, Cowboy was peeved about the presence of the new woman. It was not the woman per se, it was he had to admit, he was simply jealous that Ortega had something and he did not.

Stupid, yes, but Ortega always carried the favor of Castillo.
Sometimes the two of them, who were both born in Mexico, would converse in that damn Aztec tongue.
Or they would laugh together about some event that happened in Peru. The Pole did not seem to mind, but it always wounded him, that their conversation left him out.

Ortega pulled himself into the saddle and held an arm out to the woman. Kessie. He spoke calmly to the new woman.

"Be a good lass and jump up behind me now," said Ortega. Tanatacura looked about her, then relented and grasped his open hand. Surprisingly strong muscles lifted her onto the back of the horse with one pull.

Ortega gently grasped her hands and placed them on his hips. Then adjusted her hand to grip his side.

"Hold on now," said Ortega.

Lightly kicking the horse and they trotted around the glade.

She gripped him hard at the unfamiliar bounce and loss of balance, at length a small giggle escaped her. She smelled the heavy musk of his scent and held tighter. She had been walking for…for a moon cycle? No, she could no longer recall how long she had been walking away from the dead city.

Now, however, she was flying like the little hawk, or at least running like the white-tailed deer.

"East," said Castillo. "We journey east and southeast until we find those ships."

He kicked his war horse, following the trail of the single horseman.

Apalachicola Village.

Three gray spinsters who bereft of children and guardians of the drum sat around a wiry woman beating upon a small oblong drum. The spinsters slowly became animated as the unfamiliar smile lines creased normally dour faces.

Music was known to attract good presages and bring births to the clans. Their task was to sing and oversee the dance of the bountiful woman.

Their chant and the rhythmic drum beat brought maiden and widow alike into a circle around a low fire, dancing one behind another with nippy, swaying steps, signifying they were available for suitors or husbands.

Tanatacura joined in the bountiful-woman dance following the other swaying women around ruddy embers, although her eyes were only for Ortega, and while she danced she stroked the beautiful red and blue ribbons woven into her hair. The beautiful ribbons, a gift from the strange warrior.

She smiled at him as she danced, attracted by his features, fascinated by his prowess as a warrior. Outlandish at first, but she had decided to be his woman.

"Together we will replace my son," she swore to the gods, and, though she shuddered to realize it, she had no regrets. Life was life. Yet she said a silent prayer for her lost son "May he find his way through the trackless forest to the Great Sun."

Perspiring from the dance, Tanatacura rested on a log by the fire, sitting next to Ortega. Ortega stared at his woman, *at his wife* and she stared back.

Both tiring of the mild flirtations, the frustrating overtures in mutually unintelligible languages, and casting demure side-glances, she at length swept him a coquettish glance that meant they understood one another.

He spoke hushed alien words hardly above his breath, but her black eyes held his stare. The more Ortega looked at her, the more he admired this survivor, bewitching, pretty, hawk-eyed woman.

Throughout the day he had watched sunbeams reflecting off her ebony hair and inhaled her scent of woman and wood smoke. His breathing had quickened, mesmerized by her eyes and how the red firelight had outlined her womanly figure while she danced.
Indeed she made a fair representation of her people.

Tanatacura for her part found that she was breathing heavily, regarding him in speechless admiration of the warrior.
He stooped over her, and on her lips pressed a tentative kiss in the manner of the Spaniards, the kiss itself an alien gesture of affection but she accepted it with parted lips.

When she did not resist, he almost lifted her from the log, stopping only long enough to pick up a horse blanket-saddle pad in one hand and grasping her other hand guided her away from the village.

She giggled the sweet low laughter of the Florida woman and went with him eagerly towards the copse that edged the savanna and together they hurried through pine-fringed glades heavily scented with flowers that slumbered in the chilly silver light.

In the darkness, under blazing stars, she pushed him down upon the needle-strewn forest floor and rubbed his manhood.

"One would think that the devil had broken loose today," moaned Ortega.

He laughed naturally, pleasantly enveloped in her warmth, and rolled her, pine needles and all, onto the horse blanket.
The dawn found them under the branches of magnolia trees, thick with fragrant pink-and-white tinted blossoms, unnoticed the night before.

They held each other wrapped in the warmth of the saddle blanket, enjoying the tremors and sweet agitations of love as the stars faded and the eastern sky altered from grays and purples to gold and at length illuminating vast stretches of uncut forest. The singing of birds and agitations of squirrels carried on the morning breeze.

They returned to the village to find the scouts packed and waiting for them. Beaming bright with gaiety and happiness, the ardor of their joy could scarcely be repressed as Ortega mounted his horse and lifted *his* woman into the saddle behind him.

Cowboy sullenly ignored them; Rybowski slapped Ortega on the back, saying only "Love, Chance and God, my friend."

But Castillo seemed calmer, seemed almost healed at the occurrence of their contentment.

Your happiness is an experience that many men miss; be thankful for it.

"Let's move out; there are ships waiting to be found," said Castillo.

Book one: Part 17: Tampa

He awoke with a stifled cry.

Another fucking nightmare had disturbed his sleep again.

It was the butchered boy again, the dream, otherworldly, perhaps a dream of hell itself... The sun slightly out-of-focus, the air dense as molasses flecked with noxious effluvia, and the little river rippled in the miasmatic air, the sparkling reflections from the shallow waters strangely muted.
He walked across the meadow, stepping over intertwined bodies or around those that shuffled about despite their terrible wounds.

Across the meadow, men, women, and children bludgeoned, fang-ripped or sword-cut, all dead, walked about without apparent purpose, except for the joy of movement.
The lifeless appeared to be hemmed by the tall weeds and muted river. All this he found strange naught. Normal even.
He found the Pensacola boy waiting for him, twirling the bloody flint knife like a jester. The boy spoke in perfect Castilian Spanish, and that seemed normal also.

"I missed you, Luis," said the Pensacola boy.

Castillo took the child's hand, ignoring the cuts and tears, the small body, savaged by the wolves and sliced upon by the cut-noses, smiling up at him, an innocent face that lacked lips and tongue.

They walked hand in hand towards the tall tuber weeds where yellow-eyed shadows darted furtively weeds and was instantly awake.

Fuck.

Agitated, unwilling to risk another dream meeting, Castillo slipped on his boots and walked out of the hut they sheltered in.

Above him, brilliant stars, both the big ax and little ax, could be identified.

Below him, a white blanket of fog covered the horizon in all directions. Only the tall flat-topped mound upon which he stood, jutted out of the opaque mist.

Tired, yet unable to sleep, he sat upon a carved log to watch the growing pink and orange glow on the eastern horizon. Disturbed, shamed even, that his dreams were a weakness not fit for a conquistador. Ortega and his new woman, Kessie walked out of the hut and cuddled together near him on the log. *I must have woken them.*

A quiet morning and no one spoke.

From within the hut came the light snoring of Rybowski and Cowboy, nearby one of the horses snorted, and somewhere deep in the fog came the whooping cry of a nightjar.

A new day was breaking in the world. *On Florida*. The womb of civilization, about which scholars and priests crowed about so often, concealed the grinding ugly truth: an underbelly of death, poverty, slavery, and stagnant waters of disease and decay.

Coupled with pride, ambition, greed, and the obstinate jealousy of the church, made the Spanish into a scourge as dire as anything that had ever fallen upon the inhabitants of Florida.

Castillo contemplated Ortega's words and his own guilt at bringing the miseries upon the inhabitants of both the Andes and Florida.

The conquest of Peru was fading into a dream of distant arid mountains, yet he could still vividly recall his shock and revulsion upon seeing the first slave with the nose hacked away; the cruelty was done to a proud Incan warrior, who had not been cowed by either the cruel damage to his face or the lash. The revulsion, the act itself, he had shrugged off as a necessity of war.

Thankfully, such harsh treatment was not required on a large scale in the dry Andes or even during the rebellion with the obstinate Mayans in their festering jungles.

A slave could be released or made into an ally, but a man horribly disfigured was a potential enemy *forever.*

Of course, it was de Soto's fault, the mistreatment of the slaves. Castillo had recognized the problem even before leaving the fertile lands of the Tallahassee.

For while the Governor-General was attempting to emulate the startling successes of both Cortez and Pizzaro, and doing so with a vastly larger, better equipped, and better-fed army; he had ignored the basic reason for the other two Conquistadors legendary success. Cortez and Pizzaro knew how to make allies or at least temporary allies. Cortez had been trained as a lawyer and Pizzaro weaned in the Royal Court before Conquistadors.

But Hernando de Soto was the opposite of Cortez; the Governor-General was a professional slaver.
His pride and training mostly guided him to make slaves, not allies, and then per God's will, to treat the slaves as harshly as deemed necessary to break them.

Castillo stretched sore muscles and cruelly mocked his own insipid virtue, by which he had wasted good years of his life keeping the faith as a fanatical follower of de Soto.
Twice sullying himself by linking his honor with the reprehensible actions of the governor.
Once, in his not-so-far-away youth, there had been the kernel planted of the ideal concept of a warrior. Conquistador.

Now.....*I am no different than my father* and shuddered at that thought.
Fuck, where did that come from? Fuck, is it too late now to change? And change to what? And the army, what will become of them, the cream of Spain, Portugal, and peculiar nations of the old world.

What if, pondered Castillo, *What if... the Army had possessed allies such as the brave archers of the Ocala, Potano, and Timucua? What the hell, and the club-wielding hordes of the Apalachee?*

... Say twenty thousand bowmen from the south, as our allies, instead of destroying and enslaving them.
We would have swept this land from ocean to Mother River, Governor de Soto would even now be presiding over an empire that rivaled any in the lands of New Spain or the Inca.

But *no*, De Soto had left a track of blood and tears across the world. He was like a gem, with a hidden flaw, strong and beautiful on the outside, but rotten on the inside, ready to fall apart.

The eastern horizon grew lighter, and then painful orange-pink as the first rays of dawn crept over the light fingers of the palm trees. With no allies, the grand expedition would push deeper into the vast land of Florida, fighting on until final defeat.

The warbling call of a mocking bird perched on the roof above, caused him to glance away from the impending sunrise. The budding light revealed another flat-topped mound crowned with a small hut, a twin to the one they now rested on.

"I remember this place of the twin mounds," said Ortega.

The words trailed off to a whisper and he ceased talking, for in the distance two other items protruded out of the fog. Nearly the same color as the mist, yet the morning light glistened upon dew-covered sails. *Sails.*

"The Ships!" yelled Castillo.

He jumped to his feet, teetering on the edge of the mound, but quickly turned to wake Rybowski and Cowboy.
The five stood on the lip of the mound, unable to speak, staring at the sun-dappled masts of *one* ship, the fog still hiding the deck and the bay or river upon which the twin masted ship floated.
Castillo knew it might be two hours or more before the mist burned off, the fog could even get worse before it got better.

"Let's go find that ship and deliver the Governor's message," said Castillo.

Moving cautiously off the mound they skirted a fog-shrouded village, the sagging houses long abandoned. Yet, they reined in sharply to a halt in front of a line of bodies tied to stakes.
Someone had crucified the entire village. Rotten posts holding desiccated bodies canted sideways or lay fallen upon the sandy ground.
From out of the mists came a deep Spanish voice.
"Tampa," they called themselves and their bay Tampa. In their language, it means "Bay of sticks". Who would have guessed their name foretold the manner of their death?"

Out of the fog, leading a lame horse walked a conquistador, his once fine clothes now little more than rags.

Marquès Don Queipo Antonio Primo de Rivera, the nominal leader of the minor houses of the Hidalgo Cavaliers; and a noble who had at every turn, protested the Governors' efforts to make the Hidalgos work as scouts.

Cowboy soured at the sight of Don Queipo.

The very Hidalgo that had set upon him the day he had first met Rybowski, Ortega, and Castillo. Cowboy's disappointment was palpable. They had followed the lone scout's trail for several hundred miles, admiring the pluck of the conquistador and fellow scout.

To see Don Queipo standing there…..

Rybowski's eyes narrowed in recognition of Queipo.

"How did you come to know what these people called their harbor?" asked Rybowski.

Don Queipo, dirty and thin, looking more like a lean highwayman than the son of a noble, pursed his lips.

"That Vasquez, the bastard captain? He assigned us to the rear guard. Can you imagine how great an insult that was? Well, very near here. The Spaniard castaway that the Governor-General took as a translator for these savages' guttural utterances…?

It was a *very* touching scene, the castaway and his Indian slut and breed offspring weeping buckets. The Tocobaga cacique was standing around mumbling his barbarian spittle, rubbing on his new crucifix and I asked the translator what lies the leader was spewing?"

Don Queipo snorted at the memory.

"The translator, was he a Basque? Anyway, the Basque translated the savage's words. A savage translating a savage eh? The northerner said something like: The Cacique says that he will be punished for helping de Soto's army."

Queipo gestured at a desiccated body with a crucifix hanging around a desiccated neck and giggled. "Look they all got their very *own personal* crucifixes," said Don Queipo.

Castillo, for his part as the leader, rode up and grasped the hand of the Hidalgo.

"We have been on your trail for weeks. Good to see a familiar face. Grand news! From the mound where we spent the night, we spied the masts of a ship. She cannot be more than a league from this accursed village," said Castillo.

Don Queipo smiled, flashing yellowed teeth; however, his dark eyes did not match the smile.
For standing before him were misfits unequal to his association, three peasants and the bastard son a foreigner, albeit of noble blood.

"Ah well, indeed! That is the best of information! Let us proceed to this ship of yours," said Don Queipo.

Don Queipo mounted his lame horse ignoring the looks of disapproval from the three scouts, but the devil be damned that he would appear before the sailors afoot while peasants rode.

Dense blinding mists eddied and swirled around the group, saturating clothing and gear as they moved past the line of posts and followed an old shell-strewn track towards the unseen bay.

Castillo hung back to confer with Ortega, whose women clung tightly to his back.

The end of their difficult assignment was at hand. A pressing decision would have to be made. What would they do if the ship was only a Brigantine that could not pick up their horses? *Specifically his horse.*

Cowboy, keeping a secure grip on the rope to his colt, led the way through the cloying blanket of white. Visibility was down to less than the shaft of a spear. In the center, the bastard son of a Polish count and the son of a Spanish Marquès kept an uneasy silence.

Marquès Don Queipo Antonio Primo de Rivera y Sáenz de Falange savagely whipped his limping horse. At first, briefly elated upon learning that a Galleon or Brigantine was nearby. Now he smoldered at the thought that he, and this bastard foreigner riding beside him and the peasant scouts would reach the boats simultaneously.

I would have found the ships today without the peasants' help!

Don Queipo fumed at the thought of sharing in the exaltation of success and the stunned revelation when he presented the code word "Cortes" to the supply ships.
Accolades from the Governor-General should be his and his alone. Don Queipo had long ago lost count of the lonely days and dangerous nights that he had traveled since his men had been ambushed by the feather-and-skin-festooned band of Choctaw warriors.
He had been the only survivor,-well he had had to shove Gonzalez off his horse as a distraction or neither man would have escaped.

The story of his unlikely journey would become legendary across Spain, equaling or surpassing the adventures of his ancestor's battles with the Moors.
He fumed. Now at the end of his journey, to be greeted by the very peasants that had been his bane since landing in Florida.
For some unnatural reason, the veterans of the Peruvian Campaign had unjustly shone as favorites in the eyes of de Soto.

But that would soon end.

Upon reaching the ship, he would declare the three peasants and the bastard to be deserters, ordered by the Governor himself to be whipped and then hanged from the highest tree or mast. The Indian slave could be given to the sailors for their entertainment, then thrown overboard or sold in Havana. But that
horse, that stallion ridden by Castillo, he would claim for his own.

The fog momentarily broke and Rybowski could see Don Queipo beaming like a youth on his wedding night and then the white blanket fog quickly obscured the smiling Spanish Don.
Is the Don addled?, wondered Rybowski, but then a warning shout, the mists became alive with writhing shouting men, unseen arrows flew overhead, and grasping hands pulled him roughly from his screaming horse.

Cowboy, who had led the group towards the water mostly by instinct, breathed a sigh of relief as he could, at last, see the top of a sunlit mast protruding from the fog; his mare snorted as she stepped into the unseen shallow bay.

However, the shoreline was animated with motion. At the water's edge, around him, to his front, left and right, silent warriors with strung bows and shell-topped war clubs quietly pushed dugout canoes into the bay, lifted dripping paddles, and silent, as apparitions quietly disappeared into the silvery mist, making their way to attack the unseen ship.

Those warriors to his immediate left and right stopped to stare open-mouthed in surprise at the tall apparition that had appeared in their midst. Behind them, barely detectable, other warriors continued loading their boats.

Calusa, thought Cowboy, observing the top-knot hairstyle and shell clubs. For a moment, no one spoke. Cowboy, at last, broke the strained silence and yelled a warning.

"Ambush!" yelled Cowboy.

Startled men screamed in defiance and charged at him from both directions.

An arrow thumped into his saddle and with no other option he kicked his horse forward into the shallow bay, the colt reluctantly followed but panicked at the grip of the sucking mud and salty waters; the colt reared up against the rope, pulling him from his saddle.

Cowboy floundered in muddy sand and knee-deep water attempting to get his footing, while the horses, mare, and colt disappeared into the mist. A Calusa warrior pounced upon him, landing knees first upon his chest pinning him to the muddy floor. Air was forced violently out of his mouth and saltwater flooded his lungs.

Castillo had time only to drop the lead to the pack horses, slip a hand into the shield loop and unsheathe his sword when the first shell-topped club broke upon his shield. Without a clear view of his assailant, he struck into the fog to strike bone and flesh. The shrill scream attracted unseen archers and arrows passed by, the sound of their fletching was the buzzing of angry dragonflies.

Adelantado reared up kicking and screaming and another unseen man went down below sharp hooves. Two faces appeared in the fog and he rode them down. An invisible thrown ax bounced painfully off his shoulder, an arrow banged upon his helmet and he slashed his way clear of grasping men and stabbing spears. His charge carried him into concealed low trees whose branches attempted to tear him from the saddle and his shield was ripped from his grip, yet the same grasping trees inhibited the screaming men who sought him out. Catching his breath he called for the rally.

"Ortega! Cowboy! Rybowski!"

The only answer being defiant screams in a cruel tongue and the sound of arrows peppering his strand of trees. None of the scouts answered his calls.

At the first call of Cowboy's warning, Ortega drew his sword and shield, severely handicapped by the woman clinging to his back.
Briefly, he thought to lower her to the ground as he attempted to decipher the sounds of horses whinnying and men dying.
Someone splashed in unseen water and a chorus of war cries erupted from his left and right. The fog simultaneously muffled and inflated sounds in a confusing reiteration of pain and anger.
Had they wandered blindly into the middle of some warrior camp?
A man running full out, bounced off his horse, threatening to unhorse him and he gained control as another warrior swung a shell-topped club that he easily blocked and stabbed the man in the mouth. The dying man wore his hair in the top knot fashion of the Calusa, the fierce warriors who ruled the south of Florida.

Three or a dozen arrows rattled off his shield and he turned his horse so more of his body and shield protected the unarmored woman.
Nevertheless, the woman screamed as someone attempted to pull her from the saddle.

A kick of the stirrup and a downward swipe of his sword and a hand whistled through the fog trailing black droplets.
The owner of the hand yelped in surprise and more yells answered in response, growing closer, searching him out.
It was time to go; the others would have to catch up. He turned his horse into the blinding fog and disappeared.

Rybowski, unhorsed, rolled upright into a fighting stance. Shield high, helm low, shiny blade snaking from the safety of the shield. The blanket of fog hid both him and the unknown enemies in the white blindness of the pre-dawn. Men yelled, screamed in pain, rage, frustration. Voices of a hundred or a thousand? Bodies ran past to unknown destinations. The buzzing of arrows flew overhead, unseen to thunk into unseen chests or ricochet off of his helmet.

There was no retreat, no safety, friends in peril. He thought he heard his name called from the whiteness from one direction; then a scream and Spanish words called for help from another direction. Water splashed, the air thick with the miasma of mangroves. Of Florida.

A berserker rage overwhelmed him, the warrior ethos when flight was impossible, attack with all dedication of the spirit.

To the rulers of South Florida, the Calusa, fierce, tall and fearless, out of the blinding fog came a winged apparition chanting unknown words of Slavic and Latin, protected by iron and steel. Dew-shiny eagle wings were outstretched, ready to take flight like an ibis or strike like a dawn owl; the white wings splattered with blood, flapped with each motion of the sword.

To the Calusa who knew the religion of the Christians, the Archangel walked among men, harvesting souls.

The Calusa, who had visited the Yucatan and knew of the old gods, witnessed the feathered serpent strike with poisoned fangs.

Yet fearless warriors attacked the winged creature, and like swamp magic or lightning, the charging warriors quickly fell away. One by one, the Calusa fell holding pumping wounds, as the steel blade nearly invisible in the dawn, took their souls.

Rybowski found the wounded Don and briefly stood as his protector, then still gripped by the killing rage, charged after a fleeing warrior. The warrior had been to the pyramid of K'uk'ulkan, had witnessed the sacrifices, and realized the very serpent god stood before him, ever famished for souls. The warrior, fearless of any man, fled into the fog with a terrible feathered serpent chasing him.

Out of the whiteness, other hands grasped the wounded Don and pulled him into the blind fog.

Cowboy choking on muddy water fumbled for his fighting knife, his grasping fingers, at last, finding the smooth handle and before blacking out, drove the blade to the hilt into the naked thigh of the man who pinned him below the water.

He could not hear the corresponding scream, only that he was allowed to rise above the warm bay waters to vomit mud and seagrass and finally gasp a ragged breath.

The Indian he had stabbed moaned nearby, flailing in the water and Cowboy pushed away puking water through his nose and coughing, bumping into an empty canoe which he held onto while attempting to clear seawater from his lungs.

In the sightless fog, he found himself almost alone while the bank was alive with screams and shouts of angry men.

Canoes full of alert men paddled past him towards the hidden battle on the white shore. One warrior released arrow after arrow blindly into the fog, before also disappearing into the white.

A Calusa, the last man paddling a boat full of warriors, accidentally struck Cowboy with his paddle and yelled with recognition as he spied the European's bedraggled head protruding from the dark waters.

But then the Calusa was gone, the canoe propelled by eager warriors.

Cowboy slipped into the boat upon which he leaned. Lying low he awkwardly paddled and pushed away from the disaster in the fog.

"They call this place *Tampa,*" he groaned.

Book one: Part 18: Calusa

Even before the strong Florida sun burned away the blanket of fog, Castillo could hear the savage cheers of approval and directed his horse cautiously towards the sound.

He discovered one of the supply horses, the mare grazing nervously in a pine flat-wood and he easily caught up the lead rope. The mare flinched each time the sound of cheering resonated through the pines and he gently patted her neck, whispering quiet assurances.

From the mare, he retrieved Ortega's crossbow and three stubby quarrels, cocking and loading the crossbow, he guided both horses towards the wavering noise. He was truly bothered by the fact that he had seen neither Ortega, Rybowski, Cowboy nor any sign of the Don or Ortega's woman since the confusing confrontation on the shoreline.

The vicious cheering like the thundering heartbeat of a giant beast led him to an abandoned village of ruined huts and greensward of Flat-topped earth mounds.
Tethering the horses to the roots of a storm-tossed oak, he crept silently up one of the mounds and peered cautiously over the edge.

The azure glare of Tampa bay and the sight of a Brigantine momentarily caught his attention. *The ship is still here!* Nonetheless, his eyes were drawn first to the lone sentry occupying the tallest of the mounds and then to the gathering below him.

Once again the ferocious roar of approval as a man wearing a fully antlered deerskin capered about with two flaming brands and at length poked a naked man bringing forth a groan then a noisome cheer from the avid spectators.

The man was tied spread eagle to upright stakes on the village commons, a small fire burned beneath the captive, whose skin was as pale as clouds and bleeding from multiple burns and cuts.

Don Queipo.

Around him, over a hundred warriors, top knotted and tattooed woad blue, as any Pict of the old stories, waved bows and clubs.

Calusa, thought Castillo, the tribe that controlled the southernmost area of Florida. So fierce was their renown that even De Soto had chosen to land his grand army north of their kingdom.
The dugout canoes told the story; a war party from the disease-free south, come raiding their northern frontier.
A second Calusa tormentor, this one wearing the hide of a panther stepped up to the Don, viciously jabbing him multiple times with a pair of thorns or stingray spines and a dozen new rivulets of crimson appeared upon the Spaniard, whose anguished cries set up yet another round of ferocious approval.

Of the other three scouts, there was no sign; however, there were bodies of Calusa stacked neatly in a shallow grave. He looked again towards the distant ship; no help was forthcoming and Castillo grimaced at what had to be done, controlling the rising bile in his mouth.

Fuck me.

He dropped below the mound, inspecting all three quarrels for defects and finally re-cocking and loading the crossbow. The sentry on the mound was the first problem. The guard was actually higher than Castillo - uphill and downhill shots were always the most difficult. He gauged the distance, not an unmanageable shot, but the drop on the heavy quarrels was always a bitch to gauge correctly.
A quick look at the smoke from the torturers' fire - no wind to speak of and he pointed the crossbow at the guard and waited, not watching the scene below for the cheer he knew would come.

A piteous mewing issued from the captive; Castillo refused to look and at the height of the roar of approval, he pulled the trigger of the crossbow.
He had misjudged the angle, aiming too high and the heavy bolt suddenly appeared in the sentry's left eye, the impact knocking him backward out of sight.

Castillo quickly loaded the second bolt and placed the crude sites on the Spanish Don.

"I'm truly sorry," and pulled the trigger.

The crossbow bucked as it released the bolt and the crossbow's braided steel cable snapped in half, lashing a red stripe across Castillo's dark skin.

Ignoring the pain, he strained to see where the quarrel would impact. Castillo groaned when the bolt passed through the Spaniards, leg just above the knee, to sink deep into the foot of the antlered torturer.

Fuck.

Brief silence from the crowd and then a growl louder than any of the cheers heard so far.

"I have truly pissed into a nest of ground hornets," hissed Castillo.

Despite the yells of protest from the Calusa warriors and screams from the man in the antler headdress; a wave of relief swept over him as he watched a growing puddle of crimson spread beneath the Don. The fouled shot had evidently severed an artery and suffering would soon be at an end.

An arrow thudded in the earth beside Castillo, handsome hawk-feather fletching quivering at the sudden stop.

A Calusa archer appeared on the mound where the sentry had fallen, screamed a warning to his companions, and released another arrow. Castillo rolled away from the top of the mound, dropping the useless crossbow, and scrambled down the slope, using the green mound as cover from stone-tipped arrows that flew uselessly overhead.

At the horses, he slashed the reins holding the mare and untied his stallion, mounting his horse as the quickest of the Calusa warriors crashed into the clearing made by the fallen oak.

Castillo spurred away, the mare following close behind to escape the clamor of frustrated warriors.

The Brigantine still patrolled the great bay, and he set off alone on a circuitous route of the bay and the eventual meeting with the captain of the fleet. The code word 'Cortez' from a mad Governor-General may have cost him friends.

Ortega whispered his prayer and stepped into the open.

"The Lord is my rock, and my fortress, and my deliverer; my God, my strength, in whom I take refuge; my shield, and the horn of my salvation, and my high tower."

He had waited for the sun to be just right, before walking onto the open sand, spit, and flashed his sword at the ship.
A family of monk seals barked loudly at him and slipped into the safety of the blue-green bay. After an eternity of waiting, a signal mirror flashed in return and he pulled back into the shadows where his woman waited with the horse.

Ortega prudently waited for the sailors in their small oared boat to beach on the sand before he cut the saddle girth strap and pulled the hackamore off to set the horse free. A slap on the rump and it was gone. There was little sentiment towards the mare that had carried him for nearly three years across an unknown land. Horses were horses, but recalling Rybowskis'-spoken words about family and happiness; he smiled at his woman Kessie, knowing that he had gained the real treasure of Florida and led her out onto the tan sand and blinding sunlight.

Cowboy jumped out of the boat splashing sailors, getting cursed for not waiting, and waded to meet Ortega. He grasped Ortega by the arm.

"You made it!" said Cowboy.

But then he looked deeper into the tree line, searching.
"The others? Castillo, Rybowski?" asked Cowboy.
"Not with us," replied Ortega, studying the worried face of Cowboy, whom he had never really cared for until this moment.

At length, Ortega spoke.
"Let's go; we should pick them up in a day or two. Keep the Governor's code word to ourselves until Castillo shows his ugly face. He is not going to be happy about cutting that overpriced stallion of his loose."

They piled into the crowded boat and the oarsmen pushed them away from the wilderness someone had named Florida.

Onboard the supply ship Arrow, Ensign Esquivel scanned the mangrove-lined wilderness, the King's map makers had christened the "Bay of Tampa."

Juan García Esquivel said a hasty prayer to the virgin that he would never have to touch the sandy beach of that wasteland.

"Blessed is the day that a plague or the Moors took every savage of Florida," muttered Esquivel. He scanned the blue waters for Calusa war canoes and made the token sweep with the borrowed spy-glass for more Christian deserters.
The single disheveled soldier-not the first deserter they had picked up, had insisted there were four more soldiers and a slave woman.
And indeed there were at least two more; the Captain had dispatched a launch to pick up the man and woman who had walked into the open and signaled the ship.
Maybe there were a hundred deserters, maybe only four; however, the savages, like avenging wolves, seemed adept at taking care of the problem of deserters.
Ensign Esquivel scanned the blue; there were porpoises aplenty, and the ugly mermaid manatees flapped rounded tails.
He stopped his spy-glass on a spit of beach where a hundred pelicans and cormorants took flight. The seabirds circled away, leaving one large bird on the beach.
Esquivel adjusted his glass. The giant bird spread its wings to dry in the sun like buzzards were wont to do. But waved arms? A griffin? The first live one he had seen.

Esquivel hastily crossed himself, and the Captain barked, "What did you see? Calusa again?"

The Captain watched with satisfaction as his launch pulled away from the beach with the rescued man and woman.

"No, not savages. I am not sure, Captain, a giant bird with wings and arms," said Esquivel.

The Captain gestured for his glass. He wanted to admonish the young officer; however, there were stranger things in this Florida.

The Captain adjusted his glass to find the giant bird. Such things were not uncommon. There were stories of Condors from Mexico and the Moors; the converted Christians had stories of a giant bird, called Roc. This bird flashed a mirror or sword blade at the ship and indeed waved its arms. *A trap like a honey jar for ants?*

"Dispatch the other launch," ordered the Captain. "Esquivel, you have the honor of discovery. Lead the sailors to that beach. If it is a griffin, kill it and bring it back. If it is only a man - one of the deserters - bring him back."

"Yes sir," replied Esquivel, rubbing his crucifix to fortify himself.

Book one: Part 19: Ais

1542 A.D
Territory of the Ais, East coast of Florida, Southwest of the Cape of Canaveral

They almost killed him the first day.....

Colucuchia of the Ais, specifically of the northern Otter Clan, paddled silently through the towering moss-draped cypress trees. Turtle traps were piled in the center of the canoe. A basket woven from lithe willow branches held a collection of hissing turtles, both the soft and hard-shelled varieties.
The turtles represented two days of fine eating and not even all the mornings' traps had been checked yet.

A fine morning for paddling and he contemplated the ending of the storm season and the clan returning to their winter town on the lagoon. There would be tasty terrapins and finned turtles to trap in the lagoon.

Large grandfather woodpeckers, crested, brilliant red-headed with black and white wing feathers flitted overhead from tree to tree. The wind whistled through the tall trees, yet the dark water beneath the boat was as still as a looking glass, reflecting the tall trees, wispy clouds, the dugout canoe with its two occupants.
He could see himself and Savochequeya, the eldest son of his sister, kneeling at the front of the boat.

When had my hair turned so gray, he wondered? My hair grows like the hanging tree moss, a concept he found humorous.
Well, he had been elected to the council of the elders and none of them were exactly nursing whelps. A curling white egret feather drifted lazily through their reflections, the only surface indication of the winds singing in the tree limbs and stirring the gray moss.

Colucuchia quietly rested his paddle across the boat, reached down into the reflection, and cupping a handful of tannic water, lifted it to his mouth tasting, considering the quality of the water.

Yes, it was good turtle water.

The complicated flavoring of the brown water hinted of pungent bat droppings, the fishy taste of fish hawk and eagle droppings, the bitter tang of acorns, perhaps hickories, and …. *Yes*, overripe Paw-Paws. The water also had the slight ammonia odor of red-eared shell crackers bedding somewhere nearby, hidden under the dark water.

Yes, it was good turtle water.

Yet, he thought studying the shadows, there was also the taste of alligator. Not just any alligator, which was in the taste of all fresh waters, but the specific acrid taste of old bull.

The concept of an *old* alligator in the Ais tongue was the same meaning of a *large* alligator, a grandfather bull.

Colucuchia tasted a second cupped palm of water and considered it. How close? Bull urine was distinct and spread freely when marking food or a good hunting area. A warning to all interlopers.

He watched as a large spider pulled a blue dragonfly up the rippled bark of a cypress tree. Grandfather spiders, whose legs spanned the size of a man's palm, perched upon every tree in their sight.

Harmless to the people, these quick hunters were no web builders; instead, they stalked and ambushed their food near the waterline.

As did the Grandfather Alligators.

"Good turtle water," said Colucuchia.

"Also, there is the taste of a Grandfather alligator," and began his quiet paddling anew.

Savochequeya understood the implicit warning. There were always alligators, perhaps slightly fewer in the saltish waters of their winter village, but they were always present. Their taste was in all waters.

For his uncle to give a verbal acknowledgment, meant there might be a threat or something uniquely dangerous about this particular Grandfather.

Paddling through the maze-like twisted openings between the trees, they soon found the alligator watching over its intended meal.

Their efficient, yet simple turtle traps, consisted of locating a fallen tree or log, which the turtles naturally climbed onto for the sun's warmth. The people would assemble a willow branch entrapment just under the water around the log. At a later time, usually the next day; upon the approach of a canoe to the fallen tree, the turtles would scuttle off the sun-warmed wood and dive into the trap.

In their panic, the turtles hardly ever found their way free. No easier food, so tasty, could be caught so simply.

However, this time, they had caught something besides a turtle in their trap: *something*.

From the dappled shadows, they paddled into the sunlit opening of a fallen cypress tree and the location of their next turtle trap.

Savochequeya, kneeling in the front of the boat, was the first to spy the *incredulous* sight of forest nymph perched on their tree.

The nymph, *Man-like*, half otter, skin dark to match the surrounding water, covered in mud and blood, wearing torn buckskin leggings, its dark feet and hands grasped at the cypress branches, The nymph even had an obedient servant! Floating below the branches drifted a grandfather whose scaled and armored body spanned the length of two grown men and a boy.

The nymph's dark eyes followed them as they slowly glided from the shadows, the canoe stopping well short of the tree, the nymph, and the grandfather alligator.

Savochequeya expected any moment the nymph would, like a turtle or otter slither off the log, to disappear forever into the murky water. Perhaps the nymph would get tangled in their turtle trap!

Savochequeya considered the attention and envious faces of the villagers if they returned with a captured forest nymph.

Savochequeyahe reached down and grasped his barbed fish spear.

Colucuchia, a little less given to witches' tales or children's stories, observed something quite different.

A man *clung* to the branches. A man distinctively dark of skin. Perhaps the dark man was wounded and seeking refuge from a very large alligator.

True, the stranger in the tree branches was like no man he had ever seen before. However, he had perhaps *heard of this man's tribe.*

But Colucuchia, ever given to the practical side of survival, observed many details of the unique scene. First, the stranger was nowhere near high enough to be safe from the floating alligator. The grandfather could use his powerful tail to jump at least twice as high out of the water as where this stranger now sought shelter.

So why then was he still alive, pondered Colucuchia, observing the congealed bloody teeth marks that were raked across his bare chest and back.

Below the stranger, the grandfather floated silently with a rag twisted around its toothy snout. Nearby, caught up to the cypress branches was a floating log, perhaps this stranger had been crossing the black waters on *that?*

Further out in the waters he glimpsed many dark eyes, intently studying *him and Savochequeya.* So the grandfather was keeping other alligators at bay, safeguarding *his meal.*

The stranger was still alive, at least for the moment. The muscles on the back of his sister's son slowly tensed as he quietly lifted his spear from the bottom of the dugout.

Well, everyone wants a trophy.

"Not yet," he commanded his young charge.

They may well kill this stranger, but not just yet. It was not every day that you happened upon a man whose skin matched the color of the dark watered swamps.

He turned his attention back to grandfather, who at the sound of his voice had submerged silently beneath the still black waters; why had it not fed?
But the answer was self-evident.

In his many years, he had observed other alligators and their more dangerous saltwater cousins, crocodiles, with torn animal hides twisted around their snouts, the rare outcome of the spinning powerful death roll practiced by both types of hunters.

Once an alligator or crocodile had animal skin wrapped around their snouts, they had no option but to patiently wait for the skins or hides to rot away before they could free their mouths to feed again. He had seen these animals survive two complete moon cycles, not eating until finally released of their skin enfoldment.

So the grandfather had the stranger's cloth wrapped around its mouth. Good fortune for the stranger or an unhurried death by starvation? To kill him now would be a merciful death.

Savochequeya, at last having noticed the other alligators that surrounded them, exhaled a curse that verbalized as a grunt; for the other hunters began to cautiously circle closer to the forest nymph, now that the grandfather had submerged.

However, even more worrisome were the tiny bubbles rising from the black water. Bubbles were released when something moved across the leaf-strewn mucky bottom of the swamp.

The tiny round bubbles that expressed the odor of rotten eggs upon breaching the calm surface; small round bubbles that were moving *towards* their dugout canoe!

So intent was Savochequeya on following the approaching bubbles that he yelped out loud when a snake bird abruptly surfaced next to the boat, the startled bird immediately disappearing back into the murky waters. The unmanly yell was deeply embarrassing to the young man who hoped to one day become a renowned warrior.

Colucuchia would have laughed, but he too was intent on following the progress of the submerged grandfather as it placed itself between the intruding canoe and its food. The alligator slowly surfaced, primordial eyes appearing first, then two clawed hands, each hand larger than a man's head, broke the surface on either side of the enormous scarred snout. Under the wet twisted rag were rows of massive ivory teeth.

He knew the grandfather had to defend its food, and although it could not currently crush them with its powerful jaws and spin them under the brown waters, the alligator could still tip over their dugout, spilling them into the swamp. And there were other hunters with their jaws unhindered.

"Be ready to steady the boat!" Colucuchia hissed.

Quick as a cat, he lifted his club, a sturdy oak shaft topped with a heavy conch shell. The powerful club could kill any animal short of an adult bison or a grandfather alligator. With all the force he could muster off-balanced and with one hand, he struck the grandfather between the eyes.

A fountain of water exploded from beneath the canoe, lifting and nearly upsetting the boat as the stunned grandfather rolled away diving for the shelter of the mucky swamp floor.
Savochequeya expertly corrected the tipping canoe by quickly slapping the water with his paddle, pushing hard against the rippled waves, and preventing the boat from spilling its passengers.
Colucuchia dropped his club, knowing he had not even injured the grandfather with his blow; the hit had simply startled the great beast. It would return soon and would possibly be angry. *He would be angry if a stranger had struck him on the head and stolen his food.*

He paddled the dugout up close to the fallen cypress tree, pushing the front of the canoe deep into the branches. Grandfather spiders scurried away from the disturbing boat. Colucuchia, grasped the tree trunk and a branch, leaning his weight over the fallen tree to steady the canoe.

"Get him into the boat," ordered Colucuchia.

For at last he, like the young man in front of the boat, had also considered the attention and jealous faces when they brought this odd stranger to the village.
Up close, Savochequeya realized his first impressions had been incorrect, not a forest nymph sitting in the tree but a man.
The man, shirtless, had dark skin, crisscrossed with scratches, welted from a myriad of insect bites, and torn from talons and teeth. Savochequeya thought he recognized festering claw marks from a panther, and above all the wounds and markings, were deep gouges that still oozed, cutting rivulets through cached mud; the gouges roughly matching to the grip and teeth of an alligator. The stranger's only possessions seemed to be a small pouch that hung from his neck and his torn leather leggings.

The dark man spoke for the first time, unintelligible words in a guttural tongue.

"De Soto!" said the stranger.

The words that had no sense or meaning.

For the first time, Savochequeya looked deeply into the man's eyes to find the vacant look of those who were fevered or dying.

"Quickly, into the boat," ordered Savochequeya in the Ais tongue.

The man was surprisingly heavy and reluctant to release the cypress limbs.

At last, the stranger's eyes focused clearly on Savochequeya and his uncle, then glancing around the black water swamp he was evidently startled to see nothing but water and trees.

"Jesus Christ," exclaimed Luis Castillo and then louder "Where is my horse?"

But at last, releasing his grasp upon the tree branch and consented to let the young Indian assist him into the narrow boat.

As he attempted to settle onto the turtle traps, lightning shot through the entire world and Castillo dropped heavily to the bottom of the canoe, his face settling into muddy water next to a cage where angry sharped-nosed green turtles struck at him over and over. Then the world faded to black.

Colucuchia dropped his club to the bottom of the boat, admiring the handsome tattoo of a seahorse on the stranger's bicep.

The stranger's words had meant nothing to him, just nonsense of the addled. Yet, that was not why he had struck the delirious man.

When Savochequeya had assisted the man into the canoe, Colucuchia had recognized the scars of a warrior. Puckered scars of arrows and healed slashes from shark-toothed-edged weapons.

A man yes, but what exactly had they rescued? He *had*, after all, heard of this man's tribe.

Book one: Part 20: Manny

East of the Cape of Canes, east coast of Florida, 1543.

Manuel Cabrera, master of the sloop *God's Banner,* smiled his yellowed teeth into the brisk wind and salt spray. Off to the starboard, winged fish glided over the waves.

Good sailing, good crew, God is great, he thought. But his guts hurt. Fucking shark.
Manny smiled into the salt spray. "Marcos ware the Bulls," ordered Manny.
Warm sunlight shone on his weathered face cracked and toughened from years in the Florida sun, as he turned to watch Marcos expertly lean on the rudder and turn the ship seaward of the Bulls of the Canaveral Cape, those submerged reefs that triggered rogue waves which swamped the unaware or careless.
To sink anywhere along this coast would cause one not only to deal with the creatures of the deep; but to land on the Canaveral Cape. Home of the Ais. The name the royal map makers should have given the jutting lowland, Cape of the Damned.

A Christian would be far better off in the jaws of some Kraken or shark than to be captured by the Ais. It was known the Ais were cannibals of the worst sort. Their appetite for Spaniards put the Caribs to shame, it was said.
"God is great," said Manny Cabrera. He grinned again at the wonderful day.
He looked to the green blur that was the Cape of the Ais; he would only go ashore on *that* land at his time and choosing. When slaves were available for the taking.
The sails shifted, rigging creaked and groaned at the sudden shift in the wind. The crew, anticipating the unpredictable winds off the cape, reacted instinctively, pulling hard on ropes and pulleys keeping the sloop under full sail.

The shift in winds brought the foul odor of shit and vomit from the hold and Cabrera shifted his position to remain upwind. In this part of the world, *many people* fell ill and died when exposed to foul miasmatic odors.

And he was a survivor.

The shift in winds drenched his miserable cargo with salt spray, yet they remained silent. No more flogging was required to silence the captives.

"God is Good, God is Great, God is...."

Manny glanced down at the men and women chained to the deck, frowning at the unfilled spots. A dozen more slaves needed to make a full cargo and he would return to Cuba.

With luck, he could even toss the less profitable Indians into the ocean and replace them with more valuable cargo, some bucks, or young women to provide a little entertainment on the way home.

God is good, but he frowned at the slaves. Every year the animals became harder to catch.

The result was his having to travel further north on each voyage. The Florida tribes had become wary of the white sails. His crew no longer believed his oft-told stories that once upon a time... fifteen years past? The Indians would walk right up to the boats and be plucked easier than a tall man picking fruit from a short tree.

Cabrera laughed at the memory of easy gold. *God is indeed great!*

But now the Bahamas were nearly empty of Indians, the few remaining Lucayan-Tainos having fled to the Calusa lands.

"Good luck with those bastards," he snorted to himself.

Along the east coast of Florida, the Tequestas seem to have been trapped out or fled inland and the coast from the St. Lucia inlet to the Canaveral Cape was afire with murderous Ais and Jeega.

"Pray for the day when the Ais are all dead," said Manny.

Hell, I'll attend service on that day!

Manny chuckled.

"Yes, God is Great and blessed be those who help themselves," said Manny.

That fucking shark.

But seriously, if wishes were fishes, the catch was fewer and less profitable every year. Yet the ravenous slave markets of Cuba had not lessened.
More and more the wealthy Dons turned to the Portuguese merchants to provide slaves of the Niger delta and Guinea-land for the Spanish plantations and mines. Who could have ever, ever foreseen profit in sailing across the ocean?
He sighed; those greedy Portuguese would put an honest Spaniard as himself out of business. A formal protest to the king was in order. He would need a lawyer.

From the deck, the son of the Guale, Cacique glared at him with pure hatred.
Well, that pup-buck may require another whipping. Guale-Brule-tits-and fuck them. He laughed out loud again thinking of the shark. Oh, Damn his guts hurt.
He had never laughed so hard in his fucking life. That shark. *Fuck.*

At the mainmast, his witch stretched her chain to the full length and urinated over the edge of the ship. The witch was a valuable bitch. Witch-bitch, bitch-witch. She was worth more than even God's Banner. When at length he tired of the sea, decided to settle down he would sell his witch and buy a whore house with the profits.

For his witch could accurately predict hurricanes.
Witch-bitch-bitch witch. He gave LaMacha anything she asked for except her freedom.
Good is Good- witch bitch, she has nice tits, but oh no Manny, you don't put your seed in that witch-bitch. Henry had, and he fell off the mainmast. Philippe had, and he was shot in the balls by an Ais warrior.

"No-no-no, witch-bitch-snitch-stitch-twitch-bitch."

LaMacha had asked for Seal meat.

Fucking seals; only the Indians ate fucking seals. But God is Good.

He had ordered Marcos to put in at Dead Seal River and send a boat to get his witch a seal.

Rodriquez had come back empty-handed. Cleft pallet fuck, foul-breathed swine of Gehenna, monk seals were easy to kill but Rodriquez had expounded that the shoreline and bars were empty of seals.

When he told the witch no seals could be found, she replied only, "I know." LaMacha studied the clouds.

"I know the seals are gone. A hurricane is approaching," said LaMacha.

Witch-bitch-fucking twitch! When the witch said a hurricane was near... No hesitation.

"Marcos, get us off this fucking ocean!" ordered Manny. They had let the tide pull God's Banner up Dead Seal River.
God was good, for, at a bend in the river, they discovered a little town of the Guale peoples.
The Guale Cacique had sheltered them in his little village for the price of a few hatchets and a felt hat.
LaMacha, bitch-witch, she was priceless.
LaMacha was of the Lucayan Bahama tribes. And like him, her pock-marked face proved she had and could survive fevers. His bitch-witch spoke understandable Spanish taught by the groping hands of some monk.

She did have nice tits.

With little warning, the hurricane roared over the Guale town and the storm exposed the ocean for the gray killer of ships that it really was. God's Banner strained on her storm anchors, riding the tempest out on Dead Seal River.
Without the witch-bitch-tits-witch warning, they would have been sunk or stranded on some godforsaken shore full of cannibals. He could almost kiss his witch, but-oh no, no arrows to the balls.

Whatever she wanted....

151

The hurricane passed and the stunned Guale were exceedingly easy to capture. The pups were kept with their mothers.
Manny knows God is Great, witch-bitch-tits-God is Good, the slaves were always more controllable when the children were kept with them. The Old Cacique leader and some of the warriors needed a beating.

Bitch-witch-fuck them.

The fucking shark. That fucking shark. With the most valuable Guale had been chained securely to the deck, they set the little ones and the old free.
And the betting had begun in earnest.
The winner would get first use of the Cacique's daughters.
Fucking Marcos won the bet, witch-bitch-tits, not right, the Captain should always get the first choice.
"Fucking shark," grunted Manny.
As Captain of God's Banner, he chose the slaves to be set free and those who would be kept for sale for Cuba.
Bets were placed on who would make it to the shore.
"Be free," and he tossed a boy pup into the river.
The mother screamed but she would breed more pups. His crew cheered and the outgoing river tide pulled the pup out of sight.

"The next! Bigger!" yelled his crew.

But instead, three shitty babes were tossed high into the air, over the railing with no bets placed. Carlos whooped
"If babes could fly!" and then a girl child was put on the edge.
Chains rattled against the deck and the Guale wailed in anguish.
"Bets!"
The child who had not said a word, cried out in panic as she hit the water.
"She's saying 'Free at last!'" snickered Carlos.
The girl child struggled against the tide, splashing and spitting water, and half of the crew groaned when the child actually crawled up on the muddy shore.

Well God is Great; I should have kept that one for Cuba, thought Manny. Then the old Cacique himself stood on the edge of the sloop.

"Bets!"

"I'll wager the old King does not make it to the shore!" exclaimed Marcos. He had taken that bet.
The Guale, like their cousins, the Timucuans, bathed daily. All of them could swim like god damned river otters. *An easy bet.*

"I'll match you, and the winner gets first use at the King's plump daughter," said Manny. "Be Free! Tits-witch-bitch!" yelled Manny. He had spun the old man around five times and shoved the skinny old fuck over backward into the brown water.

"Be free!"

The village leader floundered about like a drunken otter, but first one foot then another foot gripped the river bottom and the Cacique pushed his way towards the shore.

That was when the Bull Shark had risen from the dirty water and grabbed the old fuck by his skinny rib cage and quick as lightning, the old man was gone!

How they had laughed!
He had never, never seen anything so funny in his entire goddamn life. Fuck-fuck-fuck-fuck.
All of them had rolled on the decking, laughing, tears flowing freely from his eyes until his very guts ached.
Marcos with wet cheeks claimed his winnings.

"I won the bet! The mighty king did not make it to the shoreline!" yelled Marcos. And that had brought on another round of gut-busting laughter.
God is Great, tits-bitch-Guale-Brule-son of a bitch, and the devil. Oh fuck, he did not think he could have used the girl anyway after that shark.

The rest of the children and elderly were set free, the shark did not reappear and a few Guale made it to the weeded shore.
Most did not.

"Be free and breed little ones, Manny will return to this seal shit river!" yelled Manny to the shocked few lining the river's edge.

With that, they had pulled up the anchors and let the tide take them towards the ocean.
He looked upon his witch-bitch-tits, but LaMacha only studied the wispy clouds far above.

The Lucyan Tainos were like that. And they had been nearly hunted to extinction.
Fucking priests. Until the Crown had intervened; the Inquisition had gleefully burned anyone who could predict the killer storms, as witches.

They were just a little bit too quick with the torch-scorch-smoke-Had he not named his sloop after those insane little bastards?
He quickly crossed himself. It was ill-luck to think bad about the inquisitors and he was a survivor. God's Banner broke easily through the surf, into the still gray waters.

"Marcos, turn us south towards the Cape," said Manny.

He followed the gaze of LaMacha. The witch was studying the flights of gulls.

Bitch-witch-tits was a watcher. She watched the gulls and terns, the diving pelicans, snake-birds, blue herons, fish crows, Florida parrots, and Cara-Caras. She should really be called the bird-witch-bird-bitch, but then she would lie for hours and watch the movement of jellyfish under the ship, the passing of manatee shit, and whale vomit. Witch-bitch-tits-bird-turd-God is Great-I think… I… ate a grape.

Anything she wanted.

And she definitely requested witchy shit: Acorns and turkey berries and beach cactus flowers, and drift-wood and she used all to predict hurricanes.
God is Great-I think I ate a grape-tits-hit-shit. Manny thought he might be in love with his witch.

"Marcos, get us near the beach once safely past the Bulls of Canaveral!" ordered Manny.

Perhaps that storm cut a new inlet into the Ais Lagoon. Inlets drew Indians and Manny Cabrera was after all a hunter of Indians, a survivor, and a lover of tits.

As God's Banner edged closer to the distant shoreline the captain sang cheerily to his men.

"Daring, daring, the witch warning of hurricanes, Swiftly, swiftly, the seal river slips after rain. Lightly, so lightly the lingering shark- leaps after Guale. Gold and silver for the festooned jackanapes hoo-ray!"

Book one: Part 21 Panther

Pain. Overpowering.

A deluge of fiery itchy hurt washed over him, assaulting his senses upon return to the world of the waking. His eyelids were sticky with mucus and with unaccustomed effort, he forced them open to see an ink dark sky, speckled by the brilliance of stars, like distant ships on the ocean.
A single insignificant star shot across the night. His eyes traced the star's path, the effort bringing on nausea.

Thirst.
His throat was as dry, d*ry as a Peruvian desert* he might have said if in a pleasant mood. But where in the name of Commander De Soto and St. Christopher, was he?

Around him, he recognized the hushed sounds of an Indian village settling in for the night. His head shot through with pain as he swiveled to view several cook fires, red coals giving off minimal light. He could make out children, little Indian dogs, and a sitting man concentrating on straightening an arrow shaft.

The odor of cooked meat assailed him and he realized he was ravenous.
Thirsty, hungry, and hurting were disagreeable circumstances, *but they were good*. It meant he was somehow *still alive*.
And his name, he could recall his name. '*Castillo*;' that fact alone meant he had not lost his mind, not yet anyway.

Castillo gingerly raised a hand to one of the many sources of his pain, craving to tear, to scratch at the cause of his discomfort but stiff fingers discovered poultices had been placed across great swaths of his body.
Years of training took over and he forced his hand away from the poultices.

His wounds, whatever they might be, for he had no memory of them, had been deterged and medicated. From experience, he knew the poultices must not be disturbed. An involuntary shudder swept him from head to toe, at the thought of being awake while his wounds had been treated.

In the campaigns, he had often assisted the barbers with their treatment of the injured and sick. Pinning men to the ground while the healers cleaned and deterged wounds, retracted arrows, cauterized with red iron, or worst of all, treated men for the bane of all conquistadors, the gangrene rot.

The thought of gangrene caused him to sniff the air around his body and then to forcibly wiggle the toes of both feet and flex all of his fingers. For in the starlight he could see neither hand nor foot, only the blocking of stars when he lifted an arm.

Where in the hell was he? Mexico? Peru?

This Indian village could be anywhere in New Spain, but then he recalled the last two brutal years.... He was in *Florida* with the army of Governor-General De Soto.

His horse! Where was his horse?

At length, he recalled his lone ride around the bay of Tampa and the *cat*.

Riding his prize Andalusian warhorse under a sweeping oak tree, his lance resting on the pommel and the panther, heavy as a man dropping upon his back.
The tan cat had grasped his helmet in crushing jaws, raking the horse's flank and his mail shirt with powerful rear legs and sharp claws, his armor saving him from immediate evisceration. The cat's curved claws became hopelessly entwined in his shredding chain mail.
Fetid hot breath washed over him, the panther's powerful bite crushing his helm to his head, and snarling so loudly into his ears that he could not know that both he and his horse were screaming almost as loud as the cat. A triple cacophony of fear, frustration, and rage rocked the otherwise silent forest.

The panther and himself tangled as lovers; fell from the rearing screaming horse. The cat twisting to force him to hit the earth first.

The air was stolen from his lungs, forcing a silent scream from painfully landing on his sword pommel.
A powerful paw had smashed into his head, breaking the chin strap and sending the helmet flying away. Like a boxer, the cat hit him again and he lost his grip upon his lance.

The panther now only sought to free itself from the infuriating woven metal of the mail armor, snarling and rolling, kicking and biting as it pulled Castillo through thick undergrowth, through sharp palmetto bushes, ferns, and ripping blackberry bushes.
Helpless to stop or even slow the panicked cat, helmetless his head had smashed into a sturdy elm tree, bringing unconsciousness.

Of becoming free of the panther, he had no recollection.

The days following the attack were a confusing haze of nausea and searing headaches wandering lost through unending forests and prairies. Wading foul-smelling waters and pushing through grasping mud that threatened to swallow him whole. Collapsing at times from ill dizziness, the clouds above spinning like a child's toy.
Each day, growing ever weaker from lack of food. He was certain that he had eaten something unclean, yet mercifully had little memory of exactly what he gorged upon.

The sudden onset of noise, the nocturnal calls of river frogs brought him back to where he lay in an unfamiliar Indian village. Thousands, perhaps millions of frogs roared their song into the night.
His final thoughts were again of his missing horse as pink streamers then blackness darker than the night slipped across his vision, forcing him back into an edgy slumber in which he dreamed of the arid mountain passes of Peru, of gold and burned temples.

In his dream, a golden mask changed to desert sand, and the sands cupped in his trembling hands, morphed into dark waters. Lost... he was lost deep in the heart of a black water cypress swamp. Laying upon a rough-barked log that changed into a tree; his brown skin covered in mud and welted from hundreds of insect bites. Too weak to move from his temporary island, he slowly became aware of nearby men, Indians in a dugout boat, fishing spears held in the striking position.

He mumbled something in Spanish, and the two men in the boat jumped with a startled gasp, nearly upsetting their cypress canoe. *They had not known I was a man,* suspecting he might be one of the two-legged man-demons that haunted the deepest Florida swamps – those holy places where only the most powerful shamans or priests dared to search for their medicine plants and potent mushrooms.

Castillo dreamed on, sleeping on a palm mat in the village of the Ais; while overhead, above the Florida night sky, little shooting stars skipped, lived, and died. Below him, on a plain of reeds and water, thousands of green frogs sang and chirped in songs older than the very land.

Somewhere, not far away, sitting around a sparking fire, beaming at their new fame, however fleeting; Colucuchia and Savochequeya again repeated to all who would listen to the tale of how they had captured the dark warrior in the swamp of the grandfathers.

Book one: Part 22: Mother's milk

Castillo awoke to the sounds of a familiar battle; the dueling songs of break-of-day mockingbirds, one bird nearly overhead, imitating first the brash screech of a parrot and then a red-winged blackbird.

Close by, another mockingbird answered with the piercing melody of a meadowlark and finally, to the screech of a fish hawk. There had been similar calls at dawn on the Tampa mound.

He opened his eyes in the dawn light; above him were the rafters and palm thatching of a shelter. Wood smoke whirled in patterns, collecting in the palm fronds before escaping into the soft drizzle of rain.
Someone had moved him during the night. The shelter he now lay under was intimately familiar - open-sided to catch cool breezes; the women would raise woven palm fiber walls during cold weather or mosquito season.
He was still in the south then.
The Army was?

The expedition in their long march north and west had long since passed through the lands that constructed this type of shelter. A "Chickee" as the Potano and Ocala called their huts with adjustable sides.
We, what had happened to Ortega and Cowboy? Where was his horse? Soto? Rybowski?

In the light, he was surprised to see that someone had removed his crucifix from his pouch and draped the silver cross around his neck. He wished he could trade the cross for his missing Toledo steel blade. For in the dawn light he saw that his ankle was tethered by a palm fiber rope to the shelter's corner post.

So then, I am a captive.

His attention was drawn to the labored sounds of puffing and blowing. He shared the small shelter with an Indian man who stared at him and a woman squatting over coals, blowing into embers and adding twigs to a budding fire. On the packed sand between them, a basket of whitish roots and river snails. To be cooked to break the night's fast?

The two Indians, their noses and ears pierced, wearing only woven loincloths were tattooed in unaccustomed patterns. Their tattoos inferred they were not of the Apalachee, Ocala, or Timucua.
A fortuitous bit of luck indeed, as those three southern nations having been crushed and enslaved by De Soto's army and survivors would have demanded retribution. The conquered peoples would very well have legitimate reasons to kill him *slowly*, for which he could not blame them.

"They had lost and to the victor, the spoils," reflecting an oft-told quote by his father.

Outside the shelter, standing in the misting rain was a crowd of people, men, women, and children; they jostled and laughed, not so quiet and very curious about him. As he was of them. Since losing the horse he was certain these were the first people he had met.

Only the children lacked the eccentric tattoos in strange designs unknown to him. Where had he walked? Certainly not back to Apalachee?
The tattooed woman, at last, noticed that he had awakened and brought him a gourd full of sweet water which he greedily gulped down.

"Thank you," said Castillo in Spanish.

The tattooed Indian man, his eyes crinkling into a gap-toothed smile.

The woman whose face was disfigured by abstract patterns of tattoos, began speaking a string of sentences that although the words were unintelligible, the articulated words reminded him of the melodious language of the Indians of Cuba.

The woman returned to her cooking fire and used forked branches to retrieve the river snails, which she expertly cracked and skewered the steaming meat on pointed sticks.
Blowing on the morsels, she popped them into her mouth ensuring they were cool to eat and spit them onto a soot-stained palm leaf. She then loomed over him, forced open his mouth, and shoved both snails in without asking.

The snails were delicious

"Thank you," he said hoarsely. He wanted, he needed more. And weakly gesturing at his mouth. She shook her head, the universal gesture of "no" and began talking until he fell asleep again.
My mother once fed me thus.

As he slipped into unconsciousness, he dreamed the Indian man spoke in perfect Spanish.
"She says, sleep now, your guts cannot take any more snails."
Once more he slipped into a dream; their first day in Florida at the Bay of Horses.

Luis Francisco Castillo watched tensely as the sailors unloaded his stallion from the Galleon. The blindfolded horse was hoisted over the railing and lowered carefully towards the warm waters of the shallow bay.

"Careful now!" he warned.

The sailors did not care that his superbly trained Andalusian warhorse had cost him a lion's share of his Inca gold. Only that once the livestock was unloaded they could back away from the unfamiliar Florida shoreline.
To Castillo, the familiar sounds of arrows whipped overhead, and before he could sound the alarm, a feathered arrow appeared in the eye socket of the sailor working the davit hoist.

With a squeal of pain, the sailor who would be dead within a minute, released the davit, dropping the snorting stallion the final two feet into the blue-green water of the bay. The Bay of Horses.

Without hesitation, Castillo waded into the warm waters; ignoring the arrows that bounced off his helmet and mail, cursing at the brief pain of impact but fish spine-tipped arrows not penetrating his mail shirt.
Grabbing the halter of the blindfolded stallion and ignoring the screams of wounded sailors, he pulled his prized horse out of arrow range.

Castillo woke with a start.
My Horse! Adelantado…?

Full morning sunlight caressed one of his legs, the other in the shadow of a hut; the rain had stopped and the crowd of villagers gathered around; his pallet had grown larger.

He briefly recalled the dream in which the Indian had spoken to him in Spanish.

Men and women equally tattooed, clad only in woven breechcloths; women nursed infants at their breasts, naked children and dogs scampered about; the men stern-faced, armed with bows and arrows. He noted the arrows were not set in bowstrings.

Other men carried the universal weapon of the Floridas, war clubs topped with a conch shell.
From the crowd stepped a fierce form, a stocky warrior whose entire body was painted red and black. The paint accentuated the pointed deer bone through his nose and clawed turkeys' feet piercing both ear lobes.
The painted warrior barked at him, his words unintelligible, yet a different tone from the tattooed women. He alone carried no weapon but stomped his feet as if in a challenge.
The painted man switched to one of the bastard Timucuan dialects.

Castillo recognized the tongue, perhaps Potano, yet could not understand the warrior.
When Castillo did not respond, the warrior began to dance, elbows out, spinning until finally calling a perfect imitation of a Gobble, the call of a wild turkey.

The crowd laughed and the warrior stomped around the hut repeating his gobble until at last stopping and pushing aside his breechcloth he urinated on the sand in front of where Castillo lay.
Head held high, chin jutted out, the painted warrior marched away. His point, whatever that may have been, apparently satisfied.

Many of the other warriors faded slowly away, the women going off to clean their babies, only the children staying to stare at the stranger.
The two tattooed Indians returned with a bundle of sticks, this was, after all, their shelter.

Upon watching the painted warrior urinate, Castillo was reminded that he too had a fierce need to relieve himself.

"Where can I piss?" asked Castillo.
Dismayed at the weakness in his speech. He could scarcely believe it had come from him.

The women responded with a blank stare but the man reached up and grabbed a large gourd hanging from the rafters of the shelter.

"Sorry," said the Indian in Spanish, his accent inflections hinting of being raised near the border with Portugal.

"Did not realize you had not seen the cup to make water," said the tattooed man.

Castillo gaped at the Spanish-speaking Indian. But grabbed the gourd, gingerly stood up, and glanced at the surrounding crowd; as best as he could, turned his back to the largest group of the watchers and urinated noisily into the gourd, groaning with relief.

"Don't mix up your piss gourd with your drinking gourd," chuckled the tattooed man.
"Name is Carlos de la Rocha," said the painted Indian.
Castillo stared intently at the Indian.

"How is it you come to speak Spanish so fluently?" asked Castillo.

Carlos replied,
"I could ask you the same question, my friend. How you come to speak Nahuatl so well?"

Observing the dark-skinned man's uncomprehending look.
"You spoke Aztec words in your delirium," explained Carlos.

"But the answer my friend is we both learned our words as children, me in Spain and you, I suspect in Mexico," said Carlos with a smile. "And my dark companion, be it known, you are now a slave of the Northern Ais," said Carlos.

Castillo lost his grip on the piss gourd, clumsily reached for it, knocking over the container, the sour liquid spilling into the fire, pungent steam filling the shelter. The Indian woman screeched loudly and rescued her baked tubers from the coals.

Carlos, the Spaniard-turned-Indian, stifled a snicker.

"Conquistador, there is not a faster way to make an enemy, than pissing on my wife's artichokes. Her name is "Kondewekcha" in one of those island dialects, it means "Conch Woman", or perhaps "Conch eater", depending on the island the speaker is from. Those island Indians sure do like their snails." Gesturing at his woman, he said, "Her folk, those few who could escape the slavers, have settled upon the Florida rivers."

Carlos contemplated the stranger for a moment. His fancy crucifix did not mean he was not a slaver.

"You one of those slave hunters? Didn't think so when they brought you in from the *west*. If you had wandered in from the east, well let's say the Ais would not have been so….nice to you."

But Castillo couldn't give a fuck about godforsaken island conch eaters.

"Sorry," he said, carefully placing the piss gourd away from the cook fire. "Ais," Carlos had pronounced it "Aeceece"

He had never heard of the "Ais" and be damned if he was going to be a slave of the Indians-fucking snail-eating Indians.

He owned Indian slaves; his father had owned Indians and African slaves. Hell, his step brothers and sisters were the children of Indian slaves, ignoring the fact that his own mother was a slave chattel from the Ivory Coast.

Instead, he thought, *There is going to be a fight, a damn bloody one.*

But just not yet, Castillo sank heavily back to his sleeping mat as vertigo overtook him.

"Carlos, where in the hell are we?" asked Castillo, in a weary voice.

For when he stood to relieve himself, he saw that he was in a village on top of a large hill. As far as the eye could see, was a flat expanse of broom grass, tall puffy reeds, and winding rivers. A broad silver lake was in the distance.

It was going to be a bitch to escape.

The tattooed man moved upwind of the foul-smelling smoke and squatted down, his position of comfort, looking out over the waving sawgrass.

"Well, I'm not exactly sure where we are. You know as a foot soldier, I was never concerned with maps. That was the task for the Navigators and Captains. I was just a fighter," explained Carlos. Carlos squatted in the fashion of the natives, looking out over the plain of reeds,

"I can say for certain, only this, our summer camp is a day's journey from the Ais Rivers and canoe paddle to the Atlantic Ocean. But, don't rightly know how far north of Cuba we are and never had a lot of chances to find out.
'Carlos de la Rocha' –Do you know I have not spoken my name out loud for years," cautiously repeating his European name as if unsure how to pronounce the words.
"I landed with Adelantado Narváez and his brave six hundred. However, I became separated, lost, as I suspect you are," said Carlos.

Castillo noted a hint of sadness in the tattooed man's speech.

He studied this man Carlos, who claimed to be a member of one of the first Spanish expeditions into Florida, his hair graying, the shells in his ears and nose, the numerous Indian tattoos. An Indian in every outward appearance, however, Castillo could make out the sharp hawk-like features of those Spaniards whose ancestry included the blood of Moorish invaders.

How many years does it take one to forget your ways and become an Indian?

"I'm Luis Castillo, horseman for the army of Governor-General Hernando De Soto. We landed not far from where Narváez came ashore."

Carlos nodded, expecting an answer like that.

"I once heard of a slaver named Soto, who worked the Nicaragua coast. Never considered slave traders much for generals. Well in twenty or so summers, I have never been able to determine how far north of Cuba we are. However, if I had to conjure up a number, I would say we are only two weeks north by fast canoe."

Taking a stick from the fire he drew a crude map on the sandy floor.

"To the south, the Jeega, the Tequesta, and then the powerful Calusa." Carlos spat at the name of the Calusa.

"Impossible to paddle through their lands without the risk of capture, and they are right bastards. And to our north are the hostile nations of the Timucuan bowmen."

Carlos gestured with his stick.

"The lands of the Ais. *The Lagoons of the Ais* are roughly here, in-between those two powerful peoples. Inland, there are other nations to the west, smaller than the Timucuans and Calusa. No friends.
There is great hatred between the Ais and their neighbors, there is ever tension, yet the Ais is a small numbered people. Outnumbered twenty to one and sometimes there is war, sometimes the Ais give tribute, though it galls the young and old alike."

A child walked up to them showing off her parrot, a braided grass rope attached to the bird's reptilian-like leg. Carlos snatched the girl and placed her on his shoulders, bouncing the giggling child and screeching parrot.

"One of my many daughters," said Carlos.
Placing the child on the ground, she ran off with the bird flying in short circles.

"Well Castillo, you are one of the few live Spaniards I have seen, in well, perhaps....four summers. There have been Spanish raiders captured and some shipwreck survivors - a Basque one year and a Gael, another storm season... .neither spoke Spanish and well, they lived only long enough to spread their seed as the Ais are collectors of unusual peoples. They *will* be interested in you, Dark-Moor."

Carlos and Kondewekcha assisted Castillo down to the river where most of the people gathered. He leaned heavily on them as they traversed a steep path winding alternately between skinny palm trees and open-sided palm-thatched huts; finally past smoldering drying racks holding rows of fish, eels, turtles, and alligators.

Old women, gray-haired with heavy dugs, tended the smoky fires; sharp-eyed, guarding the drying food and armed with willow flogs, they swatted at skinny mongrel curs whenever the dogs dared to approach too close.
One elderly matron screeched loudly as one of the dogs, cleverer and braver than most, ducked the swinging stick and snatched a low hanging perch, ears back darting quickly away, the other curs yelping on its heels.
The villagers laughed in their approval of the dog's bravado.

Castillo was mildly amused to find the hill was not as large as he had first assumed, and in fact, the hill like many in Florida could be more accurately described as a large mound situated on a level plain. The mound was constructed almost entirely of the shells of mussel and river snails, bones, and discarded pottery shards.
At the sandy river's edge, the vast plain, the winding river with its multitude of lacing channels and the distant lake were no longer visible, for along the river course grew fluff topped cane reeds, taller than a thatched hut and obscuring anything but a wide pool created by a bend in the watercourse.
At either end of the bend of the pool was a tall platform holding a boy who scanned the water.

Watching for Alligators Castillo assumed.

The Ais, like many of the natives of Florida, were consummate bathers; men, women, and children gathered to cleanse themselves in the sluggish brown water. Families gathered to wash, lovers groped each other, and children played games of chase through rows of dugout canoes. On the west shore, was an outcropping of brown-black clay where women sat coiling pots and younger daughters attended to toddlers.

Castillo halted at the water's edge.

Balking like a shy horse; have I not seen enough water?

Like most conquistadors, he was not keen on bathing. It was well known by learned scholars that washing often killed people.

Yet Conch woman issued forth commands and Carlos translated.

"She says sit, you will stay out of the water until your wounds stop dripping."

Castillo, relieved, sat heavily upon the damp bank, his wounds itching as if he had rolled in the poison itch vine.

He observed the Ais at rest, however, his thoughts were about the whereabouts of his horse, and companions, Ortega and Cowboy. Had they survived the Calusa? What of De Soto and the grand expedition?

Slowly he sank into one of his dense moods of brooding which seemed not far removed from torpor, yet which his body required for recovery. At length, the warm sun lulled him to a dream sleep while the Clan of the Northern Ais played and loved and considered their odd captive.

As he lay on the reedy shore of an uncharted, river he dreamed of Cuba. Specifically, the tavern, known by all as "Mother's Milk".
De Soto had used an entire year to outfit his expedition to Florida.
A year to plan, to hire ships, gather supplies and livestock, purchase slaves, and arm the poorer
soldier-conquistadors, while cataloging the nobles and sons of wealthy houses who possessed their own expensive equipment.
A year to pick commanders and confer with sailors for a spring tide date into which they could sail the shallow waters of the land they would conquer.

The Hidalgos and Grandees of other countries, spent the year drinking, betting, whoring, and racing their costly coursers and chargers brought from all kingdoms of Iberia, Europe, or the two Sicilies

After his own Stallion had savaged the horse of a Burgundian cuirassier, he had wisely opted out of the racing; instead, becoming a spectator to such events. Days were spent exploring the exotic island of Cuba, betting on the horse races and besotted by the powerful Island rum.

It had been at one such race outside, of a tavern - *he refused to admit it was a brothel*, on a sweeping veranda, scented rose and honeysuckle bushes were set in cultivated terraces, draped with fern and lantanas.

Gleaming hummingbirds flitted about under a flaking sign proclaiming "Mother's Milk" and a carved relief of tropical wood of two great breasts with pointed rose nipples.

Sitting in the shade of the veranda, he had glimpsed the woman.

He had been critiquing a drunken party of Hidalgos queued up to run their expensive horses. The Hidalgos, of noble birth and haughty mien, sweltering in their plumed hats. The tropical sun glittering on their rich embroidered clothes and gleaming intensely on the jeweled pommels of their swords.
It was still early, the sun not yet directly overhead, no breeze, the air thick as water. The gay banners of the horsemen hanging straight down and even under the veranda, the heat fierce, driving rivulets of water down his dark forehead.

A half pitcher of mother's milk- rum and coconut water already consumed, had made him very drunk. A trio of whores giggled, sashaying towards him, gauging his affluent clothing. Their painted faces and beaming smiles did not match their avaricious eyes, nevertheless, they were whores and he pushed his face deep into the large bosom of the first woman.

"I am very drunk," he slurred, "But can always make the effort for some good topping."

The third woman, a Negress, at whom he could not get a decent look, for his eyes were surrounded by mounds of flesh and cotton; exhaled a sharp gasp, and fled as if he were a leper.

He had glanced at the fleeing woman and it was his turn to gasp. The first whore grabbed for his crotch.

"Don't you worry yourself about the crow, she's too old for you anyway. But Rosita and I will make you very, very happy."

But the fleeing woman-*he had seen her backside a thousand times as she washed the laundry at the Hacienda pond.*
The running woman *had to be….could only be* his mother, sold some five or six years previous when his father had tired of her.
Her sale had mattered little to Papa. He had married her only to placate the priests, his father choosing whatever concubine had been bedded at the time and dragged her down to the church.

In the dream, as in truth, he had brusquely shoved the two whores aside, upsetting the table and shattering the milk jug, and unsteadily lumbered down the veranda to find only an empty cane field and dry creek bed.

No, He had to be mistaken. Damn the drink… But…

During the years with De Soto's scouts, he had often vacillated. Had he seen true or had it simply been a delusion of the potent rum?

He awoke from his old dream to find himself encircled by six aged men, their long hair turned silver-white, appraising him. The old men and an apprehensive Carlos crouched around him, studying him as if he was a unique shell or odd beast washed ashore upon some beach.

Behind the elders stood silent warriors, curiosity on their faces but weapons held ready.

The stocky warrior who had pissed near him, still painted red and black, was now armed with a shell-topped club. The warrior pushed his way forward and barked several words, gobbled again, and stepped back into the smiling crowd.

Castillo attempted to rub the fog of sleep-away however he was simply too exhausted to do anything but sit upright.

"Am I going to have to kill that turkey fellow?" mumbled Castillo. Carlos spoke gently, beaming with pride.
"Don't mind my son, he is young and envious of your reputation as a slayer of the Timucua, and enslaver of the Potano and Ocala."

"Your son?" exclaimed a bemused Castillo.

"Well I could not give him a baptism and Christian name, but he is prideful and is known by the name of "Timucua-Killer" by the elders and "Turkey Dancer" by the women; both, by the way, are quite accurate names."

Carlos gestured at the old men that stood around them.

"These are the elders and they have questions that will decide your fate, Conquistador," explained Carlos.
One of the old men, face like weathered granite and massively scarred, where once there had been an eye, asked him a question and Carlos translated.

"He-who-knows-where-to-hide-and-kills-a-man," asks that you show everyone the sea-horse tattoo," Castillo responded by lowering the woven cloth shawl from his shoulders, that he had no recollection of having worn before falling asleep and lifted his arm.

The old men muttered among themselves and Carlos explained their consternation.

"These six are the 'Council of Elders.' They govern the Northern Ais clans, except in times of war and *they* select a battle leader to lead. The elders, from oldest to youngest are: 'He-who-knows-where-to-hide-and-kills-a-man,' 'Kills the Sentry,' 'Three-wives,' 'Spear-through-the-Bear,' 'Kills-the-raiders-from-the-east-sea,' and 'Colucuchia' which translates as 'Killed-Calusa-in-the-boat,' in the Pontano tongue."

Carlos paused and added, "Colucuchia is the person who captured you in the swamp, west of the lake of the reeds.

He did not recall ever having seen Colucuchia, although there had been an odd dream that had slipped away like a sparrow.

"Why are the old fucks - uh, elders interested in my tattoo?" asked Castillo. Carlos, briefly listened to the elders, before replying.
"Well, Conquistador, in their language, 'Ais' means ''The People' or even 'The first People' and their legend of origin is that the God of Thunder mated with a Sea-horse and the offspring was

the first Ais who waded out of the lagoon, with the full-grown head of a man growing from each ear.
The Seahorse is their totem, at least the northern clans," explained Carlos.

Ignorant fucking savages, Florida is rife with them, thought Castillo.

"Luckily for you," Carlos, stressed, "The tattoo may just spare you from, uh certain unpleasantness that has been meted out to the slave raiders who ply the coast."

An elder who was missing three fingers asked a question and Carlos translated again.

"Spear-through-the-Bear asks, 'Did you wash ashore from a shipwreck?'"
Castillo shook his head.

"No, I landed with the army near the village of Tampa, in the Tocobaga lands," explained Castillo. Another old man questioned him and Carlos spoke at length.

"'Three-wives' asks if you breed true to your skin color or are you only stained by the juice of the walnut?"

"Tell them I breed true if they let me bed their mothers," said Castillo.

"I have assured them that you breed true otter-color like babies and there are many such as you among the Spanish," replied Carlos with a wink.

One of the younger elders spoke words of passion, and Carlos translated.

"'Kills-the-raiders-from-the-east-sea' wishes to know if you are a slave hunter of the salt sea? Of the east or west sea."

Castillo, weak, was becoming agitated.

"Fuck, tell him again, I landed with Governor De Soto, to the west. *I am no slave hunter.*" "Steady Conquistador, these elders hold your life in their decision," replied Carlos.

"To live, follow my instructions; show them your scars, and name of the clans that this Governor of yours and you have defeated."

Castillo rose on unsteady feet, dropping the shawl and pointed to wounds he had received in Peru and Florida.

"This one - Apalachee, this one, Choctaw, these arrows, Timucua, this one, Ocala, this, Tocobaga, these….gesturing at the unhealed wounds, I think these are from a puma. This and this, I have no memory of receiving, but they itch like hell. Tell them to kiss my ass," said Castillo.

The elders spoke among themselves for a while and Castillo settled back upon the riverbank, for the plain of reeds had begun to spin in his vision.

At length, the elders spoke to Carlos and then all six removed their clothing, their naked wrinkled bodies crosshatched and scarred like Castillo's, waded into the river to bathe.

Carlos sat down next to the dark Spaniard, a glum look on his face.
"Well, they have allowed you to live. *And*, you will not be tethered anymore. But if you flee, *my* life is forfeit. So don't run away, conquistador," said Carlos.

Carlos skipped a shell across the tannic river water, watching the ripples slowly flow north. Castillo had never heard of a river that flowed north.

Carlos would just have to go with him when he ran from this land of reeds.

"Oh and they have ordered you to breed," smirked Carlos.

As his wounds had healed, it seemed so healed his mind. Although he fiercely missed his weapons and stallion, it seemed that lacking sword or helm, his nightmares had ceased to plague him.

He felt as if it had been years since he had the luxury of sleeping throughout the long night without visits to the apparitions of cut noses or cannibal victims. Instead, there were the pleasant dreams of his childhood, siblings, and mother.

No more in his dreams did he revisit the tavern of Mother's Milk and only once did he return to the bloody meadow of the walking dead and field of waving tuber plants.

In the final dream, he had stood at the fearful edge of the tuber field, hand in hand with the deceased Pensacola boy, staring intently into the rustling stalks and near shapeless beasts.

Slowly and stealthily, a shaggy form crept from shadows; malevolent amber eyes peered eagerly at Castillo and the child. Nearer and still nearer the form approached, until close against the tall plants where it could conveniently pounce. The beast paused to feast upon the fear that its prey should be shedding.

Milky eyes shimmered, a fearful growl rumbled from deep within the beast, ears flattened, drool strings glittered from yellowed fangs, nostrils dilating at the heavy blood scent upon the meadow, tail bushed, bloody paws scratched at red clay as it tensed to seize man and child.

Castillo no longer feared the malevolent fiend and the snarling watchers. He produced a crossbow, the very crossbow that had slain Rybowski.

The weapon loaded and cable no longer broken, he pulled the release, and the quarrel sunk deep into the throat of the approaching creature.

The beast roared, flipping backward, howling in the voice of his *father*

At that, he was instantly transported away to stand alone on the mist-shrouded twin mounds of Tampa, listening to the unseen whippoorwills, and faded into sleep.

Upon the following days and nights, the haunted dreams no longer tormented him as they had for so many years.

In this, he felt renewal and restoration, eagerly joining the men and slaves in the hollowing out of a giant canoe of cypress that had been cut down the previous year.

He arched his back, flexing his mended wounds, his strength had returned and he helped the men roll the log into place and pack dark clay around the sections not to be burned. With fire and adze, they chopped upon the log.
The Ais swatted him again with the willow switch. The ancient Indian, silver-haired, and savagely wrinkled, screeched and clicked in an unintelligible wail that sounded more like a befuddled owl than any of the languages of man.

The willow hissed across his healed wounds, the sting a mere annoyance compared to the vicious bites of the oversized horse flies that occasionally stole onto his sweating shirtless back.

The men of the clan, warriors, and untested youths alike, laughed good naturally for none of them were safe from the stinging willow branch of "Ach-coot-tsusi " which loosely translated loosely as "Guardian of the Boat Fire."

Savochequeya hooted at Ach-coot-tsusi when the old man hit the dark man, "his captive" and Savochequeya was, in turn, welted with the willow switch.

The wizened little self-appointed sovereign whacked and screeched at all, overseeing the laborious process of burning and chipping the immense cypress log that would one day become a canoe.

Castillo had been given an adze if one could stretch your imagination to the farthest use of the word. For the Ais had no iron, and the so-called adze was the lip of a conch or whelk shell tied to a sturdy branch.

Castillo briefly considered burying his adze in the craggy head of the old man, but that thought passed quickly, and instead, he laughed along with the others.

So he allowed Ach-coot-tsusi to reposition his hands on the adze and mimic how to lightly chop at the charcoal in the boat. A gentle stroke that would not shatter the brittle shell blade.

For without iron tools, the Ais boat builders utilized the methods of their ancestors, a combination of controlled fire and shell topped adzes to burn and shape their boats. Slow by any standard, however, the result was as good as any log boat he had seen.

His mind, spirit, and body mended.

Unexpectedly, his evenings among the Ais became far more agreeable. And two of the Ais women became heavy with his children. A fortuitous combination causing many sundry feminine eyes to look approvingly after him and he was the foundation of much gossip among the clan women

The days grew shorter with less sunlight and one evening around a warm fire roasting whole frogs Carlos spoke.

"My friend, the elders have decided," said Carlos. "On the morrow, we pack our belongings. The Ais are returning to the winter village on the saltwater lagoon."

Book one: Part 23: Oath

Moving from the summer village to the Ais winter village, affected him with melancholy.

There had been the day-long journey away from the freshwater river and tall mound and stopped on the palm-lined edge of a great saltwater lagoon. Rows of dugout canoes were staged upside down on logs.

"The Ais River," said Carlos. "We go to Jaguar Island, now that the season of the hurricanes has passed."

Castillo could not find any island, only the other side of the lagoon, a green blur on the horizon.
"At least the water is calm," said Castillo.
There had been questions he refused to dwell upon while he healed. And now the Ais were moving east. Further away from anyone who might know of his horse or word about Ortega and Cowboy. What of De Soto and the expedition? Their fate? New questions formed. Could he use a canoe to escape on this river?

Carlos spoke to his newfound friend, who was too interested in the canoes.

"Conquistador if you flee," said Carlos as they paddled across the wide lagoon, "the elders will have me killed."

The conquistador made no reply to this fact. Fish hawks hovered above the Ais and dropped into the lagoon. The hawks shook the water from their wings as they carried fish away gripped by sharp talons.

The Ais have me in their talons using Carlos, thought Castillo.

"The elders' oath, my life is forfeit," repeated Carlos. The dark-skinned conquistador emitted a great sigh.
"My oath, Carlos. I will not attempt to escape from this winter camp," said Castillo.

The words were spoken with bile in his mouth. It chafed that he was a captive to savages and he had given his word.

They paddled into an excellent sheltered harbor and arrived at the winter settlement; two giant mounds of oyster shells and a village surrounded by a log wall.

The men set to evicting noisy serpents with rattling tails from the unused houses. With gusto and cheers, a great game it seemed, as many of the snakes were caught alive and tossed into the open ground where fearless children threw tiny darts at the snakes.

One of the winter village shell mounds was even higher than the one he had awoken upon after his capture in the swamp. Carlos took Castillo up the mound for a view of the two lagoons.
From the tall mound, one could view that they were actually on a longish island, with immense rivers or lagoons to the east and west. An enormous cypress tree stood outside the village wall.

"The Sentry tree," said Carlos pointing to the tree. "From on the top of the Sentry tree, on a clear day, you can see the ocean to the east," said Carlos.

Escape by sea? Cuba was somewhere to the south.

Below them, in the village, the men were repairing roofs with palm thatch, while the women waded into the lagoon to collect the evening meal. The women returned within the hour and with minimal effort had harvested such an abundance of sustenance that everyone feasted until they could eat no more.
Some of the women still tended coals stacked with oysters, small conches, and the skates-with-stingers had been easily stabbed in the shallows. Others saw to the sweeping of huts and burning of last year's floor mats.
More than a few of the younger women slipped out of the palisade and into the bushes with young men.

Castillo sat cross-legged upon the shore of the lagoon, engorged upon so many oysters, that he felt ill. Enormous gray-black clouds formed to the east. With the wind picking up, several of the Ais men and boys pulled their canoes out of the choppy waters into a grove of palm trees.

Carlos sat nearby, his tattooed face pointed into the freshening wind. Castillo had learned his fellow Spaniard loved to talk about food, almost as much as he liked to eat food.

"Have you had the flesh of the little whale?" asked Carlos.
"I do not believe so," said Castillo.
Had Cowboy shown them water cows? He had eaten things on his stumble-walk from Tampa.

"The little whales, are called the water cows in Cuba, or in Hispaniola, they name it Manatee? It is greatly esteemed by these Ais, but even after all these past years, I do not find it very palatable," admitted Carlos.

He held out both arms in a sweeping gesture to the east and west.
"The Ais River," said Carlos.
He belched loudly rubbing his distended belly.
"Oh… I ate too many oysters," moaned Carlos.

Gesturing towards the building clouds and the distant ribbon of emerald land to the east.

"The ocean lies under those thunderclouds and to the south, live the middle and southern clans of the Ais. South of the Ais are the Jeaga and Tequesta towns.
At length, you reach the shell mound towns of the Calusa, to whom all pay tribute," explained Carlos. He belched again, the noxious effluvia reaching Castillo.
In the palm trees above him, noisy parrots brawled with one another until a hawk warning was screeched. A sparrow hawk chased a broken-winged dove through the camp and the entire flock of parrots sallied forth to attack the wayward raptor.

One of the warriors pointed at the hawk and jocosely cried, "Timucua," which brought forth a round of chuckles from those in hearing distance.

Carlos, interrupted by the parrots, began talking again. It was as if the captive Spaniard was driven to release years' worth of details and since their arrival at Winter Town Carlos never ceased his nonsense about the lagoon and the winter town island.

"Many and many a time, in truth I have overeaten and lain in the warm lagoon, breathing in the slumberous fragrance of Florida that filled the air until at length I could stir," admitted Carlos.

Castillo pretended to listen, but mostly watched the Ais children of both sexes, armed with miniature darts and dart throwers as they stalked noisy grackles that picked at freshly harvested conch shells. At least one of the grackles was hit and placed in the red coals.
The young learn the skill of the atlatl at an early age he thought. Carlos continued speaking.

"As for beasts that live upon the Lagoon? There are many bears, some lions and they say some Jaguars also; for they have been trapped at the Canaveral Cape and this island upon which we will winter is named for the Jaguar.
And here, as at the summer camp, the hunters return with bears, wolves, foxes, otters, spotted wild cats, two types of alligators, tortoises, and once, when I was first a captive, they brought in a great beast called a Bison, as big as an ox but now only resides in the grasslands to the west.
There are others. I forgot to mention my favorites. Here resides a giant rat, white in color, which when poked, pretends to be dead and is easy to catch.
There is the ring-tailed little bear-dog that goes about masked as a highwayman and is held in great esteem during feasting celebrations. There also is a great stock of squirrels, black-faced or gray and a smaller one that, by a certain skin, will fly from tree to tree and are greatly redeemed by the women who sew them into wraps. You don't believe me? Indeed it does fly! There are many many deer, easy to trap. Some of the hunters bring back several from the same hunt."

Carlos belched again and emitted a tiny groan.

"But this inland sea, a lagoon, is a treasure house of food stocks! There is a great store of seals, whales and porpoises, sea turtles and sawfishes, and such abundance of trout that it would astonish one to behold; likewise, drum-fish as big as a man are plentifully taken.

"There is a fish called the mullet-bass, the most sweet and wholesome fish as ever I did eat. Of this fish, the Ais take many hundreds together,

both net and trap, but their favorite method is to paddle the river at night and the mullet so startled, they jump into the boat to be clubbed by children.
Besides mullet-bass, we take plenty of skate and catfish, a wealth of crabs, and the least slave captured by the clans may catch and eat what he will of them.
You have yourself seen the acres of oysters that carpet the lagoon floor; an equal or greater amount of sweet clams lie hidden in the sands waiting only to be uncovered. Verily, I have oft been cloyed with them as they were so luscious," said Carlos.

A screeching yell rose from among the children and Castillo laughed when a girl paraded past showing off the parrot she had slain by an accurately thrown dart. Her parents admired the kill and added it to the fire with the grackle.

The Ais, toil-spent and travel-stained, gathered around family fires or lounged on the lagoon edge, laughing at the antics of their children and their tiny wars upon the birds.
The laughing and yells of the children brought a new sound to his front, as far out on the distant river, a raft of ducks disturbed by the noisy children, lifted to cloud and darken the azure sky.
"Now the duck and birds…" explained Carlos.

Castillo could not recall when he had last laughed and the smile lines on his face were an alien thing.

Book one: Part 24: Flint Trader

Castillo painfully followed the boy up the giant cypress tree.

"Slow down boy," he wheezed.

Arms and legs burning as he pulled himself to another of the handholds. Steps of sorts that had been hacked into the tree, and polished from a hundred generations of Ais hands climbing the ancient sentinel.

Yet he soon ceased his grumbling as the thinning branches allowed him to view more and larger patches of green and blue. Until at last with a final grunt, arriving at the oscillating top and he pulled himself into a clearing of sorts.

The boy lounged in a swaying woven willow basket-more spider web than substance. Castillo gripped the branches tightly and stared.

"Jesus wept."

For just as Carlos had described, from the tops of the springy branches, cool wind in his face, the blue Atlantic could be seen curving out of sight on the eastern horizon.

Below him, he could just make out the sandy trail that twisted snake-like to the oval mounds of the winter village and beyond the village, the longish island on which it sat between two emerald green lagoons or sluggish rivers. One or both rivers were named for the Ais, as Carlos had explained.

To the west, the afternoon sun shone upon a vast pine and oak forest, staggering in its primeval immensity. Somewhere to the west, invisible in the huge blanket of emerald, he knew was the summer village of the Northern Ais and their freshwater river that flowed lazily to the north.

Further west on the dim horizon jutting into the sky like giant anvils, at least two fires raged across patches of forest or on the distant prairies.

The prairies, unseen, knew of their existence beyond the pines because he had wandered lost across those flatlands.

He would never tell anyone how to his everlasting shame, he had wept at the endlessness of the prairie.
But mostly he could only recall agonizing headaches, elusive recollections of crossing a land bereft of trees, and endless nights shivering on a weeded savannah where wolves howled from dusk to dawn.

I nearly starved to death in a land thick with fierce bison and wild cattle, he contemplated.

He was not certain, but he thought there had been horse droppings also, or perhaps the manure had only been a desperate hallucination because every painful step caused his vision to swim.
Beyond the prairies, unseen and even further west was the bay of Tampa, where conceivably, his stallion still lived. Perhaps Ortega and Cowboy lingered in the area, although surely they would have returned to Cuba by now.

His guide up the sentry tree; a youth who wore only a shark tooth knife and breechcloth, but whose voice had not yet deepened, called out a warning.

"Wings!" said the boy who pointed at the distant ocean.

Squinting, his eyes focused on the broad expanse of blue, Castillo attempted to comprehend what the boy was pointing at, and at length, he could make out a large gull or pelican flying north.

No, the distance was too great, *not a bird.*

Finally, it dawned on him; the tiny white speck on the far ocean could only be a sail! A galleon or frigate was plying the waters, sailing north.
They were his countrymen on a trading mission or perhaps a mapmaking expedition for the King. That ship or one like it was his escape out of the Florida wilderness. For him and Carlos. Their ride back to civilization in Cuba.
If Carlos escapes with me then the ex-soldier would not then forfeit his life, thought Castillo.

He contemplated the island below him, his prison. The broad lagoon between him and the beach; he would have to steal a canoe and somehow signal the ship.

What if there was not another ship for… years? That thought was too disturbing.

The Ais boy talked excitedly and Castillo with only a minor understanding of the Ais language, watched the distant sail disappear from view.

Scanning the lagoon Castillo tapped his young guide,
"Hey look! Big canoe coming our way," said Castillo.
When the boy, at last, stopped talking and looked to where Castillo was pointing, two large canoes were approaching the village from the north.

The young sentry yelped in his native tongue, grabbed a conch shell from a basket, and blew a long warning honk on the shell.
Searching the area below the tree, he called out and dropped the shell through the branches to the far ground. When he did not get the answer he was expecting, he tossed another shell from the tree.
A faint voice echoed up through the branches and finally a matching conch call. The youth who blew the responding call was shortly seen racing down the trail to warn the village.

Castillo understood some kind of a signal had been given and his guide slithered down the tree like a Mayan monkey, leaving him alone.

"Don't wait for me," he yelled at the boy. "Fucking monkey boy," and lowered one foot onto the step below him and carefully began the long climb down.
He was surprised when at last his shaky feet stepped onto solid ground.
He was alone, except for a single scrub jay that screamed at him. The jay, he knew, was telling him to make his escape attempt. Castillo briefly considered simply walking away from the village.

Carlos.
His limbs shook from the strenuous climb and any flight would result in Carlos's death.

By the time he made the trek back to the village, the sun had settled through the treetops but still shone across the western lagoon.

The Ais had formed a loose cluster around a stranger and nearly as curious as the Ais, he pushed through the crowd to see trade goods displayed across three deer hides.
Upon one deer hide were displayed egg-shaped flint blades, on the middle pelt, tiny serrated arrowheads, and the last, deerskin held rocks, small boulders that appeared to be fossilized coral.

One of the elders lifted a chunk of fossilized coral and expertly struck it with a whelk shell knocking off a palm-size flake of rock.

Carlos stood amid his adopted people, inspecting a large stone blade, and held up a green glass bottle that must have washed up on the beach.

Castillo, his curiosity whetted, pushed his way through the crowd to locate a bowl or skin of freshwater. A small gathering of young Ais warriors stood off to the side glaring at the trader. Carlos's son appeared to be the leader and as Castillo walked by them, Turkey Dancer spoke in perfect Spanish.

"Timucua Flint Trader!" said Turkey Dancer and he spat in the sand.

Castillo was surprised, but then he wondered why he should be. Carlos would have taught his son the King's words for the day when they were rescued from the Ais lands.

The son of Carlos gave Castillo a conspiratorial glance and spoke quietly.

"The elders protect the traders, but perhaps this Timucua will meet an Alligator or Panther on the journey back to his village? What you think O killer of Timucua?" asked Turkey Dancer.

"Gobble, gobble," said Castillo and walked away to find his water.

Castillo squatted Ais fashion in the shade, and Carlos soon followed, squatting next to him, twirling and showing off his new flint knife.

"Carlos, from that sentry tree we saw a sail going north in the ocean," said Castillo.

He was not about to say out loud, he saw their *escape ship.* For who else in this village could understand Spanish?
Carlos, still admiring the blue and crimson of the flint blade, was not surprised at the information about the ship.

"Yes, yes, slave hunters. Look at the colors of this stone," replied Carlos, mesmerized at the spinning flint knife.
"*Those* raiders have been stung along this coast and avoid Ais lands. Well, the clever ones anyway. There could always be more dumb raiders. There are old slave raiders and dumb slave raiders. Rarely both," replied Carlos.

The Timucua flint trader halted mid-sentence in his haggling with an elder. Halted upon hearing the alien words of Spanish speakers. The flint trader searched out who was speaking Spanish.

Castillo looking over Carlos's shoulder could see the trader's back stiffen, turn, and with cold black eyes searched the gathered Ais.

"Oh shit," mumbled Castillo.

For he looked upon a broad face, heavy-browed and facially scarred to mark him a survivor of the pox. Yet, where the traders' nose should have been, was only a healed scar, a stub that dripped mucus.

Someone had hacked the man's nose off and branded the cheeks. Castillo suspected there would be other scars beneath the trader's deer hide shroud.

The trader studied him like a captured insect. Taking in his torn breeches, the heavy crucifix, the lack of weapons, and at last smiled at Castillo.

A smile that sent shivers of dread up his back.

Shit, shit, shit, I should have left when I climbed down the tree.

Neither turned their gaze and Castillo thought desperately where there would be a weapon close at hand. The boats were only feet away.

Carlos thrust his new knife at Castillo.

"Look at the quality of this flint," said Carlos oblivious to the stare of the flint trader.

Castillo held the blade before him, edge out ready for a backhand slash across the eyes if attacked, however, the trader went back to haggling, bartering for his flints.

Shit, he thought, but said nothing to Carlos of the Governor-General's baggage slave that now traded in flint.

"It is of fine craftsmanship and shade," said Castillo.
He handed the blade back to Carlos, adjusting his stance, he stepped back to where he could see the flint trader who was now talking with an elder as the sun dropped below the horizon.

Castillo lay upon his mat. Sleep was a long time coming but the determination had been made.
Before the sunrise, I escape this place.

Yet at length the needs of the body took control and he slept and dreamed of his former life.
In Luis's restless dream, Governor-General De Soto looked on with disinterest as three Gahanna-men soldiers firmly held the Indio captive.
A Castilian applied the cherry red branding iron to the Indian's cheek, while another, a gray-haired Portuguese in stained clothing, dropped his whetstone into a leather pouch and easily cut the man's nose off.
A priest with bulging eyes of a codfish recorded the enslavement, looked up from his ledger manuscript, and spoke to the Governor-General.

"This slave claimed he was a merchant of colored flints and shark teeth, Sire," said the priest. De Soto, whose thoughts had been elsewhere, only replied "Pearls?"

"No sire, like the others; these savages hold greater worth in their stones than pearls or gems," said the priest.

"Merchant eh? Well, he may be of some use as a translator. Do not work this one to death. Perhaps if he can learn a civilized tongue he can teach you some of his words…"

Castillo was roughly woken from his dream to see the stars blazing overhead. A dark man-shaped shadow suddenly blocked out their brilliance and he groped for his club.

"Luis," a harsh whisper spoke to him out of the darkness and he recognized the voice of Carlos. "Luis, wake up! Up man! There is a problem!" said Carlos.
A shell cover was lifted from a torch.

In the flickering glow of a palm torch, he could make out Carlos and his son Turkey Dancer, and other younger warriors who followed the young war leader, Turkey Dancer.

Then from out of the darkness walked the very two who had brought him to the Ais as an invalid; the elder Colucuchia and the young warrior Savochequeya.

"The flint trader?" asked Luis. Knowing the answer to his question as if some fortune-telling gypsy or moor.

"Yes," replied Carlos, answering Luis's question curiously, half mirthfully, half wrathfully. "What do you know of the merchant; ah no, what have you done to him?" hissed Carlos. Luis stood up rubbing the scars of old wounds.

"Specifically, I have done nothing to the man, but the Spanish…"

His words trailed off. Carlos the soldier, should be the last person to ask about the Spanish treatment of conquered peoples.

Colucuchia interrupted the two.

"The elders have agreed to sell you to the Timucua trader. The trader has forsworn all future trade with the Ais if they do not sell you," said Colucuchia.

"The trader will not see the dawn," hissed Turkey Dancer. The other warriors nodded eagerly in agreement.

"Yes," Carlos agreed.

"But, Luis, you must be shielded from the elder's wrath. As a slave, you will be punished for what is about to happen. There is but one way to protect you. You must become an Ais," said Carlos.

Carlos held out two carved heads the size of a gull egg. From the wooden faces protruded a nose as long as his finger.

"The long-nosed twin gods," explained the castaway Spaniard.

Luis looked at the odd carvings, then to Carlos and Colucuchia without comprehension.
From his pouch, Carlos pulled out a spine taken from one of the great flat-fishes of the lagoon.

"Luis, you need the protection of the clan. You must be adopted by the clan, you must be acknowledged as Ais. Then they cannot sell you, but instead are obligated by clan decree to protect you from all outsiders," said Carlos.

"Alright then, I'm in," said Luis cautiously, feeling the lie upon his lips. Carlos dropped to his knees.
"To be formally accepted into the clan, you must wear the twin gods. I did, as you must now. Lie down," instructed Carlos.

Castillo crouched ready to spring into a fighting stance.
"What is with the carvings?" asked Castillo.
"Down, on your back," ordered Carlos.

With a cautious sigh, Luis complied with the request. Trusting the man he had learned to be a friend. Carlos said something in a dialect that he heard yet did not fully understand. Southern Ais, the language of Colucuchia he would later learn.
At Carlos's command, all the Indians seized upon him pinning his limbs to the damp earth. Colucuchia settled down and grasped his head.

"What the fuck!" demanded Castillo.

He had been betrayed to the cut nose trader?

"Be still Luis," instructed Carlos, who then proceeded with a history lesson. "The Ais, which means "First People" believe their origins lie with the lightning god striking the lagoon and impregnating a sea-horse. From this union, out of the Lagoon walked the first man, the first Ais," explained Carlos.

As he spoke, he positioned his fish spine as Colucuchia grabbed Castillo's head and stuffed a section of twisted deer hide into Luis's mouth. Castillo could only think of De Soto's unmanning of the Indian slave and began to struggle.

"The first Man walked out of the lagoon and from each ear, there hung a tiny human head with the long nose. The long-nosed twins. The same twins who also bent the sapling, teaching man how to make the bow. And so those who wish to become members of the Ais, they must also wear the twin gods," explained Carlos.

With that Carlos thrust the fish spine through Luis's ear-lobe, threaded the oozing hole with sinew and attached the carving of the long-nosed god.

Luis attempted to scream through the hide but powerful hands held his mouth closed around the buckskin.

"You, my friend, already carry the marking of the sea-horse, and the Ais suspect you belong to clans already. Still….. it must be official," explained Carlos.

Carlos switched sides and repeated the procedure, tying the second god to the bleeding ear then stuffed a poultice of mud, tree moss, and willow bark into the wounds.

"All must wear the gods. Do not remove the twins until all in the clan acknowledges your formal joining. They will now fight for you and you will fight for them," said Carlos.

"Rise warrior, I see you," said Colucuchia.

The warriors released him and he jumped up spitting out the buckskin, wanting to rub his ears, but they hurt far too much to touch.

"Fuck! Holy Mary mother of God! Jesus fucking wept, Carlos!" hissed Castillo.

He wanted to kill someone. Around him, there were only smiles in the dim torchlight.

Dawn broke pink, the stars faded from the sky and Colucuchia paraded the new Ais around the clan huts to the awakening community. Many of the Ais were not surprised, only wondering why it had taken so long for the dark man to join the clan.

"I see you," came the greeting from the awakening Ais.

One by one the elders came out of their huts to find themselves annoyed, or worried about the future of the flint trade.

"He-who-knows-where-to-hide-and-kills-a-man" laughed heartily at the cleverness that had been played upon the council of elders.

"That Timucua trader-dog should have been slain long ago," he said and laughed some more.

At the river's edge, near his two large canoes, the flint trader blew on coals he had kept hot all night. He waited for the dawning, listening to the night herons, listening to his guards and his paddle slaves stir to the light in the east.

He had been unable to sleep; the dark Spaniard had awoken too many memories.

Old memories, horrible memories of his time as a slave to the wolf-faces, and the fresher memories of how women, *even* slave women reacted when seeing his disfigured face.

There had been a time, before the coming of the elk-dogs and fur-faced warriors, when women came willingly to his fire. Now he had only slaves available to him and they always hid their faces in disgust when he bedded them.

In his hand he twirled his sharpest knife, listening to the sound of his fingers lightly rustling over flint, the rock spirit bragging it was good flint.

"Stone Singer" that had been his name so long ago…

When there was enough light to see his fingers, he put down his favorite blade and chose another knife, jagged and dull.

This would be the blade that he would use to remove first the nose then the manhood of the dark man. Stone Singer stirred the coals again.

His new slave could not be allowed to die quickly; the wounds would be packed with red coals.
If careful he would keep the dark man alive for years. And Stone Singer was nothing if not careful. One of his guards arose and made water in the river, turned back towards the fire adjusting his breechcloth when suddenly he was knocked back into the water with a grunt of pain.
The guard recovered, for he was a solid warrior, and staggering from the mud he was shocked to find that an arrow had sprouted from his chest.

"What the...?" stuttered the guard. Another arrow hit him again. Then from out of the shadowed huts came a withering fire of arrows and darts. However, from the waters of the lagoon came mud-smeared warriors.

"Stones Singer" his plans for vengeance were suddenly forgotten as a heavy shell-topped club crashed through his skull and he slipped into the forever darkness.

Book one: Part 25: Shoots Ducks

The lone survivor of the flint trader's hired guards stared sullenly at his Ais captors.

"Shoots ducks in flight" was his name, barely of seventeen summers on his first journey as a guard for the flint trader.

These southern Indians. He had been warned they were unpredictable. Small in numbers compared to his people and all the more vicious for their fewer numbers.

These Ais did not even grow beans or maize, so ill-cursed was their mosquito-infested land.
Yet strange and wondrous things, unknown peoples and beasts washed ashore onto the cape from the eastern sea. So despite their reputation for treachery and murder, traders would often risk death for the profitable Ais trade.

He knew that his time would soon be over.

"Shoots ducks in flight" harbored no illusions of what fate lay before him and he swore that he would be found worthy of his clan and his death song would receive approval from his ancestor spirits.
Bound upright to a tree trunk set in the center of the village plaza, he watched with interest something of a dispute between the clan elders.
Doubtless concerning the murder of the trader and the future of flint trading.
Warriors and elders had split into two rival parties.
Yet, he doubted it would come to blows because warriors were already peeling away from the elders.
Guffaws or yawns coming from the stocky warriors.

Seemingly unconcerned with the dispute, a muscular warrior wearing turkey feathers slowly stomped around his post, bloody scalps hanging from his belt.

Soon other younger Ais warriors shuffled around him, stomping in rhythm behind the one wearing the turkey feathers, one warrior proudly danced with the braided scalp of his friend, Lightning snake.

Ignored by all was the tall dark man wandering around with the long-nosed gods hanging from his ears, secure in the protection of the clan. "Shoots ducks" recognized the significance of the long-nosed twins.
To wear the twins, Gods who were the bringer of the bow and tobacco, was the same in his own clan, and "Shoots ducks" smiled at the joke that had been played upon the elders who had agreed to sell the dark warrior.
For undoubtedly, a warrior is what he was, as suddenly the dark man stepped into the growing circle of warriors that were dancing around him.
Firelight illuminated white scars on dark skin. Lots of scars.

"Shoots ducks in flight" began to tap his foot in timing to the warriors' slow dance. His voice with a will of its own, began to sing his death song. It was time to die proud. Two figures hovered around the dancing warriors and arguing elders.
One, an ancient wisp of a man, toothless and stooped, the elder was tattooed with faded markings of a Calusa, a Calusa *conjurer* no less, the evil eye was imprinted on his bony chest.
The other, a maiden, *Illaca* was her name, pretty with a pouty mouth, intelligent eyes, and unusual hair, a shade lighter in color than normal.

Only yesterday the girl had giggled with him as they attempted to understand each other.
Only yesterday he had presented her with a gift of a blue and red feather found on the shore of the lagoon. Well, that opportunity was also past.
It was time to die proud.

The debate of the elders ended with two storming off, while the remaining nodded with approval at the Timucua singing his song of death and the old men shuffled painfully into their own slower version of the warrior dance around "Shoots duck."

Carlos sided with Colucuchia and "Spear-through-the-Bear" and they watched the elders
"He-who-knows-where-to-hide-and-kills-a-man" and "Three Wives" walked away in frustration.

"Well they should not have sold the conquistador without full consensus of the council," mumbled Carlos, turning towards the fire to see his daughter, Illaca, standing near the circle of shuffling warriors.

She stared at the young Timucua tied to the torture post. In her hand was a twirling small blue-red feather.

"Jesus wept," Carlos groaned.

Had not his family gotten enough attention this day?

"Kills-the-raiders-from-the-east-sea" and "Kills the Sentry" shrugged their shoulders, the deed was done. There would be other traders. There were always collectors of the oddities that washed ashore in the Ais lands, be it beast, man, or item.

Colucuchia spied the Calusa conjurer slave, suspecting the slave was going to request the honor to be the torturer for the captured Timucua.
An involuntary shiver swept Colucuchia, the Calusa elder well knew his work.
"Fuck it," said Colucuchia.

And they all joined in the dance around the captive.

Luis Castillo sat down by the fire. Dancing had been a really stupid idea, fresh blood trickled down his neck, hell he did not think he could shit without grimacing. The pain in his pierced ears throbbed like two drums.

He used a clump of tree moss to wipe at the blood running down his neck.
"How long do I have to wear these?" muttered Luis Castillo of the Ais nation. Illaca stood twirling her feather as her father walked up and simply said
"No."

Carlos studied his daughter, always the rebellious one. A trait admired by the Ais, but she would have been hell in Spain. Probably even forced into a convent.

"No," repeated Carlos.

However, he could see in her stubborn features he already lost this particular war.
As much as the people loved to torture enemies, they needed warriors more. For the common defense and to marry the widows.

Defending the land was a costly process for warriors. Consequently, any maiden or widow could save any captive from death by simply walking up and proposing marriage.

Carlos rubbed his tired eyes, nodding his head in approval, but really thinking "no" and Illaca gave a tiny squeal and hugged her father.
She then strolled into the circle of dancing warriors, stepping past Turkey Dancer who snarled at her, but inside was pleased with his little sister's bravery.

"She will breed brave children, even *with* the hindrance of the Timucua blood," said Turkey Dancer.
"Be my husband and become one of the People," said Illaca to "Shoots ducks in flight".
The prisoner had temporarily ceased his death song.
"What did you say?" he said to the beautiful girl-women before him. The dancing had come to a halt, all eyes upon the two.
The ancient Calusa conjurer appeared from the shadows to translate.

"This tasty one says 'marry her and you will live.' Seems like a good choice, boy as much as I would love to ply my skills," said the Calusa.

"Shoots ducks in flight" only briefly considered his options and nodded in agreement to the Ais woman.

"Yes, I will marry you. You will be my wife. Where are the twins?" said "Shoots ducks in flight"

For he knew he too would have to wear the heads of the twin gods. The Calusa cackled to Illaca.

"He says he wishes to have many, many children with you," explained the Calusa conjurer. . The crude statement caused Illaca to blush and the older women to laugh.

Once again, the sharp spine of the lagoon flatfish was brought out to puncture holes in earlobes. Only this time the warrior held still without anyone holding him and never uttered a sound. The silence also brought murmurs of approval from the watching clan.
At last, the Calusa conjurer had the attention of the elders, those that had stayed around.

The Calusa tossed cowrie shells in the air, studied them, and explained to the stupid northerners what he already knew.

"There is a hurricane coming to Ais land. Coming to the Ais Lagoon. Coming at us," said the old Calusa.

A groan, unasked for, escaped the gathered Ais. The old man had never been wrong about his storm predictions.

Book one: Part 26: Hurricane

Carlos and Castillo climbed the giant cypress tree to seek verification of what the old Calusa had said. Castillo climbed slowly as his new earrings pained him greatly with every branch grabbed.

"How long do I have to wear these things?" asked Castillo upon reaching the top of the sentry tree.

But Carlos was preoccupied with the large white outer band of cloud formations to the far south. For the first time, Castillo noticed the wind had picked up considerably since his first climb up the tree. Carlos was shaking his head.

"But the acorns have already dropped," Carlos muttered to himself. "
What?" said Castillo.
A branch snagged at his left ear, nearly bringing tears to his eyes.

Carlos looked at him as if he was a dullard and remembered the conquistador was new to the seasons on the Ais coast.

"The acorns have ripened and dropped. That is a reliable sign that the season of hurricanes is over. However rogue storms *like rogue* Spaniards are not entirely unheard of," explained Carlos.

Carlos took a final look at the approaching clouds.
"Let us go, Luis. We must prepare for the winds," said Carlos.
They began the long descent to the ground.

When Castillo's shaking legs, at last, stepped onto the solid ground, Carlos was waiting for him,
holding a small shark tooth. He gestured towards the long-nosed gods hanging from Castillo's ears.
"The twins have served their purpose," said Carlos.
As an afterthought, Carlos gave a mild apology.

"Brace yourself, Conquistador. This will not be pleasant," said Carlos.

Using the shark tooth, he sawed the cords that had been so roughly pushed through Castillo's earlobes. Castillo ground his teeth, almost fainting as the cords were pulled out.

"Tisk, tisk, those are some angry wounds. If they get worse you will need a maggot. Go pack the holes with sea-weed mud poultice and come help the clan to prepare for the storm. My guess is we have perhaps a day and a night to get ready," said Carlos.

Castillo helped the men drag the heavy dug-out canoes,-twenty-two by his count; far above the low area and rolled the boats over, upside down on large logs.
Palmetto leaves, new and old, were stacked under the boats and the woven wall and floor mats were placed upon the leaves.

"Why the mats? asked a confused Castillo.

"That is where we will lay during the storm," replied a stoic Turkey Dancer.

Savages thought Castillo.

Palmetto leaves were then stacked over the upside-down canoes to fill in the gaps. Over these palmetto leaves were stacked sundry logs and rocks crossed to hold the leaves in place. Small pots with smoking red coals were suspended inside the boats where no rain could get to them along with fuel to keep the small fires fed.
During this time, the wind increased bringing hot gusts from the south and heavy clouds raced overhead. On the mound, the Ais used ocean shells to dig out cavities high up on the tall mound. Drain trenches were cut into the floor of the depressions and heavy palm mats taken from the huts and placed into the cave-like shelters, which were then covered with palm leaves. Logs were leaned against the palm leaves
Heavy logs grunted Castillo.

"What are these?" asked Castillo.
Carlos was busy passing gourds of water and smoked mullet into the mound holes.

"Have you ever experienced the Florida Hurricane, my friend?" asked Carlos.
Luis Castillo only nodded, *a storm is a storm he thought.*

"The women and children will stay in the nooks in the mound. They are safer than where the men will wait. There is no chance of flooding on the mound," said Carlos.

The implication that the canoes could get flooded at their new location was bullshit, he thought. The lagoon would have to rise twelve feet to reach the canoes.
Carlos looked at his friend, understanding his disbelief.

"It is impossible that the flood tidewater could reach the boats," protested Castillo.

"The water *has* flooded the boat storage area in the past, although not since I have lived on the coast," replied Carlos with a shrug.

Horse shit, thought Castillo.

"The very unpredictable nature of the storms is why the Ais move inland to the freshwater during the season of the storms. The coast is a dangerous place to reside. Conquistador, *If the* water reaches the boats, make for the top of the mound and wait for daylight. It will pass, but you will not be very happy," warned Carlos.

Even as Carlos spoke, a violent wind gust shook the village, tearing palm leaf thatch from the roofs of huts or ripping palm leaves from the tall trees.
Children laughed and played in the wind until a furious torrent of rain chased the final holdouts into the shelter niches cut into the mound.
Hours later the outer bands of the hurricane swept across the island. The fishnet stands and fish drying racks could be heard snapping and breaking as they were rendered to their original individual pieces. Rain pounded upon the heavy thatch covering, anchored by logs wrestled in place just to hold the shelter covers in place. The coming of night compounded fear of the storm and keening wails of terror could be heard over the roar of the wind.

As the sun disappeared below the horizon, there came the far-away muffled rumble of distant thunder and before full dark, the storm burst upon them in the wild howl of the tropical tempest. The men crawled under the canoes for quiet waiting and the women hushed children with stories.

It poured.
The water came down in sheets and in torrents, first vertical and then at an angle.
There passed through the forest a terrible gust of wind which made the trees bend and maple branches break to fall heavily to the ground.

Palm fronds flew about like some giant attal dart.
The village dogs crawled into the questionable shelter of the boats to curl up with the men and set off a series of howls as if they were hunting game. Only to cease their howling when the roofs were lifted off the huts and hurled into the lagoon.
Castillo settled in with a cur for warmth, composed himself to wait anxiously for the first ray of morning, making a pillow for his head from his arm, and stretched to restless sleep. His ears hurt. Never in his life had he heard the howl like what now screamed at him in the night.

A demon howled in the night.
Castillo could hear trees breaking like twigs.
A sand pine fell over to crash into the palisade wall, the deed heard and felt through ground vibrations but not seen in the inky blackness.

Women wailed and hardened warriors cried out in panic.

Whatever demon had arrived with the storm, now closed in on the villagers.
Sticks, branches, and shells pelted him, blowing in from under the boat along with stinging rain. Smoke assailed him, as the ember pots stuffed way up under the boats, smoldered.

In truth, Castillo curled under the boat hugging his legs, paralyzed with fear as trees snapped all around him and he prayed to the Lord God of the Spanish, he prayed to the forbidden gods of his Ibo ancestors and then to the god of the Turks. He even considered praying to the forbidden blood goods of the Aztecs.

Daylight arrived later than usual, for the hurricane had not yet passed, and the dawning of the day allowed him little peaks at the blusterous morning and naked trees.

Then, in a convoluted descending wail, like the howl of prairie wolves, the hurricane died down to absolute stillness.

Castillo relieved the storm was over, crawled from under that boat, and made water. He smelled of wet dog.

"Mary, Mother of God! I'm glad that's done with," said Castillo. From under another boat, Carlos chuckled.

"Done with? No, no!" exclaimed Carlos as he wriggled from under a canoe. "Conquistador, the worst is to come! We are merely in the eye of the hurricane."

Quickly the Ais scattered about the shattered village, relieving body functions and grimly inspecting the remains of their huts before returning to their rabbit holes.

Moving slower than the others, "Shoots ducks in flight" and Illaca emerged from a mound hole to make water.

It seemed as if both could not stop touching the other even when urinating.

Castillo chuckled to himself; the Flint trader-guard is rewarded with a willing maiden, and my reward is a wet dog and smoke reddened eyes. He smiled at his people. The Ais.

Well, there was also the fact that he was alive.

The hurricane conjurer pranced around bragging of his abilities, extolling the virtues of a tree-frog god. Yesterday Castillo had deemed the old Calusa slave- "He who Wears Human Heads" well-nigh demented, yet, the old conjurer had known,-somehow, that the hurricane was coming towards them.

"Carlos I do not believe you about this hurricane eye," said Castillo.

"The hurricane does believe in you, Conquistador," joked Carlos.

But the wind began to increase and the rain began anew as the Ais mothers ushered their children to their shelters.

A cold rain began to pelt him and Castillo could only mutter.

"Fuck," and he too crawled to his mat under the boats trailed by two tail-wagging wet dogs.

Book one: Part 27: Wreck of Gods Banner, Cape Canaveral

"As for your male and female slaves whom you may have, you may buy male and female slaves from among the nations that are around you." Leviticus 25:44

Manny scrutinized his witch with indecision. Should he take her with them on the raid?

LaMacha, the hurricane witch chained to the mast, chaffed at her manacles watching the sailor-raiders anchor "Gods Banner '' on the shoal of a new hurricane-formed inlet.

One of the sailors with more Indian blood than Spanish ancestry gazed nervously at the croaking noise from the tree.

He knows, she thought.

In a nearby Manchineel tree, the storm stripped of all its poison leaves perched a family of orange-beaked eagles croaking in alarm at the presence of the slave-ship. The Kara-Kara eagles, half carrion buzzard, half eagle were steadfast harbingers of disasters.

Disaster for whom, she wondered?

She studied the crew, *so it's not just the mixed-bloods that are prescient of the dangers....*
The sailors normally insufferably loud, now only whispered to each while furtively turning quick anxious glances to the shoreline while they busied themselves lowering the fast paddling canoes to the water and supplied the narrow boats with coils of bondage rope.

They're ready to piss themselves, as well they should be whenever touching ashore on the Ais coast.

The attention of the orange beaked eagles, an evil omen scoured from her old memories. The image of Father Acevedo followed by helmeted soldiers and her stunned parents on the morning of the day the good father had turned upon her after she had twice accurately predicted hurricanes.

"I pronounce you witch!" said Father Acevedo.

He had screeched like a Kara-kara, pointing with a trembling finger and the soldiers had stripped her naked and bound her cruelly on the threshold in front of the family home.

Once bound tightly, the good Father Acevedo sprinkled her with holy water speaking magic words of Latin; and had been greatly disappointed that the powerful water did not immediately engulf her in cleansing fire.

Undaunted, the priest had nevertheless alerted the village. Their very souls had been rescued by his quick action.

"The Lord has broken the rod of the wicked!" said Father Acevedo.

And she had been led away to the stockade for deliverance to Inquisition clerics and trial by fire for the accusation of witchcraft.

"Those who burn," her father whispered about the dreaded Inquisition.

The image of the village priest and her recollection of his last words was the very confirmation she sought of the eagle's croaked warning.

"The Lord will break the wicked," whispered LaMacha.

She tossed a cowrie shell into the waves and fervently prayed both to the powerful god of the Spaniards and to the ancestral gods of her people, that the foul sailors of the slave ship Gods Banner would be destroyed, their essence devoured by the all creator frog-divinity who brought the great summer storms.

Her prayers to the frog god of the island clans were careful and restrained, for, in its hunger, the three-eyed-one always answered the prayers of its patrons.

It was a gift and power to be used sparingly for the god was capricious.

While waiting to be conveyed to the Inquisition, she had prayed to the Three-eyed- ancient-one to rescue her from the Christian devils in black robes.

And indeed she *had* been rescued from torture and fire but had instead been sold by greedy soldiers. The action that landed her on the deck of the slave raider's ship.

Though she had been saved from the cleansing fire of the frenetic churchmen; life on the slave ship had not been easy or pleasant.

The sailors of the slave ship 'Gods Banner,' had at first treated her coarsely, her status simply that of another Indian captive to be sold at the marketplace, and because she could speak the language of her enslavers; they had christened her the insulting gibe of "Daughter of the tavern-slave."

However, the Captain "Manny" as he liked to be called, an insane little man, foul, leader of even fouler company, had at last silenced his men when she had accurately warned them of the hurricane and after the first storm they simply referred to her as the "Witch."

When Manny had acquired her from the unscrupulous guards; *and he obtained many slaves from the guards who waylaid unaware Christian Indians,* Manny had been disinclined to heed her warning of the approaching storm. The day was becalmed with no indication of the approaching bad weather unseen over the horizon.

At great risk, she forced upon him her urgency by digging her nails into a tender spot.

"Oweeee! You little bitch!" he had roared slapping her to the deck and administering kicks.

Manny watched with evil glee as his first mate used her roughly.

Resistance was of course in vain, and with a grunting moan of a swine, the act was over quickly. She was manacled, bruised, and weeping to the open deck with the other freshly caught captives.

But they had no sooner weathered the grand bank of the Bahamas when the horizons blackened, the seas grew to the size of mountains, and there fell upon the tiny slave ship a gale so powerful that nearly all the canvas had been torn free of the bolt-ropes.

After somehow surviving that storm, Manny never again ignored her warnings. Instead, permanently chaining her to the mast. A spacious solitude on a small boat and the superstitious sailors mostly ignored her.

Manny, having for many years harried the Ais and seal rivers coast and bays, resolved at last to land south of the Canaveral Cape at which the recent storm had fissured the barrier island slicing a new inlet between the gray ocean and jade waters of the Ais Lagoon.

Never, never pass up investigating a new firth, thought Manny.

Profit was always to be had at new cuts in the dune line which attracted Indios like hornets to carrion. The slaver deliberated about his pet witch. At length, he pulled a hanging key from beneath his stained tunic and unchained her.

"Something tells me, we might need your skills of language," muttered Manny.

His black-nailed fingers sank painfully into her arms and he hissed the odor of rotten teeth in her face.

"Run from me, and I swear by the Water-devil, I swear by the beard that I wear on my face, that I will blind you, my witch bitch," hissed Manny."

Marcos opened the weapons locker and twenty raiders, mostly second-generation Cuban Spaniards, but including a sprinkling of Portuguese, Indian and African bastards took pikes and cutlasses, two Harquebus, two crossbows, and diverse cudgels for the taking of captives.

Manny nodded with approval as he divided his villainous slavers equally into three canoes with plenty of good hemp rope. The remaining crew was left to guard God's Banner; to water the slaves, toss them a raw fish if one could be netted and if required dispose of bodies to the sharks that had learned to shadow the slave ships. Gulls and ravens screeched overhead as the three canoes paddled silently through the new inlet, disturbing a group of sea-cows, huge, ugly seal-looking things that nearly up-ended the first canoe with the panicked flip of a dozen round tails.

"Satan-spawn foul creatures," muttered Manny. Relieved that his bitch-witch never requested Manatee meat.

He swept the lagoon with a spy-glass searching for high land where the Indian animals would have
taken shelter during the storm and he was immediately satisfied at finding at least two tree-covered locations.
From one of the high spots, gray smoke of cook fires spiraled into the air and Manny laughed with evil glee.
He did not need a voluminous amount of slaves to complete his cargo and return to Cuba, a dozen or two would make up for any losses on the voyage home.

"Fucking shark," he chuckled, putting away his spy-glass. "South," ordered Manny.

He pointed to a tall barrier island topped with oak and pine. Gauging where to come ashore as not to cause his animals to flee.
The three boats moved quickly over clear water and flowing eelgrass, stopping a league from the high point and came cautiously ashore in a little sandy cove, beautiful in its exotic setting except for the stench of decaying sea-weed that was heaped high upon the shore sprinkled with sea-horses and upturned spiky horseshoe crabs.
The practiced raiders jumped out of the canoes and pulled the boats over the seaweed and out of sight in the palm trees.

LaMacha collected a handful of tiny stiff sea-horses, the totem she knew of some of the Ais clans.
Another sign she understood.

Away from the ocean breezes, sizzling summer air savaged them, as it was always hotter after a hurricane. Parrots and grackles piped among the tall palms and the lulling hum of a thousand bees gathering nectar on storm bent wildflowers greeted them. A seemingly normal day, a good an omen as any, and there were fervent prayers mumbled to catch a clan of Ais unaware, napping in the warm heat.

"Quiet!" warned Manny from the rear. "I hear a noise! What is…? Indians?"

Manny forced his witch to lie prone on the ground and he ducked behind a palmetto tree. His raiders followed his example crouching motionless as the sound of at least two animals, perhaps men pushed through the undergrowth towards them. Marcos and the other crossbowman aimed their weapons at the approaching noise ready to kill.

LaMacha squirmed to get away from the pressing knee on her back. She turned back towards the directions of the canoes and saw eyes watching her!
Three painted faces, red ochre stained with deep black circles painted around their eyes, stared at her, then quickly disappeared.

Marcos's scalp itched whenever someone spied upon him and he spun his weapon around but there was nothing but palmettos and vines.

"Witch-bitch-god-dammit-Jesus-wept," cursed Manny under his breath.

Stepping ashore upon this accursed land was always the most dangerous part of his burdens. Walking into these coastal jungles risked death hard by, and if not death, bloody red ruin or serpent bites. Suddenly, quite near, there sounded the loud honk of warning, primeval, and inexpressibly uncanny. Manny hissed at his men,
"Cranes!"
He pulled his knee from his witch pinned to the sand.

"You bastards, don't you dare fire those monstrosities!" said Manny to the two harquebus men.

Two red-headed cranes, tall as any of the raiders, honked again spotting the slave-raiders, and the birds half sauntering, half fleeing skirted from the men, suddenly taking flight with a great swoosh of powerful wings.

"Good as turkey, those things I tell you, but we can't alert the slave stock to our little visit," said Manny, quietly reassuring his slave-raiders.

A few more paces and all at once, every one of the raiders grinned knowingly.

The humid inland breeze that greeted them hinted at the subtle perfume of mangroves, but there was also the scent of smoke mingled with the suggestive smell of roasting fish; furthermore, they were downwind and their body stink would not alert the Indians to their presence and they might even get to feast after the seizure of whatever village or clan awaited them.

"Kill the dogs first," growled Manny and they started up a sandy ridge.

Dogs always worried him. No other animal had alerted the Indians as much as their mongrels, resulting in numerous slaves escaping his raids. *Fucking dogs.*

There were no dogs, only bodies. A pagan cemetery.

Hidalgo, the half-caste Negro Indian was the first up the hill, cautious as a ferret, his thin body was at home equally on the swaying masts furling canvas or slipping quietly through the forest in search of human gold.

Up the hill he walked, weaving between palmettos and sea-grapes, stepping over fallen palm trees and when needed, silently slicing through the clinging thorny vines with his cutlass until at last cresting the hill only to swear an oath to the virgin and make the sign of the cross.

There was death to be found on the long thin hill; the sandy ridge was an oft-used depository of bodies.

The raiding party followed him, scrambling through the storm-stripped trees, and upon reaching the summit, they discovered it was a burial hammock. A ceremonial mound shunned by Indian and Spaniard alike. A place only to be trespassed upon when depositing a corpse. Neither the witch nor slave hunters favored the place of the dead.

And corpses there were plenty, for as everywhere else in the unexplored land of Florida, fervor and plagues had swept the coastline, taking their deadly toll, decimating all of the clans.

Tall platforms dotted the ridge in various stages of repair or construction. The corpses had been set upon open platforms so carrion birds and buzzards could cleanse the bones before actual burial in an ancestral earth mound.

And the buzzards sat thickly in barren trees bereft of leaves, refusing to move from their assigned meals; the ground beneath the buzzards painted white with bird droppings and a foul order assailed the raiders. Both the Spaniards and Portuguese crossed themselves to ward off the evils that resided in the miasmatic atmosphere. Bad air ofttimes made people ill or insane.

They crept past posts topped with the skulls of panthers or tigers and frog-shaped clay pots that still held the lingering odor of stale tobacco. The skulls and tobacco served as a warning to the spirits that resided on the mound as if to say "Keep away spirits! The spirit of the cat protects me!"

Bodies. Perhaps natives drowned in the recent hurricane were wrapped in moss cloth and had recently been placed on upright platforms. The odor of rot was only just emanating from the deceased.

One by one the raiders pulled the corpses off the platforms, inspecting them for gold. There was nothing of value to be had from the bodies. Manny shivered violently, as one of the corpses was missing a nose.

"Fucking savages," murmured Manny.
It was only right that he enslaved these animals and tamed them.

Some of the older platforms had been knocked over during the hurricane, spilling bones on the trail.

An empty skull with the long hair still attached lay upon the sand watching as the raiders assembled on the edge to view an Ais encampment below.

LaMacha the witch, watched the long-haired skull for any indication of motion; she knew spirits could and often did live in angry old bones. Just as they inhabited the trees, lakes, even boats like God's Banner.

Spirits good, evil, and indifferent, some phallic in nature, others nurturing, sometimes appearing as water-spouts, whales or land animals, also flying creatures-fish, bird or bat *and* bones of the dead.

One could capture the benevolent spirits with sacrifices of a bird or alligator, skunk-cat, or, in the season of raids, a captured slave.

However, as no sacrifices were performed, she could feel the anger in the dead and the skull with the stringy hair could easily be of the malevolent type of ghoul, the kind that would cause one to break a leg in a turtle hole or step on a stinging flatfish.

But then as she fingered her seahorses, she was certain there would be a sacrifice…..soon.

They crept over the wind-stripped hill, crouching behind palmettos to observe an Indio camp below them.
Two huge fires burned to make coals for the pile of clams and oysters still sitting in the water. Eight to ten canoes were pulled above the waterline. Indians, men, and women certainly of the Ais clans, busied themselves with the construction of fish racks. But the majority of the Indians were knee-deep in the lagoon, busy constructing an elaborate fish weir. None in the water had any weapons save a few whelk-shell hammers.
A song wafted up from the green waters, then a woman's laughter as she splashed water drawing attention to her near-naked body.

Manny briefly wondered why there were no children? *Well, there will be no little ones to teach to swim.* So they had happened upon a burial party and the Indians had stopped long enough to catch fish. No doubt the storm had ruined their stock of smoked mullet.

He smiled his lopsided smile again.

No dogs to be seen. Witch-bitch-fucking twitch, rope, twine, these slaves are mine!

There were enough animals to make a full cargo if they could be trapped and not be injured during the capture. He snorted in approval at the cemetery ridge and the Indians below, more or less already trapped. He had used death mounds before with great success. The slave animals would normally fight fiercely to protect their families, but an armed group swarming from the hill of the bones… *now that had placed terror* in the soul of many a stout warrior.

Even the fucking dogs had fled away yelping in terror. The thought made him laugh, Bitch-witch, fucking dogs-Indians ate fucking dogs-*animals eating animals.*

Manny's eyes rested on his witch.

Love, he realized not for the first time; love was the real reason he risked the fickle anger of the church by keeping his pet witch.

"Thou shalt not suffer a witch to live," Exodus 22:18 said the priests.

Yet, Manny had allowed her to live and had fallen in love with his hurricane witch.
He sang a lightly soothing tune "I thought I was loved!" whispering with questioning mock pathos. The crew snickered at their crazy captain.
Manny discreetly turned away his head towards the animals below, wondering if there was more merchandise to be had at their main village?
But his thoughts went back to his witch's tits, for there was in them a malicious need to be kneaded, seeking suckle, *teat dominance*, that's what it was, Teat *Dominance*. He had to bite his tongue to keep from laughing. Teat dominance was for suckling pigs.
It was said that a quarter of the population of Spain was converted Jews and a quarter was converted moors. I am, bitch-witch–swine–tits, must be full Galatian because the thought of tasty roasted suckling pigs did not bother him in the least.

"My swine," whispered Manny, gesturing to his raiders back over to the hill.

"Just as usual, we spring a trap but leave an escape route where we will rope the animals. Hidalgo, you take the guns and your six and capture the canoes. Sanchez, you will take the main group and a crossbow and charge down the hill screaming like banshees. Here…."

Manny took a pike and stabbed the bottom of the skull lying on the trail; a few stiff tendons still holding the jaw in place and long black hair streamed down the pike. He handed the pike to Sanchez who took it with some reluctance.

"Goddamn, Captain, it stinks," said Sanchez.

"You run down the hill screaming "Banna! Banna!" It means mother or something in the Ais tongue," said Manny.

He had heard those words often enough from his slave captives on the journey back to Cuba.
Manny giggled at the thought of the Ais reaction when their mother or sister returned from the grave.

Bitch-witch it would be funny!
LaMacha was horrified as the skull was thrust high, the jaw flapping as if it was trying to wake the warden spirits of the bone-mound.

"To me, my swine," said Manny.

Manny took the remaining sailors and crept down the ridge to hide at the chosen escape route. When his men sealed off all directions but one, the Ais would run right into their ropes and cudgels. He smiled. *God was good.*
At the prearranged signal, Hidalgo had a sailor fire his Harquebus and rose screaming running down the ridge to capture the canoes and Sanchez stumbled down the steep sandy slope, holding his grisly banner aloft, calling out the native word for mother.

The Ais fisher-folk hesitated, then scrambled out of the water and away from the Europeans towards Manny's trap.
Marco crouched next to Manny and his witch, waiting to spring the trap closed. Fingers gripped the crossbow tightly.

"Marco the wary," he was often called. Ever susceptible to the wildest suspicions and most chimerical fears, he hissed "Silence!" swearing he could hear wolves!
And suddenly they all could hear the howling and yelping of wolves.

"Ware you must not linger here," hissed Manny's witch in her island accented Spanish, listening to the approaching wolves.

Sea-wolve, she thought, for the little bodies of the seahorses had begun to vibrate in her palm. She smiled for the first time in ages.

"Have you marked out a line of retreat?" asked the witch. Knowing they had not. But the old slaver would not leave empty-handed.

"Witch-bitch-tits, it's not in Manny's nature to come off empty-handed, however hard-pressed," snarled Manny.

However, the slave-raiders charging down the hill were suddenly violently overwhelmed with a hurricane of bone-tipped missiles, arrows, and darts that sailed through the air to stop the raiders with a series of sickening thuds.

More arrows fell upon the raiders and Sanchez dropped the pike and skull as arrows pinned his arms to his sides. He struggled to run and a warrior pounced upon him driving a deer bone-leg knife deep into Sanchez's spine.

A rush of warriors, swarthy men painted and tattooed, burst from dark mangroves to fall upon Hidalgo and his men guarding the canoes. The slave raiders standing by the canoes went down as if a giant scythe had taken their lives.

The sound of conch shell horns sounded from *behind* Manny and the panicked natives running from the water suddenly veered to a fallen tree where they picked up pre-staged weapons. War clubs and bows suddenly appeared in their wet hands and they turned upon Hidalgo's men who writhed and screamed at the arrows that impaled them.

A fucking trap, no, no nooo! A fucking trap!

The unreality, the impossibility of the situation assailed Manny with a fury as if caught in a maelstrom. Rodrigo holding club and rope was suddenly thrown back with a hawk-fletched arrow in his throat and a tiny serrated arrowhead protruding from the exit wound.

He dropped his club and ropes settling onto the sand, gurgling with eyes bulged. The arrow pulsated with a throb that matched Sanchez's elevated pulse.

"Pull the goddamn arrow!" commanded Manny.

Perhaps it was time to fly.

"Stand to your arms, you coward mountebanks!" cried Manny.

A slaver running from a howling Indian turned and used his pike to stab his pursuer, pinning the writhing man to the ground.
Manny jumped up to club a warrior who had appeared from the foliage behind them. Manny cuffed his witch, pointing at Rodrigo.

"Pull the goddamn arrow, damn you to hell!" ordered Manny.

"The moment I withdraw the arrow he will die!" protested LaMacha.

"God Dammit! Jesus wept! Any damn fool can see the truth to that. He is a dead man! Withdraw the arrow, bitch. Take off the point and pull the shaft and we get back to the boat."

"O, you screech-owl!" protested LaMacha. "May your offspring be tied to a Manchineel tree! Bastard of Cuba. Nay, I will not! Manny, on my soul you use me ill."

"Bitch!" said Manny.

Manny slapped LaMacha cutting his fingers on her teeth. Turned to the bug-eyed Rodrigo and placed a cudgel in the palm of his hand, closing the stiff fingers around the handle of the club. Then snapping the arrow so the barbed point fell to the ground, he violently jerked the arrow from Rodrigo's neck.
Manny forced Rodrigo to his feet and screamed

"Fight!" even as blood pumped from the arrow hole.

"Time to fly," said Manny to his witch.

Manny grasped her hand and ran towards the canoes, leaving four-fifths of his crew dead or dying. Attempting to escape the trap and flee to their ship was a mixed gathering of desperadoes willing to trip any of the others if it meant they could reach the safety of the boat. Villainy and greed had been written on every countenance, but now the slave hunters only showed panic and the Ais cut them down.

The first mate and boatswain ran after their fleeing Captain and Marcos. The first mate managed three paces before an arrow took him in the thigh. Screaming he turned at bay with a long pike and jabbed at the painted savages who still howled like wolves.

Out of the group of savages, came a wild-eyed dark man, far darker than any Indian and swinging two clubs, edged with sharks' teeth. Without hesitation, the dark man batted the pike aside, running up the shaft to slash the slave-raider across the face.

Luis Castillo was possessed by the *fever of battle. Oh, it had been too long!*
His arms tingled with the familiar clasp of edged weapons gripped just right in his hands, felt the joy, the battle joy-rage that came with physical combat, his body twisting and slashing, his muscles knowing the moves without thinking.
Even as he slashed the raider across the eyes, there was disappointment at the ease of the kill, the quickness, and the dissatisfaction of how untrained his opponent had been.
Castillo ached with a physical need to find an enemy who could offer him fulfillment, quench the ache that quivered down to his gut. With the rage fully gripping him, he ran after the other raiders, wolf-howling like the others, spittle-drool leaking across his dark skin. It was now a race with the Ais warriors to be the first to grapple and kill the raiders.

Rodrigo was the next who stood to meet Castillo and with his life-blood pumping out of the arrow wound; Rodrigo simply fell over just as Castillo reached him and the conquistador screamed in frustration, doubling his effort to get ahead of the Ais.
At the next clearing, a Cuban Indian wearing sailors clothing waited for him and expertly lassoed his slave lariat around Castillo's neck and jumped behind a scrub oak, causing the rope to tighten and pull Castillo off of his feet and slamming his body into the tree, where the rough tree bark removed a knife's length of dark skin.

Rather than fight the lasso, Castillo dropped his shark-tooth clubs, rolled forward around the tree, surprising the Indian, for as ever before, slaves had immediately pulled back to free themselves. Castillo rolled around the tree, pulling on the rope, and sank a knee-deep into the man's groin. The Indian sank to the sand in a fetal position. Castillo pulled the noose free of his neck, retrieved his shark tooth clubs, and resumed the chase with another howl.

Afterward, he would have no remembrance of how his shoulder and chest had gotten the skin shredded off, nor the origin of the pain around his neck.

Manny ran as fast as he ever had in his entire life, pulling his witch behind him. There was the attachment of love, a nurturing deep affection for the love of his witch, a love that kept his grip tightly clasped to her wrist; when to release her would have guaranteed reaching the canoe before the howling Indians. At least three arrows pierced Manny's clothing as he twisted and dodged around bushes and palm trees, never giving the savages the straight open shot.

"Hurry!" cried Marcos, panting, aiming the cocked crossbow, waiting, he stood by a canoe he had already dragged from under the palms and pushed in the shallow green water.
Manny understood that Carlos had not waited for him, but anyone who could paddle. The heavy canoes required at least two paddlers to move quickly.

A wolf called from the forest and an Ais warrior sprinted into the clearing carrying a tall bow and a handful of arrows, stopping only long enough to place a turkey-fletched arrow on the bowstring and in one motion pull and aim his bow.
However, the bowman was thrown backward in confusion, firing his arrow high into the lagoon as Marcos's crossbow quarrel passed through him so fast, the warrior did not comprehend what had just punched him. His life-blood poured out as he attempted to notch another arrow with numb fingers.

Manny pushed his witch violently into the canoe and the two men began paddling with all their strength.

"Wait! Wait for us! Captain please!" yelled Pascale, the Boatswain.

Pascale stumbled out of the jungle, followed closely by the Second mate Alonso. The large canoes could carry twelve and more when required. When the Captain and Marcos did not turn back, the two sailors, betrayed, frustrated, and terrified, pulled their own canoe to the green water and began paddling after the other canoe. Within seconds the boat began taking on water. Marcos had knocked small holes in the two hidden canoes. *Villany.*

Four men dashed out of the forest howling like wild animals. Manny and Carlos looked back with apprehension, surprised to see a tall African, nearly naked as the Ais, howling with the others, fall upon Alonso and Pascale.

The two slave hunters paddling for their lives, could not help but think of how much gold the dark African would have brought into Cuba. They silently cursed their ill luck but wasted no breath, panting too hard to speak any words.

But then an arrow hit the boat and they looked shoreward to see Indians running along the shallows parallel to the boat and firing arrows. The witch, one by one, dropped the little seahorses into the lagoon chanting an invocation.

Manny stopped paddling long enough to cuff her. "Shut up!" wheezed Manny.

And hence, the race to God's Banner. The two men paddling their boat out of arrow range and a little army of Indians howling on the shore. Others pushed through the grasping foliage making for the anchored slave ship.

An exhausted Manny and Marcos pulled alongside the slave ship just as six of the Ais scrambled onto the bowsprit, and made a determined charge at the crewmen.

A native armed with a shell-topped club knocked down a sailor at the same moment another sailor thrust him through the body with a cutlass.

Another raider, knife in one hand, hatchet in the other, backed too close to the chained captives and was pulled off his feet and twenty sets of hands yanked at his hair and groped for eyes.

Another slave hunter fired his crossbow, pinning an Indian to the mast, just as Manny clasped the manacles tight, securing his witch to the mast.

There was close fighting on the deck and the crewmen with long pikes, pushed the Indians towards the stern, having the advantage of numbers, weapons, and familiarity with their ship; when a creature of their nightmares, dark of skin, dripping sea-water jumped into the mass of raiders swinging shark-toothed clubs and screaming.

For the dark man fought precisely as he had been trained since his youth, swinging, elbowing, and kicking, letting the force of others carry them past while those in his circle of reach were killed or blocked.

Marcos could not get an open shot with his crossbow and finally yanked the trigger to miss and sent the bolt through two chained captives and into the deck.
Castillo broke his shark tooth club upon the crossbow but rolled and came up with a crimson cutlass, hacking at the crossbow stock held defensively until the steel blade found the fingers and Marcos dropped both crossbow and fingers.
So quick was the blow that Marcos did not even realize his fingers were gone and Castillo sank the crude sword deep into Marcos's chest where the ribs gripped the blade.

Manny was on Castillo then, swinging ax and cutlass so that Castillo had to jump into the mass of chained captives. Castillo rolled off the screaming Indians and found a pike dropped upon the deck, and in one motion threw the shaft like a spear to punch Manny in the belly with a 'whoof'.
Other Ais scrambled from the ocean and pushed past.
Castillo dropped to his knees laughing at the closeness of his death only to find a beautiful woman chained to the mast and staring at him with admiration or fear. He did not know or care, for his mind was full; all he knew was that he was sated, the battle fever leaving him.

And he had a ship.

Book one: Part 28: Conquistador

The woman chained to the mast was of pleasing aspect. The same woman he had seen the slave-hunters push into the canoe. Her face of calm demeanor but expressive features, cat-like-black eyes, abundant hair, black and straight. Dressed in a shift of Spanish make, the series of tattoos upon her forehead and arms bespoke of childhood in the upper Carribee islands.

Castillo studied her imploring look, those long, dark lashes fluttering on high tattooed cheekbones; the soft rise of high breasts and her parted lips trembled as she pleaded in slightly accented Spanish.

"The key," said the woman.

Castillo drew nearer to the woman. She seemed to falter under his gaze, Fever? The woman's voice trembled, but she threw back her slender neck with a gesture that became her. The woman held up her chain and pointed at the moaning slaver-leader impaled by the thrown pike.

"The key is about his neck," said LaMacha.

She felt both curious and slightly hostile at having to grovel before the dark stranger.
The brass key was attached to a blood-soaked leather thong and Castillo, with a swift tug, snapped the raw hide and tossed it to the woman at the mast.
That she spoke Spanish so well, was intriguing. "The keys for the others?" asked Castillo.
The woman freed herself and spat upon Manny, the slave raider.
A great smile spread across her tattooed face when she realized that the Captain who had kept her chained to the mast, *was not dead*. Yet.

"Manny," murmured LaMacha as she freed the pirate's belt knife.
Castillo ignored the screaming slave hunter and found a hatchet. Three hard blows and the Indian captives slid chains through iron rings set the deck and the Guale were free to gather weapons and mutilate the dead or wounded crew.

More Ais climbed aboard God's Banner, exploring the ship, claiming weapons and clothes, glass, and rope.

Castillo suddenly weary, jumped over the side and helped the captives, including the woman he had freed from the mast, climb off the boat and stumble through the surf.

There was a cheer and he turned from the woman; to his great dismay, the boat was ablaze. The cheers changed to panicked yells and Ais began jumping into the surf as the speed of the growing fire caught them unawares.

"No! My escape from this coast!" Castillo yelped as God's Banner burst aflame like a dry pine cone. Blood chilled in his veins and his heart sank from the sight of the blaze.

The Ais and Guale bellowed and stomped their approval but Castillo charged into the surf and scrambled up the bowsprit. He began stomping burning embers, but with a roar, the sails and tarred rigging were consumed in a sudden conflagration and it was Castillo's turn to jump from the ship. The deck planking caught fire, the wood crackling, and the pitch rising in blisters, the intense heat forced even those on the beach to retreat.

Castillo crawled from the surf, knees in the sand.

"NO, no!" hissed Castillo.

He scrutinized the inferno even as the Ais and freed captives wandered off into the sunset to the west. Someone brought him a gourd of water.

"Thank you," muttered Castillo.

It was the woman he had freed from the mast; she that had brought him water to quench his thirst.

For the witch LaMacha, every ember lifting to the starlight represented a soul of each dead person that had perished on the terrible ship and the orange of the burning embers resembled the orange beak of the Kara-Kara eagle, as she had been forewarned.

"You wanted that ship?" asked LaMacha.

Orange embers shot into the star-filled Florida sky. They sat in the sand, close enough to the burning ship that sweat glistened on their foreheads.

Castillo did not respond; his eyes no longer made tears.

"Are you aware of the pain and suffering that has seeped into the timbers of that ship?" asked LaMacha.

No response.

"I would have that cursed ship burn. Fire is the only way to release the souls trapped in the blood-stained planks. God's Banner was bane upon this coast. It would have changed you, Conquistador. It would have sucked your soul to the deepest frozen pits of hell," warned LaMacha.

Castillo looked at the woman who sat next to him.
He realized that she had spoken to him in good Spanish. *A slave?*
But he said nothing. He was marooned on this coast for how long now?

"On the wharves of Havana, I have seen the Sea-horse tattoo on many a hawk-eyed Conquistador warrior. The only good thing I can ever say of Spain is that they grow the best warriors in all the seas. *Else* their god of the cross would not have conquered so many other gods. These Conquistadors, carried about them the twin masts of both arrogance and power," said LaMacha.

No response from the dark man.
"I have witnessed warriors of your SeaHorse clan, in numbers greater than all the gulls of all the seas, sail from Havana to the northernmost outpost of the king's empire. I have even seen one or two return to Cuba. Their armor rent and torn or covered in green moss, their long beards tangled and their eyes… Well, conquistador, their eyes had the vacant look of having lost their soul on some faraway plain," said LaMacha.
Three warriors and an Indian woman had returned from Florida.

Castillo turned back to the embers of the slave ship. *His ship.*
LaMacha was unsure. Had she misjudged the warrior?

"I have even beheld the grand fleet of Hernando de Soto on his embarkation to conquer the empire of Florida," said the witch.
At the reference of de Soto, Castillo jumped as if one of the tiny Florida vipers had bitten him.

Yes, thought LaMacha.

"The slavers on God's Banner, on their return from the brothels. They would often speak of Governor de Soto's "Grand Expedition" and the glorious progress through the savage Empire of northern Florida," said LaMacha.

"That was *my ship*. I captured it," said Castillo, finally breaking the silence.

LaMacha simply calculated the number of sailors it took to move God's Banner through the currents of the Florida straits.

You, conquistador,r would be lucky if you were only cast ashore in the Calusa lands and tortured. Although the greater possibility is that you would simply die of thirst in an endless sea of blue water.

"Do you really desire so greatly to return to lands of the black robes, that you would risk the serpents and storms of the eastern sea?" asked LaMacha in a quiet voice. "What draws you back to Cuba? A dark-eyed beauty? You have sons?"

"Shut up," replied Castillo.

Half of his face was illuminated by the burning ship.
Her nagging made him reflect that the only thing he had ever cared for was his stallion, now lost in some hell-hole, named Tampa.

"I will never return," she spat. "I have had enough of the black robes and their 'just' tortured god. On the wharves in Cuba, the orphans would cry all night from hunger, their extended bellies… They looked like baby robins and would be still in the morning. And the fat priests on the way to visit Manny no less, they would lift their robes and step over the lifeless children," said LaMacha.

Castillo winced at her description of starving children. He only recently stopped dreaming of the Pensacola boy in the field of tubers. And true, he had seen enough of the empire to know it was an ill omen to be parentless in the old or new world.

"The Franciscans set up orphanages," he stammered.

"So, what then draws you to return Conquistador? The fighting? It would appear you have fallen in with the correct clan if you wish to fight. These people, these Ais, are of the smallest of the Florida clans, yet they hold nearly the entire east coast. And they do so despite the overwhelming power of the Indian clans on their very borders. The Timucua to the north and the Calusa to the southern water-lands," said LaMacha.

She made the sign of the cross at the mention of the Calusa.

"I have seen you fight and I thank you for my release from the foul ship. However, I also see that you are not a simple killer. Else you would have put the Guale to the sword or like all Spaniards, sold them. Instead, you set them free. As well as giving me the key to my chain," *said LaMacha.*

You could have sold me.

"Please shut up," croaked Castillo.

He did not know why he wanted to return to Cuba or Mexico. The rum? His ship hissed where charred timbers touched lapping waters.

"You allowed me time with Manny and I thank you for that also," she beamed in the darkness," said LaMacha.

Manny's penis was packed in sea salt and tucked away in her power bag.
"Do you know that I loved Manny?" admitted LaMacha.
That piqued Castillo's interest. Such an odd confession.
"The slaver Captain?" asked Castillo.
"Yes, I cannot explain it. But after a year chained at the mast, I came to love him. I would have gladly given my body to the crazy bastard. There is no explaining it. But the more I came to be associated with the ship, the more I felt as I was part of the crew. I am not proud, but for a time I actually translated with the coastal tribal elders on behalf of the slave hunters. I actually felt a sense of accomplishment when we turned for *home* with a full hold of slaves. I turned away at the use of the girls by the sailors, justifying that they would receive far worse in Cuba or Hispaniola," said LaMacha.

"Then why did the slaver Captain keep you chained at the mast?" asked a genuinely interested Castillo.

"Conquistador, he kept me because I could reliably predict the coming of hurricanes, such as this last one," said LaMacha.

There was a hint of pride in her voice. "A witch then," said Castillo.

He held no grudge against hurricane conjurers, as did the Catholic Church.

"Indeed, a valuable talent not to waste," he speculated out loud.

"My name is Luis Castillo, originally from Mexico. I was a lancer and scout for de Soto. But now it appears I am a killer of slave hunters and owner of haunted ships. Your name?"

"I am," she hesitated, not exactly sure who she was anymore.

"I was baptized "Mary" until the day I predicted the second hurricane and the village priest, a good man, turned on me and handed me off naked to the Inquisition," said LaMacha.

Castillo struggled in the darkness with his imagination to see Mary naked. The Indian women, unlike the Spanish, did not possess the shaggy wool coat of pubic hair.

"I was then a nameless slave and finally christened "LaMacha" by Manny the crazy. Mary was an innocent girl. LaMacha, however? I fear for the reckoning when the Three-Eyed Frog calls in his debts," said LaMacha.

Luis Castillo nodded in the firelight.

Not many of the sea island people who worshiped the frog god remained alive or free or dared to admit a debt to a foreign god.

"Mary, I like the name, Mary. Always been my favorite name. If ever I have a daughter that will be her name," said Luis Castillo.

"That Mary is gone," LaMacha said under her breath.

"I like your name also. Castillo is a name of strength. It has power," said LaMacha.

However, the Conquistador had slipped back into himself. Back into the embers of the accursed ship.

"Conquistador, you must place the loss of God's Banner, your escape from this coast, in the story of your life. 'Perspective' is the Spanish word Manny would have used. Is the burning of that cursed ship, and your escape from this coast; the worst or best to have ever happened in the story of Luis Castillo?" said LaMacha.

He winced at the memory of cannibalism in the frozen Florida mountains. *I killed Rybowski. The other Mary who had drowned herself in a muddy river. My mother.*

"Have there been times in your past when all seemed hopeless? Did you ask yourself: Can I survive this?" she asked in a hushed voice as if asking herself the same questions and not the dark warrior sitting beside her.
Castillo felt a stirring towards this witch. Pity perhaps? Yet her questions dredged up the nightmares of the de Soto expedition. Memories he had striven to forget.
LaMacha continued.

"I was betrayed by my village priest. Given unto the Inquisition, the very worst of the black robes. Then I was raped and chained to a mast of a slave ship to witness every horror man can inflict upon fellow man. I miscarried the slavers' child on the deck of that ship," said LaMacha.

She nodded at the burning embers.

"I cried for the lost child, who was just another of the countless who perished on that ship. Have there been times in your past when all seemed hopeless?" She asked again.

"Again and again, I asked myself: Can I survive this? To my greater horror, a fog of the devil settled upon my breasts and I fell in love with the captain and eagerly warned the slavers of the coming of hurricanes. The Christian god should have told me to allow the evil to drown. Manny loved me too, although he was terrified at the thought of treating another person with kindness," said LaMacha.

Castillo stirred uneasily on the sand. "Please stop," he croaked.

"Then one year we actually visited my village in the outer islands," said LaMacha.

She continued speaking despite the plea from the conquistador. She was no longer telling the story to the dark Spaniard but telling the story to herself.

"The village was named 'Red Bay' and Manny stopped to catch the finned turtles. Slave hunters had long before captured my clan. My parents and sisters were gone. I have witnessed the horror of such raids. Red Bay was a place of ghosts and I dared not admit to the slavers that this was once my home. The skeleton of our priest lay sprawled in the plaza, yellowed bones poking from his robes. The skull had been split with a cutlass. What value does a slaver have with an island priest? Manny had reached down and plucked the cheap pewter crucifix from the bones and like a child, skipped it across the blue waters where my family once floated their fishing canoes. A barracuda as long as a man, flashed across the top of the water to capture the silver cross in its great teeth. The slavers laughed, they found that hilarious.

Yet I know a bad omen. These men whom I had come to form an affection for, they were doomed and so was I," explained LaMacha.

"You do not need to tell me more," complained Castillo. "Please stop"

He was thinking of his own crucifix, displayed when in the presence of the Governor-General.

"I stared at the bones of the good father. There had been love for this kindly priest and for the first time since he had given me over to the Inquisition I recalled his words to speak to those who would do me harm," said LaMacha.

"May you have peace," I said quietly to the bones.

229

Manny cuffed me about the head.

"This priest will never attempt to burn you, my witch," Manny had quipped.

"However, back on the boat, chained to the mast again. I sank into a black morass of despair, grasping at the words of my priest and repeated them over and over.

"May you find peace. May you be free. May you have grace and courage," I repeated these words over and over and at some point; the memory of my dead baby on the deck of that ship did not hurt so much," said LaMacha.

"I'm sorry for your child," Castillo said at last.

"Yes" replied LaMacha, "However, there will be other children, strong proud children, now that I am free of *that* boat."

She took a calming breath. Her daughter had been tossed over the side of the boat.

"Luis Castillo, may you find peace. May you be free. May you have grace and courage."

By the time she had repeated the mantra three times, Castillo found himself repeating the words and the calming effect was an addiction. The memory of his mother at the brothel did not pain him as it had. And for the first time, he admitted to himself that yes, that *whore* had been his mother.

At length, the sky to the east paled ever so slightly and he truly asked himself, *'Why do I want to return to Mexico?'*
To join yet another killing expedition?

Here on a backwater coast, he had found an escape from the horrors of two conquistador excursions. He had found friends and people who required the only god-given talent he possessed.

At last, he turned to the witch.

"Thank you, Mary. May you find peace. May you be free. May you have grace and courage," said Castillo.
In the pre-dawn haze, La Macha only nodded at the dark warrior. Yet she was unexpectedly elated when he spoke.

"I will not return to Cuba or Mexico," said Castillo. "There are a few more slave hunters like *De Soto,*" *he* thought, "That need to be murdered."

In the paling light, he found Mary's hand, enjoying the warmth of her touch, not realizing he had been chilled by the dawn dew.
She laid her head upon his scarred shoulder and thought of *strong and proud children.*

The last thing he recalled before falling asleep was that someday he would return to Tampa and find his horse.
The sun inched on the eastern horizon, orange-red, the same color of coals of the smoking ship. Burned nearly to the waterline, the pine scorched to a deep yellow color, and black, the name "Gods Banner" still legible, although the paint was black and curled. A shark fin surfaced around the burning hulk attracted by blood.

Castillo woke with a start and stumbled back to the encampment where they had set the trap for the slave hunters. Aching muscles screamed at him as he stepped around the bodies prone on the high tide mark where little ghost crabs climbed on their trophies.

He was followed by Mary.
Since watching the ship burn and the freeing of the Guale captives and woman, rarely had Castillo taken his eyes from LaMacha.
Not even while Turkey Dancer tortured the only two slave hunters taken alive.

"O black-eyed woman, do you know what temptations you are inviting?" said Castillo in the Mexica tongue of his youth.

Yet, she spoke little besides pleading for a chance to burn one of the captive slavers.
At length, the Ais and the freed Guale, with captured weapons and clothes, paddled back to the main village to be greeted like returning heroes.
Carlos welcomed the return of Turkey-Dancer and Castillo with great hugs and eyed the woman who followed Castillo, nodding with approval.

In Spanish, she introduced herself. However, when she spoke to Castillo, there was a change.

Her voice spoke one thing, a defensive coldness learned upon the slave ship. However, her eyes and gestures betrayed an attraction to Castillo.

Paradoxically, *her prayers had called upon the clans* of the Ais with her sea-horse offerings. However, her prayers had also called up both Ais warriors and a *conquistador*. a Spanish warrior who bore the tattoo of the sea-horse.
A Conquistador! She gazed upon the dark man before her, the handsome features and smooth skin. Even his scars were alluring.

Her magic had summoned this man, a shockingly brazen warrior, who stared with hungry approval at her supple figure, he stretched his body in a leisurely fashion, recognizing her mutual desire, and laughed a low, agreeable laugh.

That laugh… the Ais Indians who had witnessed his berserker fighting, suspected he was insane, as were all great warriors.
Silently, he took in her dusky face and island tattoos, the eyes were dark as a night without moon, highlighting her pearl-like teeth, and realized down to his balls how vastly he had underestimated the command of her beauty.

With a start, he realized how much of a stupor he had been in since his capture in the swamp of the grandfathers. *No*, he had been in a daze since the morning of his visit to the Tavern of Mother's Milk.

"Hurricane Witch, Mary, there is not another like you in all of Florida and I have seen most of Florida," admitted Luis Castillo.
She would not say aloud, however she thought the same could be said for the dark warrior across the fire.
He stood and walked to her and held out a hand.
She took his outstretched hand and he pulled her to his side kissing her Spanish fashion, an act taboo to her people, but her struggles were brief and she succumbed after a little wordless struggle.

And then she knew.
She had been sloppily kissed by fat priests and stinking sailors. But never like this. Not like this! His arms tightened around her waist,

forcing her breasts flat to his chest as he kissed her again and she moaned aloud.

Then he released her, beaming at the beautiful witch-woman and his release from the ailment that had so bewitched him since watching his mother flee the brothel.

Only because of de Soto's desperate need for horsemen had the Governor-General kept him in service, and had then thrown him away when his affliction had outweighed his worth.

When she felt his hands slacken she reached up and caught him by the neck. For all her beauty and magic she had rarely been excited till this instant.

It was as if she too had been released from a bewitching haze in which she had been chained to a mast of a slaver-ship.

This dark warrior had first freed her body from the mast and now had opened another door with his kiss, allowing her the capacity to desire again.

She forced her body against him, a silent desperate plea forbidden for so long. Desire and lust flowed through man and woman and they retreated into the darkness outside of the circle of firelight.

Dawn found them intertwined, lovers that had healed something that had been lacking in each.

Book one: Part 29: Matanzas inlet

"And David enquired at the Lord, saying, Shall I pursue after this troop? Shall I overtake them? And He answered him, Pursue: for thou shalt surely overtake them, and without fail recover all." Samuel 30: 8:

"They are devil worshippers who refuse god and can never be trusted. The Indian of Florida can be sold in Cuba, Santo Domingo, and Puerto Rico benefiting all the colonies involved"
-Pedro Menedez de Aviles, Governor of Florida. Proposal to the king, for the enslavement and removal of the Florida Indians.

"Parlez-vous Français?" Heron said again, attempting to wrap his tongue around the odd words.

"Parlez-vous Français?" echoed "Yellow-flint-snake" from the front of the canoe and both men laughed.

As flint traders, they were collectors of languages and information. Heron's father and crazy Grandfather both had stressed that information was always more valuable than any stone, fur, or shell.

They paddled their canoe loaded with trading flint, away from the castaways. As in previous years, the summer storms had wrecked strange boats upon the eastern beach.
Two of the winged boats broken by the hurricane had washed ashore south of Seal Inlet and another was beached near Mosquito inlet.

The bedraggled and mosquito-bitten survivors were slowly trudging north towards their "Français" settlement they had named "Fort Caroline."

The "Français" had been eager to talk with the two flint traders who had bargained all of their food for valuable colorful ribbons and priceless iron knives.

Information was valuable.

Heron and "Yellow-flint-snake" had both been trained in the concept of numbers. Numbers and language skills were necessities of all traders. Both had agreed upon the number of the "Français" trudging up the beach - thirty times two open hands and another four open hands.

His grandfather, Luis would say, "Three-hundred and forty" men had been cast ashore and were making for their fort along the Seal River.

Information was valuable, and the traders had learned that another three hundred "Français" had come ashore at Mosquito inlet and had only now passed the Tomoka River on their journey north.
The "Français" armies were weeks apart. They foraged for sea turtle eggs, moving beetle slow up the beach.

"Parlez-vous Français?" both said together but in a drawn-out mockery of the words. It was truly astonishing what the ocean would cast ashore, strange beasts, and stranger people.
The two men stopped their canoe at the mouth of Seal Inlet to study the tidal flow, check for boat flipping manatees, and to locate the Spanish encampment.

"No seals," observed Heron, as he watched a pelican feather spin quickly towards the ocean.
"Outgoing tide," commented "Yellow-flint-snake."
"The seals have still not returned from their Hurricane shelters up the river. They will be back soon enough if you wish for a feast. Ready for the crossing?" asked "Yellow-flint-snake."

Heron stretched his muscles, lifting the paddle with both arms as high as possible. "Aghhh," groaned Heron and said, "Let's go."
They paddled into the seal inlet with powerful strokes to keep from being swept into a gray ocean still angry from the recent hurricane.

On the paddle across the inlet, both men dwelt upon the fact that the Spanish army across the inlet was less than half the size of the approaching "Français" army.

The army from the north consisted of seven double open hands plus one open hand of Spanish soldiers.

This will be interesting, contemplated Heron. How well do the strangers fight? They have opposing gods?

Once across the inlet, they let the outgoing tide pull them to the Spanish encampment, marked by two flapping banners.
They pulled their boat above the high tide mark, all the while being scrutinized by armored men holding wicked spears or the tiny bows that could kill at a hundred paces.

"Parlez-vous Français?" joked Heron to the soldiers who guarded the encampment, however, most of the strangers did not react.
At last, a soldier, gray-bearded and gap-toothed smiled, lowered his spear, and leaned upon it.

"All right then, let's get our Frenchie guests to see Admiral Avilés," said the soldier.

The two flint traders were taken before Admiral Menéndez de Aviles and seventy-five dangerous-looking Spanish soldiers.

"Their body stink alone will slay the other army," said "Yellow-flint-snake" in Ais. For the first time, Heron was aware of a row of chained captives.
He recognized women and children from the "Français" of the captured Fort Caroline.
Most were red-faced from crying and occasionally when one of the women or children began wailing. A Spanish guard would cuff them until the wailing ceased.

One "Français" woman stood out from the rest, not from her lack of tears, but her skin tone. Her dark skin was the same walnut smooth color as of his Grandfather Luis Castillo.

The interpreter, a Tequesta slave, captured on the south Florida coast and taken to Spain for training was shoved forward. The Tequesta bore scars from having survived a disfiguring disease, but then many of the soldiers bore the same scars.

"They are from Fort Caroline?" asked Heron of the Tequesta while nodding towards the captives.

"Yes, the Admiral has captured the fort and put all the men to the sword. The women and their children will be parceled out as rewards as the Admiral sees fit. However, the fat one, Father Escobar has said *that is not to be allowed.* Even though they be Lutherans under the sentence of death for their hearsay. The good father is certain he can persuade the fair ones to return to the folds of the True Church," explained the Tequesta in passable Spanish.

"And the dark woman?" asked Heron.

The Tequesta looked at the line of captives and turned back to Heron with a knowing smile.

"The Congo woman is naught but a slave, as I. You wish her?" asked the Tequesta.

"I will trade for her," replied Heron.

Heron attempted too late to pretend only *passing* interest that would lower any price.

"She looks old," replied Heron. "Probably does not have all her teeth," said Heron. Behind him "Yellow-flint-snake" groaned at the thought of the cost for the dark woman. "And I have a boat," beamed Heron.

Admiral Avilés pondered his dilemma.

"Three hundred and forty men, say the Indio traders and another three hundred only weeks behind. God truly has blessed both church and crown by wrecking Ribault's fleet for us," he said to his Sea Captains.

However, he could see the doubt in his captain's eyes. Not a coward among them, but they were pragmatists. The Spanish expedition in Florida was divided and outnumbered.

Most of his soldiers were constructing a fort at their new settlement of St. Augustine and another large contingent held the captured Fort Caroline. Standard combat protocol would be to fall back and regroup his expedition for a proper battle.

"My suggestion, Admiral...." said Father Escobar.

"Shut up!" snapped Admiral Avilés. "This is a council of war and the church has no say. You do your work priest and we will do ours," said Admiral Avilés.

Father Escobar's face turned bright red and retreated hastily from the circle of soldiers. Admiral Avilés blew out a deep breath, he had just made an enemy and everyone knew it. "What has the Indian proposed?" asked Admiral Avilés.

The Tequesta who had sat in silence next to the two flint traders, stood up cautiously; unsure of the Admiral's status. The humiliation of a priest *always* meant burning.

"The Ais flint trader says 'Offer terms of surrender to the Français' castaways. And in trade for the African slave woman he will paddle the 'Français' across the inlet in small groups," said the Tequesta slave-interpreter.

At this, the Tequesta Indian paused because the following words could result in his own execution.

"The Ais says, he believes that seventy-five Spaniards may be able to overpower ten Frenchmen. However, he says if you need assistance, he will find some Ais warriors to help you."

The Admirals' eyes bulged starkly outward and he and the entire Spanish encampment broke into gut-wrenching laughter. Off to the side, the French captives wept for slain fathers and husbands.

One woman however stared at Heron in horror.

"Yes!" said Admiral Avilés, wiping tears from his eyes. "This trader has the balls of a bull! He does present a bold and clever plan. Why my seawolves did not think of that is embarrassing."

But the Spaniards still laughed at the bravado of the words.

"Bring the Congo woman to us," said Admiral Avilés.

The slave woman was unchained and pushed forward.

Admiral Avilés studied the captive and the Ais flint trader who now pretended little interest in the slave, even mumbling a few words of disgust.

"What did he say?" asked the Admiral, enjoying the game and gaining respect for the native. The Tequesta looked uneasy, but shook his head and translated.

"The Ais Trader says he has changed his mind. The dark-skinned woman is old, ugly, and has rotten teeth."
The Spanish encampment broke into laughter again.
It was obvious that the woman was indeed none of those things.
"Cochon Putain!" shouted the dark-skinned woman at Heron.
She showed strong white teeth in her anger. Those who knew French fell to the sand laughing.

"What did she say, what did she say?" begged those who did not understand the language of their ancient northern enemy.

Someone shouted,
"Are these Ais one of the lost tribes of Jews?"
"Nay, they are Venetian spawn!" shouted a soldier in response.
"Worse!" shouted another.
"I think he might be my Genovese brother-in-law!" shouted another soldier. More laughter and guffaws.
"Yellow-flint-snake" observed the mirth and merriment his friend had started with the strangers and spoke with some admiration.

"My friend, are you sure you want that she-panther?" asked Yellow-flint-snake.
Heron had been surprised at the dark woman's reaction. Had it been something he had said?
"Well… " Heron stuttered.
"Deal!" roared the Admiral. "You will ferry the French across in small groups and your reward is this woman. May God have mercy on your soul!" said the Admiral.

And the encampment broke into another bout of laughter.

"Hold," said an emboldened Father Escobar, feeling the desperate need for recognition and knowing he was correct.

This is my business, Admiral, he growled silently.

"It is against the edict of the Holy Church to sell Christians to pagans. "Even Christian slaves.""

Menéndez de Aviles looked irritated. Escobar was correct. There was such an edict issued in a vain attempt to stop the Venetians from selling Christian women and boys to the Turks.
However, the Italians were right bastards and the Turks offered huge sums for fair-haired slaves.
"We do not wish to offend the church," replied Admiral Menéndez de Avilés.
He again was frustrated at the impositions of this Escobar.
The priest's effrontery had worn thin. *This man is not a bishop and he must know his place.* Yet there was the arrogance of the Inquisition about this fat priest... *Tread lightly.*
Looking directly at the two Indians, Menéndez de Aviles spoke to his Sea Captains

"Of course, we can easily torture these two to ferry the French, but then they would be of no further value and might even flee. And they did bring us the word of the French army across that inlet. Torture... for their reward? *Nay."*

The Admiral had come to like the Indian stone trader.

"Treachery would not be the Christian thing to do, would it Father Escobar?" replied Admiral Menéndez de Avilés

Father Escobar pushed aside the African slave woman and stepped into the circle of captains gathered about Menéndez de Aviles. *At last, the admiral has realized the value of my counsel,* thought Escobar.

"The solution, Admiral, is simple and will only make the Holy Church stronger. This Indian shall become a Christian and you can sell him the slave without offense," replied a beaming Escobar.
"The Holy Church is never wrong," stated Menéndez de Aviles. "After the French are destroyed, the Indian rock trader will be immersed in the lagoon. Father Escobar, you will baptize our new Christian."
Escobar was furious; baptizing the Indios was far beneath his station, but only bowed.
"Yes Admiral," said Escobar.

Book one: Part 30: Demands

At dawn, the first of the French banners appeared on the south side of the inlet.

Lacking boats to cross the wide inlet, they made camp and began cutting pine trees to build rafts. The Spanish for their part began marching in and out of the dunes, waving various banners to make it appear there were many more of them than the actual number.

"Yellow-flint-snake" and Heron unloaded the heavy flint from their canoe and readied their boat for a crossing.
Admiral Menéndez de Aviles himself took a seat in the canoe, carrying only a rolled-up flag. Quickly, the Tequesta translator sat nimbly in the boat.

"The Admiral orders us to cross the inlet," said the Tequesta.

"But do not beach this… boat. Can you fit ten of the Frenchmen in this log?" asked the translator.

"Easily the number of two hands," said Yellow-flint-snake.

"Seals!" called Heron from the front of the boat.

The incoming tide pulled the canoe and a family of barking seals towards a quickly-disappearing tidal island. Hundreds of Pelicans, gulls, and snake birds took flight in a low roll of thunder.

"The leader of the Spaniards requires no guards?" asked Heron as they paddled across the inlet.

The Indian slave shook his head.

"Admiral Aviles has a reputation as King Philip's man. The Admiral brought the treasure fleet from Cuba to Spain and is famous across the known world. His word is law, his actions from wisdom," replied the Tequesta.

Stopping near the French encampment but without actually landing the canoe, Admiral Aviles stood up and began speaking Français to the cautious stranded French army.

Upon close inspection of the enemy, the Admiral was heartened; the Lutherans, although outnumbering the Spanish forces, had suffered greatly at the "Winds of God" hurricane and the inhospitable terrain of Florida. *They are a beaten army and not a shot has been fired,* thought Admiral Menéndez de Avilés.

"What does he say to the Français?" asked Yellow-flint-snake.

"Shissh!" replied the Tequesta, listening to the demands of the Admiral and the eruption of heated debate raging across the French camp.

Heron observed rows of starved, sunburned, and insect bitten Français. He saw hatred in the face of some, but desperation in most. One man placed his face into the tidal inlet and attempted to drink. Only to puke up the saltwater.

"They are like children, these Français," observed Yellow-flint-snake. "They do not know how to dig for good water?"

The Tequesta quickly explained the debate.

"The Admiral demands unconditional surrender as his terms. All arms are to be deposited on the south shore. The Admiral tells them that we have captured Fort Caroline," explained the Tequesta.

Admiral Menéndez de Avilés unrolled the flag he had brought and held it aloft. A groan swept the French camp.
Heron recognized the banner he had seen hanging upon Fort Caroline upon his first visit to the strange fort.

"The French soldiers seek to know if their lives will be spared and the admiral replied that 'He makes no promises.'"

At length, a Frenchman, better dressed than most, walked up to the shoreline and unbuckled his belt, and dropped it to the sand. Next came the helmet and breastplate. Others followed his example and soon the Fleur de Lis of France and the flag of Coligny were carefully rolled up and deposited next to the growing pile of weapons.

A smile of satisfaction swept across the face of Admiral Menéndez de Aviles and he began speaking again to the Castaways, his voice more impassioned than before.

The Tequesta Indian translated.

"The Admiral asks, 'Is there anyone in the camp who will return to Glory and salvation of the Holy Church and reject the teachings of the Heretic Martin Luther?'"

A chorus of angry yells erupted from the French encampment.

Admiral Menéndez de Aviles swept his eyes across the camp from one end to another. For the first time, Lutherans had shown backbone by rejecting the Holy Church. A few Frenchman dropped their eyes to the sand, remaining silent.

"So be it and may God have mercy on their souls," said the Spanish Admiral in icy words that caused Heron to Shiver.

Once back on the Spanish side of the inlet, Admiral Menéndez de Aviles stepped out of the canoe and walked to where the French women and children stood, in full sight of the shipwrecked French army on the opposite shore.

A soldier guarding the captives stroked a wreath of brown curls that cascaded from the head of a captive.

"My poodle," said the soldier admiringly.

Beneath his calloused hand, the French captive sobbed. A widow at sixteen years of age and an uncertain future awaited her.

"Take her Rodrigo," said Admiral Menéndez de Aviles. "She is yours as reward of your bravery storming the gates of Fort Caroline."

"Thank you, Sire! Where is that turnkey?" shouted Rodrigo while simultaneously groping for the breasts of *his* French captive.

"Hold!" ordered Father Escobar.

Father Escobar placed his heavy body between the approaching soldier assigned to guard the keys to the captives. A worried Brother Phillipe followed the Inquisition elder.

Admiral Aviles snarled to himself, *What now?*

"The captives are under the protection of the Holy Church. This woman had taken Mass with me. There are rules of civilization," said Father Escobar, who had burned more Indian and Moor heretics than he could remember, was smug in his own justification.

Insult a member of the Inquisition at your own peril, thought Father Escobar.

Book one: Part 31: Spoils of war

The Admiral was enraged.

"These captives are spoils of war. Place the children under the cloak of the church. The women are just rewards for those who storm gates or stand in ranks risking death for the Holy Church and Crown!" said Admiral Aviles.

"Leave us, priest!" spat Admiral Aviles. "Now!"

I will be free of this man, thought Admiral Aviles.

But he turned to watch the first seven Frenchman, all officers, being escorted from the canoe and marched behind a dune to where a line of spearmen stood.

"Kneel, dogs," spat a Sergeant-at-arms.

The French captives expecting to be fed, kneeled in the Florida sand and were quickly stabbed.

"We shall call this Matanzas Inlet," said Admiral Aviles as he observed the canoe loading up the next group of Lutherans.

Good.
Brother Phillipe returned at a fast shuffle, brown robes flailing in all directions, and dropped to one knee in front of the Admiral.

"Admiral! I beg your pardon for my impudence," said Brother Phillipe. "I beg you, sire, allow me to question the captives and ensure they are not Christians before you put them to the sword," said Brother Phillipe.

Admiral Menéndez de Aviles, seeing his plan come to fruition, was suddenly in a better mood with the church.

"Of course Brother, it is our obligation to shepherd Christians," said the Admiral. Admiral Menéndez de Aviles gave new orders to his captains.

"Spare any who are members of the true church. Assist the good brother and question the prisoners for any Christians. Catholics are to be spared the sword but chained. Also question them for skills. Our new settlement of St. Augustine will require carpenters. Find the ship carpenters and secure them with the women. Spare any of the Lutherans with some value......Tanners, cobblers, smiths, even musicians," ordered the Admiral.

Then, recalling the small head of a starved-looking boy among the French.,

"Spare the drummer boys also," ordered Admiral Menéndez de Aviles.

"Yes sir," said Captain de Cordoba.

"Thank you, Admiral," said Brother Phillipe.

The Brother stood and bowed. Then frowned at the small exceedingly sharp burrs, tan in color, lining the hem of his robe. One spur drew blood as he attempted to pluck it from his clothing.

"However," warned the Admiral, "spare not the 'Sudden Converts,' those that march over the dune and only upon viewing the garlic tainted blood watering this wasteland, do they swear fealty to the Pope. *It is too late for those Heretics,*" growled Menéndez de Aviles.

"Go now, the Indian boat nears," pointing at the approaching canoe overburdened with French captives. "Matanzas Inlet indeed," the Admiral said to no one in particular.

The sun was setting in the west as the final group of Frenchmen crossed to the northern side of Matanzas Inlet.

Admiral Menéndez de Aviles had the final group of Lutherans brought before him.

"Your comrades are a week's walk south of here," said the Admiral. "Marching to the relief of Fort Caroline," explained the Admiral to the last of the French.

A few captains laughed quietly at the joke. It had been a good day for the crown.

A burly Huguenot Sergeant, who had spent the day convincing his ever-shrinking group of comrades to keep to the order of surrender. Nevertheless, some soldiers had fled south to find the other army. They trusted not the Spanish mercy.
The Sergeant removed his cap.

"Yes sir."
To comment beyond that, or supply any additional information to the Spanish pigs would be treason.

"Father Escobar!" called out Admiral Menéndez de Aviles. The Fat Priest shuffled to the captives.

"How may I be of service Admiral?" said Escobar.

"Have one of your scribes make me a sign. Paint the following words: *Hanged not as Frenchmen but as Lutherans.*"

"Certainly Admiral," beamed Father Escobar and turned to locate Brother Phillipe.

The French Sergeant's eyes widened and he turned vainly, searching for the French army that had spent the day being ferried across the inlet.
Admiral Menéndez de Aviles nodded to the Frenchman.

"Hang these heretics so the entire world knows the folly of Luther," said Admiral Menéndez de Aviles.

Yellow-flint-snake and Heron dropped exhausted to the sand and watched the tidal flow. Porpoises pinned huge schools of mullet against the inlet shore, causing the fish to jump out of the water and flop on the beach. The Flint traders were too tired to even pick up the fish attempting surrender for their meal.

Their hands hurt, their knees hurt, and their back muscles ached. Heron rubbed his sore neck.

"Thank you," said Heron to Yellow-flint-snake.
Yellow-flint-snake waved a stiffening arm.

"You are my partner," said Yellow-flint-snake motioning a stiffening arm. "Name your firstborn in my name," he said jokingly.

The Tequesta approached and stared at the inlet. It was so much like his childhood village of Santa Lucia.

"The Admiral is pleased," said the interpreter. Yellow-flint-snake and Heron did not answer.
"The Admiral requests you to ferry the next group of French across the inlet," stated the Tequesta. Both traders looked up but said nothing. The trade had been to move one army for one woman.

At last, Yellow-flint-snake spoke,
"This Admiral is slippery as a saber-fish."

"And," said the Tequesta Indian, "The priests say you cannot have the woman until you accept our god. You will become a Christian."

Heron flexed his stiff hands.

"One thing is for certain, you can never have enough gods," said Heron. He curled into a ball, dropping off immediately into sleep.

Book one: Part 32: Christian

Grandfather would indeed be angry, he thought.

Heron lay in the lagoon and allowed the warm salty waters to flow over his face.
The outsiders intoned enchanted *powerful* words above him. The words became muffled as he slipped underwater to lie upon a bed of scratchy water weeds. Tiny fish pecked at his body. Normally, the nibbling of the little brothers would have made him smile, however, the strangers, were a somber lot when the subject was about their magic.

Far off, muffled by the lagoon waters, the sound of thunder echoed.
How long would they keep him immersed?
If the sky-fire struck while he lay upon the itchy grass villages of the sea-horse, would he arise from the waters with two human heads growing from his ears, like fist Ais man?

Nevertheless, as if hunting a nervous deer, he ignored the approaching storm. He calmed his mind, opening his presence to capture and absorb the magic of the strangers.
When he arose from the water, he was to eat part of a stranger, *eat part of their god* to fully absorb the magic. *Perfectly logical request.*

All the clans he had visited as a flint trader would often distribute a mouthful of panther or hawk, even a small portion of the throwing arm of a fearless adversary. The act of ingesting was required to absorb the power of the hunter or warrior.
Once there had been a jaguar slain and three villages gathered to share in that power feast, for the checkered cats were less common than when his grandfather was in his prime.

At last, a hand tugged at his elbow and he was allowed to rise above the green-blue water.

The same gentle hand guided him to kneel in the mud, with only his chest and head rising out of the lagoon; he quickly felt his ears, relieved that no long-nosed gods had sprouted from his pierced earlobes that sported only the iridescent heads of hummingbirds.

The Spaniard's shaman fell into a deep trance while repeating the power words; behind and above him a black storm cloud towered into the heavens.

Heron shook water from his eyes as a slave or acolyte brought forth a burnished cup and cedar container in the shape of a tiny coffin that held the offering.

The shaman, his head shaved in an outlandish pattern, spread his arms wide, calling upon his gods. One of the gods, their favorite it seemed, had been murdered and nailed on a cross.
Heron watched as a lighting streamer shot horizontally across the sky. His people who spent much of their life in canoes, called this "empty sky fire" because it was less dangerous to boaters than the lightning that killed trees or fish in the broad lagoon. However, "empty sky-fire lightning" was normally a herald to the deadly sky-fire that had created the first Ais and the accompanying thunder-clap noise that slew people and sometimes even killed entire herds of bison.

The *strangers from the eastern sea,* their magic controlled the sky-fire to direct death at their enemies, and to gain that power, Heron would allow the strangers to immerse him in the lagoon. Sky-fire *power and the dark woman.*
Grandfather tried to persuade me the sky-fire weapons were not magic… but ground pine knot in a tube that sparked.

From the kneeling position, the shaman's amulet swung back and forth in front of Herons' face.

The tortured god. And the very *same* charm his Grandfather unwrapped during the season of the hurricanes or to show it to castaways when the clan elders needed a sacrifice.

The shaman's slave held out the container to the shaman who spoke more alien words to the heavens, opened the box, removed a piece of the dead god, and held it up to the rumbling heavens.

Heron narrowed his eyes in suspicion at the sight of the dead god portion. He had expected dried meat, tough old jerky, yet the round object looked more like a thin acorn flat cake that had been placed on a hot rock and forgotten about.

The shaman waved the offering in front of Heron's face, waiting for him to open his mouth, annoyance becoming evident and finally, Heron allowed the god fragment to be placed into his mouth.

He crunched down upon the sacrifice and was surprised, actually disappointed at its blandness. For no reason he could explain, he had expected the burn of an island pepper to accompany the giving of power by the strangers.

The shaman held out a wood cup and Heron sipped upon the foul liquid that tasted of spoiled sea grape.

The shaman said in Grandfather's language "This is my body… this is my blood."

Thunder louder than any cannon burst over their heads and a lightning bolt cracked nearby, sending palm fronds flying from the struck tree.

"Jesus wept!" Heron exclaimed in Spanish.

His outburst or the violence of thunder and close sky-fire appeared to cause great consternation between the two shamans.

Father Escobar and Brother Philippe, their robes soaked to their waists, jumped at the unexpected thunder but were shaken by the unexpected words.

Using god's name in vain was punishable by flogging.

Brother Philippe asked gently, "Where did you learn that phrase, my son? From the Lutherans?" nodding towards the great oak tree holding the swaying bodies of the dead Frenchmen.

But Heron, lifelong paddler of the lagoon, only gestured at the safety of the forest and waded towards the palm-thatched huts of the smoke-shrouded Timucua village.

The soldiers holding their iron-tipped weapons, were quick to follow his example, leaving the two shamans in their long robes to flounder through the seagrass, and mud.

Heron had to think.

Why were the shamans so alarmed that he could speak some of their God's words?

Flint traders, after all, had to speak many varied words. He winced at the memory of Grandfather's willow-switching when he pronounced the Spanish words incorrectly.

But regardless, Grandfather would be angry with him for partaking in the stranger's magic.

"Their god is a jealous God," he had insisted.

The sky darkened, cold rain hesitantly pattered the forest leaves and suddenly the heavens opened up, like the hooves of a million little water kelpies; thunder boomed again across the lagoon.

Soldiers and Timacua Indians sheltered under the large trees, while children splashed about the puddles running and laughing with skinny wet curs.

All avoided the tree with the dead men hanging from it.

Brother Philippe stood under a palm tree that offered some small protection from the shower. Next to him stood Heron, with goosebumps raised across his chilled skin.

"Do you know other words of our Lord?" asked Brother Philippe. Heron concentrated on the alien language and nodded his head. "Some words, yes," replied Heron.

Small ice stones began to fall from the gray clouds, melting almost immediately when touching the sand.

"Father Escobar will wish to know where you learned Spanish. How did you come by the Christian words?"

"My Grandfather," said Heron.

Scooping up a handful of the ice pellets and crunching them in strong teeth.

Philippe shuddered at the thought of placing ice next to his aching teeth.

"Grandfather taught me the words of many clans. Words to be useful in the flint trade."

Heron furrowed his brow: "Bottle," "Musket," then "Son of a Bitch," "Although a bitch is a wolf, a dog, is it not?"

"Where did your Grandfather learn Spanish?" inquired Brother Philippe.

Heron concentrated on the words, not exactly certain what the Shaman's assistant was asking, and finally responded,

"Grandfather said, those were words of his birth tribe. He also cautioned me, warned everyone; that your winged ships would return and not just the slave raiders, but ships with armies, although Grandfather made no mention of *your* enemies," pointing towards the ancient oak.

"These French bastards, is that not the name your warriors give to those swinging from the great tree?" asked Heron as he collected more sky-ice.

"Grandfather resembles that warrior" shouted Heron over the rain, gesturing towards a dark-skinned soldier wearing a Cuirass and holding a crossbow.

"Is your grandfather a maroon, a dark moor? Where is your grandfather now?" asked Brother Philippe over the roar of the rain.

"I know not the words 'maroon or darkmoor' and I learned the other words in the town of Ulumay," said Heron.

Brother Philippe looked with renewed interest at the newly christened Indian; *Yes there could be Dark-Moor blood in the young man shivering before him.*

"We have chosen a Christian name for you, now that you have been baptized," said the Brother.

"Grandfather warned me about your names. That is why all of his children and grandchildren, he named from his clan. Names that sound like gravel being chewed when attempting to learn them. Learn we did well with Grandfather's stinging willow branch!" said Heron.

"Your name then?" asked Brother Philippe.

"My name is José Diego El Gato De Castillo. That was the name of his father. Crazy Grandfather! My name was first learned under the tutelage of the willow switch and later the pinch of the blue crab.

Until I could say that name correctly and in unexpected moments. Have you ever had a surprise crab on your ear?" asked Heron with a hint of mirth.

"Indeed a very Christian name," replied Brother Philippe with a smile, recalling his painful learning of letters.

At length sunshine saturated the morning again, spreading drying warmth upon chilled skin and sodden
clothes; the baptismal group ambled back to the village, following the smoke and scent of fresh food; stepping across fresh puddles, hurrying down a twisting trail through stalks of Custer-apples and Itch-weed Ivy. Every step shaking loose clinging pearls of raindrops from willow and oak.

Above them, in the leaves and moss of ancient oaks, Florida parrots and jays vibrated their feathers dry while squawking harshly at the departing humans. Squirrels crept from their hiding places in leafy palm trees. Grackles and crows settled upon the dead Frenchmen to pick at their unseeing eyes.

At the village, a feast was being cooked to celebrate the great victory of the strange Spaniards over the strange French. Except for the noise they spoke, Heron could see no difference in the warring strangers. Heron had to admire their cleverness and bravery of how the Spanish had destroyed their enemy, storing that kernel of information for future reference.
But then Grandfather was clever as a wily bull raccoon, except for those days when he capered about as if bitten on the nose by the double fanged water snake.
Lately, those days were more often than not, he thought sadly.

A soldier led the Congo woman to Heron and handed him the rawhide rope that was attached to her neck.

"Does she have a name?" asked Heron.

His new woman stood face downcast and at length lifted her head and asked him in accented French, "Parlez-vous Français?"
Heron smiled.

Book one: Part 33: Savochequeya

"If they were free they would just be idle and fight, which would cause loss of lives, souls, and the property of settlers."
Bishop of Santiago, 1544

Of the Florida Indians: "They are great bowmen, and very faithless. I hold it certain they never will be
at peace, and less will they become Christians. Let the Indians be taken in hand gently, inviting them to peace; then putting them under deck, husbands, and wives together, sell them among the Islands, and even upon Terra Firma for money, as some old nobles of Spain buy vassals of the king. In this way, there could be management of them, and their numbers become diminished. This I say would be proper policy, and the Spaniards might then make some stock farms for the breeding of cattle, and be there to safeguard the many vessels that are wrecked all the way along from Carlos (Calusa) the port of San Agustin, and river of San Mateo. There the Lutherans of France had made a fort, and found a nook whence to plunder as many ships as should come from Mexico or Peru."
-Castaway Hernando D'Escalante Fontanda 1566

"With the help of divine grace to employ all one's strength, for the salvation and perfection of your people."
-Unknown words of the Inquisition

East coast of Florida, South of the Cape of Canaveral

A series of alarm blasts from shell trumpets called out to warn of their coming.

"Grandfather will be angry," said Ochobi Eduardo Lopez del Castillo, from his watch in the great tree.

The boats approaching were not of the people, not a tree hollowed out to ride the lagoon. They were somehow different. They were boats of Grandfather's people.

Ochobi placed the heavy conch shell in its basket and he scampered down the tree in a seemingly controlled fall.

The village had been warned that the stink-strangers were on the lagoon.

As with the preceding native settlements, the Spanish exploring party was assaulted by the foul miasma of discarded oyster shells, drying fish, and wood smoke.

Father Escobar, the official representative of the Holy Church and nominal leader of the tiny expedition made the sign of the cross to ward away the perilous odors that could kill a man as sure as any savage's arrow.

The native guide, Eduardo, a newly baptized Christian once known as "Yellow-flint-snake," pointed his canoe paddle at a scarcely noticeable peninsula.

"Savo-chequeya, a town of the Ais," explained Yellow-flint snake.
"Savochequeya. Dear Lord," repeated Father Pedro Escobar.
Scowling at the tongue-twisting name. He was aware that the savages followed the widespread practice of naming the settlements after the town leader, the Cacique.

The boats and canoes of the Spanish reconnoitering party, one by one, caught up and formed a rough line in the building breeze. Waiting until all the boats were ready. Crossbows were cranked and loaded; swords loosened in sheaths.

"We are ready, your holiness!" said Captain Alcayede, shouting across the water.
"God is with us, replied Escobar with a cultured Castilian accent.
The exploring party had paddled as one to yet another of the endless Indian towns along the "Baya Grande de Ays"; the vast inland sea of Florida's east coast that was not fresh or saltwater. A shipwrecked sailor could not quench his thirst from the brackish waters of the Ais Lagoon.

The boats paddled into a protected cove that was unseen from the wide lagoon.

Father Escobar studied the palm-fringed settlement festooned with drying nets and racks of smoked mullet; amazed at the passing thought that he *actually missed* the orderly Indian towns of the hurricane-swept Yucatan.

He made the sign of the cross again.

The Indians of Savochequeya were of the "Ais" nations.
Another of the seemingly endless clans of devil-worshiping coastal barbarians of east Florida. And for whom the Royal Cartographers had named the endless lagoon.

The Lagoon will have a proper Christian name soon, he thought and crossed himself again for good measure.
The Spanish boats holding a mixed group of two dozen soldiers and sailors, two clergymen of the true church, captive French Huguenots, and conscripted Indian servants landed their boats next to rows of Ais canoes and the stiff-jointed occupants filed cautiously onto the shell-strewn shoreline.

Flocks of noisy parrots screamed at them from the dense branches of water oaks and leafy palms. The exploring party was greeted not by flights of bone-tipped arrows but by swarms of mosquitoes and vicious yellow flies.

Nevertheless taking no unnecessary risks in an unpredictable brutal land, the sailors turned their boats around, readying them for a speedy departure if required.

Captain Alcayede ordered his soldiers to use their halberds and crossbows to usher the Indian servants to the fore; a living breathing wall to shield against arrows or darts in the occurrence that this particular Ais town was hostile.

Captain Alcayede trusted not a single one of the coastal savages.
The Ais in particular were right bastards and in general, appeared to be hostile to everyone Indian or Christian.

Moreover, the ongoing raids along the Florida coast by Spanish slave traders had tainted most of the coastal tribes against all Christians. The Ais were justifiably wary of strangers.

"Music" ordered Alcayede.

A burly soldier cuffed one of the Frenchmen who had been spared from the hanging tree.

"Lutheran justify our mercy and make these animals like us," demanded the sergeant-at-arms. The Huguenot uttered a silent prayer for his murdered comrades at Matanzas Inlet.

"Eternal rest grant them O Lord. May their spirits rest in peace until the Lord himself, with a cry of command, gathers we who are alive, who are left. Jesus will arise and we will be caught in the clouds to meet the faithful departed. Amen"

Only a few of the French had been spared the blade or noose. The carpenters built a new Spanish settlement but also the rare musicians who could play for their new masters.

The Frenchman took up his fife and played a lively tune. It was well known that European music had the power to calm the savages of New Spain. At the sound of the flute small yellow dogs awoke from their torpor and rushed to bark at the exotic strangers.

Yet no inhabitants of Savochequeya came to greet them.

"Could these Indios fear the music of a Lutheran?" asked Father Escobar. "Tell the Frank swine to stop blowing," *Perhaps I will order the Luther pig to be executed.*

When no Indians greeted them, Escobar looked first to his assistant, Brother Phillipe then to the captain, and finally narrowed his eyes on the native guide.

"Have you brought us to a plague-infested empty town?" demanded Father Escobar

Yellow flint snake, now christened as Eduardo the Christian, wilted under the anger of the conjurer of the god on the cross.

"Has the plague has been here before us?" Escobar snapped at Captain Alcayede.

For the barking dogs and cuffing of the Frenchman to silence, still had not brought forth any of the pagan Indios.

Captain Alcayede, the military leader of the expedition, only shrugged his shoulders. *Had the slave hunters brought yet another of the same killing fevers that sweep Cuba and Mexico from time to time?*

"Your holiness, anytime we are not greeted with catfish spine-tipped arrows, it is a good day," said Captain Alcayede.

"Alright then let us move in and see if anyone yet lives," Alcayede ordered to his soldiers.

The soldiers pushed their human shield wall before them moving slowly inland, swatting at the swarms of yellow flies, cursing in the many dialects of Iberia and France, and kicking at the irritating dogs whenever they came too close.

They followed an impressive shell causeway above the high tide mark towards a sturdy-looking palm log palisade, circular in design, wreathed in wood smoke. Savochequeya was much the same as every large town they had visited along the Baya Grande de Ays. Piles of oyster and clam shells fouled the air.

"Be ready boys," warned Captain Alcayede, noting the cooking smoke.

"This is no dead Town."

"Satan spawn!" said Father Escobar.
Escobar hissed through his barred teeth, crossing himself with righteous indignation at the sight of a pagan totem outside of the palisade wall.

Secured to a painted and feathered cypress post was the giant skull of a dragon or crocodile. Beneath the skull-hung shell carvings with the pagan images of the birdman and the twinned rattlesnakes. The birdman and snakes were the seemingly universal pagan religion - Satan hatched; the symbols linked the otherwise diverse Florida Clans and tribes. Unique to this totem was the addition of white and pink shell carvings of sea horses.

"Captain, mark that post. There will be a burning of witches on that affront to our lord," said Father Escobar.

"Yes, your holiness," said Captain Alcayede, as he made the sign of the cross.

The Inquisition was not to be mocked, he reminded himself, glancing at his men to make sure they also made the sign of the cross.
Escobar's chest and arm actually pained as he walked past the crocodile skull.

Admiral Menendez.

Only with monumental effort was Escobar able to hold his anger in check.
The *Commander* of the royal expedition; Admiral Menendez had stressed upon him specific instructions not to provoke the Florida natives until the Caciques or other Indian leaders had sworn their allegiance to the crown and church.

An insult to both the Church and me, by not permitting this Satan spawn town to burn... Menendez. Perhaps the Admiral should burn. thought Escobar.
Perhaps *Menendez should burn* for giving him this disagreeable assignment far below that of a representative of the Holy Inquisition. Orders to follow the fleeing Frenchmen that had survived the cleansing at the inlet. Chasing the few Lutherans was a task that could have been handled by even an incompetent officer such this Captain Alcayede.

Menendez. The Admiral had the impudence to quote a verse to him!

"And David inquired at the Lord, saying, Shall I pursue after this troop? Shall I overtake them? And He answered him, Pursue: for thou shalt surely overtake them, and without fail recover all." Samuel 30: 8:

"How dare he," fumed Escobar.

Admiral Menéndez de Aviles then had given him the obligation "To follow and capture any of the fleeing Lutherans. To explore the lands south of the new settlement of St. Augustine; record the names of towns, populations, natural resources, and landmarks. If possible, locate Christian captives who could be used as translators.

"There would be time enough to cleanse the Indio Towns of Satan's influences" the Admiral had assured him.

It is my holy duty to cleanse pagans from the lands of New Spain, fumed Escobar.

Fire and blood, hot iron, and molten lead, from Mexico City, the Yucatan, and Cuba; he had relished the souls he and his fellow Inquisitors had saved.
Discovering along the journey, that he had a natural inclination, a god-given talent to break the enemies of the church.

"Salvation and conversion of the Florida Indio would come with the arrival of additional men at arms and missionaries. Then as needed, the Inquisition would, as they had in the Moorish provinces of Spain, purify the land with fire and stake," explained Admiral Menendez.

And of course, the Inquisition was always needed

"The right hand of God," Escobar mumbled as he rubbed the painful spot above his heart.
To stand in front of the devil's very dragon skull post and not be able to push it, overstressed him like a sore tooth and physically pained him in the chest and arm.

The Spaniards halted before the log palisade, crossbows, and halberds at the ready.
Dark-eyed faces stared back at them from an arrow tower and the palisade.

"Tell the Frenchman to play again," ordered the ever impatient Father Escobar.
A gate slowly swung open.
Captain Alcayede and his sergeant looked behind him to see they had been shadowed by dozens of armed warriors, however before he could call a warning, the village inhabitants were at last released by their leader.

A tangle of dogs, women, children, and armed men flowed from the inside the palisade to the exploring party.

The town's bolder inhabitants ignoring the Indian slaves, the smell, and the iron weapons, crowded close around the Europeans, haranguing the newcomers, demanding gifts in their sing-song language. Occasionally fingering the outlandish Spanish clothing, tugging on greasy beards, and making fleeting grabs at the strange weapons.
Young women with blue-black hair, breasts perked high laughed at the European clothing and beards, but soon stepped back in confusion, wrinkling their noses at body odors of the unwashed Spaniards and Frenchmen.

Try as he could, Captain Alcayede could see no hint of treachery among this group of Indios. The warriors who had shadowed them, offered up smug satisfaction in the knowledge they could have ambushed the strangers with ease.

Of the Ais people; Captain Alcayede noted both the men and women were tall and well-formed, nearly naked, painted in outlandish designs of reds and purples, their bodies adorned with shells, flowers, and feathers which dangled from arms, knees, necks, and ears, their only clothing being the standard rags woven from fibers of tree moss covering their genitals. The town's mongrel dogs nipped and barked until the naked children chased them away with tiny spears.

The natives were however particularly intrigued by the heavy dark robes worn by the two clergymen, warily gesturing at their wooden crosses.
To the Ais, the "crossed stick" was a familiar symbol of power associated with the twin rattlesnake god.

Warriors, some carrying a heavy shell-topped war club in each hand, clearly enjoying themselves crossed their weapons in the imitation of the holy cross and capered about yelling in gleeful imitation of animals - a turkey-cock no less.

One warrior kept repeating "Son of a Bitch!" in what could have been English.

Escobar gazed with disfavor at the Indian girls, their high breasts uncovered to the world, a reminder of his first Mexica servants.

Even the devil worshipers of the Aztec Mexica had covered their womenfolk. Modesty, an apparently unknown concept to the wilder Florida savages.
Well, that would change

The good Father threw a warning scowl at the soldiers and sailors; their un-Christian leers were the same at each new village.

Captain Alcayede *noted the town of Savochequeya was indeed unique. Some of the Ais warriors carried iron hatchets and one warrior incredulously wore a women's bonnet, items that could have only come from a European shipwreck.*

Yet another warrior wore a too-small but silver-chased French helmet, hinting at contact with the shattered Huguenot army.

Of more significance, Alcayede took note that this clan of Ais was like the Caribs of the Lesser Antilles. It was readily evident that many of the Ais of Savochequeya were of African lineage, part or whole. And because of their unique ancestry, the dark skin Ais towered even higher over the Spaniards than the normal hand span's difference between European and Native.

The Indian reactions to the Europeans were much the same at each town they visited and the explorers had come to expect the behavior from the natives who had never or in the case of this village, 'rarely' seen Europeans.
However, for once, the natives did not gather around the Spanish sailors of Guinea or dark moor linage to rub their dark skin as if trying to rub off the paint.

An Indian pushed his way through the throng, conspicuous from the others because he wore clothing, a ragged cotton shirt with breeches. The Indian knelt before Father Escobar who graciously presented his signet to be kissed.

Juan was the most gifted of the Indian interpreters. A Timucua who resided near the new Spanish settlement of St. Augustine and one of the interpreters sent forward to smooth the arrival of the Spanish exploring party.

"Holy Father," said Juan.

Juan had been baptized in the tidal lagoon in front of St. Augustine, the tattered shirt a reward for being the first of his people to accept Christianity.

The kneeling Indian kissed Escobar's outstretched hand and stood, his face respectfully planted to the church man's feet until addressed by the powerful magician.

"What have you to say, Juan?"

"Powerful Father there have been more slave-raiding attacks from Cuba and these people were not permitted to greet you until a determination was made as to your intentions."

"When every Ais is baptized a Christian, the raids will cease," promised Escobar. "The Lord is our Shepherd."

Juan nodded his head at the power of the hanging god of the cross.
"The Cacique Savochequeya awaits your presence," replied Juan.
Bastard heathen! In God's name, this Florida was trying, thought Escobar.

Every reeking town had its own version of aristocrats - deceitful and tattooed, who believed themselves to be equal to *the king* and haughtily superior to any Spaniard of lesser standing.

Visitors to the towns and villages had to go before the Cacique, *not* the other way around.
That would soon change, he said to himself, thinking about the Indian leaders of Mexico who had been put to the torch by the guardians of the faith.

"Well, let's get this over with," he said to his scribe, Philippe Oreja, a youthful Basque monk. "Philippe, order a servant to bring the gifts."

The Spanish party was escorted through the gate.
The Town or fort, for it was a combination of both, was set upon a hill of shells higher than a halberd, and two flat-topped shell mounds

poked from above the surrounding palm log wall. A small hut sat upon each mound, surrounded by short log palisades.

The Spaniards had traveled through many Timucua and Ais Indian Towns, most with various arrangements of shell mounds and they had learned that usually the town leader or Cacique lived upon one mound and their most powerful shaman lived upon the other.

Once through the rough gate, they entered a grove of ancient Cedar trees whose lower branches had been cut away, creating a large shaded area. Along the inside of the log wall, was a continuous thatched shelter that was more or less communal. Additional palm-thatched huts had been constructed along the bases of the twin mounds.

The Spaniards nudged each other, snickering; these would be the "blood huts," the huts where the women were confined during their menses cycle. Their snickering ceased as they approached the Cacique and his warriors.

"Cacique Savochequeya, leader of the Northern Ais," said Juan, making another deep bow.

At the bottom of one mound, surrounded by fierce-looking Ais warriors, sat the Cacique, resplendent in a crimson robe made from the feathers of rose-colored sea birds. Thick strands of freshwater pearls were heaped around his neck, while clawed turkey's feet jutted from pierced earlobes. A stingray barb was placed through his nose. Beneath his crimson robe was a breastplate of scaly crocodile skin and placed across his muscular legs was a war club made from the jaws or bill of some great saw-toothed fish.

Savochequeya, the leader of northern Ais land, considered the group of approaching Spaniards. These were the people of the stories. The invaders who used steel and magic, horse, and dog to conquer the southern Islands of the Tainio and Lucayans.

They controlled the lightning with their fire sticks.

Yes, he could see their arrogance and swagger, so oddly out of place for such a tiny race of people. There was war in that arrogance.

Savochequeya took special note of the holy men in the black robes. There also had been stories about these magicians. Priests of the jealous god of the crossed sticks and whose love of fire were legendary.

The island peoples, Lucayans, and Tainos had long been fleeing their storm-tossed islands as the unstoppable tide of Spanish conquered and enslaved island after island. The island refugees had brought with them amazing stories of conquering warriors: sickly pale faces covered in hair, like animals, men, and women who refused to bathe, their unwashed bodies carrying the stink of corpses.

Since his childhood, he had listened to the legends about these powerful invaders, yet over the years, ship after ship was storm-driven to wreck upon the beaches; he could never envision the pathetic men and women who crashed their winged boats upon the shoreline of the great salt sea, as conquerors.
Those Spanish, who crawled out of the sea vomiting saltwater were easily killed or captured on the beach and in fact made sickly short-lived slaves.

Savochequeya no longer feared the black robes. The priests captured by his people had died quite easily, if noisy in their own fire.

However, this was his first encounter with Spaniards not cowed by storm.

In his lifetime alone, at least two great Spanish armies had landed upon the sunset coast, enslaving and laying waste to the western clans and towns until finally disappearing into the northern lands of the Apalachee. According to the stories, the armies of iron shirts had twice utterly crushed the powerful Ocala and Timucua, ancient and implacable enemies of the Ais.

Complex emotions raced through his mind: caution, curiosity, fear, more curiosity, and finally slowly simmering anger.

Outrage.

Their strut belied their self-importance; these strangers had not come as humble guests in a hostile land, but instead, their actions were more like the haughty Calusa, rulers of the Southlands,

Savochequeya considered the Spanish shaman and warriors: *these people were evil and dangerous*. These Spaniards, few in numbers, confident in the enchantments of their black-robed magicians and thunder weapons.

Despite their swagger and steel, if he gave the word, not one of these strangers would escape back to their boats without a dozen arrows in their faces.

His Taino slaves had forewarned them about the hardened turtle-like shirts that protected the child-sized chests of the invaders.

"Take their eyes," the Taino had advised.

The Spanish stopped before they reached the protective wall of painted warriors and ordered their interpreter forward for introductions. Their Juan.

"No," said Savochequeya. *Not the Timucua,* not the Juan. Send me the Flint trader," ordered the Ais leader.

The Flint trader was Ais and was well known by Savochequeya, almost *even liked,* before becoming a slave to these strangers.

Flint-Yellow-Snake was ushered forward.

The Flint trader approached and put his head to the hardpan floor until acknowledged by Savochequeya.

"Great Lord," said Flint-Yellow-Snake as he stood upright, "I bring you the rarest of all gifts. Iron," and proffered one of the knives he had traded from the French in exchange for food.

Savochequeya nodded his head in appreciation. An impressive gift no doubt.

"Trader, why do you bring these shit stinking people to my town? And where is your fellow thief, the ruffian, Heron?" demanded Savochequeya.

Flint-Yellow-Snake gestured to the soldiers and priests standing behind him.

"These men are Spanish, the renowned warriors of legend and conquerors of the salt islands. They bring offerings of friendship from their great father across the waters and seek only to pass through your land in their pursuit of the other people of the hairy face, the Clan of France.

These Français men have insulted the Spanish father and gods. They seek retribution and revenge," explained Flint-Yellow-Snake.

"Much as you have done lord, during the time of the great dying," said Flint-Yellow-Snake.

Savochequeya bristled at the choice of words; the trader was almost disrespectful in front of his people. Almost but not quite enough to kill him.

"Do you bring flint, Timucua?" demanded the Caciquie Savochequeya. Omitting the title of "Trader" that assured safe passage in all lands.
Naming him a Timucua was a humiliating insult, worse for having said it in front of the assembled Ais. Flint-Yellow-Snake had been born Ais and would forever be Ais. *For as long as he lived.*

The jubilant Ais went silent, waiting for blood.
The trader paled and visibly shook, not so stupid as not to have realized his error. The danger. The protection of Spanish magic only went so far.

"Not flint, Lord, but valuable gifts," said Flint-Yellow-Snake.

Flint-Yellow-Snake signaled a waiting slave, who fearfully approached and set a reed basket at the trader's feet.
The trader reached into the basket and brought up coils of scarlet and indigo ribbon, colorful beads, a handful of tin bells, and two mirrors. Flint-Yellow-Snake spread the offerings on the sand before the Ais leader's feet.
The gathered Ais quietly sighed at the value of the gifts. Custom demanded an equal gift be returned.

Savochequeya was impressed at the wealth of the gift. Of course, he held a secret gift to match that of the white strangers.

"I asked you about Heron, son of Ulumay," said the leader of the Ais. Savochequeya expressed indifference to the Spanish gifts.

"My friend Heron has taken a woman from these strangers. He spends much time on the river with her, yet returns with no fish," replied Flint-Yellow-Snake.

This set off a series of guffaws from the gathered Ais who were fond of Heron despite his habit of overvaluing his trade flint.

"Hmmmf!" growled one of the daughters of Savochequeya, heavy with child, and stomped away. *Traders will be traders,* thought Flint-Yellow-Snake but hiding his smirk by turning to the strangers. Flint-Yellow-Snake gestured for the fat Priest and leader of the soldiers to come forward.

The first meeting between leaders was always the most dangerous. The local chieftains or town elders expected deference and respect for their position.

While the Spanish were confident in the magic of their gods, the edge of their weapons and history of victories demanded the same respect. The two expectations could never be met, so he lied when needed, which was to say always. So far he had kept the meetings from breaking out into bloody conflict by utilizing his personal knowledge of the coastal Chieftains and then not fully translating the demands from each side.

Father Pedro Escobar and Captain Hector Alcayede de Córdoba, the military leader for their expedition approached the Ais leader.

Captain Hector Alcayede de Córdoba, a veteran of countless Indian skirmishes and fights against Protestants, respectfully fell into step behind the difficult Father Escobar.

His legs trembled not from fear, for he was brave, but from the anticipated battle. He considered the Ais warriors, their disposition, weapons, and *his* path of least resistance if retreat became necessary. Having the portly priest in *his path* during a hasty retreat could mean death. The Inquisitor would not be the first priest left to the heathen war clubs when things became hot.

To his trained eye, several things stood out to make this particular Indian town unique and in his experience "unique" could always be understood as "lethal".

First, many of the warriors had European weapons, axes mostly, but he had spied a rusty halberd and crossbow quarrel held like a knife. Recovered from a wrecked galleon? Slave raiders or perhaps trade with the Huguenots? No matter the origins, iron weapons in the hands of fearless warriors were a problem to be factored in too. Secondly, the natives themselves, many were of mixed race. There was a strain of African lineage to this town and it showed not only in their faces but in their height and muscular build. The Florida

Indians generally towered above the average Spaniard; however, these mixed-race warriors were giants in a land of giants.

"Lord," said Flint-Yellow-Snake in the Ais tongue, gesturing at the Priest.

"This is the Shaman Escobar, holy man to the gods of the Spaniards. Keeper of the fire and I have been forewarned he is a powerful magician who burns enemies of their great Father who lives across the great salt sea."

The trader then turned to Captain Hector Alcayede de Cordoba, "Captain Alcayede, renowned war leader, fearless in battle, conqueror of both the Lutherans and Sea-Island peoples."

Captain Alcayede, nodded his head at the mention of his name, while Father Escobar stared open-mouthed, his attention drawn to a masked shaman behind Savochequeya.
The Shaman capered about a smoky fire wearing a carved wooden mask with antlers and a black raven feather robe. *Satan's very attire.*

Swinging back and forth from the pagan's neck were carvings of sea horses and most jarring of all was a large silver crucifix set with a blue gem.

You will burn for this taint to the cross, thought Escobar.

Squatting near the shaman at a smoky fire, was an old woman whose facial tattoos marked her as a Tanio from the islands; however, her pocked-marked face marked her as a survivor of smallpox. The scars were common enough in Seville or Havana, yet out of place in this village on the Ais.

Her black eyes showed no fear or curiosity, only pure hatred.

Well, hatred was common enough, thought Escobar.
He smiled at the thought of breaking that hatred.
The woman stood up. Rage twisted her wrinkled face.

"These two are never to be trusted!" she spat brandishing a small wooden knife lined with shark's teeth. "Kill them. They are worse than the slave hunters," she warned.

"Shut up woman!" exploded an enraged Savochequeya, who slapped the old woman with a powerful blow. "This is my council and I alone decide when to kill the strangers!" snapped the Cacique. Without a backward glance to the old woman, "I wish no war with these iron shirts, '' said Savochequeya to the Flint trader.

"Tell them I have a gift that equals their ribbons," said Savochequeya.

The Ais leader clapped his hands and a negro-Indian mixed-blood warrior prodded a terrified

Frenchman from behind a woven mat wall.

Savochequeya savored the shock on the stranger's faces. He too could surprise.

"I offer this gift as my token of friendship, an enemy to hang upon the cross, with your gods," said Savochequeya.

Savochequeya noticed the black robbed shaman gazed upon the Frenchman with dilated pupils; as if the captive were a naked slave maiden. No one yet has claimed the stink people were sane.

"We have prepared a feast," said Savochequeya, dismissing the stink strangers.

I decide when they die, he said to himself.

Father Escobar threw the clay bowl of tough sea turtle meat at the sniffing curs and carefully picked up the platter of charred fish. The fish was at least edible.

These savages of Florida only knew to scorch their food over an open fire. Even the Mexica, corrupted as they had been by the wiles of Satan, at least knew how to prepare decent food.

He sighed, greatly missing the cooking skills of the personal chef of the Admiral. The servant, while liked by Admiral Mendez, had in Escobar's opinion far too much of the Moorish blood to be in the position to serve as a personal servant of the Admiral.
The cook could never fully be trusted.
Despite the tainted blood, the Admiral's servant did know how to tenderize and season the great sea turtles and the ability to prepare a multiplicity of other savory dishes.

Escobar watched as his scribe walked around a group of nearly naked Ais warriors with their ridiculous horse tail attire.

The natives yelled and screamed while playing a game of throwing blunt spears at a clay disc rolled by a youth. When they became Christians, the church would stop such a waste of time. They would plant maize for settlers.
As his scribe drew near, Escobar scowled again.
Basques, another people who could never be fully trusted. When a much younger Escobar had inquired why the Inquisition had not spent more time in the Basque Mountain homeland - the unsatisfying response had been "The Basques were too poor for the church to squander valuable time in the mountains."

Brother Philippe, humble in appearance, warily approached Father Escobar.
The senior churchman was legendary for his foul moods and rapier-sharp tongue.
Philippe suspected Admiral Menendez had given the lagoon exploration assignment to Escobar to divest the sour Father from his presence.

Had he…?
Philippe crossed himself at the polluted thought that perhaps the Admiral had sent Father Escobar south in hopes that he would be killed by the Lutherans or hostile Indians. No, it could not be so.

Philippe wove his way through the men of the town to the small fire where Father Escobar sat scowling as well, scowling at everything.

Philippe sighed; these poor Indios were no different from others of New Spain, children only waiting for the word of God.
He neared the Father and genuflected, an action that always improved Escobar's disposition.

"Father, you asked to be told of anything unusual. I'm sure you noticed the Indians of this town are of mixed race?"

Escobar stared blankly at his scribe, a reaction that suggested *he had not* noticed how different these Ais were from others of the other Florida clans.

"I noticed some of the Ais of this town were of darker skin than people in the other Ais settlements. I probed around the town and discovered these people harbor a Cimarrón," explained Philippe.

Father Escobar exploded in anger, "You bother me; you insult my person to tell me these savages have a wild cow?"

"No Father, forgive me, not 'runaway' as with cattle or horses but a runaway African. Cimarrón is how the inhabitants of Hispaniola name the Africans who fight alongside the Caribs. Cimarróns or sometimes just called Maroons," Philippe calmly explained.

Escobar grimaced at the name of the fierce Caribs. The unstoppable ocean-going Indians for which the Caribbean Sea had been named. Spain had conquered vast empires in the New World. The gold-rich Aztecs and then the Incas in their cloud-shrouded mountain citadels had fallen to steel and Christian bravery. Yet, the islands of the Southern Caribbean Sea could not be settled because of threats from the Cannibal Caribs.

"This runaway, or perhaps he is only a dark moor castaway, is now the town shaman. The same masked shaman who accompanied the enraged Tanio woman at the meeting with the Cacique Savochequeya.

"They say the Taino woman can predict hurricanes," explained Brother Philippe.

"A devil worshiper and a wind witch?" stammered an outraged Escobar.
"They will burn for witchcraft!" hissed the Priest. "Thou shalt not suffer a witch to live."

Father Escobar tossed his fish into the fire. No longer hungry, but once again incensed that he had been sent south by the Admiral.

"Let us talk with this runaway Maroon," said Escobar.

The two priests held their robes as they plodded carefully up rough pine log steps set in the slope of the shell mound reserved for the shaman.

Into Satan's lair thought Escobar as he struggled up the incline.
At the top of the hill, they both crossed themselves and entered a small hut enshrouded with an acrid cloud of tobacco smoke.

They were shocked to find the Taino woman feeding a small fire with the medicinal plant tobacco and the old African slave spouting indications above a prostrate fevered Indian.

"Witchcraft!" hissed the Priest
It had been a surprise in the morning to be presented with the French prisoner.
But this… To discover a feral slave and one who practiced witchcraft was an assault on the very nature of Christendom.

The old African carefully removed the carved deer mask and hide shirt, exposing his walnut-colored skin that was surprisingly disfigured by an unusual collection of old scars: round puckered arrow or dart wounds, a wide long scar that stretched horizontally across his chest that could only have made by Spanish steel blade or perhaps one of those shark tooth clubs, so favored by the Coastal Florida tribes.

One particularly odd set of curved slash marks could only have come from the raking claws of a beast, a Jaguar or Panther.

Brother Philippe, who had never considered the herbal healing rituals to be either a "pact with the Devil" or a threat to the holy church, reconsidered his opinion of the slave.

The scars were not those of a slave. The man had obviously been a warrior or soldier in his youth.
Hanging from the scarred chest and contrasting sharply with the dark skin, swung a heavy Christian cross of silver, inset with a blue jewel.

The holy cross had to have been stolen off the slave's owner, thought Father Escobar, or perhaps recovered from a shipwreck, but no, that would make it the property of the king.
So no, the cross was stolen; the African might even be an aged servant from the recently annihilated French. Huguenot possessions were automatically forfeited to the church, to his expedition.

The African seemed not at all surprised by the interruption of the two Priests and only glanced at them with a scowl while removing a wad of Tobacco leaves from his mouth and placing the wad in the mouth of the sick Indian.

He then squatted by the woman near the small fire and began talking.

"Tobacco heals so many ills. However, for most, there is no cure for the diseases the slavers bring to the coast. The Christian Spanish slavers," he added.

The old slave then began talking in an Indian language becoming agitated and waving his hands at unseen objects in the smoke.

Brother Philippe recognized Nahuatl! *Where had the African learned the words of the conquered Aztec?*

Finally, good Spanish words began to again thread into the old man's mouth; as if he was trying to remember a long-forgotten lesson.

"Have you seen my Andalusian horse, Adelantado?" he suddenly asked the priests with unexpected pride.

"Such an exceptionally trained warhorse, a killer of men, my Adelantado. His price cost me more than a small ranch, but I was young and drunk with Inca gold," said the dark-skinned man.

At the mention of gold, Escobar briefly ceased thinking of the cleansing fire that would be required for this follower of Satan.

"Adelantado, his children, and grandchildren, now roam the wide grasslands between here and Tampa.
Yet the Ais or Timucua, fearless in war, do not attempt to approach the horses… The legends you see, the great dying came with the arrival of the first horses.
Such a waste not to train the horses. They do hunt the wild cattle."

An impatient Father Escobar had thoughts only of obtaining the silver cross.
"Where is your owner, slave?" said Father Escobar.
The dark shaman, eyes blazing with an ancient fire, pulled out a wood-handled knife hafted with a single large shark tooth.
Brother Phillipe saw, with alarm, that the crazy old woman had drawn her own shark tooth knife.

"Ah, to be young," he said in mixed Nahuatl and Spanish, while reaching over and slicing into a leaf retrieved from a basket of green palmetto leaves.

The slave continued cutting into broadleaf, mesmerized by the wispy sound the serrated shark tooth made as the leaf was cut into strips.
The Maroon's Spanish improved steadily with every word spoken.

"In Peru, we never had problems with impertinent priests. In fact, I personally presented several priests to our Indian auxiliaries in Cuzco. You see the priests attempted to interfere with certain unseemly practices - the sacrificing of children upon frozen mountains. Pizzaro could not afford to insult allies.

And what was another Indian child for their gods?
However the priests… always so quick to burn anyone they disliked, nearly ruined our pact with those Indians. You see the mountain Indios, they hated the Incas more than us Spaniards." The two priests backed towards the door.
The old slave kept up his slicing and talking.

"One particularly insolent priest, I watched as our allies flayed him alive with little glass knives.
Governor-General de Soto learned this lesson well and *no* insolent Priests accompanied him on his invasion of Florida," said the old slave.

The old African looked directly at the two men as if weighing their strengths.

"Even old, I could take your eyes before you killed me," said the dark-skinned shaman.
The two robed men had different reactions to the blasphemous words of murder and Pagans. Brother Philippe hid his slight smile, while Father Escobar stammered outrage at the insult.

Brother Philippe gently held the arm of Father Escobar.

"Remember our orders from the Admiral; we are to only gather information about this land, even information from runaways," said Brother Philippe.

The African stood to his full height. His stooped frame had once been tall. His words were spoken with pride.

"I am not a runaway slave! I am Conquistador! I am Luis Castillo! The son of a conquistador and grandson of a Moor commander at Granada! I am a Cavalier for Governor-General Hernando de Soto!"

The old man suddenly turned serious.

"Arrows fell thick as rain," muttered Luis Castillo. "Have you word from Governor de Soto?

After our victory in the city of Mabila, de Soto sent us four to locate the supply galleons anchored on the Bay of Horses. All these years there has been no word of the fate of de Soto and his thousand."

"Kill these two," said the woman abruptly.

However, Luis Castillo was no longer interested in the Priests. His eyes followed the swirling patterns of tobacco smoke and memories.

"Such a fine warhorse, as ever left the plains of old Spain. At first sight, his beauty and bearing would take your breath away… His children! I have seen his offspring running wild in this and even the great cats must give the children of the Conquistador war horses respect. My Adelantado," said Castillo, who began to weep softly.

The two priests fled into the night. Insanity was known to be contagious.

Father Escobar was exultant. He stood before Captain Hector Alcayede de Cordoba.

"Do this deed and we go back to St. Augustine, our mission complete," said Escobar.
Captain Alcayede felt trapped and squirmed under the gaze of the Priest. Few crossed the Inquisition and escaped punishment.
Still, the military commander was simmering in anger.

"You would have me walk into a ground hornet nest and stomp my feet until they chase us from here to Admiral Menéndez?" demanded Captain Alcayede.

Desperately hoping the mention of the Admiral would cause the idiot to come to his senses.

The priest, however, was determined to return to any civilization, even be it St. Augustine or the captured Fort Caroline.

"Our orders Captain are to capture Lutherans and find any Christian castaways who could speak the native languages. We have found both. Would you Captain believe our orders are to carry us to the very end of this land of savages?"

"You ask too much Father," said the military man who counted the numbers of Ais warriors in his head.
Armed with iron no less.

"I only ask that you capture this African slave and we depart peacefully," purred Escobar. Captain Alcayede closed his eyes contemplating the reactions of the Ais.

The exploring party would have to fight their way out the town and then paddle past a hundred miles of Ais towns.

He clicked off the name of the towns they had visited in their journey south: Surruque, Urribia, Urruya, Suyagueche, Potopotoya, Saboboche, Pentoaya.

If *lucky*, one out of ten of the exploring party would survive to St. Augustine.

"These people are warriors," said Captain Alcayede. "We are outnumbered in a hostile land. You realize they destroyed the Lutherans quite handily?"

"I had not realized the Admiral had placed a coward in command," snorted Father Escobar.

Captain Alcayede half drew his sword at the insult. Any other man would be dead. Honor demanded no less.

Enraged, he said, "What you ask would have us dead. Including your holiness," hissed Captain Alcayede.

The Priest was nonplussed.

"Your family is in Cordoba, is that not true? Cordoba is a hotbed of Moriscos," stated the priest in an oily-smooth voice.

"Are they perhaps Moslem converts, Captain?" asked Father Escobar. "How true is their faith I wonder?"

Black eyes stared at the captain.

"The Inquisition does God's work in Cordoba," said the priest.

Captain Alcayede felt the hair rise on the nape of his neck and blood turned to ice.

The smug bastard.

"The boats must be readied and everyone at the beach when we grab the slave," said Captain Alcayede with resignation.

Alcayede was disgusted at the Priest. Good Christians were going to die. And die slowly.

"And Good Father, hold a mass by the boats. It will be the last rites for some. Then be prepared to paddle," said Captain Alcayede.

The following morning Father Escobar arranged his vestments on the beach and began the Latin Mass. The expedition soldier and sailors knelt before him ready to take communion on the shore of the wide lagoon.

Most of the Ais looked on with curiosity but were quickly bored by the lack of magic.

An impromptu spear-toss game ensued, much to the ire of Escobar, who had to speak the old Roman words over a roaring, gambling band of savages.

Captain Alcayede and three picked men looked out of the shadows at the base of the mound where they had secreted from before dawn.

"Let's do this," said the Captain.

The four men crept up the shell mound towards the small hut where the shaman-runaway slave lived.

Book one Part 34: Ulumay

From the great cypress sentry tree, Ochobi, also named "Joaquim Lopez del Castillo" by his daft grandfather, looked out across the two lagoons visible from the swaying tree.

The green ocean was visible again this morning. He could recall only once the long journey to the ocean. However, his mother had insisted he had been many times as a swaddled infant and toddler. Ochobi leaned back in the branches, he could see the village and the smelly Spanish Conjurers attempting their magic. It was said their dead god had returned to life.
Ochobi gazed upon grandfather's hut atop the shell mound and furrowed his brows. Four of the strangers made their way up the stairs to Grandfather.

Well, he hoped they found the old man lucid today. There were days.....

Suddenly his eyes narrowed and he spared a moment to verify what he was seeing and grabbed the shell conch. He blew the alarm as hard as his little body could blow.

The alarm sounded, he flew down the branches nimble as a monkey and sprinted towards the village. Ais were gathering bows and arrows, assembling around the Spaniards just as Captain Alcayede and his three men carried a fur-wrapped object into the center of the Mass.

"Are we discovered?" he asked a worried Brother Philippe.

"I'm not sure," said the Basque. Something has kicked them up like an angry cloud of hornets."

The statement caused the captain to bark with nervous laughter. But he ordered the old slave wrapped in the fur, placed on the ground and they drew sword and rapier.

The Ais, however, were all facing the lagoon as a half dozen dugout canoes paddled slowly to their settlement. A cheer swept the Indians and, incredulously, several began to gobble like a turkey.

The canoes beached and an enormous man of mixed Indian African descent hopped gracefully out of the boat followed by the ancient warrior, Turkey Dancer.

With gusto, they did the honor of picking up two baskets from the boats and upending them upon the lagoon beach.
Severed heads fell to the sticky sand. Calusa top knots adorned every head.

The children began a game of kick-head before clucking old women set the heads on the fishnet posts. Ochobi came running into the crowd and jumped into the arms of the dark giant.

"Father! Father!" he yelled in delight.
Two Huguenot soldiers carrying match-locks stepped unsteadily out of the canoes and the Spanish as one, brought up crossbows and spears.

However, the Frenchmen were protected by the recent arrival of warriors who also brought up clubs and bows.
A tense standoff, until the giant boomed out.

"Who are these people who draw weapons upon my brothers?" demanded the dark warrior giant
"Welcome home Ulumay. These Spaniards are my guests," said Savochequeya to the giant warrior.
The entire village knew Ullumay would succeed Savochequeya as village leader and on that day the town would be known as Ulumay.

Savochequeya held his tongue. It seemed lately as if some of the villagers were attempting to hasten the change in leadership.
Ulumay ignored his Cacique who wobbled in his pink feather robe.

"A great victory over the Calusa enemy, with the assistance of our new friends with their thundersticks!" boomed Ulumay.

A roar of celebration went out across the cove interspersed with turkey gobbles and English words of "God Damn!"

The noise hiding the commands yelled by Savochequeya.

Ulumay set his son down to inspect the strangers in his village and noticed the body wrapped in a blanket near the two black-robed shamans.

A bony ankle protruded from the fur wrapping. An ankle that showed coffee-colored skin. The little toe was missing.

His father Luis the Conquistador had lost a toe to one of the little leaf rattlesnakes.
Ulumay boldly pushed through the spears and swords of the strangers to pull the fur blanket from the body.

Luis Castillo lay in peace on the sand, having suffocated in the blanket.
"Father!" yelled Ulumay.
And an even louder yell again shook the cove, causing parrots and grackles to take noisy flight.
With a command from Turkey Dancer, every bow in the Ais town was pointed at the eyes of the Spaniards.
Captain Alcayede, seeing death and ruin upon his expedition, sought out Yellow-Flint-Snake who might salvage this disaster with his few words of Spanish.

Yellow-Flint-Snake also held his bow taught, arrow pulled to his cheek, and stood near his father "Shoots-ducks-in-flight" who had returned with the war canoes.

He heard his name called out by the soldier who always moved about like a panther - the one soldier worthy of joining the Ais.

"Tell them! Tell them the old man died during the night and his last wish to have Holy Communion with the priests!" said Captain Alcayede. "We have done nothing wrong. Tell them!"

The captain expected to be pierced by arrows as soon as someone even blinked.

Ulumay towering above all, bent down and picked up the pathetically light body of his father. "I speak your words in Spanish, and that is what my father would have wanted," said Ulumay.

With sharp words of Ais, the Indians lowered their bows, relaxing muscle and wood but keeping arrows warily notched in the string.

Ulumay removed his father's heavy crucifix and drooped the amulet over his youngest son's head.

"You will be the next conjurer, my son," said the pained warrior-giant. Ulumay, followed by his son, carried the conquistador, turned shaman, to the shell mound to be buried with the ancestors.

Captain Alcayede only wished to kill Escobar.

He spoke to the Priest in a calm voice that ignored the water trickling down his leg.

"With the slave dead, we have no Christian interpreter. These savages will not turn over their French comrades. So Holy Father, we have no choice but to continue our mission south and fulfill our orders given to us by our Admiral."

A look of fury and finally resignation crossed Father Escobar's face and he nodded. "So close!" his only words.
Captain Alcayede turned away, making a silent oath on the honor of his family, that the fat priest would never see St. Augustine again.

Brother Phillipe collected the holy vestments while Escobar stood rooted in shock.

With a shrill scream the old lady, La Macha jumped upon Escobar's back and with the strength from a lifetime paddling the lagoon, raked her shark tooth knife across the eyes of Father Escobar of the Inquisition.

Two soldiers quickly stabbed the old woman, while Father Escobar writhed in agony and eternal blackness at the base of the pole set in the earth.

His ruined eyes could not see the great crocodile skull adorned with feathers, and the carved symbols of the twin rattlesnakes, the spider, the long-nosed god, the flying bird man holding the head of the enemy, or the pink and white delicately carved seahorses that twirled from gut string.

The dark giant reached for his dying mother. Anger growing.

"Perhaps we should take our leave of this town," said Captain Alcayede in a hushed tone.

End of Book One.

Made in United States
Orlando, FL
04 December 2023